ABOUT THE AUTHOR

Margaret Hawkins lives and writes on a farm in south County Wexford. She is health columnist with the *Irish Farmers Journal*, author of *Restless Spirit: The Story of Rose Quinn* and her radio essays have been broadcast on RTE 1's *Sunday Miscellany*.

www.margarethawkins.ie

BY THE SAME AUTHOR

Restless Spirit: The Story of Rose Quinn

DENY ME NOT

MARGARET HAWKINS

Margaret Hawkins

BUSHEL
PRESS

ISBN-13: 978-0-9575342-2-3

This first paperback edition by Bushel Press, Co. Wexford, Ireland.

An e-book edition of this title is also available.

Cover concept by Rosemary Twamley
Cover design by Liam Furlong

www.margarethawkins.ie

Facebook/MargaretHawkinsAuthor

Twitter @MargaretHawki10

For Ruth

PROLOGUE

13 June 1988

Hannah Casey's twenty-three-year-old hands shook as she hung the framed cutting from *The Irish Times* over her bed.

She re-read the headline that had drawn her like a magnet.

THE END OF THE TERM ILLEGITIMACY

Tomorrow the term 'illegitimacy' – with all its stigmas and awful connotations – will be gone at last.

New law. New life . . .

Now she picked up the dusty frame that the newspaper cutting had replaced.

It was a group photograph of her and all the other children reared in Royle Protestant Children's Home.

She ran her finger over the glass, over the image of herself and her best friend Beryl sitting on Nanna, the housemother's knee, squinting at the sun.

What ages were they then? Five and three? Six and four?

Putting on her navy cardigan to go to work, she let the words escape into the silent room.

"Someday I will know who I am," she said as she closed the door of her room in the nurses' quarters behind her.

"And I will hold my head high."

14 June 1988

Abraham Stephenson felt excited as he climbed into the helicopter.

Not that he would ever admit that to Florrie, his wife.

"More money than sense," he'd told her when she revealed the gift she had planned for his sixtieth birthday.

Yet he knew she knew what would please him. To fly over Knocklannon – to survey all he owned.

The aerial photographs on his study wall had nothing on the bird's eye view he was getting right now.

As the helicopter gained height, he feasted his eyes on the land that lay below him – the back lane field, the big field, Walsh's grove, the twenty-two acres bought off Cribbens in '74, the marl field, the pound field, the stony field, reclaimed in '69, Ryan's rosses . . . two hundred and forty two acres in total.

He asked the pilot to take it slowly over the cattle fields where his pedigree Herefords were now like brick-coloured dots against the green grass. He saw some of them run, startled by the sound of the machine in the sky. Others stood their ground, white heads visible as they stared up at the unfamiliar noise.

Lifting his binoculars he picked out Knocklannon Lad, the bull, chain hanging from the ring in his nose, lumbering after the heifers, only mopping up work to be done now this season.

The silage fields, newly shorn of grass, stood out like yellow handkerchiefs below him.

He'd been the first in the locality to cut, as always, and now the fodder lay where it should be – fermenting in a pit ready to put weight on livestock in the winter.

The look of the crops pleased him too – the barley, wheat and sugar beet – five times more profitable than the other two – all satisfyingly clean of weeds.

"Will I sweep out wider?" the pilot asked.

"Aye."

Soon they were flying over the village of Rathbrandon – pub, the two churches, Carthy's shop, community hall, graveyard, then over his sister Vera's farm that backed onto his.

"Could do with money spent on it," he said to himself, irked by the wet corners in her fields and the pallor of the grass in places.

He would have to talk to the boys . . .

They were flying over the Blackstairs now, circling back to Wexford Harbour, over Ferrycarrig's round tower and now back to Knocklannon.

His eyes scanned his own land again as the pilot hovered over his chosen landing spot.

Pity Leo hadn't been with him – he would have enjoyed the trip. His younger nephew was hungry for Knocklannon – Abe knew that. Still, he wouldn't hold that against him. He'd been no different in his day.

He was out of the helicopter now, climbing again into the jeep that he would drive back to the yard.

The helicopter was rising, now almost out of sight on its journey back to base.

The radio turned on as soon as Abe switched on the jeep's ignition.

The one o'clock news . . .

He heard that barrister – what was her name – Mary Robinson, tail-ending a discussion about a change in family law.

The gist of it was lost on him, however, as he drove, puff-chested, back to the yard, his mind still lingering on his bird's eye view.

Not for the first time he felt a pang of regret that he had no son to pass Knocklannon on to.

"But that," he said to himself, "is what I get for marrying a dud."

Chapter
ONE

September 2004

"Odd."

Hannah Casey thought there was nothing in the envelope at first, it looked so flat. It was her mother's handwriting, she knew, but weak and spidery this time, as if control had gone out of the hand behind it.

Opening it she saw there wasn't even a letter inside, instead a few words scribbled on a piece of cut-up calendar that older women used as shopping lists.

"*Hannah,*" it said. "*News not good. Come if you like. Mother.*"

Below it was written the name and number of a hospice.

A hospice . . .

Hannah tried to take it in. She hadn't heard from her mother for over a year – now this.

It was several minutes before she got through to the nurse in charge. No, they couldn't give a lot of detail over the phone, but could Hannah please come up?

Hannah had to think. She would have to ask for time off . . . a lot of it.

"That'll be fun," she said to herself, "given that they think my mother is dead already."

"You'll have to tell them the truth," Beryl said, when she rang her at work.

"Looks like it . . ."

Phone to one ear as she cleared away her breakfast things Hannah tried not to feel resentful.

"Part of me doesn't want to run to her," she said to her friend. "That's not very charitable, is it? When did she ever run to me – that's what I keep thinking . . .?"

There was silence on the other end of the line for a few seconds.

"Yes – but does anyone deserve to die on their own?"

"No. You're right . . . I should go. I will."

The wider implications of her mother dying now hit her, though
. . . What if she went to the grave with the secret of who her father
was? It was a stonewall Hannah had always been afraid of coming
up against. Right now, she couldn't even voice that fear to Beryl.

As she quickly packed a case, Hannah thought of her mother's
age – sixty-nine – not that old. Cancer obviously – and her mother
had never told her. What sort of a mother/daughter relationship
was that?

"A non-existent one," she thought as she rang her ward manager
at Waterford General's CCU unit. Emer Boyle was brusque but yes,
she could see her at 9.30 a.m.

In the car now Hannah took the scrap of paper out of her pocket
to read it again. *Come if you like*. It was more of an invitation than
her mother had ever extended to her in the past. Did that mean
she'd changed?

Driving into Waterford city to go to the hospital, Hannah knew
she could do with a drink to steady her nerves but that would have
to wait. On the quay in traffic she had the urge to ring Matt but
stopped herself. No. Why would she? She'd ended it, hadn't she?
What was the point of ringing him now? It would never have
worked out. Not with him wanting a child. What was the point of
her having a child, she'd thought, when she didn't know who she
was herself.

As the traffic moved off again she wondered what she would
find at the hospice. How long did her mother have left? Hannah felt
the fear seeping in again.

Now she could see the disbelief on her superior's face.

"Pull the other one, Hannah. You've already had leave because
your mother died! Two mothers. For God's sake!"

"There is an explanation."

Hannah watched her nursing colleague sit back in her chair.

"I'm all ears."

"The woman who died a year and a half ago *was* a mother to me.
She was the house mother in the children's home I was reared in."

Hannah could see the flash of surprise on Emer Boyle's face. Was
it followed by one of disgust? Pity? What was she thinking –
orphan, bye-child, bastard even?

"You were reared in a children's home? God! You've never
said."

"I didn't think it was anyone else's business."

"Of course it isn't. I just hadn't a clue – as long as I've known
you. So – the woman who is dying now is your *real* mother?"

"Yes."

"And where was she when you were in the children's home?"

"Living in Dublin."

"And you had no contact with her?"

Hannah tried to control her voice.

"I did. She came to see me at the home – as often as she could."

"Wow! At least she kept in touch. How long has she been ill?"

Hannah had no option but to lie this time. What would her boss think if she told her she hadn't a clue?

"A few months."

"I'm sorry to hear that. Were you close?"

Hannah didn't answer.

"Right . . ."

"Please . . . if we could just get the leave sorted."

"Of course."

The ward manager lifted her pen.

"How much time off do you think you need?"

"A month maybe. It's hard to say exactly."

"No, a month's fine. To be honest I think it may be for the best – that you take a break, I mean . . ."

Here we go . . .

"I hate saying it – especially at a time like this – but I think we both know that's a good idea."

Hannah saw her boss turn pages of her file.

"Time-keeping issues, a medication error, being rude to a patient's family. I knew it wasn't like you – but at least I can see now that you've had a lot on your mind. Who'd blame you for going off the rails a bit."

Hannah didn't correct her.

"Like I told the medical manager, it won't happen again."

Her boss closed the file.

"Good. Sometimes we all need to take time out after we've been working for a long time, take stock . . ."

"I'll be nursing my dying mother!"

"Of course you will – and that's what you must concentrate on now. Where is she at the moment?"

"In a hospice."

Her boss waited for more detail but didn't get it.

"Right. Good. She'll get great care there. And you'll get support as well. You will let me know how things are going, won't you? "

"Yes. Thank you."

Hannah heard her boss speak again as she reached the door.

"There's no . . . shame in any of this, you know, Hannah. Being more open with people might be better in the long run. Secrets – they have a habit of eating away at us."

Hannah did some deep breathing to calm herself as she walked back into the coronary care unit to the brightness and the bleeping machines and the very sick patients. Who did her ward manager think she was? Oprah Winfrey? Concentrate – that's what she had to do – just until one o'clock when the agency nurse would arrive to relieve her in CCU . . .

In the car now she stared at her mother's letter again. The scrap of paper upset her. Could her mother not afford normal writing paper or had she not even bothered to buy some? Or was it the only thing she had in her bag that she could write on? Hannah stuffed it into her pocket again, unable to look at it anymore.

The hospice was like a hotel – the foyer with the big reception desk and the leather chairs, pseudo-marbled columns and original paintings hanging on the walls.

She could almost see the brochures for the place – *St Albert's – the hospice you'll be dying to get into* . . .

At the desk she explained who she was. The manager of the place was friendly, efficient, caring.

"Hannah – of course – Lil will be glad you're here. She mentioned you yesterday."

Lil?

The woman was showing her the way to her mother's room.

"You live some distance away, I believe?"

"Yes."

The words hung between them – like why hadn't she been here before now? Hannah answered the question before being asked.

"She didn't tell me how ill she was."

"I see, but you're here now. That's the main thing."

Right now Hannah wished Beryl was with her. Beryl had wanted to come, worried that Hannah wouldn't be fit to drive. She would ring her later . . .

A nurse was helping her mother to sip water from a beaker when she was shown into the single room.

"Look who's here to see you, Lil. Hannah. Your daughter. We'll leave the two of you to talk."

Her mother looked old, wary, trying to smile.

Hannah was shocked at how much weight her mother had lost from her face and arms, shocked too by the distended abdomen – a tell-tale sign of the cancer.

Hannah stood at the end of the bed.

"You got here."

"Yes."

Her mother was attempting to shift round in the bed but couldn't.

"Will I fix the pillows for you?"

"Please."

Hannah moved forward to fix them, careful not to disturb the morphine pump that lay beside the locker.

When she finally seemed settled, Hannah sat down in the armchair at one side of the bed. Her mother seemed even more tense now – awkward, her hands fidgeting with the sheet.

"You said the news wasn't good . . ."

"Yes."

"They wouldn't tell me anything over the phone. What did the doctors say exactly?"

Hannah watched her mother turn her head to stare out the window at the lavender beds and the pond.

"What no one wants to hear. You can talk to them yourself."

"I've an appointment for two o'clock."

"Right."

"How long have you known?"

Hannah saw her mother shrug.

"A few weeks but my stomach hasn't been right for many's the day."

"You should have said."

"I . . . didn't want to be annoying you."

The words stung. Annoying her? Any other mother would tell her daughter when something so serious was going on, wouldn't she, share her grief with her, draw comfort from her during the days of tests and results . . .? Her mother had denied her even that.

"Did you have trouble getting time off?"

"No," Hannah said. "I had holidays coming. I'll be able to stay with you as much as you want."

Was it tears Hannah saw in her mother's eyes?

The chat with the doctor took place in the family room.

"We'll make her as comfortable as possible, of course. Her pain will be controlled."

"Thank you. How long has she got?"

"Weeks, maybe a bit more, maybe less. It's difficult to say exactly. You know yourself, being a nurse."

Yes, she knew, after twenty years in the job, how slowly – or how quickly – death could come.

Hannah couldn't bear to go back to her mother immediately. Instead she went outside to breathe in fresh air and ring Beryl.

"It's in the liver. Probably a secondary."

"God love her."

Beryl had lots of questions: how Hannah was, was there anything she could do, would Hannah stay in her mother's flat?

"No."

She had never spent a night under her mother's roof in her life. It would be too weird to start now.

"I'll find a B&B."

"Ok. It's great you got time off to be with her anyway. You'll be glad afterwards."

"I hope so."

Beryl rang off eventually after promising to come up to Dún Laoghaire on Friday evening, after she finished her shift on reception in the hotel in Waterford.

"Book me into wherever you're staying. For two nights."

"Ok. Thanks."

The ward was quiet in the post visitor, post tea lull.

Her mother had very few visitors. It was one of the first questions Hannah had asked the nurse. The parish priest from Dún Laoghaire had come, she said, and a woman – a friend of Lil's, the nurse thought. She'd come every day – Kit – she was sure that was her name. If the nurse thought it strange that Hannah didn't know her mother's friend she didn't say so.

Her mother was asleep now, her mouth open, her breathing irregular. Her face had already distorted a bit, making it more difficult to understand what she was saying.

Hannah sat, an unread book on her knee, watching her. She wished she felt inclined to touch her again, but when she had touched her mother's hand it had moved away involuntarily.

"Hannah . . ."

Her mother's head lifted slightly.

"Yes. Do you want a drink?"

Hannah put her left arm behind her mother's shoulders to lift her up a bit then held the beaker to her lips with her right hand, tilting it just enough.

"Are you still with him – your young man?" her mother asked.

Matt? Young? He was twelve years older than her: fifty-one. She'd never gone out with a young man in her life.

"No. It didn't work out."

"Oh."

Her mother drifted in and out of sleep again.

Next time she spoke it was to ask what the doctors had said.

"How long?"

"They can't really say. Maybe not long . . ."

What was the point in telling her lies? Hannah was fed up of lies, of secrecy. Now she pushed herself to ask . . .

"Is there anything you want me to do? Anyone you want me to contact?"

Her mother shook her head.

"Is there family who don't know about me?"

"No . . ."

She watched her mother's crepey hands pull at the sheet again.

"None at all?"

"Your grandad died last year. There's no one else."

Her mother had turned her head away. Hannah felt hurt at the matter-of-factness of it. Her grandfather was dead and she had never even been given the choice of knowing him. Was he the man in the photograph she'd asked about when she visited her mother's flat for the first time when she was nineteen years old? The next time she'd gone there the photograph had been put away.

"There's so much I want to know."

Lil Casey had her eyes shut.

"Where you're from, about my grandparents, where they lived, where you went to school . . ."

Hannah kept going in spite of her mother's silence.

"You owe me that much surely . . ."

Her mother was trying to shift in the bed.

"Is the pain worse?"

Half an hour later, when the medication had been adjusted, Hannah watched her mother close her eyes again. That's it, she thought – her mother is trying to escape – close her eyes so no one can ask her any more questions. No big ones like the name of the man who fathered her child . . .

Hannah felt terrified at the thought of time running out. What if her mother never told her?

"So much for thinking I'd come to terms with not knowing who my father is . . ." she said to herself. It had been a way for surviving, she knew, pretending not to care, but right now, with her mother so close to death, the pain was raw – visceral.

After getting into the car later, exhausted, to go back to the B&B Hannah rested her arms on the steering wheel for a few minutes. What if her mother said nothing? Stonewall.

Hannah was amazed at how her attitude to the hospice had changed.

Two weeks ago when she'd come here first she'd thought it such a step up from hospitals, impressed by the size of it, the opulence of it. Now she only smelled the stench of death.

Three people had already died. She'd arrived in the morning from the B&B to see rooms being cleared and disinfected and family members pale and tearful getting into cars. Already new people had taken up the beds.

It was like an airport, she thought, people queuing up on the runway, ready for departure.

Her mother wouldn't last much longer; she knew that. Her kidneys were packing up. Food intake was non-existent.

She'd tried to broach the subject of her father three times. She had the right, hadn't she? She wasn't being cruel, was she? Wouldn't her mother have been the same if it were the other way round?

The first time she'd attempted it a nurse had come in and the moment was gone. The second time her mother had feigned sleep then eventually told her a bit about her grandparents and her grandfather working on farms and on the roads but very little else. The third time she had eventually said "No good'll come of chasing him" and refused to be drawn any further.

"You can't blame me for wanting to know . . . Mother – please . . . it's such an important thing."

Her mother was agitated after that, even in sleep.

Sensing strain in the room, the nurse had said to Hannah that her mother needed as calm an environment as possible. Had she overheard her trying to get answers?

Hannah couldn't help resenting the implication. How come it was always about what her mother needed? Even death was giving her a reason to keep Hannah at arm's length.

Beryl tried to console her friend but it didn't work.

"It's probably hard for her," she said. "She's kept the secret for a long time."

"And in the meantime I get told nothing, is that it?" Hannah said, her head in her hands at a canteen table. "I don't even know where she wants to be buried or what sort of a funeral she wants, for God's sake! I don't know all sorts of things like if she ever broke her arm falling off a swing, if she hated her teacher, when she reached puberty, if her mother made poultices like Nanna did when we got boils on the back of our necks."

"You're tormenting yourself – thinking so much." Beryl said.

"All the questions are doing my head in. Once she's gone how will I ever find anything out?"

The nurse interrupted them.

"Hannah – I think you should come back in. Your mum wants you."

Mum. She'd never called her that in her life.

"Hannah is here, Lil."

Hannah saw her mother's hand move as if she wanted something near the television.

"Is it your bag you want?"

"Yes."

The nurse put the navy handbag on the bed beside Lil and smoothed the covers.

"I'll leave you two alone. If you want anything, just buzz."

"Thanks."

Her mother's fingers were fumbling at the bag.

"You want me to open it?"

Her mother blinked again.

"What do you want? Your purse? Your rosary beads?"

"No."

The only other thing in the bag was a padded brown envelope.

"You want this?" she asked, removing it. She was surprised to see her name written on it.

"May I open it?"

Her mother seemed to nod.

The envelope was torn at the corners – as if it had sat in the bag for years.

She took out a folded document, a receipt of some sort, a few photographs, a post office book, a newspaper cutting and two sets of keys.

Her hand shook as she looked first at the receipt. It was for a burial plot in Dean's Grange Cemetery. At least she now knew where her mother wanted to be buried.

The folded document was a last will and testament.

Her mother was fingering the second set of keys that Hannah had placed on the bed – the older set, one huge, old-fashioned key and a smaller Yale one.

There was a label attached to them.

Hannah read the words.

'Casey, Drumcadden, Rathbrandon, County Wexford.'

"Are these for where you were born? Your home place?"

Her heart lurched at hearing the address for the first time. She tried to figure out what was happening here. Did this mean her mother was giving the house to her — a house she'd never even seen . . . God!

She looked at the photographs – ones obviously taken when her mother was a child outside what looked like one of those two-up, two-down cottages.

She looked at the backs of the photos – Drumcadden 1948, Drumcadden 1956 . . .

Angry tears now stung Hannah's eyes. Why hadn't she seen all these things years ago? Why hadn't she been let visit? Why hadn't her grandparents been told about her? Ask a stupid question . . .

The post office book looked ancient. Hannah opened it at the first page.

She was shocked to see that her name was down as the holder of the account. 1965 . . . The account was opened two months after she was born! Heart pounding, she turned to the next page and the one after. There were only twenty entries or so in the book, the biggest ones in the two years after she was born.

She couldn't even guess how much that would add up to now in euro.

How could her mother save money like this?

"Where did it come from?"

The expression on her mother's face told her.

"*He* gave this to you, didn't he – my father? To help rear me?"

The words choked off in Hannah's throat.

"But you never used it."

Hannah sat down in the chair beside the bed, unable to take it all in. All the deprivation at Royle came back to her – the hand-me-down clothes that never fitted right, the too-big shoes that sligged off her feet when she ran, the doing without when all the time the money was there?

Her mother had paid what she could afford towards Hannah's keep in the home out of her cleaner's wages – Nanna had told her that only in later years.

"It couldn't have been easy for her," Nanna had said.

Now she knew there was all this money . . .

"You have to tell me who he is – please . . ."

Her mother's hand was moving again, as if to locate some other object.

All that was left on the bed was some old newspaper cutting. What use would that be?

Her mother's fingers were fumbling over the cutting. Had it something to do with her father? Hannah almost grabbed it out of her mother's hand. One side only had ads yellowed with age, the other had a photograph taken at what – an agricultural show? It was of two men, she saw, one holding onto a cow that had a large rosette tied to its halter. The second man was presenting a trophy to the taller man who was holding the cow.

Hannah's eyes scanned the caption hungrily.

Wexford farmer Abraham (Abe) Stephenson (left) being presented with the Reserve Champion trophy for his pedigree Hereford cow Knocklannon Glory, by the chairman of the Royal Dublin Society, Ballsbridge yesterday.

"Is one of these men my father? The RDS guy? The other one? Abe . . . Abraham Stephenson? "

Her mother seemed to stare at her for ages before finally blinking "yes".

Christ! Thirty-nine years old and she finally knew . . .

When the tears eventually cleared she stared at the cutting again, scanning the man's face for similarity. Was there a resemblance? She wished the photograph was clearer. He looked tall. Was that where she got her height? She always knew it hadn't come from her mother's side.

She had to ask . . .

"Is he alive?"

Hannah saw her mother eventually nod then clutch her arm as if she was trying to say something but couldn't. Then the grip loosened and her mother's head sunk deeper into the pillow. Her face had distorted further. After several seconds Hannah pressed the bell for the nurse. She knew enough about dying people to know that it wouldn't be long now.

When death finally came two nights later, Hannah was glad Beryl was with her at the hospice.

Her mother had been agitated for hours, deep, guttural sounds breaking the silence of the room. She'd seen enough patients die to know that her mother wasn't at peace. Was her unconscious mind worrying about what Hannah would do with the information she now had, she wondered? Or was she simply sorry for holding back for so long? Hannah kept telling herself it was the latter.

She checked her mother's pulse again. It was barely there.

When her mother finally puffed out her last breath, no tears came. She knew she should be feeling grief for the woman who had died and compassion for her but all she felt was sadness and anger at her mother's escape. She still had so many questions. How had her mother met this Abe Stephenson? Where did he live? What was he like? Had her mother loved him or he her?

She and Beryl stood by the bed, the palliative care nurse at the other side, Hannah's brain somehow registering the coldness of her mother's hand on one side and the warmth of her friend's on the other.

Her mother's eyes were still open.

"I'll do it," Hannah said to the nurse and slowly she drew her hand downwards over her mother's face to close them.

October 2004

Abe Stephenson cursed. His prize Hereford bull was lame. Damn! The last thing he needed was an injured animal.

Something must have gone up in the animal's foot and let infection in; a sharp stone or a piece of rusty wire maybe.

He cursed again. He had always been so careful about making sure the field the bull was in was swept for anything that could cause damage. The vet would have to be called – more bloody expense!

Memories of losing one of the best bulls he ever had flooded back. The fever associated with the footrot had made the animal infertile and Abe unfortunately hadn't had him sperm-counted before the breeding season started. It had been an expensive lesson that year, finding that none of his pedigrees were in calf when they should have been. Luckily the breeding season was a long way off now. He'd have the animal well checked-out by then. A bull firing blanks would be no use to anyone.

Getting Knocklannon Esquire into the crush would mean hassle though. He'd need Leo. The days of him being able to handle a bull by himself were over – he wasn't stupid enough to think otherwise.

Leo's phone was ringing out. He was probably in the shed working on the corn drill.

With the good autumn weather and clay falling off boots it was time for sowing winter crops. He briefly considered ringing Roy. No, no point. The bull would smell the fear off him at twenty paces. Abe walked back to the yard. He would drive the two miles to his sister's place instead to find Leo. It'd be quicker that way.

After telephoning the vet he walked to the farmhouse to tell his wife, Florrie, where he was going.

She was at the piano again. The music met him as he came in the back door. Jesus, did she ever leave that thing alone these days? He stood listening for a few seconds, though, suddenly shocked at the standard of her playing. When had she become that good? Time was she could only play the three hymns for church – and that was after weeks of practice.

She closed the lid when he went into the drawing room.

"What?" she asked, hands in her lap.

"The bull's lame. I'll have to get Leo."

"Do you want some tea before you go?"

"I'll get some at Vera's."

"Whatever you like."

The music started again as he went out the back door – some loud, classical shite this time, the sort he'd switch off if he came across it on the radio.

The fact that she hadn't tried to persuade him to have tea annoyed him. There was a time she'd have humoured him into it with niceties, almost pleading as she told him that she had baked something or other he liked.

Still, at least she didn't neglect the house. He'd never been ashamed to have anyone step across his threshold. He never had to search for clean clothes either. Being turned out well every day was important to him, even now.

His mother had drummed it into him. "Look like a businessman and you'll be treated like one". Early on, he had taken to dressing smartly when he went to the mart, even wearing beige trousers sometimes, stuffed into clean Wellington boots. He knew he had presence – and that people turned to watch him when he passed. Yes, they might smirk at his smartness but they all paid attention when he was bidding. And he was easy to find when they were looking for him after they'd turned down the price in the ring but didn't want to bring their animals home.

Checking his wallet for his cheque book and his pocket for his glasses, he put the key in the ignition. There was a time he could see a midge on Mount Leinster. Now he couldn't read the back of a Corn Flakes packet without the specs.

As he reversed the car he remembered the prescription in the dashboard. Angina, my eye! Doctor Dunne didn't know what he was talking about. A little bit of pain after exertion never killed anyone. He'd never been sick a day in his life.

Glancing round the yard as he took off, he was pleased with what he saw. Cemented yard, gates properly hung, outhouses in good repair, doors all painted red – it looked well. What matter if he'd had to cut down on farming in the last few years? Hadn't the arse fallen out of the price of almost everything anyway, so what was the point in killing himself at the age of seventy-six? As long as he could hang onto the few pedigrees he'd be all right. The empty slatted shed where he'd once housed cattle was now earning tidy money as a storage area for a local builder. What matter that it didn't pay to fatten large numbers of stock in it anymore? With farming in a slump you had to grab opportunity where you could find it.

And contacts with builders would come in handy if – when – he got the green light for his own building development plans. Get in early, clean up. Only fools were held back by sentiment. It might have been bred into him never to sell land, but the world had changed. He'd make more money out of those five acres joining the village than he'd ever make by farming it – that was for certain. He left the yard, the engine of the '03 Mercedes purring as he moved out onto the road.

Vera's place was only two miles away, less as the crow flies.

Marrying Harry Kemp who owned the land adjoining Knocklannon had been a cute move on his sister's part, especially the way things worked out with her being widowed young, but what could you expect with an eejit who couldn't even handle a gun properly?

Neighbours had gossiped at the time his sister married, about Harry Kemp being old enough to be her father, he knew, but Vera knew what she was doing. If there was one thing his sister had it was balls. She might never own Knocklannon but she would own the land beside it.

On the straight stretch of road before he turned right for Vera's he passed Lil Casey's cottage.

It was the only piece of property he didn't own on that side of the road: a cottage on half an acre. He made a mental note to ring Flynn, the auctioneer, again, to see if his bid had been accepted yet. Flynn hadn't been able to contact Lil Casey in the last few weeks, he'd told him, so had had no answer for him. Maybe she'd moved house. The delay irritated him. Especially as he needed the cottage if he was to be sure of meeting the council's sight line requirements for the housing development entrance.

Lil's father, Jim Casey, was dead eight months now. Surely she'd had enough time to make up her mind about selling?

He'd gone to Jim's funeral and had scarcely recognized Lil, she'd aged so much.

He'd caught sight of her only once since then at the cottage, filling a skip with old furniture and rubbish a few weeks after the funeral.

He hadn't stopped to talk then, even though he would have liked to have known her intentions. Better to let Flynn handle it. He'd make his move when the time was right. He didn't need tongues wagging if his car was spotted parked outside the cottage. The word would be out in no time that he was trying to buy the place and he didn't want that. Or people putting her up to looking for a higher price.

Driving down his sister's lane now he saw that Roy had been out with the hedgecutter. At least he had done a half decent job. He might make a few bob out of it the way he was going. Sheep'd never make his nephew a rich man. Nor being stuck in that shed chipping away at some old stone. Good job he wasn't the only son Vera had or she could have shut up shop years ago.

Abe saw his sister feeding the dogs when he arrived into the yard.

Three sheepdogs were around the saucepan, snarling at one another to get the lion's share. He saw his sister Vera aim a kick at the noisiest one to shut him up.

"Leo around? I couldn't get him on the phone."

"In the shed. What's up?"

Shouting over his shoulder about the bull, he headed across the yard.

"I was just going to ring you. Come in when you're finished, will you?" his sister shouted after him.

"Aye."

Abe found Leo a few seconds later, face smudged and grease gun in hand, standing on the steps of the corn drill.

The sight of his nephew's bald patch shocked him. Both his nephews were now over forty – where had the years gone? It only seemed like the other day they were chaps.

"Well?"

The conversation with his second nephew was to the point as always. He needed a hand. Right. Just give him time to finish this and then he'd be over, Leo said.

"Which field are you sowing first?"

"The twelve acre – it's fit enough."

"The back lane field at home is pretty near it too. The seed'll be out from the co-op tomorrow, ready for you."

"Right."

"Where's the lad?"

He saw Leo grin.

"Michelangelo? Can you not hear him?"

Sure enough, Abe could hear the sound of Roy tapping away in an outhouse further down the yard.

Abe threw his eyes up to heaven. "He's easy amused. There's a few calves to vaccinate when you're over as well. I'll be weaning them in a few weeks."

"Give me half an hour or so."

"Right."

In the kitchen, Abe had to move two dirty coats, a bottle of sheep injection fluid and three old copies of the *Irish Farmers Journal* from a chair before he could sit down.

Vera was wetting the tea. Finishing that, he saw her plonk that day's *Irish Times* on the table in front of him.

Her finger was pointing out a death notice.

"Who's snuffed it now?" he asked.

His sister didn't answer as he scanned the surnames in bold print.

Barrett, Browne, Carr, Casey . . . Jesus!

Elizabeth Mary Casey (Lil) formerly of Drumcadden, Rathbrandon, County Wexford . . .

Abe forced himself to speak calmly.

"Must have been sudden . . ."

"Cancer. Riddled with it – according to Tom in the shop."

His heart began to pound as his sister tapped the paper again.

"Keep reading."

. . . *sadly missed by her daughter, Hannah* . . .

Jesus! Abe Stephenson forced his breath to flow freely. Stay calm, stay in control. If he kept pretending to read he wouldn't have to answer.

He could hear his sister getting mugs from the dresser.

"That'll surprise a few people. Not me, though. That one had a gamey eye on her, if you ask me."

His sister placed the teapot on the table now, covering it with a tea cosy that had seen better days.

"It's a pity the paper doesn't say what age the daughter is. Jim Casey can't have known. Not that he'd have told anyone if he did. She'd have been the talk of the parish."

Abe forced a reply out.

"Aye!"

"Might throw a bit of a spanner in the works for you, though."

Abe's heart pounded. Christ, what was coming now?

"What?"

"You wanting to buy the cottage as a rental property – what if this daughter of hers wants to keep it?"

Abe swallowed.

"A city one'd hardly want a place like that."

"Maybe you're right. Wouldn't be grand enough for her, probably, the way women are going now. When's the burial?"

When Abe didn't answer he saw his sister turn the paper round so that she could see it herself.

"Day after tomorrow. Private, if you don't mind. I don't know who from around here'd be going anyway. When she was home she hardly set foot outside the door."

Abe took another gulp of tea, then stood up.

"The vet'll be out."

"Right."

Vera was reading the death notice again.

"Doesn't say *loving* daughter, did you notice that?"

Abe saw his sister put the paper down before taking a sip from her mug.

"*The Irish Times*, no less!"

Abe had his hand on the doorknob when his sister spoke again.

"Posh name for her sort too. Something less than Hannah would have done her."

Abe wiped the perspiration from his forehead with his clean handkerchief.

What could he do? What should he do? He had to get into the car quickly. No stress, that's what the doctor said, and here he was sweating like a pig.

Think rationally, he told himself.

Of course Vera had been all talk about Lil Casey having a child – the whole parish would be. That was just a normal reaction, he told himself. It'd pass.

Still, he felt nauseous at the thought of all the speculating and guessing that would go on, but then why should anyone think that the father of Lil's child would be in this locality? Lil hadn't lived here. They'd all think it was a fella in Dublin. The gossip'd all blow over in a few days.

The Hannah name was a shock, though. What was she thinking of? If he had known she was going to call the child that he'd have put a stop to it. He should have made it a condition of her getting the money. Hannah was his grandmother's name. What right had she to use it? He didn't care if she'd always liked his grandmother, running messages for her and bringing her cups of tea in her room when the old woman had been forgotten about on threshing days. The child . . . He squeezed his eyes tight to stop himself imagining her.

What age would Lil have been then? Twelve or thirteen when she started helping out in the house for a few pence while her father, Jim Casey, manned a rick or did his day's donkey work in the yard?

Abe let the engine idle at the end of Vera's lane. He had to think . . . If the truth came out . . . No, that was impossible! He would recognize no bye-child no matter what law there was in the country . . . A sudden recollection of the helicopter ride twenty years before unnerved him, though. The Status of Children Act . . . no more illegitimacy. He'd heard the news that night on the television. Effin women's libbers with nothing better to do but make trouble for decent people . . . Now he thought of his parents – his mother – what would she have said if she'd found out? He stopped himself before he got to the end of that thought.

Feck! What had he brought up all that old stuff for? It was all in the past. Buried. And if Florrie had been able to have children none of this would have happened. It was her fault.

Why did he have to go so far to prove that the problem wasn't with him, though? Was that what he'd done? He remembered how the worry had eaten away at him and how tongues had started to wag when two years had gone by and there was no sign of a baby.

It wasn't that he didn't know what to do. Hadn't he lived on a farm long enough?

After a year of nothing happening he had dispensed with any displays of affection, preferring to get down to business, grunting the seed out of him in the hope of it germinating.

Seeing Lil at the RDS that year had been a surprise. She was skittish enough even though she would have been what – twenty-nine? Thirty? No spring chicken. And old enough to know how to protect herself. She'd always fancied him, ever since she was a girl. The knowledge had turned him on. That time he'd grabbed her in the dairy and shoved his hand between her legs she hadn't complained . . . He used to catch her watching him as he went about his work, too, waiting for him to wink at her.

The job in Dublin had happened suddenly when she was seventeen. After the hen house incident. What age was he then? Old enough to have had more sense . . .

He could still see her that day in '65 when she had told him she was pregnant.

She'd been afraid to come near the house, knowing his wife would be there. She was apprehensive, too, that her father would see them speak.

There could be no phone calls, no arrangements, so she had walked up and down the roads for hours when she was home on holidays until he had driven past in the car.

She'd told him through the car window, her face pinched and white.

She was sure, she said. The news had horrified him. And elated him. He had lead in his pencil after all. No, he told himself, Lil Casey wasn't the sort to be having it off with several men. He was the father of her child. And she'd say nothing.

"What do you want me to do?" he said, finally.

"I don't know," she said, her voice quavering.

"You'll need to go somewhere for a while."

Her hand was gripping the rolled down window.

"I'm not going to the nuns – I might never get out! Can you get me a place in one of the mother and baby homes your church runs? That way I'll be able to get out when it's all over."

"It won't be easy. Your father knows nothing about this, I hope."
Lil had blessed herself before uttering "No".

Abe found a pen and a piece of paper in the glove compartment and passed it out through the window.

"Write your address on that and I'll contact you when I sort something out."

When Lil had scribbled the words, he placed the piece of paper in a bulb box in the dash.

"You'll need money."

Abe revved the car as he spotted a vehicle in the rear view mirror.

"I'll be in touch."

And he left her there, her arms wrapped around herself to ward off the shivers on a warm June day.

It had been difficult enough to get the information without putting himself at risk of exposure.

In the end he had gone to Dublin for a day and walked into two Protestant churches before he found a clergyman he could approach.

What the clergyman thought he didn't know, but he didn't care. He felt far enough from home to be anonymous.

He didn't care if the clergyman believed his story or not. His sister, he told him, had got herself in trouble, and he wanted some advice about what to do. His parents were elderly, he said, and it would kill them if they knew. His sister worked in Dublin, he said, and she could disappear for a while. Did he know of a place that could take care of her?

"God bless your brotherly concern," said the rector. "I'll write an address down for you. She must write to the woman who runs this place. She can stay there until after the child is weaned. How many months on is she?"

"Two."

"Good. There'll be time to organize it."

"What will it cost?"

"She will be expected to help out with the work of running the home while she is there and while she is able. A contribution to the home would, of course, be appreciated. It is God's work and those who do it should be supported."

"Yes."

His mind was already working out how much he would give – anonymously, of course. Luckily Florrie had little to do with keeping the books at that time. He put money on the table every

Friday morning for the house and that was enough. Anything special she had to ask for.

On the steps of the church, he looked at the address, Bethany Home . . .

Yes, it was far enough away from where Lil worked to give her privacy. If she stayed out of sight she'd be all right. She'd still be able to write to her father without him suspecting anything.

He had heard nothing until the following spring. Easter, was it? He was sowing potatoes in the pound field.

Lil had come home on the bus for a few days' holiday. He had made sure to give Jim Casey a few days tidying up work, even though he was now laid off from Knocklannon and trimming the roads for the council. That way he got to know if there was any news of Lil.

Abe had sent the money to Bethany Home in the form of a draft. "Towards Lil Casey's confinement" – that's all he had written on the envelope.

Fifty pounds – the price of an average cow – it had taken a lot of collecting, but it was harvest time and he could afford it. He had thought several times of paying nothing but decided against it. He wouldn't have her saying that he didn't pay his debts.

The day after Lil had told him she was pregnant he had sent Florrie to the doctor and then to a consultant for tests. Two months later they'd been told that Florrie would never have children. Blocked tubes.

The news had got out and the laugh was on the other side of the neighbours' and the workmen's faces now. There was nothing wrong with Abe Stephenson. It was his wife who was barren. They could put that in their pipes and smoke it.

He knew his attitude to his wife had changed from then on. He was harsher with her and she took his criticism as if it was her due. For years after she had been more anxious, more compliant. Part of him had enjoyed it. Part of him wished she'd stood up to him. He'd have respected her more if she had.

Lately, though, that had changed. There was a stand up in her now. When she was dressed up she was still a fine looking woman. Her breasts still drew his eye. Pity they didn't do what they were supposed to do and he mightn't be in the mess he was in now.

He tried to remember what time Lil's funeral was at. Would he go? Could he go? Maybe he could keep his distance, sit in the car and watch what was happening and who was there?

He would see her, the child . . . A shiver ran down his spine . . . No, he couldn't think of her as a daughter. He had no connection with her and she'd get nothing out of him. He'd told Lil Casey that.

He had met his obligations on that score. That was the end of it. They'd agreed on that.

He checked his watch. 11.55. He picked his mobile phone up off the seat beside him and rang his solicitor's number.

He couldn't have an appointment so soon, the secretary said.

"Tell him to make time," he told her. "I'll be there last thing this evening."

He was pulling into the yard at home when the mobile rang.

"Mr O'Connell will see you at five o'clock, Mr Stephenson," the secretary told him.

"I'll be there."

It would work out all right. Florrie would be at the day care centre working on that book she was putting together for them. She wouldn't even know he was away. Not that it would worry her if he was. Sometimes he wondered if she would care if he never came back.

Hannah was jealous of Kit Bermingham. She knew she should have more sense but that was the feeling that surfaced now.

Kit was with her in Lil's basement flat, helping her to sort through her mother's belongings.

Kit, Lil's friend and co-cleaner at the hospital, had had so much of Lil's time. Hannah felt upset that Kit knew her mother so much better than she did. She'd even given her her cat when she went into hospital. Why hadn't she asked Hannah to take it? It would have been some kind of connection.

"Is it ok if I have these?"

Hannah turned to see Kit holding up two tins of cat food that she'd found in the tiny pantry.

"Of course. Whatever's any use."

Hannah saw Kit's eyes light up.

"I'm serious," Hannah said. "I wouldn't have room for all this stuff in Waterford."

"Are you sure? Anything at all?"

"All the furniture, if you want it. I might want a few small things but that's all."

"You're joking! God, that's great!"

Hannah was sorting through an old biscuit box of photos. There was none of her – not even as a baby. Maybe no photographs had ever been taken of her.

"Maybe it would have been too painful for her to have them," she thought as Kit rooted out more cat food in the pantry. "Or maybe she was afraid to have evidence lying around in case someone saw them and asked awkward questions . . ." Either way, it hurt.

"I'll be really glad of this – and the sideboard, if you're sure," Kit was saying, as she ran her hands over the arms of the sofa.

"We've turned a shed in the garden into an extra room. Jimmy's put electricity in it. With so many in the house it's a refuge for us sometimes."

"Take whatever you need."

Kit told Hannah she had two sons and a daughter. Her daughter was a single mother with a two-year-old child, living at home.

"God knows if times had been different Lil might've been able to rear you herself, but there was no lone parents' allowance nor nothing then but at least she kept in touch with you. Shows the sort of person she was. Must have been desperate on her going to visit you then leaving you behind each time."

Hannah bit her tongue, stopping herself saying, "What about me being abandoned until the next time it suited her to come?" The pity shouldn't be all for the mother, should it?

"I'm sorry, I didn't mean . . ."

"She never, ever mentioned me?" Hannah asked. "Let my name slip or anything?"

Kit looked embarrassed.

"No, but I wish she had. I thought she'd have trusted me enough, seeing as we knew each other so well. God, we even slept in the one bed on one of those bus holidays to Connemara. We talked about everything under the sun – or so I thought."

God, they'd gone on holidays together!

"She loved Connemara," Kit was going on. "Couldn't get enough of it. The wildness, I think. You can't take the bog out of the girl, she always said. Then she'd tease me about being a Dublin jackeen. It was a sort of a cant between us."

Hannah turned away.

She'd never known about Connemara.

"You see that picture there?"

Kit was pointing at a framed print over the sideboard, one of a barefoot girl wearing a shawl. Two goats stood beside her on the side of a hill.

"You should keep that. Your mam loved it."

Hannah took down the print, wiping dust off the frame as she did so. Augustus Burke. *Connemara Girl*. What was it in the picture that had connected with her mother? Had she owned goats as a child? What? Now she'd never know . . .

Hannah took another look around the room. Most of the stuff had been placed in a pile in the centre of it, clothes and bed linen in black bags ready to go to Oxfam, ornaments and crockery in boxes.

Kit could take the picture of the Pope and the Sacred Heart lamp. Hannah felt strange handling them, never having been brought up with such icons.

"I'll think of your mother every time I look at them," Kit said glancing round the room. "It'll be hard to believe she's not living here anymore . . ."

"Yes."

Hannah tried to remember how many times she had visited her mother here – ten times? Twelve, maybe? It was scarcely more. Even then she was seldom on her own. Whenever her mother invited her she would tell her to bring Beryl too or some of the others from Royle. Eventually, though, she'd realized that this was a ploy for preventing the discussion getting too personal.

After that she'd gone on her own as often as she had the courage to, but she could sense her mother's discomfort. She'd been distant, wary, saying that she had to go out later as if to cut the visit short.

The memory of the day she qualified came back to her. They'd had their tea in the Montrose Hotel. The occasion had been spoiled, though, when someone her mother knew had come into the restaurant just as they were leaving. A few strained minutes of conversation followed during which Lil did not introduce Hannah. Hannah was more hurt by it than she let on. Would she have been happier if Lil had introduced her as a friend?

It was only then that it had really hit her what she was: her mother's dirty secret.

The man was a retired solicitor that her mother had cleaned house for years before.

Her mother had only said who he was reluctantly and looked over her shoulders a couple of times as she crossed the road to get the 46A bus back to Dun Laoghaire.

Hannah had been glad to leave her. She didn't remember much about the evening. She met up with some of her friends from the Adelaide and stayed out late, sidestepping any questions about how she'd celebrated with her family.

It surprised her how raw the memory was still. How many times had she told herself that she had let all the pain of her past go? Lots of people had crosses to bear, didn't they, and they got on with life. That's the way it had to be if you wanted to survive. She took a deep breath . . . Now her mother was dead, though, and she'd just found out the name of her father . . . Stuff that had been repressed for years was bound to come to the surface in circumstances like that, wasn't it?

Her phone rang. It was the undertaker. Everything was organized for tomorrow. Had she seen the death notice in the paper? Yes, she had, she said. Yes, it was what they agreed.

She had chosen *The Irish Times* deliberately. Protestants read it. She knew that from boarding school. Goosebumps rose on her arms at the thought of her father seeing it.

She still couldn't understand why she'd been reared Church of Ireland. Religion went deep with people, didn't it? Surely her mother would have wanted her to follow her faith?

It was a mystery. And how had her mother ended up in Bethany Home? And how come she, Hannah, had been sent from there to Royle? More goose bumps rose on her arms . . . Did that mean her father had chosen the place she was reared? Or was it just because her mother, a Roman Catholic, had given birth to her in a Protestant baby home that she had been sent to whatever Protestant children's home there was a space in?

"You look wrecked tired," Kit was saying. "Have you slept at all?"

"Not very much."

"Maybe you should go back to the B&B for a while? This can't be easy for you."

"No, it's a distraction. I'm all right. Honest."

She had intended to leave the sorting until after the funeral, but what was the point? The flat had to be cleared for the landlord.

Was there more information about her father hidden somewhere, she wondered. So far she had found nothing.

"Your father – did Lil say who he was?"

"Not really."

"Oh! It's none of my business anyway but I wish you well – if you're trying to find him or anything . . ."

"Thanks."

Hannah stood up to place the last sorted box with the others in the middle of the floor. Not that much to show for a life, was it?

"I was thinking – would you like to travel with myself and Beryl in the car tomorrow? To the church and that?"

She could see tears in Kit's eyes.

"I'd love that – thanks very much."

"Good. That's sorted then. Do you think many that have been invited will come?"

"They will of course – Sister Ambrose and as many staff as can get off. It's the least they could do the length she worked there."

"Are there any neighbours around here that I should ask?"

"I don't think so. Your mum kept to herself and a lot of people she knew are either dead or they've moved away."

"We'll see who turns up then."

"Yeah."

Kit was putting on her coat.

"I don't know what I'd have done without her sometimes, to be honest. I used to come down here, have a fag and a cup of tea and get things off my chest. She was a good friend."

Hannah swallowed hard to quell the feeling of jealousy again.

"Right. Could you collect whatever you want to take on Thursday, do you think, or maybe I'm rushing you? I told the landlord I'd give the keys back to him on Friday morning. No point in delaying things really."

"You're right. That'll be no problem. A friend of ours is a carpenter and has a van, so Jimmy'll ask him for a hand out. It's very good of you. I won't know myself with all these extra bits and pieces."

"Don't forget these."

Hannah handed her the tins of cat food.

"I'd forget my head if it wasn't stuck to me."

With Kit gone the place seemed empty. Weird.

She rang Beryl.

"I'll be home at about four. I've just the solicitor to see first."

"At least your mother sorted out her affairs," Beryl said. "Must have been hard for her, building up to giving you all that stuff . . ."

There it was again: the sympathy for her mother.

"You don't think it was about time, do you?" she snapped, then regretted it.

"Sorry. I didn't mean . . . Look we'll talk when you get back."

She looked now at the phone number written in small, neat print in her diary: Abe Stephenson's landline number. She'd looked it up in the 05 directory. There was only one Abraham. And only one Knocklannon.

Getting out of the car in the multi-storey car park by the shopping centre, she toyed with the idea of making the call.

Who would answer?

She keyed in the digits, after setting her mobile phone not to display her number. That would give him more information than she wanted him to have right now.

How was he feeling now, she wondered? Indifferent? Scared? Part of her hoped he was.

053 . . .

She felt scared as she put the phone to her ear. Eventually it was answered.

"Hello. Stephenson's."

Feeling panicky, Hannah hit the "off" button. It was a female voice, older, kindly . . . saying the name Stephenson like it belonged to her .

Was it his wife?

Hannah was trembling. How could she have done that? Of course his wife answered. What was she going to do if he had answered – say, "Hello Daddy"? What was she thinking of?

Still shaking, she put her phone in her pocket as she walked up the street to the solicitor's office. She wouldn't tell her about the post office book, she decided. It was in her name, after all. She felt for the book in her pocket, though, anxious that it was still there. Beryl had suggested she get it updated as soon as possible. She would need ID, but that wasn't a problem. Identity . . . She wondered where her father was when she rang. Near the phone? In from feeding or bedding cattle? Back from the mart maybe?

The thought of her father being a farmer excited her. Sowing crops, feeding cattle, sheep maybe . . . She tried to imagine him at all those jobs – jobs she'd helped out with almost thirty years ago as a child when she went to stay at Watson's or Deacon's – Protestant families who took children from Royle to kill two birds with one stone: give the charity children a holiday and get help with hay-making or harvest time or at Christmas when cattle were housed and the daily workload was heavy.

"It's in your blood," Mr Watson had said one day when she'd been walking the fields and was the first to spot a cow with blood murrin.

Was it in her genes? She remembered the welts on her hands from stacking bales in groups of four so that the rain wouldn't destroy them before Mr Deacon had time to put them in the shed, the roughness of calves' tongues when she was putting her fingers in their mouths to get them started on the bucket, the squelch of her wellies in muck as she walked back to the dairy, putting a new filter in the milk strainer before she poured the next unit full of milk into the milk churn . . .

By the time she reached the solicitor's she had almost made up her mind. She could ask for more time off work, couldn't she, and go live in her grandfather's cottage for a while – in Drumcadden. What would be wrong with that? The map she'd looked up had shown it to be north of Wexford town in the direction of Enniscorthy, a couple of townlands away from Knocklannon. The cottage was hers now, wasn't it? She got butterflies in her stomach

at the thought of it. Being close to where he lived . . . Would she have the nerve? She wondered what condition the cottage was in. Maybe it was a kip, but she could do it up, couldn't she? She had lots of choices now about what she could do. Suddenly she felt a bit freer. She was financially better off. She'd be able to clear her credit card and a lot more if she wanted. Beryl was always giving out to her about spending so much, saying she didn't need designer labels to prove she was someone. True, she'd gone over the top a bit since Nanna died . . .

"But that happens a lot, doesn't it, when a parent dies?" she said to herself. "You let your hair down a bit when the control factor is gone."

Pressing the bell at the solicitor's, she tried not to admit the real reason she wanted to go live in Wexford. To be near him, find out what sort of a man he was. Suss out the lie of the land . . . She felt nervous again at the thought of it.

Florrie Stephenson put down the phone.

"Odd."

"What?"

"Whoever was ringing – they said nothing."

"Probably a wrong number."

She picked up the fork that her husband had accidentally knocked off the table and put it in the sink.

"Maybe."

Silent calls made her uneasy. Still, Abe was probably right. No use jumping to conclusions . . .

Eating lunch now she wished he didn't clack his cutlery off the plate so many times before putting food to his mouth.

What was it they said about familiarity and contempt? Still, maybe she was annoying him with something she was doing and he was thinking the very same thing. See the big picture – accept people the way they are – that was the thing to do if ever serenity was to be achieved in this life. Easier said than done, though . . .

"I'll be away tomorrow," she said.

"Oh?"

"The day care centre's going on an outing to Kilkenny. I've been asked to help."

"What time will you be back?"

Florrie put her own dishes in the dishwasher. She couldn't believe it. No caustic comments about that effin place and how much of her time it took up.

"Five o'clock or so. They'll have to be back for the buses at half-past four."

"Right."

"Do you want me to leave some dinner for you? You can heat it up or wait till I come back."

"Stop fussing! I'll be all right," he said, getting up from the table.

Florrie watched him leave his dirty dishes behind him.

"Will you check the sucklers in the big field? I haven't time," he said at the door.

"When I tidy up here."

Filling the dishwasher, she thought of the following day. Headspace – that's what Roy would call it.

She wished that Abe's eldest nephew could come with her. It was ages since they'd had a cultural day out together. Soon . . . Florrie was glad that Abe hadn't asked her questions about the next day's schedule. What he didn't know wouldn't irritate him.

The staff of the day care centre would only need her on the bus trip up and down, so she'd have most of the day to herself. She couldn't wait. Bookshops beckoned, music shops . . . With a bit of luck there would be a lunchtime concert on in the city somewhere. She would sit there drinking up the sounds.

She tried to remember when she'd been in Kilkenny last. Was it the day she'd run away and got as far as the marble city before regrets started addling her head? What year was that? 1966? '68? She'd sat there in the lounge bar of a hotel for hours, eyes like a rabbit with myxomatosis from a night of crying, not looking at anybody.

His words had cut deep. About what use was she when she couldn't have children and how if she'd been a cow she'd have been culled. Eventually, two days later she had gone home, her running away money spent. He had told anyone who asked that she'd been on holiday.

Frank had helped her see a way through it.

He had found her in the church that Saturday, staring at the organ keys instead of playing the hymns that she had gone there to practice.

Her rector had talked about forgiveness, lamented how things could be said in the heat of a row, about how Abe could be trying to deal with his own pain about not having children and how acceptance and peace in their relationship would come in time and with the help of God.

His words had kept her sane. She resisted the temptation now to sit down at the piano. It would have to wait till later. Instead she ran the duster over the polished wood. Abe had brought the piano home in the cattle box, telling her he'd got it cheap at an auction.

She doubted it. The quality was too good. In time, she'd accepted it as some kind of peace offering.

The sucklers in the big field were grazing happily. Walking among them now with a stick she looked from one to another of the cows and calves, looking for signs of illness or unease. There were none. They were fine cattle. Healthy. She'd spotted the champions among them when they were calves just as quickly as Abe had. And she was the one who had trained most of them to the halter, ready for the show ring. Whatever Abe might say, she was due just as much credit for the Knocklannon herd as he was.

Their contentment won't last long, though, she thought, as she closed the field gate.

The calves would be weaned from their mothers next week. She wasn't looking forward to that – the bawling would go on for days.

She was picking windfalls when Max's barks announced her sister-in-law's arrival in the yard.

"I'm in the orchard," she called, hearing the car door close.

Vera was round the side of the house in seconds.

The sight of her sister-in-law irritated her, though she tried not to let it do so. Why was it that Vera's ferret eyes always seemed to get in amongst everything she said? No, that's not very Christian.

"You're at the apples?"

"Yes."

"Are you baking for Friday night?"

Friday night was the night of the harvest thanksgiving.

"Yes. I'll bring some of these to the Centre as well."

"They won't starve in that place with you around anyway."

Florrie picked up the bucket to carry it to another tree.

"Better than letting them rot."

"Abe about?"

"No."

"Will he be long?"

"Didn't say. Gone to town, I think."

Florrie could see Vera now begin to pick a few apples herself.

"Well, what did you think of the Casey one?"

"Who?"

"Don't tell me he didn't mention it?"

"I don't think so."

Florrie listened while Vera told her about Lil Casey and the death notice and the daughter.

"Jim's daughter? Lil? She's dead? She wasn't that old, was she?"

"Sixty-nine."

"She used to work here when she was a child, didn't she? I remember Jim mentioning it."

"If you could call it work. Mother used to give her a few days here and there when she was busy. Wasn't she the sly one, all the same? Jim Casey can't have known about the child, but then she could have had a dozen fellas in Dublin and no one'd have been any the wiser."

Florrie threw the apple she'd picked up away. There were wasp holes in it.

"Still, it must have been hard on her – giving up a child."

"And what right had she bringing one into the world in the first place? Them as do things outside the rules have to pay the price. At least they used to. Nowadays they're getting paid for it, as far as I can see."

Florrie didn't reply.

"Funeral private, if you don't mind. Like she was someone."

"Some people don't want a fuss."

"Or deserve it. Not that anyone from around here'd be going anyway. She's too long out of the place."

Florrie picked up the now-full bucket to go back to the house.

"I suppose. Is Roy busy? He said he'd pick what's left on the trees for me. We can use them for decorating the church."

"He's hedge-cutting today over at Emmet Doyle's. Should have done it last week but he was stuck in the shed at that stonework. Out there till one o'clock in the morning if you don't mind – there's no talking to him."

"It's good to have something that absorbs you. Not everybody has that."

"If there was money in it there might be some sense to it . . ."

"Maybe there are more important things than money. Roy doesn't look at things like that. Was it urgent – what you wanted Abe for?"

"Not really. He said he'd have a look at the ewes with me. I'm picking a few out to sell."

"I'll get him to ring you when he comes back then."

Florrie was glad she hadn't invited Vera in for tea. An invitation always meant her sister-in-law running her eye over the house for sign of improvements and new purchases.

"Isn't it well for some?" she'd say, standing back to look at whatever the new item was. Or "It's all right for them that has it."

Back in the house Florrie left the apples in the back kitchen ready for washing.

The phone rang.

She lifted the receiver.

"Hello. Stephenson's."

There was no sound on the other end.

"Hello."

Still no sound – then the unsettling "click" of the receiver being put down. Florrie replaced the receiver at her end, feeling uneasy. She would ring Eircom if it continued. And she would mention it to Abe when he came home. So much for thinking it was a wrong number.

Getting a parking space near the solicitor's office wasn't easy. Abe Stephenson fumed as he was forced to drive around a second Wexford town car park.

Spying a car about to pull out he turned right against the arrows to get into the space, ignoring the angry blow of the horn of another motorist who had been about to drive into it.

"Feck her!" he muttered. "She should have moved quicker."

When he walked into the solicitor's building the receptionist looked at him nervously from behind a too-high wooden desk.

When he gave his name she told him to go straight up.

Bill O'Connell was waiting for him at the top of the stairs, hand out.

"Abe, how are you?"

"Fine."

After small talk about the weather and farming in general Abe took the chair that was proffered.

"Now, what can I do for you?"

"I'm looking for some advice. For a friend. Confidential."

"Assured, as always."

Abe wasn't so certain. What about all those staff who did the typing? Not to mention the startled hare of a one on reception.

"He's trying to deal with a . . . let's say, a situation . . ."

"What sort of situation?"

"There's a woman claiming that she's his daughter. He's asked me to help him find out where he stands legally."

Bill O'Connell sat back in his chair and made a steeple with his long, clean fingers.

"I see," he said. "And *is* your friend this woman's father?"

"He's not sure. The mother could have been with any number of men for all he knows."

"I see. Well, if she can prove that your . . . friend is her father, she can claim against his estate when he dies. Since the Status of Children Act in 1988, children born outside wedlock have rights equal to those born within it. If your . . . friend has a daughter she would be entitled to one-third of his estate, with his spouse, if he has one, getting two-thirds. If his wife pre-deceases him, his daughter would be the sole heir."

Abe swallowed hard before replying.

"And is there any way . . . he can stop her getting anything?"

"As I say, if she has proof, no. He can deny paternity, of course, but if she goes to court to demand a DNA test and that proves positive . . ."

"He's fucked?"

"I wouldn't put it quite that way but there wouldn't be any way out of that person inheriting. Has your friend met his alleged . . . daughter?"

"No."

"Is the mother alive?"

"No, she died recently."

"Was the alleged daughter mentioned in the death notice?"

"Yes."

"Was she adopted or was she reared by her mother?"

"In some class of orphanage."

"Is there anything to connect your friend with this woman's mother? Paper evidence of financial support for the child, for example?"

"I don't think so. He says he was careful."

"Mmm . . . Was this an open relationship – I mean, could others testify to there being a relationship between your friend and the mother?"

"No. No one knew."

"A name on the birth certificate?"

"No!"

"Has this woman – the alleged daughter – contacted the person she believes to be her father yet?"

"No, but there have been silent phone calls. He thinks it was her."

"I see. Does your friend have a wife?"

"Yes."

"Has he considered discussing this . . . allegation with her? The truth, if it is the truth, while difficult to admit, might be better in the long run."

Abe Stephenson stood up.

"There's no question of that."

The solicitor adjusted his cufflinks.

"Well, there's not really much your friend can do unless this woman contacts him directly. It may be that she doesn't want contact or that the mother hasn't actually told her who her father is. Your friend may be crossing a bridge before he comes to it."

"Aye and sometimes people lose the run of their head when they're dying. God knows what she's told her."

"Was she reared using her mother's maiden name?"

"Yes."

"Your friend – does he have a will made already?"

"You know I have!"

Abe Stephenson cursed himself for letting it slip.

"Ah! It's better to be clear about everything, that way I can advise you best. In confidence, of course."

Abe knew he was sweating. All this talk was rattling him.

"One of your nephews benefits, if I remember correctly, along with your wife?"

"Why should he lose out because of someone turning up out of nowhere thinking she can get something out of me?"

"Well, all I can say is if she's not your daughter – and you have intimated that you are not certain she is – then you've nothing to worry about. A DNA test would sort it out once and for all, as I mentioned. You could do that voluntarily and that would clear up the matter immediately."

Abe Stephenson had his hand on the doorknob.

"There'll be no test."

"I'm trying to play devil's advocate here, but is there a chance that you might feel differently if you got to know her – if there was a possibility that she is . . ."

Abe nearly twisted the knob off the door opening it.

"No!"

"Well then, the best thing to do is not to anticipate the future. Until she makes a move you won't know what she wants. If she contacts you then you'll have to decide what to do, but that is the situation to the best of my knowledge. What age is she now?"

Abe tried to think. 1964, no 1965.

"Nearly forty."

"I see. I'm sorry I can't be any more help to you than that at present.

"Aye, but you'll send me the bill anyway."

"I hope I've taken instruction related to your business satisfactorily over the years."

"Aye."

Pity it wasn't some land purchase he was handling now . . .

Driving home Abe almost forgot to stop at a junction. Damn new one-way systems in the town – why couldn't they leave the roads alone?

"It'll be my word against the word of a dead woman – simple as that," he said to himself.

If the child, this Hannah, took after her mother she'd be soft-going and he'd have nothing to worry about. As he swung the car into the yard, his wife's hens scrawked and fluttered to get out of the way. Fucking hens, he thought, and fucking chickens coming home to roost . . .

Hannah was pleased to see Beryl's car parked in the driveway of the house they owned together in Waterford.

She had dreaded the thoughts of a cold, dark house, especially today.

The journey from Dún Laoghaire had been long and slow because of traffic and rain, and she'd been preoccupied thinking of the two phone calls she'd made to Abe Stephenson's number.

A woman had answered both times. Was it his wife?

"If he had answered, what would I have said?" she asked herself, almost breaking into a sweat as she took her bag out of the boot. She wondered now how she'd had the nerve to ring at all.

Beryl must have got off work early so that she'd be there. What would she do without her?

Beryl always joked that Hannah had become a nurse just because she'd had so much practice with her.

When Beryl had asthma attacks as a child, Hannah had often sat up with her, trying to keep her calm or she had gone to the hospital with her and Nanna when the attack was bad, Hannah holding Beryl's head out the window so that she could take big, gulpy breaths as Nanna drove.

The aroma of dinner hit her now as she opened the door.

She remembered, then, that she had eaten nothing since breakfast.

Beryl hugged her tightly before taking her bag.

"You ok?"

"Numb."

"Food'll warm you up. Come on. You're as pale as a ghost."

The house was warm, welcoming.

"I gave Kit some of my mother's stuff – furniture and that," she said as she finished her Spaghetti Bolognese. "Whatever she wanted."

"Right."

"She seemed glad of it."

"That's good. Was there anything you wanted to keep?"

Hannah shivered as she told Beryl about the goat girl print.

"My own mother and I didn't even know what she liked or didn't like . . ."

Beryl's hand on her arm was comforting.

"There's such a thing as dwelling on stuff too much. Come on – coffee!"

In the sitting room Hannah took the mug that her friend handed her. Right now she felt like drinking a bottle of wine instead but she had to keep herself together for tomorrow. How was it that she was always looking forward to wine now – she usedn't to need it at all.

"Did you find anything about . . . him?"

"Nothing. Some photographs – grandparents mostly. Not very well-off looking. Lived-in kind of faces. And I never even saw them in reality . . ."

"I know, it's tough . . . I forgot to tell you. Fr Brophy rang. You're to ring him back."

"Right. I'd better do that now."

Quickly she dialled the number of the presbytery in Dún Laoghaire.

"Fr Brophy? Hannah Casey here."

The priest sounded friendly, caring. He had everything arranged for tomorrow, he said. He'd meet her at the funeral parlour at 10.30 and then go ahead to the chapel. Her mother would be proud of her for organizing everything so well, he told her. He asked her how she was herself.

"Surviving. It's all a bit strange, to be honest."

"Of course it is, but our Lord will help you through the loss and the pain. He is with all of us in time of need, even though sometimes we can't see it."

Hannah put the mobile phone down on the coffee table.

"I didn't even know if she went to any church. He said she went to Mass every Sunday – and to confession – can you imagine that? I wonder did she have to confess having me, confess . . . doing it?

"Now you're tormenting yourself."

"Being thought of as the product of sin – not a great feeling, is it?"

"No."

"I remember going there to help Nanna to collect a baby once – to Bethany Home – do you? We went on several buses and all the way back in a taxi. The baby was only a few weeks old. I was that baby once."

"Yeah."

Hannah hugged a cushion.

"She must have loved him, mustn't she? My mother wouldn't be the sort to . . . do it lightly, would she?"

"I don't think so."

"She wasn't a drinker either so that wouldn't be a factor. Kit said she never touched the stuff."

"There you are then."

"Not like me so!"

"You didn't need the stuff one time either."

"Don't start . . . Will you listen to me, wanting to be conceived in love! I've known enough men to know it doesn't matter. Most of them only need to be in the humour for it."

"We'd all like to be wanted. Feeling like that's only natural."

Hannah was sorry she had spoken. Beryl had no idea who her father or mother was. At least she'd had a mother – of sorts. Maybe if she was able to understand more, she'd be able to forgive . . .

"God, I wish Nanna was still here," Hannah said.

"Me too," said Beryl.

She thought of the night Nanna had died, the thirty of them singing her into heaven.

Rock of Ages, Cleft for me, Let me hide myself in thee . . .

And Nanna had waited for Hannah to arrive from London where she'd been on holidays, opening her eyes as if in final recognition of their presences before puffing out her last breath. She was eighty-six.

"Organizing funerals turns you into an adult very quickly, doesn't it?"

"Sure does."

The phone rang, startling the two of them.

It was Rita, another of the Roylers. She'd be at the funeral tomorrow. Noel would too, and Ivy and Sharon.

The others were abroad and wouldn't be able to come at such short notice.

Hannah was glad Beryl was fielding the phone calls. Right now she was very tired. She couldn't remember feeling as exhausted as this in a very long time. She hoped she'd sleep but right now she didn't want to be on her own.

The doorbell went.

Beryl was still on the phone, giving Noel directions from Cork.

"I'll get it," Hannah said, pulling herself up off the sofa.

It was Matt. He stood there on the doorstep, collar up and hands in pockets, greyer than she remembered him.

"I saw the death notice in the paper. I didn't know whether you'd want to see me but I'm here anyway."

"Come in."

She pulled away from his touch. No point in giving him mixed signals now.

She showed him into the sitting room, glad that Beryl was here.

"Matt."

"Beryl, how are you?"

"Ok. Can I get you a cup of tea?"

"No, thanks, I won't be staying. I just wanted to . . ."

Beryl got up.

"Right, I'll go polish my shoes. Will I do yours for you?"

Hannah nodded.

"That'd be great, thanks."

"Right."

"Sit down," she heard herself say.

"You should have phoned."

"I'm ok. It was good of you to come but there was really no need."

"It isn't a crime to ask for help or accept it."

"Beryl's been great – everybody really."

"That's good."

"She must have taken ill suddenly . . ."

Hannah heard herself give him the details. It was as if someone else was telling him.

"Did you have a chance to talk to her . . . before she died?"

"Not that much."

"So you're still in the dark . . . about a lot of things?"

"Yes."

She knew he meant her father. She'd spoken to Matt about him a few times when her guard was down after a few glasses of wine.

"A name, that's all she gave me."

"Right . . . Will you look him up?"

"I don't know. I want to get the funeral over first."

"You should talk all this over with someone."

"You mean a shrink?"

"Shrink, counsellor, there are lots of good people out there."

"That's up to me."

"You're right – I shouldn't be so nosey. I'm just worried about you. Old habits die hard and all that . . ."

"Yeah, well , I'm a big girl now."

"What if he's at her funeral? Have you thought about how you'll cope?"

Panic rose in Hannah's stomach.

"No . . . Yes . . . What if he is? That's my business. Please . . ."

"You're right. I should go."

At the door she could still see the concern in his eyes.

"Did you get time off work?"

"Special leave."

"Good."

That wouldn't surprise him.

He'd shouted it at her one day, about the drinking, about how she was losing it sometimes, how she needed to take time off to sort herself out before she lost her job and everyone important to her . . .

"I'd better go."

"I should have asked how you were – school . . ."

"First term – I think I'm getting too old for it. Anyway, if there's anything . . ."

"Thanks."

"Say goodbye to Beryl for me."

"I will."

Beryl came out of the kitchen as Hannah closed the front door.

"You ok?"

"Yes."

"It was good of him to come, I suppose."

"I wasn't that nice to him."

"No one's themselves at a time like this. Listen, I've put on your electric blanket. What about some hot milk to help you sleep?"

"You're really doing a Nanna on it now! I'll have a bath, I think. After I sort out what I'll wear tomorrow."

"Good idea. I'll bring up the milk when you're finished."

"Thanks."

In her bedroom later she opened her wardrobe doors.

No, she wouldn't wear black. It was dismal, inappropriate. She would feel hypocritical in it.

She thought of her mother's fashion sense. It hadn't stretched beyond floral dresses, flesh coloured tights, plain cardigans and flat shoes that gave rein to puffy ankles. She eventually chose an olive green trouser suit. She'd bought it for work, when she had once been asked to be a nursing spokesperson at a coronary care conference.

With a black polo neck underneath it she would feel all right. Green suited her, she knew, matching her eyes.

"Not my mother's eyes."

She could still see Lil's watery blue ones staring at the ceiling of the hospice room.

Opening a drawer, she fished out a small box and removed the newspaper cutting. She stared again at the image of the man she now believed to be her father: Abe Stephenson.

Were his eyes green? She wished the photograph was in colour. She told herself she could see a resemblance. He was tall, too, unless the other man in the photo was very small. She must have got her height from him. What other genes of his would she have, she wondered? If she ever met him would anyone, seeing them stand together, know they were father and daughter?

Later in bed, she tried to quell the emptiness and the lack of compassion she felt.

She hated her father for not recognizing her, but what if he hadn't been able to? What if he was married? Sending money counted for something, though, didn't it? Didn't it mean he had some kind of feeling for her?

Did he have other children? The thought both disturbed and excited her. A brother? A sister? Brothers *and* sisters? Half blood. She tried to imagine what they'd look like, what the family was like. Family . . .

As a child she had seldom been asked to a friend's house after school. Most parents didn't want their children getting too close to the charity children.

Holly Warren's mother had been different, though, inviting her to Holly's birthday parties along with all the other children in the class.

For weeks after each birthday party Hannah had daydreamed about living in a real family. She could still remember Holly's birthday cake being brought in by Holly's father. He seemed to fill the room with his kindness. She had envied Holly so much, getting a hug and a present from him.

Books had given her daydream fodder too. Sometimes she imagined living in *Little Women's* March family and her father was away at the war and when he came back everything would be all right and he and her mother would take her home with them to a house that had high ceilings and big fires and a posh clock that chimed on the quarter hour. Other times she felt more like Robinson Crusoe, alone on some kind of noisy island, surviving, making do but essentially alone in the world.

She opened the post office book that her mother had given her then slapped it shut again. She still didn't believe it. What had made him pay it? Was he an honourable man who wanted to face up to his responsibilities or was it the action of a coward: a pay off when he wouldn't give anything else of himself?

She felt agitated again – why hadn't her mother told her about the account before? On her twenty-first birthday, for instance? No, that would have brought questions with it. Questions asked too soon.

Now she felt cheated of answers.

So much for happy endings! Walt Disney should have been shot.

Beryl was at the door with the hot milk.

"Night then."

"Night – and thanks."

"That's ok. I'll give you a call at seven."

"I'll be awake."

Moving into a foetal position, the resentment towards her father bubbled in her veins again, but at least now she felt more certain about what she would do . . . If he didn't find her, she would find him and right now, she knew, nothing would give her more pleasure than to see the whites of his eyes.

Chapter
TWO

"Farming's fucked!"

"You could sing that if you had an air for it . . ."

Abe Stephenson wouldn't stay at this farmers' association meeting much longer. No point.

The two men in front of him were right – farming was going down the plughole. In the packed hall he could smell fear under the whiff of sweat, cow dung, sheep shit and diesel oil. Most farmers in the room, including himself, had their arms folded as if to ward off the message coming from the guys at the top table.

Decoupling . . . modulation . . . payments from Europe separated out from production . . . All around him people were struggling to make sense of it all.

Not only would you not need to farm at all to get a cheque from Europe in 2005, the future of the Irish sugar beet industry also hung in the balance.

Abe found it difficult to take in, especially the beet uncertainty. He'd grown sugar beet all his life, and right now it was the only crop there was profit in. Now another beet factory closing, this time in the nearby town of Carlow, was a distinct possibility. The writing was on the wall – he could feel it in his bones.

His chair scraped noisily as he pushed it back to stand up.

When he got to the door he took several deep breaths of night air to ease the tightness in his chest. Jesus, the last thing he needed now was pain . . . No, he was ok. Farming was finished – at least the way it had been, he thought, as he walked the short distance to his car.

He'd heard the smaller farmers' anxiety in their questions.

"We've to go out and look for jobs, is that it?"

"Everyone has to make his own decision: diversify, take off-farm employment, do what's necessary to survive," was the advice from the top table.

For many, used to thinking of themselves as self-employed and proud of it, it would be a bitter pill to swallow.

Abe was glad he was wealthy enough and old enough not to have to worry about the likes of that. He was glad, too, that he had his own plans for wringing opportunity out of change. The building development would give him something to focus on and he had the money to get it off the ground, unlike some.

Not that he agreed with farmers getting EU money for doing nothing.

That's what had upset the apple cart in the first place. Handing money out to bring people into farming, creating beef mountains and milk lakes until the arse fell out of every enterprise.

Subsidies – there was no dignity in them either. You might cash the cheques in the bank but you could never get over the fact that they were handouts, not to mention getting it in the teeth in the pub about farmers being propped up when other sectors of society weren't.

Abe felt nauseous now. His chest felt even tighter. Jesus! He had to get home.

He felt in his pocket for his indigestion tablets, fingers fumbling to get one out as quickly as he could. With a bit of luck that would stave off trouble.

Breathe . . . Stay calm . . .

As other farmers came out of the centre he pretended he was on the phone so that no one would approach him to talk.

Good, he was all right.

A few minutes later he manoeuvred the Mercedes out onto the street.

He would have to distract himself – that was it, think of other things, not of farming, not of her either.

Christ! Her . . . The child . . . He concentrated hard on the road. Think of something else – think of the killing you are going to make out of the new houses . . . He'd be in clover! That's what he had to do: forget farming and funerals and trying to make his mind up about going to Dublin tomorrow.

At least his gut feeling about the building project had been correct. Farmers had to look at alternatives, other options. Site and house prices were climbing all the time. Pride never paid the bills – he'd learned that a long time ago. Sticking in a "we should be able to make a living from farming" and an "it's not fair" mode didn't pay the bills either. Facts were facts. There was either money in something or there wasn't, and at the moment it wasn't in farming. Everyone had to face up to that. Close to a hobby – that's what it would be for the moment – and then only if you could afford that luxury.

When he reached home, Abe felt relieved but weary. Max ran to him, tail wagging madly, after recognizing the sound of the car.

"Good boy!" he said, patting the dog's head as he approached the back door. At least someone was glad to see him.

Damn! Florrie was still up, her fingers clacking on the laptop in front of her on the kitchen table, surrounded by notebooks and paper. Still typing up the histories of ould ones at the day care centre. Would she ever get sense?

He waited for her to say something, but she didn't.

He hung up his coat thinking that there was a time she would have coaxed a greeting out of him.

"Did you check the cattle?"

His wife was closing down her computer.

"Half an hour ago. They're fine."

"Right," Abe said, sitting by the cooker to take off his boots.

He was glad he hadn't to go out to check the stock. If she said the animals were all right they were – he could depend on that.

He heard her laptop click shut. The sound of her shuffling papers irritated him. He would go into his study where he'd have a bit of peace.

He found the bottle of whiskey in the filing cabinet where he'd left it.

She was at the door now, as he turned to get a glass off his desk.

"A cup of tea would be better for you."

"It would in its arse!"

"It's your funeral. How did the meeting go?"

"Waste of time."

"Right."

The word "funeral" made him break into a sweat again. For a split second he thought she knew. Lil Casey's funeral was tomorrow. He had to decide whether to go or not.

"I'll be gone early – about eight," she was saying.

"Right so."

He waited until he heard her footsteps on the landing before he took out the two-day-old newspaper to look at the funeral notice again.

"Funeral private", it said. Good. That way no nosey parkers from around here would be going up to Dublin for a gawk. Not that Lil had kept in touch with anyone around here, he was sure of that. Apart from Peg Travers, who had a key for the cottage, there was no one else that Lil communicated with in the locality as far as he knew and Peg, he was certain, was in England at the moment, visiting her sister.

He stuffed the newspaper back into the drawer he'd hidden it in. No, he was going to no funeral. It had nothing to do with him, he told himself. He'd washed his hands of all that years ago, hadn't he? It didn't concern him now.

The whiskey tasted good. He sat back in his leather office chair, a Christmas present from Florrie twenty years before. He had condemned her extravagance but he had liked the chair – he knew quality when he saw it.

Closing his eyes he took more deep breaths. Stay calm, stay in control. He'd got out of other sticky situations in his day by keeping his head. This situation was no different. Bluff it out – that's what he had to do. It would be Lil's word against his and she was dead. What was he worrying about?

The aerial photographs on the study walls caught his eye. The photographs were in sequence, one taken every ten years since he took over Knocklannon. It was an indulgence he had been unable to resist.

He liked seeing the progression in them – the improved buildings, more fields reclaimed, trenches cleaned up, the yard cemented. Even the silage pits were bigger than in the 1960s – he could see the increase in the ground taken up with them as he looked around the room. More silage represented more stock. He knew he had improved the farm since he got it. No EU bollocks could take that away from him. He had worked hard, taken risks and bought more land when he could and ploughed what money he could back in, through difficult decades. A good fucking operator, a bank manager had called him once. It had put a grin on his face for days.

What would he do now, given "de-coupling"? He would cut back on tillage – only sow a crop if the field was good enough to yield more than two and a half ton of corn to the acre – that's what. Sowing would be a waste of time and money otherwise. The pedigrees – that's where he would concentrate his farming energy now. His hand ran over the farm's Hereford register that lay on his desk. He had filled in registration forms for hundreds of pedigree calves over the years. Herd *Knocklannon*. Breeder *Abraham Stephenson*. It was something to be proud of. So what if they were a bit of an indulgence and he had to pay Aidan down the road to help him on a part-time basis now that he had slowed up a bit? He could well afford it and, anyway, people were still prepared to pay a premium for a Knocklannon Hereford. That wouldn't change.

His hand shook as he lifted the glass. Damn it! He concentrated on it until it steadied again.

Would he go to the funeral? Florrie would be away all day tomorrow in Kilkenny – he would be free to go where he liked without her knowing, if he wanted to.

He could even take her car to Dublin, if he gave her a lift to the bus in the morning and collected her in the evening. She'd be none the wiser and it wouldn't be as obvious as having his own car at the cemetery, just in case someone who knew him was there and recognized it.

He looked at the newspaper again. 11 a.m. from funeral home to the chapel in Monkstown. That would mean it would be at least half past twelve before they'd reach Dean's Grange for the burial. He could go there. It was a huge cemetery. He could pretend he was visiting some other grave, couldn't he? There would be lots of people doing that – and he could watch from a distance. See her . . . The child . . .

Abe Stephenson fastened the cap on the whiskey bottle tightly to stop the remorse seeping in. *Know your enemy*, he whispered – that was how he'd survived all his life. To know her – this woman who would now be, what, almost forty years of age – he would have to see her. He'd know by the look of her what he was up against. He prided himself on being able to judge animal or human character just by the way they carried themselves. Would this Hannah be like Lil Casey – soft and round shouldered and too quick to smile – or would she hold her head up, look the world right in the eye and damn him to hell?

The solicitor's words came back to him. *Until she makes a move you won't know what she wants . . .*

Even if he did go she would never know he was at the funeral and even if she did make a move in the future he knew what he had to do. Deny absolutely everything.

Hannah tightened her coat around her as she double-checked that the door of the house in Waterford was locked. It was time to leave for the funeral in Dún Laoghaire.

She hadn't slept well and she shivered now as an east wind clipped her face. Why was it always freezing on funeral days, she wondered, as she got into the car.

Beryl already had the engine running.

Hannah took the checklist from her pocket before fastening her seat belt.

"Better run through this before we leave in case we've forgotten something."

"Definitely."

"Wreath, *check*, reading, *check*, money for priest, *check*, money for hotel refreshments, *check*, phone number of hotel so we can ring them to tell them we're leaving the graveyard . . ."

"I'll do that," Beryl said. "You'll have enough to do, talking to people."

"That'd be great, thanks. How long do you think it'll take to get there from Dean's Grange?"

"Fifteen minutes or less, depending on traffic, Fr Brophy said."

"Not too bad. Do you think soup and sandwiches is enough for everyone? Maybe they'll think I'm mean – that I should be treating them to a proper meal."

"No one'll think that. They'll be glad of whatever's there. It's you they want to support."

"Yeah. Or gawp at . . ."

"Don't think like that. Have you decided whether you'll sing or not?"

Hannah had thought about it. She had sung solo at Nanna's funeral – *Amazing Grace* – Nanna had always loved it and Hannah had been glad to sing it even if emotion had choked it towards the end.

Hannah shrugged.

"No. My mother never heard me sing. She didn't even know I had a good voice. Why would I sing for her now?"

"She'd have been proud of you though – if she had heard you."

"I don't even know if she liked music. Or if she did, what sort . . ." More questions that she might never get answers to.

Hannah wondered now about her father's family. Were they good singers? Did she get her interest in music from them? Her head ached already. She hoped it would lift before they hit Dublin.

Hannah was glad Beryl was driving. Beryl's car was old and small but it was fine. She'd left her own VW Golf at home in Waterford.

It always amused her how she and Beryl had such different tastes in cars. Beryl didn't worry about what she drove as long as it got her from A to B. Hannah preferred a flashier model that she felt good behind the wheel of, even if it cost her an arm and a leg.

"One day I'll drive a sports car," she'd told Nanna one time.

"Course you will, pet, and you can take me for a spin when you get one."

And she had, too. She'd bought a soft-top, red MG when she was nursing for five years, the engine nearly clapped out and a bad buy but she had loved it. She'd taken Nanna for a drive around Greystones and Nanna had laughed and said she felt like Grace

Kelly and then they'd both laughed and said all they needed now were a couple of Bing Crosbys.

The smell of the carnation wreath on the back seat brought Hannah back to reality. She didn't even like the smell of them. Why hadn't she chosen her own favourite flower – stargazer lilies – to put on the grave? Lilies. Even the name would have been appropriate. Hadn't she always loved it when Matt arrived with a bunch? She could almost smell them now. No, they were Matt flowers, not funeral flowers. She would stick with the carnations.

Imagine – she didn't even know what her mother's favourite cut flower was. She did know what her favourite pot plant was though: geraniums. There were several of them in the flat, cluttering the windowsills and weighting the room with their heavy smell. That stink, mixed with the faint aroma of cat, had made Hannah feel nauseous and she had put the houseplants outside the back door the first day she went there.

She had said no when Beryl had suggested a single red rose to place on the coffin.

That was Nanna's tribute.

The traffic was heavy as they got to Dublin. When they reached the funeral parlour in Monkstown she saw Kit Bermingham standing at the door, eyes scanning the traffic.

Kit was dressed totally in black, her thin face more pale and gaunt than ever because of it, Hannah thought. Kit's cheeks were sucked in as she dragged hard on a cigarette.

"That's Kit, that I told you about," Hannah said. "The priest is here too, thank goodness."

"Good."

After parking they walked along the terrace by the hire-all centre. Friends she was reared with from Royle came towards her, hugging her, one after another, saying little but Hannah felt their warmth and support.

She wasn't an only child really – she was actually blessed with a lot of family. Who needed blood bonds? These were better.

Kit gave her a hug, too, crying as she did so.

"She was the best in the world," Kit was saying, after Hannah had introduced her to Beryl and some of the others.

Hannah said nothing. Why were dead people always elevated to sainthood, she wondered?

Kit introduced her to the nun in charge of the cleaning staff and two other women who had worked with Lil.

"Very sorry for your trouble."

"Very glad to meet you. Your mother was a good woman."

Hannah could feel their eyes boring into her. She felt anger seeping in again, as she thought about how if her mother had fully acknowledged her she'd have met all her friends and work colleagues long before now and today wouldn't be half so weird . . .

"Hannah."

Father Brophy was there, asking her to go in.

"We have to keep to time or there'll be problems at the graveyard. There's another burial straight after your mother's, I'm afraid."

"Of course."

"Shall we go in?"

She linked Beryl's arm as she did so.

The funeral parlour was dimly lit and small. Beryl guided her up to the front seat to take her place nearest the coffin. She had asked for the coffin not to be left open.

Hannah beckoned to Kit to sit beside them, and seeing her gesture, Kit burst into fresh tears. Hannah felt envious of Kit's emotion. Why couldn't she feel that kind of grief?

Hannah was glad her mother had had a good friend, though. It made her mother seem normal somehow, not the distant, weak, wary woman she knew and had tried to love.

"How many people are here?" Hannah whispered to Beryl.

Beryl looked around, discreetly doing a head count.

"Sixteen, seventeen . . ."

"Maybe I shouldn't have made it private." she said.

She felt Beryl squeeze her arm.

"She probably wouldn't have wanted crowds anyway."

Hannah looked round herself now, looking for elderly men. What age would her father be now – in his seventies?

No one in the room fitted that description. He hadn't come . . . She'd been a fool to think he would. He probably didn't even know her mother was dead. Would he even care? Was she stupid to be expecting him in the first place?

"Brothers and sisters in Christ . . ."

As the prayers continued, Hannah tried to mouth the response.

At last – the first stage over. Suddenly everyone was on their feet and the undertakers were wheeling the coffin out.

Beryl guided her to follow the priest.

He had said it would be easier to walk the couple of hundred yards to the church. The Gardaí were already stopping the traffic.

Hannah didn't like all this fuss. She'd have gone straight to the graveyard but the priest was having none of it.

"Lil would want it done properly, I believe. She always attended Mass. Her faith meant a lot to her."

"Of course," she'd said. She wouldn't deny her mother a proper funeral. She felt conspicuous, exposed, though, walking behind the hearse. What right had she to hold up traffic with her bereavement? She could imagine drivers cursing the delay all the way back to Dalkey.

The church was dark after the brightness they'd come from. Her friends from Royle had lifted the coffin with the undertakers and her mother was now once again being transported up the aisle.

She would never have been up the aisle in the real sense. She wondered if her mother had dreamed of being married, of white dresses and big weddings and a good husband.

The priest began to speak.

The grave attendants looked stressed. Hannah had insisted on the whole group being together before they made their way to the grave –

that was what had made the men anxious. The next funeral was due in and this one was running late.

"We should go," Father Brophy said.

Seeing Kit and her husband finally hurry towards them, she nodded. It wouldn't have been fair not to wait for her mother's friend.

Kit's hand felt damp in Hannah's as they walked the few yards to the grave. At least it wasn't a wet day. There was less wind here than in Waterford and crows still "kraacked" in the trees, undisturbed by the human traffic.

"*Ashes to ashes, dust to dust.*"

The two graveyard attendants lowered the coffin.

"Hail Mary, full of grace . . ."

Hannah could see the purple thread veins on the priest's cheeks. She scarcely heard the words. Odd the way the brain picks out detail in the most serious of moments . . .

The two workmen had moved away now, walking quietly but quickly toward the other end of the cemetery where their services were awaited.

It's a dispatch line now – coffins waiting to be put into the ground, one, two, three, she thought.

Now the priest was speaking.

"Lil's daughter, Hannah, would like everyone to join her for some refreshments immediately after this. Beryl here has directions to the hotel typed up for anyone who needs them, so we look forward to seeing you all there."

And it was over. Beryl squeezed her arm.

"I'll ring the hotel."

"Thanks."

Hannah wished the whole charade was over. She hadn't even cried. Would people think she was hard? There would be some, she knew, who would comment on it.

She was glad of the heat that met her as she entered the hotel. Making her excuses, she went to the Ladies and entered the cubicle furthest from the door. She needed silence – isolation for a few minutes – and a glass of wine or five, but that would have to wait.

The sound of Beryl's voice brought her back to reality.

"Hannah – you in there?"

"Coming."

She applied fresh lipstick and ran a comb through her hair at the sink while Beryl watched.

"You ok?"

She could see the concern in her friend's reflection.

"Fine."

"They're ready to serve the soup."

"Good."

She found herself sitting beside the nun who was Lil's boss at the hospital.

"Your mother was a great worker," she was saying. "You could always expect the others to ring in sick or have some excuse for not coming to work one day a month or so, but you could always depend on Lil. The only time she didn't turn up was the day she got news of her illness. She was due to work the afternoon shift after getting the results from the consultant. 'You'll have to page Sister Ambrose', she told the consultant, 'she'll be wondering where I am.' So they did. I stayed with her while she was being admitted. She had a strong faith and that stood to her."

"Really?"

So many things she didn't know about her mother . . .

"You're a nurse, I believe?"

"Yes. Coronary care."

"A caring person, obviously, if you went into that profession."

"I suppose."

Hannah wished the nun would stop talking. She was finding it hard to concentrate.

"And have you had a chance to think about the future? You will take some time off, I hope. Bereavement is a strange thing. Sometimes the shock doesn't sink in for a while and you have more pain than most to cope with, God knows. Do you know your father at all?"

So – even a nun couldn't hide her curiosity. Looking around at the group of people in the lounge she was sure that's what they were all thinking. She hated to see the pain in the Roylers' faces, though. None of them knew their parents. Some, unlike her, who at least knew her mother, hadn't a clue who they were. That has always made her feel strangely guilty – and sometimes superior.

"Excuse me, I must check that everyone has had enough to eat," she said, side-stepping the nun's question.

She checked on Father Brophy, who was sitting at the end of a table talking to Ivy. She wondered what they were talking about – her?

"Hannah, child, that was lovely food – just the thing on a cold day."

"Did you get enough tea?"

"Yes, and biscuits and me supposed to be avoiding the same objects. That's the trouble with being a priest, you have to visit people's houses and, God love them, you're not five minutes in but you are offered sustenance. Roll on Lent when I'll have an excuse for not partaking."

The priest stood up.

"And now, my dear, I must go. I've a christening at five o'clock, so I'll say goodbye."

"Thank you. The service . . . the Mass was lovely. I think my mother would have liked it."

"Course she would and she'd be proud of how the day has gone and of how you organized it."

"Thank you."

As the last of the people left to go home Hannah felt relieved. They had all promised to be in touch soon and she knew they would be, if she wanted them to.

"What do you want to do now?" Beryl asked.

"Go back to her flat, I think. Maybe there's something I missed."

"Right, I'll get the coats."

It was freezing in the basement apartment.

Hannah plugged in the two-bar electric fire.

"You sorted a lot already by the looks of things."

"Yeah, there's just the kitchen stuff left to do. Maybe you'd give me a hand tomorrow taking what Kit doesn't want to Oxfam."

"Of course. We could have left all this until tomorrow, you know. Maybe you'd be better taking it easy."

"No, I'd rather be doing something. What's sitting around a B&B twiddling our thumbs going to achieve?"

"If that's what you want. Kitchen cupboards first?"

"Yes. There are some old newspapers in that corner. We can use them to wrap the crockery."

"Good idea."

Her mother had been a hoarder – that much was evident. Behind the jugs in one cupboard Hannah found a clump of bills and bits of paper. She took it out and placed it on the counter, looking at each item one after another: old ESB bills, a receipt for a shoe repair in 1976 and some old birthday cards . . . Then she stopped. Her hand shook as she unfolded some familiar pieces of wallpaper. They were drawings she had done in Royle and given to her mother as presents when she was a small child – that's why the wallpaper was so familiar. It had been on the walls of the hall in Royle for years.

"She kept them!"

Hannah couldn't see clearly anymore. She'd kept them.

"She wrote on them," Beryl said.

Hannah turned one over to look. She had written "H, 6", and "H, 9"

H – She hadn't even written her full name!

The hurt surfaced again.

"She couldn't even stick them on the wall or the fridge like normal mothers! God! Why couldn't I have just lived here with her?"

"In an ideal world you could have. Sometimes secrets are just too big . . ."

"Too big, my granny, the secret was about self-protection, so no one would think bad of her, so that Father Brophy would think she was a good person and Sister Ambrose wouldn't look down on her as a fallen woman. She put herself before me all the time – how can I stop resenting that?

"She loved you, I'm sure she did."

"I wish I had your confidence!"

"She wouldn't have come to see you if she didn't. She'd have forgotten all about you, never come near Royle . . . Some of us'd have given our eye teeth to have a mother nearby."

Hannah pulled herself up short.

"I'm sorry . . . Christ, I should be grateful, I know, but sometimes you get fed up being grateful."

Hannah felt a tissue being pushed into her hand.

"If she'd even acknowledged me a few years ago – five, ten . . . ? The world has lightened up so much. It would have been a nine day wonder."

"Maybe she wanted to – who knows? Maybe she was afraid of what her own father would say. Could be any amount of reasons."

Hannah blew her nose again. Always protecting herself or someone else's feelings . . . Why hadn't her mother thought of her? Put her feelings first?

"Right now – compassion – I can't feel a lot of it for her," she said. "Or for him."

"You don't have to apologize for your feelings."

Hannah almost laughed.

"Feelings! When were we ever allowed to have them? When we got angry we were punished, when we cried we were told to stop – and now all that crap is in there somewhere ready to erupt . . ."

Beryl was looking away.

"There's a bag here that we can put the drawings in," she said. "You'll want to bring them with you."

"Yes."

"Hannah . . ."

"What?"

Hannah heard the nervousness in her friend's voice.

"What? Say it!"

"You know the picture of the man you think is your father?"

"Yes."

"Maybe I'm wrong . . . I shouldn't be getting your hopes up when it mightn't have been him at all."

"What? Who?"

Hannah grabbed her friend by the shoulders.

"Was he there? Jesus, tell me!"

"I don't know for sure."

"Tell me exactly what you saw!"

"I wanted to ring the hotel when the burial was over but I realized I'd left my phone in the car, so I left you there with everyone else and headed back to where we were parked. It's just that I saw this tall, elderly man on his own watching us for a minute. When he saw me he turned and walked off towards the other funeral. I thought maybe he'd lost his way but the expression on his face . . . it was . . ."

"What did he look like? God, why didn't you say before? Why didn't you tell me there and then?"

"It all happened in a split second. One minute he was there, the next he was gone. He just looked a bit like the picture – his face, that's all I'm saying. And the hat was the same – tweed."

"What else?"

"I don't know, tall, seventies maybe, carried himself well – I don't know . . ."

"God!"

"There's no proof it was him."

"Do I look like him?"

"Stop! It mightn't have been him at all. I should have said nothing."

Hope . . . did she have a little bit now?

"I'm glad you did. Maybe someday we'll find out if he really was here . . ."

Going back to clearing the cupboards, Hannah couldn't take her mind off what Beryl had said.

It had to be him. Why would a man be standing on his own if he'd been with the other funeral party? The other burial was far enough away and if he'd been watching them, as Beryl thought, he must have had a reason.

So her father did know her mother was dead!

"Now I know I'm right to go to the cottage."

She could see uncertainty in her friend's face.

"Do you . . . not think it's a bit soon? Maybe you'd be better to leave it for a while – until you get your head sorted a bit ."

"And spend another few years wondering who I am – is that it?"

"Don't rush into things – that's all I'm saying."

"My mind's made up."

Yes, she was sure of her plans now. She glanced again at the drawings that her mother had kept.

"If me being there puts the cat among the pigeons then so be it," she said, trying to sound confident.

Abe Stephenson helped himself to a glass of whiskey when he got back from Dublin.

Letting it down quickly he was tempted to pour another but didn't. Florrie might smell it off him.

Now he held his hands over the hotplate of the Aga to get some heat back into his body.

No, drink wasn't the answer. That was for weaklings.

The traffic on the way home had been horrendous and he'd had a near miss on the Shankhill roundabout. Goddamn roundabouts!

He regretted going to the funeral now. The day had been long and stressful.

He'd checked with the cemetery office where Elizabeth Casey was being buried and had stood at a distance in the cold, checking his watch every few minutes.

The fact that another funeral was taking place soon after Lil's suited him. There was the hearse . . . and the hired car behind it. He squinted to get a better view. Which one was *she*?

First he thought she was the thin woman all dressed in black, then he thought it was the stouter, younger one with the glasses but finally he decided that she was the blonde, short-haired woman in the green trouser suit, because the priest was talking to her more and had shaken hands with her first when the graveside prayers were over.

Her height shocked him. She was a good head above most of the crowd there.

Hairs stood up on the back of his neck too with the realization that she had the build of his grandmother: tall, thin yet not skinny, evenly proportioned. Christ!

Professional of some sort, he decided, by the look of her. Good looking. The shock made him sweat. Any man'd be proud to call her his daughter. No – he couldn't let himself think like that.

He'd forgotten that there would only be a small crowd at the funeral, too, because of it being private and he'd had to think fast when he made eye contact with the friend as she left the funeral party all of a sudden.

At first he'd worried that she might know who he was, but how could she? He could be anyone and Lil had sworn she'd never tell. That had been part of the deal, hadn't it?

The woman probably thought he was just some old geezer who took walks in graveyards to put in the day or someone who had gone to the wrong grave area by mistake.

He glanced at the clock now – five past four. He wouldn't have to collect Florrie until six. God knows what his wife would have put in her day at – doing more research for that book maybe. Last week she'd searched through ancient newspapers to get information about what happened on the day Nellie O'Dowd was born. She was eighty-five. Now all the ould ones wanted her to do the same on their birthdays. Have you nothing else to be doing, he'd said, but she didn't seem to be listening. Women! Give him cattle any day. At least you knew where you stood with them.

He rubbed his hands together. At least he'd heated up a bit now. He was tempted to stay by the fire but his clothes had to be changed. Those twenty heifers in the lower field had to be moved to fresh grass. He'd need Leo . . .

He checked the post on the hall floor before he left the house. His solicitor had sent him a bill, the charge for the interview the other day included – eejit! If Florrie had seen it she'd have wondered what he'd been there for and asked awkward questions.

Putting the bill back in its envelope, he went into his study and placed it in the filing cabinet well hidden behind his pedigree society folder.

He shouted at Max when the dog wasn't quick enough to get into the jeep. The sheepdog now jumped in and lay down shivering, big eyes watchful and solemn.

Leo's van was parked outside the bungalow. Good – he was at home. He didn't look too happy about being disturbed, though.

Doing accounts, he said he was, at half past four in the afternoon.

There was a noise inside the house.

"You got company?"

"No. I'll be there in a minute."

"I'll drop you back when we're finished."

It took half an hour to move the heifers at Knocklannon. As usual one bitch got it into her head to be contrary and took off past the gateway she was supposed to go into. Luckily Leo was able to run and cut her off down the lane.

"I thought Aidan was going to help you change these this morning. I called over but the door was locked. Were you away?"

Damn! If Leo was wondering where he was Vera would be wondering too.

"Were you looking for me?"

"I picked up the new loader in Donohoe's. I dropped in on the way home so you could have a look."

"Oh. I'll have a look another time. It's getting late now."

"Ok. What was up with the Merc?"

"What? How do you mean?"

"It was there but the Starlet was gone."

So, Leo had noticed that he'd taken Florrie's car.

Abe tried to think fast. If he didn't tell Leo something plausible he'd mention it to Vera and then the shit would hit the fan.

"Immobilizer was acting up and it wouldn't start. I rang the garage about it. They're going to sort it tomorrow."

"Right . . . Car's a bit too new for that to be happening, surely?"

Leo was still looking at him.

"I didn't say where I was because the women'd be fussing."

"Oh?"

"I was in Dublin seeing a quack."

"What for?"

"Just the usual shite – blood pressure up a bit and that. I had to get it checked out. Fucker cost me an arm and a leg for a few minutes work."

"You never said . . . Is it going on long?"

"A few months, but don't you say anything to that mother of yours or she'll be over here doing my head in."

"Right."

Leo spat on the ground.

"So – did he put you on tablets or what?"

"Aye – bloody nuisance but that's the way it is. I'd better get back. I've to collect her from the bus."

"Right . . ."

Abe saw the curtains twitch at Leo's sitting room window as he stopped his jeep to let Leo out a few minutes later. Leo had a woman there all right. It'd be the one from the shop, Abe guessed. Probably on her day off – the one with the fine chest on her.

Still, he doubted if it would come to anything. Leo had more sense. His nephew hadn't put off marrying this long to take up with someone who had that many miles on the clock. He'd choose better when it came to finding a wife.

Heading for the village, Abe was envious of his nephew, though. Not a bad way to spend a cold autumn evening when the humour was on you.

Hannah Casey was cleaning out her mother's dresser when the front doorbell of the basement flat rang.

She stood still. God – what if it was him? Heart pounding, she went upstairs to open the hall door.

It was Kit.

"Hannah, how are you? Jimmy's round the back with the van, love. I hope we're not too early or anything."

"No, no, of course not. I forgot for a second . . . Excuse the state of me . . . I'm still sorting out stuff."

"You're grand. A bit of dirt never hurt anyone."

"I was trying to clean the place up before I give the keys back to the landlord. Lord preserve us from cats – the bathroom still reeks a bit, to be honest," she said as Kit followed her back down the stairs.

"Things got a bit rough in the end that way all right. Your Ma used to leave the toilet window open for her own cat and other cats'd get in. I think after a while she didn't smell them or hadn't the energy to deal with them."

"I suppose. I'll open the back door for your husband," Hannah said, taking the big key off the nail on the wall. "We can take the things out through the back garden."

"No rush. The man who made time made plenty of it."

Kit was looking round at the now bare rooms.

"Jesus, you've done a great job. The landlord'll have feck all to do but redecorate the place!"

"I didn't want him thinking bad of her."

"Course you didn't. She'd be as proud as punch of you, honest to God."

"I carried what I could out to the garden. Some of it's too heavy, though."

"You shouldn't have touched a thing. Jimmy has a neighbour of ours with him. They'll have it shifted in no time. And I want to thank you for everything again. It'll all come in very handy."

"You're welcome. Would you carry those kitchen chairs and I'll take these bits of the bed?"

"No bother. I always fancied an iron bed," Kit said as Hannah went out. "I'm going to polish up the brass knobs and have my own personal antique!"

Within a couple of minutes Jimmy Bermingham had a plan of what furniture to put into the van first to make the best use of space.

"If we pack it right we'll do it all in one run. If we don't, we're arsed."

"Language, Jimmy, Hannah mightn't be used to it."

Hannah laughed.

"I've heard worse. Said worse."

As Jimmy and his helper lifted out the sofa and the sideboard, Hannah finished washing out the items she had taken from the kitchen dresser, packing away the china tea set that had always been visible through the frosted glass doors at the top.

She packed the two egg cups, too, and the pink and blue salt and pepper holders that had been there the first time she had been invited to her mother's flat for tea – a plate of salad and homemade brown bread. Beryl had been invited too.

"Must be hard clearing things out all the same."

"I don't feel that much attachment, to be honest. I wish I did."

"Ah, love . . ."

"I was seldom here and when I was it was only for an hour or so at a time. It's hard to find things to talk about when you've no network of family. Once she'd finished asking about work and what everyone in Royle was doing, it all got a bit awkward."

"God love yous . . . Here, I'd better have a last look in the drawers in case we've missed something."

"No, nothing, all clear."

"Great."

Jimmy and his helper were back.

"The dresser next. If we stand it on its side and wedge the glass doors open with lots of paper they won't stir."

"Fair enough," Kit said. "You're the genius, we're only trotting after you!"

Hannah and Kit stood back as the men unhooked the dresser from its chain wall anchor then eased it down onto its side. A couple of old magazines fell off the top of it, hitting the older man on the head.

"Lucky it wasn't something heavy," said Jimmy, "or you'd have been decapitated, Pat."

"Well I wasn't wearing a cap, so!" Pat said.

Hannah looked at Kit and laughed as her mother's friend handed her the magazines.

"She probably kept them for recipes or something. I'm always sticking things on top of cupboards then forgetting where I put them."

"Thanks."

It was two ancient *Woman's Weekly* magazines – both open on knitting patterns for women's cardigans.

"Your mother was a great knitter," Kit said. "If we had all the wool she knit this minute it'd stretch to Timbuktu."

Putting the magazines into a shoe box with the drawings her mother had kept, Hannah wished she'd come across more in the flat – anything at all written down that would tell her more about her mother, a diary, a journal maybe . . . Anything that would tell her how her mother felt when she discovered she was pregnant, for example. And had she loved her father or cursed him from a height when he left her in the lurch?

The thought of being the baby that was to blame for her mother's unhappiness made her sad. No, Beryl was right – it wasn't her fault she was born! She had to put that out of her mind. Hardly a good start in life, though, growing inside someone consumed by that kind of anxiety.

"That's it, then," Kit said. "Is there anything we can do for you – drop you off anywhere, anything at all?"

"No, thanks very much, I have the car."

"You will keep in touch?" Kit said as she squashed into the front of the van beside the two men. "I'd like to know how you're getting on."

"Of course."

"You're welcome in our house anytime, same as your mother was."

"Course you are," said Jimmy, who now had the engine running.

"Thank you very much. I will ring you, I promise."

"Have you any plans – about what you're going to do?"

Hannah tried to hide her irritation at the question.

"All a bit up in the air at the moment. I'll see how I go, take a bit more time off work and decide then."

"Dead right. You take it easy and look after yourself, love."

"I will," Hannah said, as the van pulled out into the traffic.

Walking back into the garden she locked the green back door for the last time.

She shivered. She'd be glad to see the back of this place. She had never felt welcome there. She was an interloper.

She'd never even been in the garden until after her mother died. Had her mother been afraid that her next-door neighbours would pop their heads over the wall and expect an introduction? The small sitting room had always been closed off to her too. The toilet, sitting room and kitchen were the only rooms she was allowed into.

On one early visit she'd noticed the dust disturbance on the mantelpiece – photograph frames, she suspected, hastily removed. She had those photographs now – one of her mother on holiday in Connemara and one of her Casey grandparents and her mother standing outside the cottage in Drumcadden. Maybe she'd feel better in the house where her mother had been reared . . .

She had looked up the townland of Drumcadden on the map. She hoped it would be easy to find when she travelled down there on Monday. Down the country – that's all her mother ever said about where she came from. Down the country – where her mother hadn't wanted her to go . . .

Hannah exhaled loudly.

Control – her mother had finally lost it the day she got ill.

Chapter
THREE

Poxy weather! How the fuck was anyone supposed to pull sugar beet in conditions like this?

The beet season had already begun, yet tractor and harvester were standing idle in the shed while the crop was waterlogged in the drills. It galled Leo Kemp to look at the fields.

With so much rain it was looking likely that the sheep would have to be housed early for lambing, too, and he doubted there was enough fodder for a long winter. It'd mean putting the bank account under pressure – or so his mother told him and she'd know, seeing as she was the one who held the purse strings.

She still hadn't stopped giving out about the price of the new loader for the tractor, even with him putting up the deposit. It wasn't for what wages he and Roy were taking out of the place either, Leo thought. What they got was meagre enough and half the time they had to wait for it until animals were sold or the harvest cheque came in.

Building a bungalow had left him stretched but he wasn't sorry. Forty years of age and still living with the mammy! It might be all right for Roy Boy but not for him.

The bank hadn't wanted to give him a mortgage to build it at first, but he had told them that all the family business would leave the bank if he didn't get it. That made them sit up. And he had done as much as he could himself to keep building costs down. Right now he was under a bit of pressure making the payments but he'd do without stuff for the sake of having his own place. It was very handy. No more humping in the car for a start. He could bring whoever he liked to the house and his mother would be none the wiser. It had been one of the reasons he had chosen that particular site – near the top of the lane.

It had taken his mother a long time to make over the site but he'd kept the pressure on until she did.

"The country'll be saying you're settling down," she'd said.

"The country can say what it effin well likes."

It was an investment, he told her. He might rent it out for a few years to help clear the mortgage, he said. She was fool enough to believe him. He'd bought a double bed as soon as the bedroom was plastered.

Marriage wasn't worrying him. He might be hitting forty but he'd wait until the right one came along – big bust, money behind her and not too much of a brain to come between him and being the boss.

Six o'clock . . . In weather like this he wasn't going to check the sheep in the lower field. If any of them had broken out they could stay wherever they were, he thought. Maybe Roy had already done it – he was welcome to the job – and being wet to the arse when he came back.

Leo hated the drudgery with sheep – the dipping and dosing and shearing and sorting, footrot and maggots and the stink of the shite on his boots. Give him tractors and tillage any day. At least you could see your day's work when you were finished.

"Le-o!"

His mother was calling him from the back door. She was always shouting him or ringing him on the mobile phone and he only down the yard. A lot of the time he didn't answer it, pretending afterwards that he hadn't heard it with the noise of the tractor.

"What's the point in you having a phone at all the way you go on?" she'd say when he eventually got back inside.

"Le-o!"

"What?" he shouted back.

"The harvest thanksgiving – we'll be late if you don't get in here right now. Roy is getting his dinner."

Good little Roy Boy. His brother sickened him sometimes.

Not that his mother fussed a lot about his older brother. Leo knew he was his mother's favourite when push came to shove – it had always been that way, even though Leo was the youngest. In most houses it was the eldest boy that got the attention but not here.

No backbone, that's why, Leo said to himself – probably because of the stammer as well. It irritated his mother no end, even though she tried to hide it. It pissed him off too, especially after that walloping she'd given him when he started stammering himself to copy Roy when he was six. His mother had slapped the legs off him.

"Never do that – you hear! Your brother can't speak properly – and you're – not – going – to be like him."

The words had kept time with the slaps.

After that he took pleasure in tittering at his brother's delay in getting the words out and then Roy would totally block. His face'd go puce but it was still no use.

"I'll be there in a minute," Leo shouted, going to the yard tap to wash his boots.

Harvest thanksgiving! He wasn't in the humour for hymn singing and sandwiches. He never was, but he'd never hear the end of it from his mother unless he did. He'd seen her in action before. She didn't keep after him to go to church every Sunday, thankfully, but occasionally she wanted her sons there, more for form's sake than anything else, he was sure.

"You're farmers, aren't you? You'd be a holy show if you didn't go. A few times a year won't kill the pair of you."

Leo would put up with it this time, he decided – at least the corn yield had been good this year. Pity the price had been lousy. He wouldn't be raising the roof with his singing. He'd leave that to Roy Boy. It was strange how his brother didn't stammer when he was singing – weird!

With the way farming was going, though, there was feck all to be thankful about. Just as well he had plans – himself and his Uncle Abe. If everything worked out they'd clean up with the housing development. His mother might complain when she found out first, but she wouldn't be long changing her mind when she got a squint at the bottom line.

With Abe's four-acre field right beside the village and their three-acre one backing onto it they'd be well placed to sell a lot of houses. And make a lot of money . . .

There were a few obstacles to get over first, of course, but nothing insurmountable.

He saw Roy putting his plate in the dishwasher. Soft eejit! He'd make someone a great wife some day.

"There's clean shirts on the landing for the two of you."

His mother already had her brown church coat with the black collar on. She'd had it so long that it could nearly trot to church by itself, Leo thought.

He watched his brother now go to the cubbyhole under the stairs to get the polish box out as their mother dished up Leo's dinner.

What was on the plate disgusted him.

"Could you not get a bit of decent meat instead of this fat shite?" he said, proking at the food.

"Eat up and watch your language. Be thankful you have anyone to cook for you at all. I won't be here forever," his mother said.

"Thanks be to Jesus for that," Leo thought. He'd like a bit of steak right now – with onions and plenty of mushrooms. He'd cook it himself if the kitchen in the bungalow was finished. Anything'd be better than this.

"Was Abe over?" he asked, as his mother came back from feeding the dogs the dinner scraps. Roy had gone upstairs to shave.

"No, your *Uncle* Abe wasn't."

"We're not babbies."

"No, but he'll be your *Uncle* Abe to you as long as I'm around. I haven't seen him since yesterday. Why?"

"No reason."

"He'll be in church. He's never missed a harvest thanksgiving in his life."

Leaving his plate on the table Leo went upstairs to get ready.

The church was fuller than usual. Harvest thanksgivings were next to Christmas when it came to attendances. Most Sundays there were only a few stragglers there.

"Ould ones trying to save their souls before they pop their clogs," he thought as he sat down in a pew beside his mother.

Roy was up at the top with the choir.

Leo had the church scanned for new faces before he bowed to mouth a prayer. He was always on the lookout. You never knew when some parishioner would have a good-looking niece or cousin up to visit and you might make a move. No such luck tonight . . .

The organ, played by his Aunt Florrie, wheezed into action for the first hymn – *Come ye thankful people, come/Raise the song of harvest home . . .*

Voices joined in, the few people in the choir setting the pace for the rest of them to follow.

The sooner the better the service was over. At least there'd be a cup of tea afterwards – and decent food, if he was careful what he picked. All the women would have baked – his Aunt Florrie included. At least she knew how to cook. His mother, he knew, had brought one of them shop-bought excuses for a fruitcake and a plate of sandwiches that he'd be steering clear of.

The preacher was a visiting clergywoman. Knickers in the pulpit – he hadn't got used to that idea yet. At least they hadn't reached that pitch in this parish yet. There'd be blue blackbirds out before his uncle and the movers and shakers in the parish allowed that to happen.

Reverend Mundy, the rector, was all right – he didn't make a nuisance of himself. Occasionally he turned up in the yard on one of his pastoral visits and picked his steps until he got onto the cement path by the back door. He stayed for half an hour, held his teacup and saucer in very clean hands, talked about very little then picked his steps out to the car again.

"How many times have I asked you to put a bit of gravel on that yard? I might as well be talking to the wall," his mother would shout, before the rector had reached the road.

Yuk! The smell of gas heaters and damp hit him as he entered the dilapidated church hall. The smell brought him back to his childhood – Santy parties and tea a couple of times a year after special services. There was talk of raising money to build a new church hall, but the vestry could whistle for that. He wasn't signing up for any standing orders.

Roy was pouring tea into the white cups already laid out on the long tables that ran down the middle of the room.

Sap.

Their Aunt Florrie was handing out sandwiches behind him. She always had a soft spot for Roy Boy. She hated when Leo called him that, he knew. Disrespectful, she said it was. Leo grinned. They'd spent a lot of time in Knocklannon as children. With their mother trying to manage the farm on her own after his father died suddenly, their Aunt Florrie had offered to mind them a few times a week. Roy with his asthma and his stammer and polite ways was her favourite, but Leo didn't care. He didn't need her mollycoddling. He was out in the yard following his Uncle Abe around as soon as he was able, feeling happy when he heard his uncle comment to the workmen about him not being afraid of anything or that he'd outwork chaps for miles around. Wiry, he called him.

He knew his uncle liked it, too, that by the age of eight he could use a stick and a tone of voice that would show the farmyard animals who was boss.

He could drive the tractor young too – rolling fields with the Ferguson 20 when his legs were barely able to reach the pedals, his nose full of the smell of TVO.

They were two of a kind – he and his uncle – and one day he would inherit the big fields that his Uncle Abe owned.

"A farm is a little kingdom," his uncle used to say. "You have to look after it, add to it, control it. Only that way can you get the best out of it."

And his Uncle Abe had got the best out of it. He had added one hundred and forty acres to the farm in his lifetime, buying every piece joining him that came up for auction.

"You have to watch for opportunity," Leo had heard him say.

"Look at the farms around you, keep in with the people who are likely to sell – the bachelors, the feckless sons who don't know the value of what they have. If you watch and wait long enough and you're ready when the chance comes, you'll get it – and at the right price."

Leo nodded at his uncle, who was at the far side of the hall, holding a cup of tea in one hand and a sandwich in the other and talking to another farming parishioner, John Styles.

Leo tried to decide if his uncle looked sick but what would he know about heart conditions? He'd noticed that he was a bit more out of breath than usual in the last few months, but he'd put that down to him not being as fit as he used to be.

His mother knew nothing yet or she'd have been watching her brother like a hawk.

Yes, she'd be upset if Abe was ill but he knew her mind would be jumping forward with excitement – to when Leo would get Knocklannon.

How many times had he heard her harp on about how if she'd been born with a penis between her legs she would have had her Stephenson birthright but Abe, being male, had inherited almost everything, even though he was three years younger.

Apart from a few thousand pounds and some cattle that she owned herself she had got nothing. She'd had to marry to get a roof over her head.

Leo remembered his father mostly as a face in photos or an older figure who sat in the chair and said very little.

He didn't remember much of the funeral – just a crowd and a lot of black clothes and someone giving him a toy tractor to play with. He had it for years until his mother drove over it one day when she was reversing the Morris Minor out of the shed.

What did he understand about death and he only five, especially as his mother hadn't bothered to explain it to him.

"You got a minute?" he heard his uncle say when the tea was nearly over and the rector had finished his "thank you and tastefully decorated" speech.

"I'll follow you out."

"Before the women finish up."

"Right," Leo said, scanning the hall.

Roy was talking to Rachel Webb, an elderly parishioner who still wore a fur coat and smelled of mothballs.

Leo saw his uncle light up the damp road outside the hall with the beam of a flashlight.

He caught up with him near the car as he shouted goodnight to Kitty and Fred Cleaver who were walking on ahead.

Rain was falling again. "There's a hitch," Abe said.

"What?"

"The cottage has been taken off the market."

"Jim Casey's?"

"Yes."

"Fuck!"

"Whisht!"

Leo Kemp's heart sunk to his boots. They'd counted on being able to buy Casey's cottage. They needed it to be sure of getting planning permission for the housing development.

Everywhere else on the road there were sight line problems because of bends being too close. Jim Casey dying nine months earlier had been good news. His daughter, Lil, lived in Dublin and was unlikely to want to come back home to it after a lifetime in the city.

"Who told you?"

"Flynn."

Ernie Flynn was a local auctioneer.

"What did he say exactly?"

"That he'd received instruction. From a daughter of Lil's."

"The one my mother was talking about in the paper? Fuck! What did he say exactly?"

Leo Kemp heard his uncle clear his throat.

"He says she's taking it off the market while she's making up her mind what to do with it."

"Curseahellonit!" said Leo.

"Keep your voice down!"

"And could Flynn not have said the sale was already agreed and he couldn't go back on it?"

"She knew no deposit was paid."

"We should have paid the price Lil was asking instead of ending up like this – haggling . . . fuck! Where do we go from here?"

"Shush! We sit tight, that's what. Flynn is going to say he has interested buyers when the dust settles."

"What age is this one?"

"I don't know."

"Whatever age she is she'll want something fancier than that place. You wouldn't swing a cat in it. She'll be looking for ensuites and fancy views. Shit! We'd better get it or we won't have a snowball's chance in hell of building."

"This is only a minor hiccup, so keep your hair on. Have you told your mother about the plans?"

"No. I thought you were going to."

"I will. Soon."

Leo tried to read his uncle's face in the semi-darkness. Was he more stressed about all this than he was letting on? His face had looked a bit redder in the church than it usually was. Red face, bad heart – wasn't that what they said? Or was it red face, heavy drinker? Leo couldn't remember.

"Let the hare sit," his uncle said. "The architect is to have the final plans drawn up in three weeks' time. A lot could have changed by then. You said nothing to your mother about me going to see the quack the other day?"

"No."

"Good."

A crowd of parishioners had now come out of the parish hall including Leo's mother and his Aunt Florrie. Both were carrying cake tins and trays.

"You'd think some of them hadn't got a bit for a week the way they cleared the plates," his mother was saying, as she handed him the tins to put on the backseat.

"It's a compliment to the cooks if it's all gone," Florrie said. "Goodnight."

"Right so," Abe said. "Goodnight."

Leo watched his aunt and uncle walk up the road to where the Mercedes was parked.

"Night."

He got into the driving seat now, glad that his brother had sat into the passenger side. Being seen with his brother up front was bad enough, but having the mammy beside him wasn't good for his image. He definitely wouldn't be stopping in the village on the way home, no matter what his mother wanted from the shop.

He glanced at the clock on the dashboard. Would Eileen be finished work in the supermarket yet or would she still be in there? He couldn't take the chance. He wouldn't want his mother seeing him talking to her or her making familiar with him. Eileen might look all right wearing one of his shirts, but he wouldn't be making any commitment to her and he'd make damn sure he was wearing rubber. No one was going to have a hold on him.

After dropping his mother and Roy in the yard, Leo drove the car back down to the bungalow near the road.

He smiled broadly. His Uncle Abe mustn't be well – not if he'd mentioned the quack again. He felt a flutter of excitement in his stomach. He might inherit sooner than he thought!

Shit! A light had suddenly come on in his bedroom. He nearly jumped out of his skin. He'd forgotten he'd left the key out for Eileen.

She was peeping round the hall door now, wearing only a dressing gown. As he got to the door she grinned and let it fall to the floor.

He had a massive erection immediately. What a day. Maybe he'd do it twice.

So much for getting an early start! What was keeping him? The landlord of her mother, Lil's, flat, was supposed to have been there an hour ago to collect the keys.

Hannah blew on her fingers to keep warm. The damp flat was like a morgue even after only a couple of months of no one living in it.

She took the ancient post office book out of her pocket for the third time that morning. *Account closed* was now stamped all over each page. The money had been transferred to her bank account. She'd gone to an ATM to check her balance again before going to the flat. Yes, she was now over €40,000 richer than she was when she got up that morning. Excitement fluttered in her stomach. She disliked herself for being glad of the money, but parents were supposed to provide for their children, weren't they? She should have had this money years ago.

Had her mother just been too proud to touch it, seeing it as "pay-off" money – tainted? It was all right for her – she wasn't the one reared where there was never enough. Hannah wondered if that was why she'd gone off the financial rails when she started nursing. She couldn't get enough of anything. She wanted so many things to be hers – just hers, nobody else's.

The bank manager would probably faint with shock when he saw her lodgement, she thought, as she closed the post office book and shivered again.

She was permanently overdrawn up to now, always spending too much on clothes, on holidays lately, on wine . . .

Beryl had asked her one time if she thought it was a self-esteem thing, trying to prove she was someone by being so conscious of exteriors? She'd told her friend to feck off with her pop psychology.

Beryl was the opposite. She lived within her means, jam jars of money set aside for this and that bill each month and seldom splurging on anything she couldn't afford – Hannah had never been able to last long doing that . . .

How had the money arrived here at this flat all those years ago, Hannah wondered? In the post? Shoved through the letterbox in envelopes whenever her father happened to be in Dublin and drove by?

Hannah jumped. The doorbell! It was the landlord, Frank Delahunt.

"Sorry for keeping you waiting. A holdup on the Merrion road."

"Come in. You probably want to have a look around," she said, as they reached downstairs.

"You've done a great job," he said, after taking a quick peep into each room. "If you saw the way some tenants leave rental properties . . . Your mother never gave me an ounce of trouble. Always paid her rent on time. The place won't be the same without her. Now, are you sure you've taken everything you need?"

"I gave most of it away to a friend of my mother's. Just kept a few things . . . My mother never mentioned me to you, I suppose?"

The man now looked uncomfortable.

"Em, no. Our chats over the years were about everyday sort of stuff – she liked her privacy, I think – that always struck me about her. I'm sure it hasn't been easy for you. Different times, eh . . ."

She said goodbye to him on the footpath, the black gate of number three creaking as she closed it behind her for the last time.

Hannah got into her car, parked a few doors down. She felt only emptiness as she took one last look at the Georgian terrace. She was glad to see the back of it in a way. The place had never been home to her. Maybe the cottage would be different.

The plan had crystallized after the funeral. She'd gone back to Waterford, got a doctor's cert to say that she was still suffering from stress and told the ward manager that she was taking another month off without pay. For family reasons . . . Family . . .

Saturday night had been spent by the fire, drinking wine and talking to Beryl. Matt had left several messages on the landline and on her mobile but she had answered none of them. Sunday was spent packing what she'd need for at least a month in her mother's cottage.

"What if it's damp – uninhabitable? It's a long time since your grandfather lived in it – it could be in an awful state," Beryl had said, shocked that she was going so soon – and at what she was going to do.

"I'll cross that bridge if I come to it. It's hardly that bad if it was up for sale – some sort of a tidy up would have been done on it. I'll be all right. Stop worrying."

"Would you not wait until next Friday and then I can go with you?"

"No, it's something I have to do by myself. Please . . . I'll be fine, honest. I'll have the place looking lovely by the time you come down. I just need a bit of time to get my head straight."

Now at last she was on her way . . .

Good, the traffic wasn't too bad. She breathed a sigh of relief as she finally left double-decker buses and traffic lights behind.

No veering off for Greystones this time. She'd almost done it automatically. Rita and Noel still lived there and they all met up a couple of times a year.

They tried to keep in touch with one another as much as possible, calling themselves a "family". They'd never been able to stomach the word "residents".

As she put her foot down after passing Kilpedder she felt suddenly queasy at the thought of confronting her father.

How would he treat her? Had he really been in Dean's Grange Cemetery the day her mother was buried? If it was him, it showed he was interested, at least. Why bother if he wasn't? Or was it fear that had flushed him out of the woodwork to have a look? She couldn't call it paying respects to her mother. Respect – she'd had very little of that from him.

"No good'll come of chasing him," her mother had said.

She tried to not let herself be controlled by that. Surely she'd stayed in the background long enough. Now that her mother was dead she could do what she thought best.

"I'm sick of being a skeleton in the cupboard," she said to herself as she passed the Arklow exit.

She thought about how her mother had been able to persuade her to keep quiet, without even saying a word, the shame around her birth somehow there between them like a silent presence. Nanna had been more vocal.

"Don't go rocking the boat, child," Nanna used to say when she got into a temper and threatened to run away to search for her parents. "Leave well enough alone. Haven't you a lot more than the little children in Africa?"

Nanna had said the same thing to all the children in the home.

There was never any encouragement to search. It was always keep your head down and be thankful for what you've got.

"It probably made us easier to control if we were kept feeling like we had no rights and that no one would want us even if we did turn up on their doorstep," Hannah thought.

Was it that Nanna wanted to keep them all for herself so that she could be a martyr, do-gooder and a saint all rolled into one, or was she simply trying to protect them from heartache and rejection down the line? So much for thinking she'd forgotten all this stuff . . .

An hour and a half later she was lost somewhere south of Enniscorthy.

She stopped the car in a gap-way to check her map again. The village of Rathbrandon – that's what she was looking for.

Her grandfather's cottage was on a back road, close to the village in the townland of Drumcadden.

Shit – she'd passed the turnoff for the village. So much for sign-posting! How many T-junctions had she come to on minor roads and no signs to direct anyone anywhere?

Twelve o'clock already. As she studied the map she ate a bar of chocolate. Not exactly healthy eating, but who cared? Her eating patterns had gone to pot lately. One of these days she'd have to turn over a new leaf, but not today. She had to make a decision about where to go next. Yes, if she went back and took the first left it should bring her into the village. If there were no signs to speak of she would ask someone in the village for directions, she decided. She'd always been a hopeless map reader. The men in her life had always come in handy for that.

The rain had stopped by the time she pulled in at the small service station in the village – Carthy's, the name over the doorway said.

The only other customer that she could see was a middle-aged man heading for a tractor parked at the side of the building. If he had a tractor he was local and therefore bound to be able to help her with directions.

"Drumcadden – could you direct me, please?"

The tall, chubby-faced man with the diamond patterned jumper looked startled when she addressed him. His face reddened as he tried to answer.

"Wh-wh-who is it you're l-l-l-looking for?"

Hannah listened carefully, letting the man get the words out in his own time. She was looking for Jim Casey's cottage, she said.

"F-f-f-follow me – i-i-it's . . . it's n-n-not far."

"Thank you very much. You're very kind."

The forty-something-year-old blushed even deeper as he turned to get into the tractor.

She felt sorry for him. Nick in Royle had a stammer, too. Several times she'd had to sort out older boys in school who were picking on him because of it. He could speak very well now, thanks to a special course that had taught him breath control. She wished this man would do that, too. The courses were often advertised in the national newspapers. He had such kind eyes. He didn't deserve to be limited in life like that when there was help out there.

"Cop on to yourself," Hannah thought, "you don't know him from Adam."

What implement was it he had behind the tractor? A hedge-cutter? Yes.

She followed the tractor as soon as it pulled out. When he turned left, she turned left, then right again, then around several bad bends, then a long, straight stretch of road . . .

He saw him indicate as he approached a gateway on the left-hand side.

He slowed down, then stopped ahead of the gate, leaving room for her to pull in. She took the car out of gear and put on the handbrake before getting out to wave her thanks to the man in the tractor.

Roy Kemp Hedgecutting Services was written on the side of the vehicle.

At least she hadn't followed some weirdo who could have led her God knows where!

The man waved back then drove off, the orange neon flasher activated on the cab once again.

Hannah felt weird. Her father, she knew, lived a short distance away, but in which direction? Her heart thumped as she watched the tractor disappear around the bend further down. Roy Kemp. He had to be one of her neighbours . . .

The newly-painted gate wasn't locked. She stood staring in for a few seconds at the side of the cottage that faced the road.

The house looked old, in need of TLC. She opened the gate and drove into the yard, parking in front of what she was sure was the only door in the cottage. The door was painted green. Not too long ago, she decided.

Someone had tidied up the small yard. There was a shed and a lean-to attached to it where a wooden "horse" for sawing wood on still stood. Was it her grandfather's?

She felt like a trespasser again, a voyeur. No, she had the right to be there. It was her house now, wasn't it?

She walked all round the cottage.

Some of the window frames were partly rotted, she noticed. Double-glazing wouldn't go amiss.

A labourer's cottage, two-up, two-down, but that's what her grandfather had been – a farm labourer. Labouring for farmers for most of his life then working on the roads for the county council until he got the pension . . . Getting that information from her mother had been like pulling teeth from a hen.

She shivered. She had imagined this moment so many times. Yet now that it was here she felt weird – and more than a bit scared.

"Pull yourself together," she told herself, as she fastened up her coat and used the two keys her mother had given her to unlock the door.

The shake in her hand meant she had to make several attempts. The door had obviously expanded a bit with the wet weather. Finally, the big key turned and then the Yale one. She was in the cottage.

The low ceiling and the semi-darkness seemed oppressive at first. She instinctively looked for a light switch. There was one – white and modern, not Bakelite. The place must have been rewired recently – so much the better.

Fluorescent light now flooded the room. At least the place looked more cheerful now.

There was a slight smell of damp, but not nearly as bad as in her mother's flat in Dún Laoghaire.

The kitchen was empty except for an ancient table and a couple of chairs that had once been painted blue. There was an old gas cooker to the right of the sink. The sink was positioned under a tiny window. The lino on the floor had seen better days.

"I expected worse," she said to herself, as she looked around.

The focal point in the kitchen-cum-living area was a Stanley cooker flanked on each side by two ancient-looking fireside chairs. The front of the cooker was discoloured and chipped in places. She opened the door of it. It was full of ashes. She rattled the box of matches sitting on the floor beside a packet of firelighters. They were dry. The fire had obviously been lit recently.

An open stairs ran up along the wall at the far side of the cooker. It was painted a depressing brown, making the place look even smaller.

Gingerly she climbed it, one step at a time, but it was sturdy enough.

There were two bedrooms at the top. She went into the one on the left first. It had been her grandparents' in their day, she decided, judging by the double bed. The floral wallpaper was hanging off the walls at several points.

The bed had an iron frame and was shoved against the wall. The brass knobs on each corner had gone green.

"They'd come up well with a good polish," she thought as she ran her hand over one of them.

There was very little dust around, though. Someone must have been here cleaning – probably before viewings took place.

She opened the wardrobe in the tiny room. It smelled of mothballs, but it was empty. Her mother had obviously cleared the place of her father's belongings after he died.

There was a tiny window that looked out over the road and onto the fields on the other side.

"I wonder whose land that is," she thought.

She went into the other bedroom. It was the same size but a bit more cheerful. The bed was more modern, but the mattress was ancient and dipped in the middle. The walls had been painted a too-strong pink for the size of the room.

She guessed it was her mother's room.

Her grandmother, Moll Casey, had died in 1984, her mother had eventually told her. That meant her grandfather, Jim Casey, had lived here on his own for twenty years.

Lil had visited him as often as she could, she had told Hannah, and spent part of her holiday cleaning and decorating, "to keep the place together for him".

"It probably wouldn't be in nearly as good a shape only for that," Hannah thought, as she stared out the window that, on this side, looked out onto the fields behind the house.

There was a root crop in the field. She knew enough from working on farms at holiday time from Royle to know that it was sugar beet. She could tell by the shape of the wide green leaves that overlapped in the drills. It looked as if it was ready to harvest. October – of course it was. The field looked very wet, though, and opening the window to get a better look she could see from the deep tyre marks that attempts had been made to pull some of the crop but had likely been given up on because the machinery couldn't travel. Pulling beet was always a hardy winter job. She remembered Mr Watson on one of the farms she'd stayed on as a child pulling a field by hand one Christmas because the beet was frozen in the ground. She'd never seen hands look so cracked, sore and dirty. And he never complained.

She stooped as she went back downstairs to avoid banging her head off the stair frame.

A toilet! How was she to manage if there wasn't a toilet in the place? Why hadn't she thought of it before? Maybe it was one of those places with an outside loo.

Opening a door off the kitchen she was glad to find a tiny bathroom – basic but functional. Yes, the flush mechanism worked.

The bath had blue copper stains under the taps but other than that it was fine. The floor had linoleum on it to match the kitchen.

She tried to open the small, frosted glass window. It gave with a second push. Fresh air – good! Tomorrow she would open all the windows wide.

She wouldn't stay here tonight, but as soon as she had made it more homely she would sleep here. She checked the time. Two o'clock. Time to get cracking . . . She would clean for a couple of hours then go into Wexford town and look for a B&B.

She brought the two-bar electric heater and kitchen-cleaning agents in from the car.

She was glad of the instant heat. Now she filled the electric kettle she'd brought with her and switched it on.

Coffee would warm her up. Nibbling one of the Café Noir biscuits she'd brought with her, she looked in the cupboard to the left of the cooker. Yes – an immersion heater switch. She switched it on. Hot water wouldn't be a problem.

She wouldn't light the cooker until tomorrow. Already she was looking forward to the heat making the place seem cosier.

The lock on the door looked new enough – and there was a bolt she could slide over at night. Good!

Living out in the sticks by herself wasn't something she'd done before but she was nearly forty, for God's sake. And hadn't she travelled on her own a few times in her early twenties as a backpacking tourist – it surely had to be safer than that.

Right! She would drag all the furniture she didn't need out to the shed first.

The shed door creaked as she opened it. She surveyed the shelves of rusty tools and dried-up paint cans, touching them in some kind of attempt to connect with her grandfather, Jim.

No use . . .

With the place cleared upstairs and down she then dusted and vacuumed the whole house and washed and disinfected the floors.

It was a smell that pleased her. The house seemed purified somehow – more hers. It smelled of Royle on a Saturday evening when everyone was washed and ready for bed.

She closed the door on her grandfather's room. It would be the last room she would do up. Her mother's room, where she would sleep, would need attention first if she was to have basic comforts.

She would buy a new bed for it straight away. She couldn't stand using anyone else's. She had bought a new one the minute she got her first month's wages as a nurse and moved into a flat on her own. After years of sleeping in ancient ones that smelled of other people she wanted her own brand, spanking new one . . .

A double bed – that's what she'd buy now. It would make more sense than a single one, even though it would look big in the room. Beryl would need something to sleep in when she stayed over until she got the other room done up.

The bed linen and duvet she'd brought could stay in the boot of the car until tomorrow.

By four o'clock darkness had almost fallen and she felt exhausted and desolate as she looked around at the cleared-out, cleaner space. She should have known this house and her grandfather Jim but she'd been robbed of that. He didn't even know she existed, never mind knowing that she was a child of Abe Stephenson's.

She wondered what he would have said if he had known. Would her grandfather have confronted his neighbour or would he have kept his mouth shut and his head down because he was dependent on him for a job, perhaps?

"He'd probably have blamed my mother for leading Abe Stephenson astray. Or himself for not raising a daughter who could preserve her virtue. That was the way it was then, the woman was the temptress, the sinner.

Hannah had a splitting headache. Time to get out of here . . .

She would come back early tomorrow morning and see it all again in daylight and she would feel better then, she told herself.

By seven o'clock, in town, she had bought nearly everything she needed.

The man in the furniture shop in the Bullring assured her that he would deliver the double bed, the chest of drawers, the kitchen table and four chairs, the two-seater sofa and the mats by three o'clock the following day.

In Dunnes now, she finished off her shopping by buying a cheap bedside lamp, a throw for the sofa and a few coordinating cushions. The cottage would be transformed.

She had also invested in some Wellington boots. No point in dragging the ones she had in Waterford up here. Already her feet were itching to get out and about, to walk in fields if she could, in the splosh of muck if she got the chance.

Near the magazine stand she found a book on interior design and DIY – just the thing.

She could feel her adrenalin flowing with the excitement of it all – doing up the cottage, living there, being up the road from her father. She tried not to feel panicky at the thought of meeting him for the first time . . .

Realizing she was famished she ate a quick main course in the Chinese restaurant by the railway station, then headed back to the B&B where she'd booked a room.

Within ten minutes she was in a bath full of bubbles, headphones on, listening to classical music. She listened twice to the soprano singing *O mio babbino caro*. O my beloved father, the words meant, didn't they? What it would be to sing about your father with emotion like that . . .

Beryl had given her the classical box set for her birthday.

Beryl was more of a country and Irish fan, so Hannah only put on her classical CDs loudly on the stereo when she was in the house by herself. She'd have to buy a spare CD player for the cottage...

Trying to relax, she thought of the months to come. What would happen? What changes would the next few weeks bring?

One thing she did know – she was looking forward to the break from work. No more stress, understaffing, bedpans, backbiting – at least not for a while. She'd had twenty years of it. For the first time she realized how tired she was. Emer Boyle wasn't wrong – she had been slipping. God, she'd been all over the place emotionally since Nanna died.

She would do no nursing until after Christmas, she decided. Maybe she wouldn't go back to work in Waterford after that. Maybe she'd retrain for something else. Lots of people did that, didn't they? Reassessed when they hit forty, tried something different. The maybes felt exciting.

In the meantime she would manage. Finding out who she really was had to be very high up on anyone's list of priorities, didn't it? Butterflies fluttered in her stomach again. She wondered how big a job that would be. Would her father accept her? Reject her? Deny her existence? The disclosure would impact on his family – on his wife, on his children, if he had any. What if he had other children? How would she feel then? She'd never really considered the possibility of having a brother or a sister. In her dreams she was always an only child – the only one her father had to focus on. Daddy's girl...

Getting out of the bath eventually she decided that she wouldn't rush anything. She would just settle into the house and the community as best she could and wait, initially, to see what happened. That was less scary.

Her mobile phone rang as she finished drying her hair. It was Beryl, back from her hotel shift, wanting an update. Right now, she could do with having Beryl here to talk to but the phone would have to do.

Next morning Hannah was on the road back to the cottage, the boot of the car full of paint.

With a bit of luck she'd have a lot of it finished by Friday evening when Beryl would arrive. With the new table and chairs the place would look more welcoming.

This time she found the village of Rathbrandon easily. Stopping the car at the service station she went into the shop to buy a newspaper and some fuel.

"A cylinder of gas, four bales of briquettes and a bag of coal, please," she said to the man behind the counter.

"Certainly. I'll give you a hand putting them in the car."

"Thanks very much."

"You down on holiday?" the elderly owner asked as he swung the bag of coal into the boot.

"Sort of," Hannah said, putting in one of the bales of briquettes. "I might settle here – you never know. I'm not sure of my plans yet."

"Isn't that a great way to be? Are you staying local? I'm sorry, I should be minding my own business. I forget that people nowadays cling close to their privacy. Sure, maybe they're right."

Hannah liked the man. He had a gentle ease about him and an honest face, probably a great father to someone. Why did she always think of that?

"No, it's all right. I don't mind you asking. I've inherited my grandfather's cottage, actually – Jim Casey – perhaps you knew him? My mother was Lil Casey."

The man looked confused and a bit uneasy for a few seconds.

"Jim? Lil? You're Lil's daughter! Of course I knew her – and Jim! I went to school with your mother and your grandfather was as well known around here as a begging ass. Your grandmother, Moll, was a lovely woman, too, Lord rest her. I'm sorry, I should be offering you my condolences – your mother . . . I saw the notice in the paper."

Hannah shook the hand that was extended to her.

"Thank you very much."

"Tom Carthy."

"Hannah. Hannah Casey."

If this man noted the use of her mother's maiden name he made no sign of it.

"It's good to meet you. And if there's anything I can do for you please let me know."

"You're very kind, thank you."

"Have you been here before? There I go again – asking too many questions . . ."

"I don't mind. No, I haven't, apart from yesterday."

"Aye, but sure what about it? Won't you get to know the place now? And everyone else'll get to know you."

"What are they like – people around here?"

"Not bad skins, most of them. You could be in worse places."

"That's good to know. Thanks very much."

"No trouble."

"Bye."

And Hannah drove off, catching a glimpse of the elderly shopkeeper still standing in the doorway, watching her depart.

It wouldn't be long before her story would be round the village, she suspected, but she didn't care. She existed, she was Lil Casey's daughter and now she had come to live in the Casey family home. They could think what they liked.

Reaching the cottage she set about lighting the cooker first. It was a success.

Within fifteen minutes the cottage seemed cheerier. Back to work.

By twelve-thirty Hannah's arms ached after washing down as many walls and skirting boards in the cottage as she could, ready for painting. She had opened the windows wide to let fresh air in upstairs and down. She ate her lunchtime sandwich sitting on the stairs. She would get it sanded down, or maybe paint it white. That would make the room look a lot bigger. And maybe put down a laminated wooden floor in the living area. That would be easier to clean and make the space look warmer. How much would it cost for new kitchen units, she wondered? Hardly much given the small space.

She made notes. This was fun, different from when she and Beryl bought the house in Waterford. This house was hers only – and part of her history. And whatever she spent on it wouldn't be wasted, she decided, even if she did decide to sell the cottage in the future. She'd need to furnish it anyway if she was going to rent it out in time to come. What she spent would be an investment . . .

She would tackle her mother's bedroom next. A couple of hours would have one coat of ivory emulsion on the walls. By tonight she would have a reasonable amount of comfort – that's if the furniture arrived. In a couple of days' time she would do different things. Visit graveyards and churches – what better places to start exploring her roots?

By the time the furniture van arrived at the gate at five o'clock, the ceiling and walls of the tiny bedroom had had its second coat.

Within minutes, everything was where she wanted it – the new bed in her room upstairs, the blonde wood table in the centre of the kitchen with the four chairs around it and the new oatmeal two-seater couch under the stairs.

With the terracotta fleece throw and several cushions in position it already looked inviting.

She now ironed the ready-made curtains she'd bought to get the fold marks out of them.

"It's beginning to look like home," she said, as she positioned a net curtain on the kitchen window. It would block a lot of light but it would give her privacy.

In the clean bathroom she hung her dressing gown and the new towels she'd bought. She lit a scented candle that she'd brought with her from Waterford.

In her mother's room upstairs, she now made the bed and hung the curtains then unpacked what clothes she'd brought with her.

She would need a new wardrobe, but not yet. Rome wasn't built in a day.

"There! That's it," she said, standing back to admire her handiwork.

She suddenly realized how tired she was. She would sleep tonight. How long was it since she'd had a proper night's sleep, one where she didn't wake with thoughts of either her father or her mother tumbling round in her head?

What would happen? Would she dream or have nightmares in this place?

After supper she climbed the stairs to bed, bringing the radio with her to break the silence.

She wished Beryl was there. Or Matt. In the past they'd have enjoyed that first night in the new double bed . . . Had she been mad to dump him? No, it had run its course.

Her mobile phone rang as she climbed into bed. It was Beryl wanting another update.

Twenty minutes later she switched out the light.

Tomorrow would be a big day. The day when she would venture out – into the world of her father.

Chapter
FOUR

Abe Stephenson nearly lost control of the Mercedes when he saw smoke coming out of the chimney of Casey's cottage on his way home from town.

Shit!

No, don't panic . . . Probably Peg Travers airing the place. Don't let your imagination run away with you, he told himself.

Driving by now, hands clenched on the wheel, he glanced in and caught a glimpse of a black car and a tall, younger woman in jeans dragging a mattress across the yard.

She was here! Christ!

Beads of perspiration broke out on his forehead as he drove the rest of the way to the village. He squeezed his eyes shut to keep the image of a small baby from surfacing again . . .

Lil not a week buried and she had turned up . . . He never thought she would. Yes, he had heard from Flynn, the auctioneer, that the cottage had been taken off the market, but moving into it herself wasn't something he had allowed himself to imagine.

No, think rationally . . . She had inherited a house – it would be natural for her to come down to see it and clear it out. It didn't mean that she knew anything about him.

Get a grip, he told himself, shove it to the back of your mind. She was Lil Casey's daughter – nothing more. It had nothing to do with him. Lil Casey wouldn't have opened her mouth. All he had to do was keep cool and he would get through this.

Abe Stephenson cursed again as he pulled in at the service station.

Today of all days when he was intent on telling his sister, Vera, about the housing development plans. He could have done without this stress. No, he would go ahead as normal. Nothing had changed. Getting Vera onside was important. He'd have to be careful how he put the plans to her. He knew she'd always held onto land by her fingernails. Asking her to part with some for a new venture might be more than she would agree to. No, he told himself, it would work out all right. He hadn't put months of planning into this venture to be stopped now by his sister – or anyone else.

Tom Carthy nodded at him as he entered the shop.

"The very man."

"Why is that?" asked Abe, picking up an *Irish Times* after a quick look at the tabloid headlines.

"Have you met your new neighbour yet?"

Abe searched for change in his pocket, not looking up as he spoke.

"Oh? Who's that?"

"Lil Casey's daughter. She was in here yesterday – a fine looking woman too. Gas the way she's turned up out of the blue like that."

Abe feigned interest in the chocolate bar display.

"Aye."

"The cottage'll be worth a few bob these days, of course, with the way the market is going."

"She's selling?"

"Hard to say. Hadn't made any definite plans, she said yesterday, but she bought a good bit of fuel all the same. Did Roy not tell you he met her?"

Abe's stomach heaved slightly.

"No."

"He gave her directions when she arrived here yesterday. Hard to believe she didn't know her way to this neck of the woods, but I suppose skeletons in the cupboard are seldom given maps on how to get out."

Damn! What had she said to Roy? No, calm down . . . His nephew had given a stranger directions – what harm was there in that?

"Abe! Your change!"

Abe returned to the counter.

"Easy know the men with money, what?" the shopkeeper said.

Abe forced himself to grin as he took the coins.

He had to act normal – any odd behaviour would be noticed. He had known Tom Carthy since he was a chap. A bit soft with giving out credit but Abe knew the shopkeeper missed nothing. He probably had it figured already that Abe was interested in buying the cottage.

It'd only be a matter of time before the likes of him got wind of the development plans too so the sooner Vera knew the better. If she heard of it from someone else they'd never hear the end of it and, worse still, she might dig in her heels.

"Tea?" Vera asked when he arrived at her back door.

His sister was taking off her Wellington boots in the scullery. She'd been cleaning out the henhouse, by the stink of them. Abe's stomach heaved at the smell. He could never stand the whiff of hen shit.

There was hardly a pick on his sister, he thought, looking at her thin frame as she put on a pair of ancient slippers, but the muscle was still good, he knew, even at the age of seventy-three.

"You should leave the likes of that to the lads."

"Yeah – and get it done this side of Christmas."

"Roy around?"

His sister looked back at him as she took off her boots.

"There's a change! It's usually the other lad you're looking for. He'll be in shortly. He couldn't finish Brophy's hedges with the rain."

"Right."

Leo came in to wash his hands after drenching sheep.

Abe nodded to Leo when Vera had gone into the kitchen.

"I'm going to tell her now."

"Fair enough."

Abe could hear his sister in the kitchen lifting the kettle onto the Aga hotplate. She was calling to them now.

"Did you see any activity at Casey's on your way home from town?" she said.

Abe swallowed hard before calling back.

"Can't say I did."

"Lil's daughter is there, according to the grapevine. She doesn't let the grass grow under her feet anyway. That mother of hers is hardly cold in the grave."

Roy came in now, coat drenched and face red from the cold. His father, Harry Kemp, would never be dead while he was alive, Abe thought as he glanced at him.

"Roy has seen her, haven't you, Roy Boy?" Leo said as he took off his boots. "Gave her directions, no less."

Abe could hear the jeer in Leo's voice.

"S-s-s-so what?"

"I know what directions I'd be giving her," Leo said, "to get to hell, back where she came from."

"Whisht!"

"Well – what's all the gossiping about?" Vera asked when they went into the kitchen. His sister didn't miss a trick.

Leo threw himself onto a chair.

"So tell us again what sort of a filly this one down the road is anyway?"

"Sh-sh-shut up," Roy said, as he got mugs and plates and knives from the dresser.

"That's enough!"

Abe distracted himself by looking at an old newspaper in the pile on the table.

"She was p-p-p-polite, which is m-m-more than can be said f-f-f-for you," Roy said.

Leo laughed.

"I think he has a soft spot for her. By God, I'm right!"

Abe saw Roy redden to the gills. He did have a liking for her! Abe felt his chest tighten.

"Whisht the two of you!" Vera said, pouring the tea.

Abe tried to remember how many spoonfuls of sugar he had put in his tea – two? Three? He only took one. What if his sister noticed?

"Well, tell us!"

Abe cleared his throat. Stay focused on the development – that's all he had to do. That way his mind would stay clear.

"Right. We have plans – big ones – that you could profit from too."

He could see interest spark in his sister's eyes already.

"I'm listening."

He talked for three minutes, uninterrupted, then shoved a piece of paper with his costings and expected profit margin on it towards his sister.

The clock ticked loudly while she perused it.

"Putting good land under houses was never a thing we did in this family. It was hard enough got," she said.

"True, but you have to move with the times. Think of the profit. We might never see the likes of this opportunity again. If we build seven houses on those fields we could make more out of them than we would farming those acres for fifteen or twenty years."

"Maybe . . ."

"It's all about cluster development now," Leo butted in. "None of this ribbon stuff anymore, so planning permission on the edge of a village won't be a problem."

Abe gave him a look to tell him to leave the talking to him.

He watched now as his sister examined the sheet of paper again, her reading glasses perched on the end of her nose. With her bottom line brain she'd be looking for gaps in the figures.

"No contractor is going to build a house for these prices."

"Direct labour. Act as contractors ourselves. That's where the real money is. Leo can act as site manager and I'll supervise."

"Y-y-you're in on this?"

Abe saw Leo grin.

Abe jumped in to avert a row.

"I had to tell Leo because if he wasn't prepared to do it I'd be going nowhere. It'll take all our involvement to make it a success – Roy's too."

Roy was now looking at the piece of paper.

"W-w-w-here are you going to g-g-et the s-s-s-start up money?"

"I'll put in some to get us going and we can borrow the rest between us. If we sell the houses off the plans and get deposits in, the bank'll lend us the rest."

"M-m-m-ortgage the f-f-f-arm?"

"To a limited extent. Sometimes you have to speculate to accumulate. And you'd get a lot of work out of it – there'd be a couple of months work drawing away from the diggers. It'd set you up."

"You'd be in fucking clover, you luder!"

"Shush!"

Abe could see his sister looking at the projections again.

"What about planning permission – there's not much road frontage on those fields and there's the bad bend coming up to your field."

"We'll get access."

"W-w-where?" said Roy.

"We need Jim Casey's cottage."

"You won't get it without it?"

"Then you should have moved faster than you did. What's that daughter of Lil's doing back here then? I thought you had the place bought as a rental property."

"I was holding out. Flynn told me I'd get it for less."

"And now she's dead and everything's up in the air? Feck that! We could be submitting plans by now only for him?"

Abe could see the excitement he'd hoped for in his sister's eyes – the glint of avarice.

"You'll have to move steady," Vera said. "If the daughter is back here it's probably because she's curious about the place. The novelty'll soon wear off it. Townies like her wouldn't settle in a place like this. They'd want more creature comforts than that place could give her."

"Sh-she's not that young."

Leo laughed.

"Go on so – tell us what age she is."

"Th-h-hir-ty, thirty five-ish."

"She's single, isn't she? She'll have a career in some city. All you have to do is offer her enough."

"I'll be talking to Flynn again tomorrow," Abe said. His sister was right – offer her enough and she would be out of his life for good.

"What does Florrie think of the plans?"

"She doesn't know about them yet."

Abe could see the flash of satisfaction on Vera's face because he had told her, his sister, first.

"She mightn't want you taking on all this at your age."

"I'm not dead yet. We'd be fools to pass up a chance like this. Between us all, we'll manage it. This boom will only last for a few years. I'll be damned if I'm going to miss out on it."

It had gone well. His sister had reacted as he knew she would. Farmers were going into building construction all over the country. Why not them? Leo would be very useful – he had a good eye for detail and the experience of building his own house. Abe felt the excitement of a new project stirring within him.

For a few minutes he had almost forgotten about her in the cottage and who she was. She was some stranger who would just have to be persuaded to sell. A stranger, that's all.

It was ten o'clock when Hannah woke. For a split second she couldn't remember where she was. The pink walls told her. She had slept for twelve hours on the trot. Sticking her feet into her slippers to go to the window, her mind felt clear. It wasn't raining – hurrah! It would be a good day for exploring. She stared now at the fields stretching out from the cottage. Was that Stephenson land? Where did Abraham Stephenson live exactly? She had passed no farmhouse on her way here from the village that she could remember, so he must live further down the road.

She thought of her mother. How often had she looked out this window, her mind on the man who had fathered her child? Had she fancied him as a young girl, leaving her vulnerable to his charms at the age of twenty-eight? Why had he gone to her flat that day, that year? Was he just lonely between girlfriends and wanting to pass the time in Dublin?

She'd rather imagine another scenario – one where he'd finally realized he'd always loved Elizabeth Casey. One where she, Hannah, was the product of that passion, not just the result of a quick bonk. No, that was happy ever after land and she didn't live in that.

Nanna in Royle had set her straight on that one, she thought, as she dressed herself. Nanna had overheard her one day telling the other children that her father was a prince and she was going to live with him when she grew up.

She had smacked her on the hand.

"Don't make up stories," she said. "God doesn't love children who tell lies."

She didn't judge Nanna harshly now, though she'd hated her that day for bursting her fairytale bubble. She was a lucky child, God loved her and Nanna loved her and she had a home there with all the other children, but she was no better than any of the others – she was never to forget that.

Hannah shivered as she went downstairs to put the kettle on.

She had just buttered some toast when she heard a car drive in. Her heart nearly stopped. What if it was him? Bracing herself, she slowly rose to answer the door.

A smiling woman in her sixties was standing there, wearing a tracksuit, fleece and old runners.

"Hello. I'm Peg Travers. I live down the road. You must be Lil's daughter."

"Yes. Peg . . ."

"A friend of your mother's, love. I've been lighting the fire and keeping an eye on the place for her since her da died."

"Of course! I wondered who . . . That was very good of you. Won't you come in? I'm Hannah."

Peg's handshake was warm.

"Pleased to meet you. I saw the car when I was passing yesterday and I said I'd come and introduce myself as soon as I could."

Hannah felt excited.

"My mother told you about me?"

The woman now looked away.

"No, love, Tom at the shop told me about meeting you so I said I'd drop in – seeing as I have a key to your house and you might be wanting it."

"Yes, of course, thank you. Come in."

"Thanks. Your mother and I were great pals as young ones. It's still killing me that I didn't get to her funeral, but I was in England with my sister and never heard a thing till I came back."

"That's all right, you don't have to apologize," Hannah said, pulling out a chair for her visitor. "It's good to meet you now. I've just made some tea and toast. Would you like some?"

"Ah, feck it, why not? I'll be dead long enough and what my doctor doesn't know won't hurt him, isn't that right?"

Hannah now watched Peg stare at the room.

"You've transformed the place! It's a little palace, honest to God. Look – the sofa and everything . . . I hardly recognized it!"

"The new furniture makes a difference."

"The woman's touch – that's what it is – though fair dues to your mammy she always gave it a good clean up for your grandad every time she was down."

Hannah liked this woman with the big voice and the big smile. The fact that she knew her mother from childhood intrigued her. She was the first person she'd met who had.

Over two cups of tea and three slices of toast, Peg answered her questions – what her mother had been like, who her friends were, where they went to school.

"This area – are the neighbours friendly?" she asked as she offered more tea. This time Peg covered her cup with her hand.

"No thanks, love. Most of them are grand – same as anywhere. They were all very good to Lil around the time of your grandad's funeral, I know. Made the tea in the community centre afterwards and all . . ."

"It's strange hearing you call her Lil . . ."

"Lil? Why? Is that not what you knew her as?"

"I thought everyone called her Elizabeth. It was what she said her name was. I never thought of her being better known by a pet name."

Hannah heard herself laugh.

"And Nanna at the children's home always called her *Mrs Casey*."

"Ah sure what harm? Didn't it keep things a bit straighter in a confusing world? And she kept in touch – isn't that what's important? Did you see her often?"

"Once a month."

"God love her."

Her? What about me, Hannah thought . . .

Lil. Elizabeth. Two separate worlds – public and private, country and city.

Hannah tried to stay focused.

"I was going to explore the area once I'd had my breakfast – to get my bearings. I don't suppose you'd be free to come with me? I'd like to know where my grandparents are buried, that kind of thing."

"You're going to stay for a while, then? Isn't that great!"

"I have a few months off work – compassionate leave."

"Dead right too. Bereavement can take its toll on the best of us. I was years getting over Larry dying. Still feel like I've only three wheels on my wagon, to be honest. Give yourself time and you'll come through this all right. Of course I'll show you round. It's the least I can do after not being at the funeral."

"Great. And lunch will be my treat. You pick the place."

"That'd be lovely," Peg said, as she heaved herself up off the chair. "When I got up this morning I didn't know how I was going to put in the day and here we are now – isn't life great all the same?"

"I'll get my coat."

"Ready when you are!"

"Right," Hannah said, finding her keys and switching off the kitchen light. "Let's go."

"First stop, Rathbrandon churchyard. That's where your granny and grandad are buried," Peg said, putting on her seat belt. "It's the Protestant graveyard, of course, but the old burial ground at the back of it is Catholic – goes back to the days when we weren't allowed to have our own graveyards."

"I was actually reared Church of Ireland – in the home . . ."

"Oh, I'm sorry, me and my mouth. I just presumed . . ."

"No harm done. Is it well kept?" Hannah asked as she braked gently at the gateway ready to go out on the road.

"Absolutely. Cleaned up for the pattern every single year."

"Right or left?"

"Left."

It was new territory for Hannah, a straighter and quieter road as they drove further away from the village.

They had driven about a mile when she saw Peg put her hand up at a passing car – a navy Mercedes.

"Huh-ho! He must be off on business today. You never see him in the car unless he's going to town."

"Who?"

"Abe Stephenson."

The hairs stood up on the back of Hannah's neck.

"Sorry?"

"Abe. Abe Stephenson, one of your neighbours. He farms a bit further on. I'll show you the entrance as we pass by."

"Ok."

"Most people wouldn't have a lot of time for him, of course. Thinks he's a cut above buttermilk with all the land he has gathered up under him but his wife, Florrie – she's the best in the world. How she puts up with him I don't know, but she must see something in him that the rest of us can't, isn't that it? That's the entrance there."

Hannah slowed the car.

"A fine place really. He's no stranger to hard work to give him his due – his mother and father before him too – hard-goers. Everyone who worked in the place had to be too. Your mammy earned the few pence she got there, I can tell you."

"What?"

"Did she not tell you the places she worked?"

"She didn't say much really."

"She worked there as a girl – in the house. Your grandad worked on the farm half his life, too, before tractors did away with the need for him. Worked on the council after that – road repair. The late sixties or early seventies, I'd say he was there till."

Hannah's fingers were gripping the steering wheel. She forced herself to speed up a bit, not wanting Peg to notice that she was taking more than a passing interest in what she was saying.

"I didn't know that . . . Have they family? The Stephenson's?"

"No. Couldn't, I believe. Florrie had some kind of difficulty, I think. It must have gone hard on her, God love her. If any woman would have made a good mother she would. Didn't she half-rear those two lads of Vera Kemp's – that's Abe's sister, who owns the farm on the upper road. She was widowed young with two little boys. You'd often see the eldest chap, Roy, out places with her – Florrie, I mean – still. They're very close."

"Really?"

"The Vera one's a different sort, though. Harry Kemp was old enough to be her father when she married him, and there's some would say she married him to get her hands on what he had."

"Oh?"

"Love of the land. It's a disease with the Stephenson's. They'd sell their granny for it. Then, of course, there's the question marks over the way poor Harry died . . ."

"How do you mean?"

"There's some as think it wasn't a shooting accident at all – that he killed himself – but the inquest found nothing peculiar, so who are we to be questioning? It was a tragedy no matter what way it happened."

Hannah was finding it difficult to concentrate on the road.

"She had two sons – Vera Stephenson – sorry, Vera Kemp?"

"Yes, Roy, a gentle sort of chap, takes after his father. He's over forty now, of course and Leo's a bit younger. He's cut from the same cloth as his mother – live in one of your ears and let the other out in flats."

Hannah kept driving, on automatic pilot as her mind took in all Peg was saying. Her father had no other children and now she'd found out that she had two cousins! Roy Kemp – where had she heard that name before?

"Here we are," Peg said as a church came into view.

"The Casey burial ground is at the far side. God, your mammy went quick in the end, didn't she? She'd failed a lot last time I saw her but I never thought she was as bad as that. Cancer is a sneaky disease, I always think. Sorry, I'm upsetting you with all my prate."

"No, you're fine," Hannah said as she got out of the car. "I should have brought some flowers."

Peg was struggling out of her seat.

"Jaysus, what I wouldn't give for a new pair of hips. God forgive me, taking His name in vain and me in full view of a house of God! Can't you bring some the next time you come? Your mother didn't want to be buried here with her mam and dad then?"

"No. She bought a plot for herself in Dean's Grange. It was all organized."

"She was a long time in Dublin, I suppose. Still, a lot of people go home to be buried . . ."

Hannah felt suddenly agitated. Was being buried in Dublin part of her mother's plan to keep her away from here – from Abe Stephenson?

When she thought about it, if her mother had had her way the cottage would have been sold before she died. With the burial taking place in Dublin there would have been no reason at all for Hannah to come to this locality.

Her mother was trying to control things to the last! Hannah felt like a voyeur in the silent graveyard now. Her mother had never wanted her to come here. No! She couldn't think like that. She had thought like that for long enough. Surely she had a right to be here? Her mother couldn't control anything anymore. She was gone and Hannah was here, life was going on and she had the right to live wherever she wanted – and the right to know about her past . . .

Peg was now pointing at a headstone.

"That's it there. A fine one too. Cost your mam a pretty penny, I'd say, but she wanted it to be right."

Hannah stepped inside the kerb to look closer at the inscription on the polished granite. *In loving memory of Margaret (Molly) Casey who died 10 November 1979 and her husband James, who died on 11 May, 2003.*

Her mother's mother had died when she, Hannah, was 14. Her mother had never said a word.

"A great woman for the brown bread," Peg was saying. "Your mother and myself'd eat lashings of it plastered with homemade butter when we'd come home from a dance on the bikes. In the morning she'd be wondering who took the bread!"

"Did my mother have many boyfriends?" Hannah asked as she traced her finger round the letters on the stone.

"She did, of course, but she never settled on any particular one, not around here anyway, but sure she was gone to Dublin when she was barely seventeen. She probably had lots of boyfriends up there."

Hannah could predict the next question.

"She never said much about your father, I suppose?"

Hannah concentrated on removing a bit of moss from the kerb.

"No."

"Probably some Dublin fella who let her down. Women have it hard and the men get off scot-free, isn't that the way?"

"I'll bring flowers next time."

"Sorry, love, I shouldn't be prattling on. Your mother'd love that. Why don't I leave you on your own for a bit? I'll sit in the car and rest my pins. You take your time."

"That'd be great, thanks. I won't be long."

Hannah waited to hear the door of the car close.

Now she stood for a few minutes listening to the coo coo of woodpigeons and looking at the older burial ground where many of the headstones stood at an angle or had fallen altogether over the years, at dandelions shorn by the wind and the tree stump where fungi flourished.

Where all is peaceful, calm and still, I rest beneath Your care . . . That's what Nanna had wanted on her headstone . . .

Her grandparents' headstone had a simple cross at the bottom. Standing there, she felt that she should say a prayer of some sort but none came. Had anyone prayed for her when she needed it?

A shiver ran down her spine as she headed back towards the door of the church. Reverend John Mundy was the rector, she read on the sign. The graves came up almost to the church door.

"Whoever got the plot nearest the door probably thought they'd be nearest to God," she thought as she walked off the gravel onto the grass ridge.

She read the name on the newer headstone of the two – Stephenson.

Christ!

"George Stephenson died 1969, Mabel Stephenson died 1976 . . ." in gold lettering on black marble.

Stunned, she now moved closer to look at the older, lichen-covered one, beside it. *Abraham Stephenson . . . and Hannah, his wife . . . born 1881, died in 1950 . . .*

Shit!

H-A-N-N-A-H Stephenson! Her great grandmother's name on her father's side was Hannah!

Her mother had called her after Hannah Stephenson! She must have known her. Hannah tried to do the sums. She was probably the granny in the house when her mother worked there as a teenager. Maybe she just liked her.

"Or maybe she gave me the name Hannah in order to give me the only connection I might ever have with my father's family?"

Hannah had a lump in her throat. Maybe her mother wasn't such a mouse after all . . .

Checking again that Peg couldn't see what she was doing from where the car was parked she traced her finger along the letters. H-a-n-n-a-h . . . She stood there for a long time trying to stare through the headstones into the past.

So many questions . . .

Did George and Mabel Stephenson, her grandparents, know of her, the baby their son had fathered? Were they the ones who had instructed him to pay her mother, Lil, off?

What would the now dead Hannah think if she knew she had an illegitimate namesake, Hannah wondered? If her mother liked her she must have been a kind woman, Hannah thought. You don't call a child after people you hate, do you?

"And I have two cousins . . ."

Roy Kemp . . . that name . . . She remembered now where she'd seen it – on the side of a tractor. *Roy Kemp Hedgecutting* . . . The man with the stammer who had shown her the way . . . Good God! He was her cousin! He had kind eyes, she remembered. Peg was right. Maybe there was some goodness on her father's side, after all.

Taking several deep breaths to ease her excitement, she headed back for the car.

Would the truth come out? When? Would her father own up and tell the world she was his daughter or would he turn his back on her?

She shivered.

"You all right, love?"

"Yes, thanks."

Putting the key in the ignition she had no idea what would happen in the future. One thing was for sure, though, she was staying in the cottage for as long as she wanted.

"Lunch – you tell me where," she said to Peg.

"The Corner Inn in the village – I can introduce you to some of the locals."

"Sounds good to me," Hannah said.

The pub car park looked busy enough for a weekday.

"Lot of builders come here for their dinner now or go to the deli counter in Tom's shop," Peg said. "There's money in those breakfast rolls, that's what I tell Tom. Hasn't the world changed a lot all the same? A while ago it was all bacon and cabbage and now it's all pasta and paninis and them cappuccinos."

Peg introduced Hannah to sixty-something-year-old Fintan Doyle, the owner of the pub.

"Pleased to meet you, Hannah."

The lounge had a real fire and smelled of roast meat and stout.

Hannah could feel what eyes there were in the place for early lunch turn on her.

"I knew your grandfather well. Many's the night he sat there on that stool on the corner and enjoyed a pint. I hope we'll be seeing you in here too."

"You never know."

"What can I get you to drink – on the house . . . you too, Peg?"

"You don't have to do that."

"Nonsense, let him. It won't break the bank, isn't he rolling in it?" said Peg.

"Do you hear her?"

"I'll have a hot whiskey to warm up my bones. What'll you have, Hannah?"

"Sparkling water'll be fine."

"Great. Take a seat there and I'll bring it down to you."

"And the menu as well, please," Peg said. "We're here for lunch."

"No bother."

Peg had now lowered herself onto the bench seating.

"Fintan'll be glad of the bit of extra trade. Busy enough at the moment, of course, with the festival in town. It all ripples out, but local custom's what keeps any place going really."

Hannah looked around. She liked the feel of the pub. The ceilings were high and the place was clean.

She wondered did Abe Stephenson drink here – or her cousins, the Kemps?

The lunch was plain but wholesome, according to Peg, who had the Guinness stew. Hannah chose the lamb but barely tasted it as Peg chatted on about her own family and her medical history.

She resisted the temptation to ask more questions about the Stephenson's. Peg wasn't stupid. If she showed too much curiosity she'd pick up on it.

The sun was still strong when they came out.

"Will we take a different road back?" Hannah asked. "Then you can show me a bit more of the countryside?"

"Fair enough. You'll know the place backwards by the time we're finished. And thanks for the lunch and the chat – I enjoyed it. It's not a bad area around here, if you're thinking of settling.

Wexford's thriving and you wouldn't need to go out of it for much, I always say. I'm sure the hospital in there could do with another pair of hands, too, whenever you're thinking of going back to work."

"We'll see. I'm not going to think about that until after Christmas."

"You're right too. Take your time and enjoy the break. You'll be working long enough. Turn right then take the next left up Wickham's hill and go back along the top road. Then we'll take another left and go back the lower road to your place. You'll have a fair idea of the geography then."

"Great."

"It's mostly farmland around here, though there's a lot more new houses than there used to be. Farmers are selling sites now that never sold sites before because of the big money they're getting. Usually they'd chop an arm off before they'd let go of a square inch."

"Sign of the times, I suppose."

Hannah remembered how difficult it was to make a living from farming. As a child when she had spent summers on farms the work had been hard and no one seemed rich but they seemed content with what they were doing all the same. She'd asked Mr Watson one time why he didn't do some other job when he was giving out after the weather broke and he had hay on the ground. He had laughed and said, "Sure what else would I know anything about, child."

"You'll have to come over for a proper supper soon," Hannah told Peg when they got back to the cottage where Peg's car was parked. "When I'm a bit more settled in."

Peg Travers beamed.

"You're doing wonders for my social calendar! I'd love that and don't forget you're welcome to drop in on me whenever you like – I mean that. And if there's anything you need help with all you have to do is ask."

"Actually, do you know the name of any handyman in the locality? If I'm doing a few things at the house . . ."

"I do, of course, but whether they'd be free to do anything coming up to Christmas or not I don't know. Most of them have been sucked into the building trade now and they're allergic to small jobs, but they'll need the small man again someday – that's what I tell them. I'll get back to you with a few numbers tomorrow."

"That'd be great, thanks. Sorry, I meant to ask – did we pass that place – the Kemps – that you talked about earlier – Roy and Leo, wasn't it?"

"God, I've a mind like a sieve. I forgot to point it out on the top road – the way we came back. Do you remember the bungalow near the road – not quite finished, this side of the little bridge – cement blocks still lying around outside it? That's Leo's – a bachelor pad, I believe he calls it, thinks he's God's gift, God love him."

"I think I remember it, yes."

"You'll probably meet Roy and the mammy, Vera, if you go to Rathbrandon church. I don't think the Leo fella goes very often but Roy does, I know, loves the singing. He has a great voice – God bless him – he carol sings for charity at Christmas with the rest of us."

Hannah felt pleased. So she had a cousin who liked music! It was a start. Maybe it was in a gene somewhere.

"Look after yourself, love."

Hannah's mind was buzzing as she waved Peg off. She thought of what Peg had said about Abe Stephenson earlier on. Why would so few have time for her father? Why did she feel vaguely hurt to hear that? Why had she presumed he would be likeable? How could she expect to know anything about him?

"How many of his genes have I inherited?" she wondered, as she let herself in to the heat of the cottage.

Physically she resembled his family – the height, the leanness . . . If only she could meet him face to face . . . So many 'if onlys' . . . Right now the need for more information was like a physical ache inside her.

Soul food. That's what music was. At the lunchtime concert in St Iberius church in Wexford town Florrie Stephenson was struck, once again, by the power and beauty of the human voice.

As the soprano, one of the opera soloists, came to the end of Puccini's aria *O mio babbino caro* the audience broke into applause. She glanced at Roy who was beside her. He winked.

"There is a lot in the world to be thankful for," Florrie thought.

And it was good to be transported to another world for a while – away from Abe's grumpiness, from everyday concerns. She was glad she had Roy to share the concert with. The few times that her husband had come to such events over the years he had been fidgety in his seat after fifteen minutes or, worse still, had fallen asleep.

During the opera festival she and Roy went to as many concerts and recitals as they could.

Today's trip had been Roy's suggestion. He needed her help with something, he had said on the phone, but he didn't say what. Still, he seemed happier than she'd seen him in a long time, so it must be something good.

Westgate restaurant was packed when they got there but they eventually found a seat upstairs.

Once the analysis of the concert had ended they talked of other things – of how the cattle were getting on, of when Knocklannon Gem was due to calve and of how the reminiscence project at the day care centre was going.

"Great," Florrie said, "you'd be amazed at the kind of stuff that comes up. There really is no such thing as an ordinary person – even in a small, rural area like Rathbrandon. It'll be good to preserve their stories for posterity."

They then talked of farming, of the beet uncertainty that had knocked them all for six. "Your Uncle Abe is like a bear these days," she said. "I don't think he can get his head around all this EU change."

She saw the flicker of concern in Roy's eyes.

"O-o-oh?"

"It's all right. I turn a deaf ear to it. His bark is worse than his bite most of the time."

"H-h-he . . ."

"What?"

Roy stood up.

"N-n-nothing. I'll get s-s-some k-k-ketchup."

Back at the table a few minutes later his face lit up when she asked him about his sculpting. A garden centre near Wexford had agreed to take some of his stonework on a sale-or-return basis, he said, after he'd emailed them with photographs of a few pieces.

"Wow!" No wonder he was happy. "I'm not surprised. One of these days you'll realize how talented you really are. What was it you wanted help with? Something to do with that?"

"C-c-clothes. New stuff. C-c-choosing it."

At last! How long had she wished that he would take more interest in his personal appearance?

Forty-two wasn't ancient, yet he dressed like an older man, too often wearing the old-fashioned jumpers and trousers that his mother bought him for Christmases and birthdays.

"Y-y-you've got good t-taste," Roy was saying.

"I'd be delighted."

The newspaper cutting now being slipped across the table caught her by surprise.

"What's this?"

Florrie scanned the first paragraph. It was an article about a course to help people control a stammer. To be held in a hotel in Waterford in January. Florrie had a lump in her throat now. She'd wanted him to take part in such a programme for years.

"W-w-what do you th-th-think?"

"It sounds marvellous. I'm thrilled. Have you applied?"

"I-I-I'm going to. I d-decided . . ."

"That's brilliant! It'll be a new you in 2005 – in a lot of ways."

"Yeah . . . Th-Th-things are l-l-looking up."

Florrie stood up to go.

"Of course they are. And no one deserves it more. Come on," she said, smiling. "We've got serious shopping to do!"

By 2.50 p.m. Roy had bought everything he needed: a new suit, two casual but smart outfits and a jacket that would go with either.

Florrie could see the lift in his confidence as each outfit was decided upon.

"You have to like it yourself," she told him as he checked his reflection in the mirror. He seemed shy, almost embarrassed, by the trendier image that was now looking back at him.

She finished off his shopping by buying him a good navy three-quarter length wool coat as a Christmas present – medium weight, well cut – it would take him anywhere – and stop him ruining the overall new look by putting his ancient anorak on over any of it.

"You'll be fighting off the ladies," the assistant in Hore's Stores said as he packed the items into bags.

"I-I-I wish. W-w-e'd better get out of here b-b-before we're b-b-broke," Roy said.

Florrie took two of the bags.

"It'll be worth it – you'll see."

In the car park she watched him put all his purchases in the boot.

"Hang them up when you get home, won't you?"

"Y-y-yes Mammy."

"Messer!"

Florrie rushed to hide her pleasure all the same by saying that she had one last thing to get in town before she left – a small present for Lil Casey's daughter.

"I'm going to call on the way home. Your mother told me there were signs of life at the cottage, so she must be there."

Roy was closing his boot.

"I-I-I m-m-met her," he said.

"Really? Where?"

Roy slowly explained about giving their new neighbour directions.

"What's she like?"

Florrie saw Roy shrug his shoulders.

"N-n-ice enough."

Florrie was surprised to see him blush.

"She's obviously made an impression on you!"

Did the new clothes have something to do with this new woman arriving in the locality as well as going on the course, she wondered.

"So what if it does," she said to herself. "He's only human."

She wished Roy had found someone special years ago, but with his stammer and a mother who poured cold water on most inclinations he had, a long-term relationship just hadn't happened yet.

"Do you think she's going to settle here?"

"D-d-don't kn-ow."

"Well, it'd be good if she did. We could do with some new blood in the area."

Florrie searched in her bag for her mobile phone to check the time as she walked to her own car. Sugar! She'd forgotten it. She thought of calling after Roy to ask him but stopped herself. She'd learned not to ask him the time. Not since the day she'd inquired why he didn't wear the good watch she and Abe had bought him for his confirmation.

Fourteen years of age at the time, he had blocked badly.

"I-I-I-I-I d-d-don't w-w-want to b-b-b-b-break it."

It had only dawned on her days after when she heard some of his boarding school friends mimicking him.

"What's the time, Kempo? Is it t-t-t-en t-t-t-to th-th-ree or a f-f-f-f-five to f-f-f-f-f-our?"

Teenagers could be so cruel. Florrie said a prayer of thanks now that he was going to get help. It was long overdue.

Approaching the cottage in Drumcadden, Florrie thought it was all a bit weird – the fact that this woman had to ask directions to her mother's homeplace. Unnatural.

"Perhaps she was adopted and only found out that Lil was her natural mother lately," she thought as she drove in.

"And her grandfather probably knew nothing about any child," she said to herself, thinking of the weather-beaten man with the cap – Jim Casey – who had worked in Knocklannon for decades.

And even if he did know he wouldn't have said . . . Skeletons in the cupboard . . . The shame of a pregnancy outside marriage was very real in the past, she knew. Young girls nowadays wouldn't understand how bad it was.

Shame, too, for a married woman, not being able to have a child .
. . Florrie took several deep breaths as a familiar wave of sadness
washed over her. Blow out . . . one, two, three – let the pain go with
the breath . . . Her counsellor had taught her the breathing strategy.
Big, deep breaths until it passed . . .

Despite trying to push the image to the back of her mind, she
had a sudden recollection of her own mother's face when she told
her that day in the dairy about her blocked fallopian tubes.

She'd never forget the pinched, white face that looked back at
her.

"You're in trouble so," her mother said, very quietly, as the
churn came to a sudden stop.

Adoption wasn't a possibility that Abe would consider. It had
taken her months to pick up the courage to mention it.

"There are places in Dublin – children's homes . . ."

She breathed deeply again. It was the closest he had ever come to
hitting her. At the last second he had stopped himself, hitting the
sink instead. He had a bruise on his hand for days.

Breathe out – one, two, three . . .

There were lights in the cottage – someone was here – and busy –
by the look of the empty paint cans outside the back door.

The door opened eventually. A woman in her thirties stood there
wearing jeans and a jumper, her fair hair splattered with white
emulsion paint, looking wary.

"Hello?"

"Hello. I'm Florrie – Florrie Stephenson – one of your
neighbours. I'm just calling to welcome you to the locality. I hope
I'm not disturbing you."

Florrie held out the wooden presentation box that contained two
pots of locally made jam and one of marmalade.

"A housewarming present."

"Oh! It's . . . lovely. Thank you very much. Sorry – my manners .
. . Come in but excuse the mess. I'll wash my hands . . . it'll just take
a second."

Florrie looked round the kitchen.

"You've done so much – and so quickly!"

The younger woman turned her head rapidly. The wariness was
still there.

"Someone told you I was here?"

"I'm sorry – I should have said. My sister-in-law mentioned
there was a car here and Roy – Roy Kemp, my nephew – well, my
husband's nephew really – he said he gave you directions on
Monday."

"The guy on the tractor?"

"Yes."

"He did, of course. He was a great help."

"Roy is sound out, as they say around here."

The younger woman was now finished drying her hands and was holding one out to Florrie.

"Hannah. Hannah Casey."

"I'm Florrie. It's good to meet you, Hannah. And you're welcome to Wexford."

"Thank you very much."

"I always appreciated people dropping in to say hello when I moved here. It made all the difference trying to settle in."

"How long are you here?"

"More years than I care to remember and still a blow-in in a lot of ways but sure, so what? It'd be a dull locality if everyone was a native. Hannah – that's a lovely name – you don't hear it much these days."

"Really?"

"I don't think so. It's a Biblical name. I always thought it would be a nice name for a little girl . . . Anyway . . . it's good to see this place being lived in again. So many older houses are being left derelict these days while the new ones mushroom."

"I suppose. Would you like a cup of tea? I was just about to make one."

"I'd love one, thank you."

Florrie picked up a CD on the counter as Hannah filled the kettle.

"You like Vivaldi?"

"Big fan."

"Me too. Music is wonderful, isn't it – the difference between living and existing, I always think. Roy and I were just at a lunchtime concert in town. It was marvellous. Wexford's great for music, especially at this time of year. Do you play an instrument yourself?"

"No. I like singing though – choirs and that, not that I'm great or anything. You?"

"The piano. I was a late starter but I'm getting there – slowly. It keeps me sane."

"Oh?"

The younger woman was looking at her intently again.

"I shouldn't be delaying you . . ."

"You're not, honest. Sorry if I seemed a bit on edge – I didn't hear the car coming in so the knock threw me a bit."

"That's ok. The last thing I wanted to do was send you into a flutter. I should be at home working in the garden but any excuse .. . do you like gardening yourself?"

"Window boxes – that's about it, I'm afraid. Beryl is better at it, though. She's the friend I own a house with in Waterford. She'll be here later on actually. I never seem to have enough energy for anything after a 12-hour shift."

"You're a nurse?"

"Good guess."

"You have that capable look about you. What specialty?"

"Coronary care."

"No wonder you're tired! And you've had so much to cope with lately. Your mother wasn't ill very long, I believe?"

"Six weeks. It's all been a bit of a blur, to be honest."

"I'm sure it has. Let me help you with those."

Florrie put the mugs and the milk carton on the table as Hannah wet the tea.

The younger woman was looking at her curiously again.

"Did you know my mother?"

"Just to see. She wasn't home from Dublin very often, I think. I knew your grandfather well, though. He worked in Knocklannon for years."

"Knocklannon . . . ?"

"The name of the farm – the townland really."

"Of course. Peg told me that – about him working on a farm locally. Peg Travers – do you know her?"

"Of course I do. Peg's herself. Speaks as she finds, though I'm not sure if I'd tell her too much . . . Hey, listen to me, giving you advice . . . and Peg has lots of good points as well. I'm sure you're well able to suss people out for yourself."

She saw Hannah smile.

"I hope so but thanks for the pointer anyway. She said my mother worked there too – when she was very young . . ."

"She could have but it would have been before my time. Farms were big employers in those days, especially at harvest and sowing time. Peg would know, I'm sure. They'd have been around the same age, wouldn't they?"

"Yes, they went to school together. Is that a Cork accent I'm getting a hint of?"

Florrie smiled.

"I haven't lost it totally so, and I wouldn't want to either. It's good to hold onto some part of your past, I think."

"The women my mother worked with in Dún Laoghaire – they used to tease her about her bog Wexford accent – or so they told me."

"I'll bet. Where did she work?"

Florrie listened while Hannah answered. She seemed very matter-of-fact and unemotional when she spoke about her mother. Odd.

"Did you live with her?"

"No. I was reared in a children's home actually."

Florrie was taken aback.

"I'm sorry, I didn't mean to pry."

"You're not. It's not a secret. Not any more."

"You don't have to tell me if you don't want to . . ."

"It's all right."

Florrie listened as Hannah explained that her mother, Lil, had kept in touch on a regular basis.

"Where was the home?"

"Greystones."

"Oh!"

"Did you know it?"

"No . . . not that one but I visited a few places like it at one time . . . the sixties it would have been . . ."

"Oh?"

The younger woman was staring at her now.

"We couldn't . . . I couldn't . . . have children," she said. "I can talk about it now. There was a time I couldn't. I thought we might adopt but . . . Infertility is one of those things that you have no control over – at least not then. Nowadays they can do more."

"You went to the homes to see the children . . ."

"I used to knit things – baby clothes, jumpers for the older ones sometimes. It helped me somehow . . . then I'd call in if I happened to be in Dublin."

The younger woman's eyes were deep green, Florrie noticed.

"Why did your husband not want to adopt?"

"Hard to say. Some men have a thing about a child not being their own. Who knows?"

Florrie could see tears flicker in Hannah's eyes now.

"I'm sorry," Florrie said. "I'm upsetting you now as well as myself, bringing all this up. I didn't come here to do that."

The emotion had gone from the younger woman's eyes as quickly as it had come.

"That's ok. A lot of people came to the home. Women mostly at first, then with their husbands later on. We'd all have our best bibs and tuckers on."

"Maybe I was wrong to go at all – raising expectations like that. I should go. I'm sure you've things to be doing."

"No, it's good to talk to you – honest."

"If you're sure . . . We seem to have got on to very serious subjects very quickly."

"It happens like that sometimes, doesn't it? You just gel or something . . ."

"Maybe so."

"And I'm glad of the company – no kidding."

Florrie took a welcome sip of tea.

"Were you well treated? We hear so much about some of the places nowadays . . ."

The younger woman shrugged.

"So-so . . . Nanna – the house mother – did the best she could with the resources she had . . ."

"I'm glad. Society was so harsh for everyone in those days. Women – and children – took the brunt of it. But you've turned out well."

Florrie watched Hannah wrap her fingers round her mug.

"At least my mother didn't forget about me. Some kids had no one. I had status in the place because my mother came to see me – would you believe that? I thought I was better than everyone else because of it. How cocky is that?"

"That was how you felt then – it's not something you have to apologize for."

Florrie listened as the younger woman talked for a long time about her life in the home. Her mother went to Bethany Home in Rathgar to have her, she said, even though she was Catholic, because she was afraid of never getting out of a Magdalene home if she went to one of them. At least that's what she thought happened.

"We were all reared Protestant. Nanna was big on religion. We did a lot of praying – especially when things were tight – but it worked sometimes . . ."

At ten to five Florrie reluctantly stood up to go. She shook the younger woman's hand for the second time.

"It's been lovely to meet you, Hannah. You've had a tough life but you've a lot to be proud of, too – I'm sure you're making a big difference in the world with the work you do. Good nurses are always needed. I hope you're very happy here."

"Thank you. You've very kind. And sorry about being a bit off-hand at first. Lack of sleep, I think."

"A few good nights' rest and you'll be as right as rain. Rest and heal, that's what you have to do after a difficult time. And if you ever want to drop in for a cup of tea and a chat you're more than welcome. I can show you the garden and the apples of my eye," Florrie said as she picked up her bag.

"What are they?"

Florrie laughed.

"The pedigree Herefords – cattle. I'm addicted, I'm afraid. I'll show you the next one to calve – Knocklannon Gem – she's a champion – and she'll give birth to another one, I hope. It's a lot of work – training them to the halter for shows and that, but it's good to have an interest in life, isn't it? It was Friesians before I got married but my tastes changed to red and white, I always tell people, when I moved to Wexford."

"When was that?"

Florrie had her hand on the doorknob.

"June 1962. A lot of water's gone under the bridge since then but we can't stop time, can we?

"No . . ."

There's a lot of pain behind those eyes, Florrie thought as she drove home. Being reared in a children's home couldn't have been easy.

"Goodness knows what scars she has but they'll ease over time, please God."

The five o'clock news was announced on the radio. She had been gone since morning. Abe would make smart comments about the life of Reilly she had . . .

Steak and chips – that's what she'd cook for supper. The smell of it would soften his humour. Women – born to yap – that's what he'd say when she told him that she had called to see the Casey girl.

Hannah shook for a full two minutes after Florrie Stephenson left.

"I was born three years into their marriage!"

It was a possibility she hadn't even considered. Her mother had had an affair with a married man – Jesus! No wonder she'd been secretive.

She grabbed her mobile phone to ring Beryl but changed her mind before hitting the call button. Beryl would be driving and wouldn't be able to answer.

Hannah sat down to try calm herself. Florrie Stephenson . . . She had such kind eyes . . .

Beryl knew something was up the minute she arrived.

"He's been here, hasn't he? You're as white as a ghost!"

"No. His wife has."

"God!"

Hannah pointed at the jam.

"She brought a present – to welcome me to the locality."

"You're joking!"

"I'm not. I liked her. You would too. She reminded me a bit of Nanna."

"Jeepers!"

Hannah was searching the fridge for a bottle of wine.

"What's that going to solve?" Beryl said, seeing what she was doing.

"I don't want it to solve anything," Hannah said. "I just want it to make me very drunk. My mother his bit on the side – Jesus!"

"That's crude."

"It's the truth! And don't tell me she didn't know he was married – she knew!"

"I wasn't going to, but who's to say how she felt or what the situation was? What's the point in judging anybody? If she loved him she probably couldn't help herself. Maybe he cared for her too for all you know . . ."

"Enough to leave her with a child to bring up on her own? Yeah, right!"

"At least he gave her money to support you."

"Conscience money."

"If he'd been a real scumbag he'd have done nothing."

Hannah stopped, realizing her friend had gone quiet. Beryl's father had dumped her in Royle after her mother died but had kept her older brother. Beryl was eighteen before she found out she even had a family. Hannah tried to calm down.

"I'm sorry. It's just hard seeing it as any father is better than no father at all. Right now I wish she'd told me he was dead. It might have saved me all this torment."

"You don't mean that."

"I do so. Who am I kidding? She'd have gone to the grave without telling me if I hadn't kept at her," Hannah said, filling a glass to the brim.

"She asked you to get the stuff out of her bag, didn't she?"

"I know, but maybe I shamed her into it. I didn't think for a minute that he'd have been married. Am I thick or what?"

Hannah now toasted the air.

"To my father – the bollocks!"

"Hannah!"

She drank a mouthful.

"So what does that make me – the daughter of a bollocks? Great!"

"Don't!"

Hannah took another gulp.

"I came down here like a bull at a gap, thinking – hoping, I don't know . . . God, I was some eejit!"

"You knew it wasn't going to be simple."

"Yeah. Nanna was right – don't rock the boat because, guess what? It can be a v-e-r-y painful experience!"

Hannah lifted the refilled glass.

"To Nanna – a wise woman!"

"Leave Nanna out of it. You're winding yourself up. Who knows what'll happen?"

"Nothing will happen unless I make it happen! I'm not the big, bad wolf in this – I'm not! I've a right to know who I am the same as everyone else has and I can live around here if I want to. If it makes anyone else uncomfortable, it's not my fault. Maybe it's about time someone rattled his cage!"

Beryl was looking at her, her eyes like saucers again.

"Bitterness is eating you up . . . You usedn't to be like this . . ."

"Yeah, well, maybe I just got real . . ."

Her friend's voice was low.

"What about his wife?"

Hannah drank more wine.

"I don't know. I can't really think about that right now."

It was almost ten o'clock the following morning when Hannah woke to the sound of heavy rain pounding off the roof.

She tried to sit up.

"God! My head!"

"I'll get you some paracetamol," Beryl said. She was already dressed.

"Thanks. Rain! Does it ever stop? We'll be drenched in town."

"No, we won't. It'll ease off later on."

"Beryl . . ."

"Yeah?"

"Do you think she was ever here – my mother – when she was pregnant with me?" she asked as her friend left the room.

"Maybe. Before . . ."

"Before her belly got big – exactly!"

"What's the point of talking about all that? You're just tormenting yourself."

"Yeah, imagining her lying in this room thinking of him across the fields in bed with his wife!"

"You won't know how it was until you talk to him."

"I know what happened all right – he got his oats – wham bam thank you ma'am!"

"I'll get the tablets."

Hannah's body felt like lead. How much sleep had she lost in the last six weeks? Too much . . . She wished she could persuade Beryl to stay longer than the weekend but how could she? She had her job to go to. She worked in a busy hotel with a big conference and wedding business – not to mention the Christmas party season coming up. Beryl wouldn't be able to take any extra time off for a long time to come.

She listened now to the noise of Beryl riddling the cooker downstairs, of her filling the kettle at the sink and the clatter of mugs as she took them out of the cupboard.

Why hadn't she heard those noises as a child, her mother making them? Why hadn't she heard her grandfather, Jim Casey, cutting sticks outside, whistling maybe, as he worked?

She sank back into the pillows. She would have a lie-in for a while until her headache eased a bit.

"Nanna wouldn't approve," she thought. Nanna didn't have much time for alcohol or idleness.

She was never short of lectures about the dangers of drink and there was no staying in bed in Royle unless you were sick. There were always chores to do and the younger ones to get up while Nanna, under pressure, shouted from the bottom of the stairs. Then there was the thunder of feet along the linoleum-covered corridor to the long kitchen where the children took their places, in relays, at the galley counter to eat their porridge. She couldn't look at porridge ever since.

"I thought you were staying in bed," Beryl said when she came downstairs half an hour later in her pyjamas and dressing gown.

Hannah filled a glass of water.

"Couldn't settle. I was thinking, how about going to the pub tonight – the Corner Inn? Where I went with Peg Travers."

Beryl looked uncertain.

"Are you sure?"

"Why not? It's a free country."

Her friend looked uneasy again.

"What if he's there?"

Hannah shrugged.

"It has to happen sometime. Sure, I'm scared but haven't I been in the dark for long enough?"

Hannah could feel Beryl's eyes on her as she took her mug of tea to the sofa.

"You will go easy? Sometimes you're not as tough as you think you are."

"I'll be fine."

"Have you heard from Matt at all?" Beryl asked.

"A couple of missed calls. I sent him a text to say I was away for a few days. Why?"

"He rang the landline the other day. He seemed worried about you – after the funeral and all."

"Well he shouldn't be. He's in the past now. He knows that – and anyway I have more to think about right now than him," Hannah thought as she wrapped her dressing gown round her knees. Like her father's wife telling him that she'd been at the cottage . . .

"She must have told him by now. Oh, to have been a fly on that wall . . ."

Beryl had stopped tidying the sink.

"Hannah . . ."

"Yeah?"

"This . . . isn't going too fast, is it? I mean, it's a lot to process . . . in a short space of time."

Hannah shrugged.

"It's not a short space of time. I'm nearly forty. Haven't I been in limbo long enough?"

By five-thirty they were back at the cottage, carrying damp shopping bags. For most of the afternoon Hannah hadn't been able to concentrate on anything – shops or sights. She'd lingered long enough in the Arts Centre to buy a painting, though. It had drawn her the minute she saw it. *Distortion*, it was called. It was an abstract watercolour of a blonde female figure, where the original painting had been torn up into tiny squares then re-assembled. The whole figure was skewed slightly because of the reassembly.

"Bit like how I feel right now," she thought.

She already knew where she would hang it – under the stairs in the cottage. Maybe she'd even get a spotlight fitted to shine down on it just like there had been in the exhibition.

Beryl looked askance at her after seeing the price tag.

"I can afford it," she said.

They were now packing away the groceries.

"What time do you want to go to the pub?" Beryl asked.

"Half past nine or so."

"You're still sure?"

"Yes. Why wouldn't I be?"

By 10 p.m. they were in the Corner Inn. The owner, Fintan Doyle, recognised Hannah as soon as she came in.

"Do you get much of a crowd on Saturday nights?" Hannah asked.

"Not bad. The music helps. If I see anyone from your neck of the woods I'll introduce you, if you like."

"Thanks. That'd be great."

Hannah could feel the eyes of the regulars on her – red-faced, elderly men nursing their pints. She scanned their faces for some similarity to the newspaper cutting. There was none.

The traditional musicians were finger-deep in a set of reels when she noticed a familiar face arriving. Was it the guy on the tractor? Yes, it was, but dressed up this time. She smiled at him, at the same time as she gave Beryl a dig in the ribs.

"What?"

"Ssh!"

She could see the pub owner draw Roy's attention to them.

God, her first cousin was walking across the lounge towards them now!

"H-h-hello. I-I'm R-R-R-Rykemp."

"Yes, I think we've met."

"Y-y-es."

"You gave me directions."

Hannah introduced herself – and Beryl.

"She's down for the weekend. Sit down and I'll get you a drink to say thanks. What would you like?"

"Gu-gu-gu-"

His stammer got worse as he tried to force the words out.

"Your usual, Roy?" the bar owner called over.

Roy nodded and his face got redder.

Hannah wished Fintan Doyle hadn't jumped in like that. He should have given him time.

"Great. My pleasure," Hannah said.

Hannah could hear the men at the counter laugh as she went back to her seat after ordering. What had Fintan Doyle said – something about it being Roy's lucky night?

At least he and Beryl were chatting. Beryl would take his stammer in her stride. Nick, a boy in Royle, had had a speech impediment. Take time to listen, Nanna had always insisted.

"Do you come here often?" Hannah asked. "God, that sounds a bit weird . . ."

She saw Roy smile at her over-used chat up line.

"O-o-only when there's a d-d-d-d-dance."

Beryl laughed as well.

"What are you like?"

"A-a-re you s-s-settling in all right?"

Hannah told him she was and that she was trying to tidy the place up a bit. She could do with someone to trim the ditch in front of the cottage, she said. Maybe he could do it when he had a chance?

He seemed pleased to be asked.

"N-n-no problem."

Hannah scribbled her mobile phone number on a bar mat and handed it to him.

"Why don't you phone me and let me know exactly?"

"G-great."

For an instant Hannah wondered had she gone mad. This was surreal. She was giving a stranger her phone number – a stranger who was actually her cousin.

She glanced at him again.

Roy didn't look anything like the picture of her father in the newspaper – Roy's face was rounder and the eyes further apart. Maybe he took more after his father's side – the Kemps.

"Is the hedge-cutting your full-time work?" Beryl was asking.

Beryl seemed to be comfortable in his company.

"We f-f-farm as well. My b-b-brother Leo and my m-m-m-mother."

"Cattle? Sheep? Tillage?"

"Sh-sh-sheep and t-t-tillage mostly. S-s-sugar beet."

"Farming isn't good at the moment from what I hear on the news," said Hannah.

"There must be some good sides to it," Beryl said, "or you wouldn't do it."

Roy was looking into his glass.

"M-m-maybe s-s-sometimes you stay at what you know because you are af-f-fraid to try anything else."

"Like what exactly?" Beryl was asking, but Roy's attention had turned to whoever had just walked into the lounge.

Hannah followed his gaze. It was a man in his thirties – tall, light build, sharp-faced.

"Someone you know?"

"Th-the b-b-brother."

"Oh!"

Beryl's gaze had followed Hannah's.

"You don't look alike."

"Ch-alk and ch-cheese."

"No matter. It'd be boring if we were all the same," Beryl was saying.

Hannah glanced over at the bar. Leo Kemp was eyeballing her. He had obviously already taken in the sight of his brother at a table with two women and was asking the barman who they were. Was that a smirk she saw on his face?

Roy's posture now looked more tense.

"Your brother's coming over."

"Ss-urprise, s-s-surprise . . ."

"I thought I'd pop over and get the brother to introduce me to our two visitors," Leo said, slapping his brother on the back. "Hello, ladies. Well . . . come on!"

"H—h-h-h . . ."

Roy was blocking badly trying to say Hannah's name.

Leo was rolling his eyes up to heaven.

"You wouldn't want to be in a hurry with this fella, would you?"

"There's no rush," she and Beryl said together.

Leo was now rubbing his brother's back as if he was a child. Roy pulled away.

"H-h-hannah and B-Ber-ryl," he said, almost coughing the words out.

"Leonard Alexander Kemp – Leo to my friends," the newcomer said, holding out his hand to shake theirs.

Hannah didn't like the way he held on to hers a few seconds too long.

"Jim Casey's granddaughter, I believe."

"Word travels fast."

"Not much a secret in this place, is there, Roy Boy?"

With that Roy stood up.

"Ex-cuse me," he said, taking what was left of his pint with him. "N-n-nice to have met you b-b-both."

"You too."

"Woops," Leo said, sitting down on the stool his brother had vacated. "Was it something I said? A very shy boy, my brother – especially when it comes to the fairer sex."

"He was doing ok," Beryl said.

"Yes, he was."

"Sor-ry! I can tell him he has a couple of fans then. It'll make his day – even his year."

"You're not alike," Beryl said.

"Thank God, what?" Leo said, winking.

Hannah could see Beryl glancing over at the bar where Roy was now talking to one of the older men.

"So, are you ladies on holiday?" Leo asked, lowering more of his beer.

"Beryl is here for the weekend. I'm here for longer."

"Really? How long?"

"No precise plans as yet."

"Right. Still, not much around here to keep a city girl occupied."

"Who says I'm a city girl or hard to occupy?"

"Hannah's a country girl at heart," Beryl said.

"Aye?"

"Yep. I like the peace and quiet."

"Plenty of that around here – too much, if you ask me . . . What do you ladies do for a living?"

He certainly wasn't wasting any time.

Hannah could see Leo eyeing her up and down after she told him.

"A uniform – sounds good!"

"We wear blue baggies."

"And they say the world is making progress, what?"

"Hotel receptionists have sensible uniforms too, don't they, Beryl?"

"Yes."

"Pity all round."

Now it was Hannah's turn to ask questions.

"You farm, I hear?"

"Yep." He nodded towards Roy at the bar. "He's more into stock, I prefer machines – the more horsepower under the bonnet the better."

"Do you get on well?" Beryl asked.

Leo glanced over at Roy and smirked.

"The jury's still out on that one. I haven't much in common with them there artistic types."

"How do you mean?"

"Sculpting, he calls it."

"Oh?"

"Really?"

"That sounds interesting."

"Interesting enough to give you a pain in the head!"

Hannah watched Leo mimic a person hunched over a hammer and a chisel – tap, tap, tap . . .

"It'd drive you wrong! Can I get you ladies another drink?"

"No, we're fine, thank you. We're going soon."

"What? The night's young. What hurry is on you?"

Beryl was reaching for her bag.

"Just when we were getting to know one another," he went on. "Still, I could always drop in sometime I'm passing . . . ."

"I'm not sure what my plans are, so I may not be there. We have to go," Hannah said, picking up her bag too.

"You need your beauty sleep, is that it? Unless, of course . . ."

Leo was looking from one of them to the other, the lesbian implication hanging in the air.

"You are disgusting!"

Leo was holding his hands up.

"Ok, ok, I'm sorry. It would have been an awful waste of womanhood if you were."

"Excuse us!"

In the car park Hannah slammed the car door shut behind her.

"Slimeball! The thoughts of being from the same gene pool as that!"

"His brother seemed so nice."

"And the way he treated him!"

Hannah had an awful thought.

"God, what if my father is like him?"

Beryl started the car.

"There's no point in putting two and two together and getting six. You liked his wife. She wouldn't have married an ogre, would she?"

Hannah lay her head back against the passenger seat.

"No, unless it was one of those made marriages and she hadn't a clue what he was like until it was too late – Jesus!"

As they drove to the cottage, Hannah thought of Leo's weasel face.

"I wouldn't like him as an enemy," she said.

"Who?"

"Leo."

"How do you mean?"

"Think about it – my father has no other children so who is going to think they'll inherit everything he has?"

"His nephews."

"Exactly. And me turning up will be like their worst nightmare."

"Roy wouldn't be like that, would he?"

"Maybe not, but Leo's a different kettle of fish."

Beryl's voice was quiet again as she stopped the car outside the cottage.

"You will be all right, won't you – if he doesn't want to know?"

Hannah gave herself a shake before opening the door.

"My father? Don't worry. I won't go off my rocker," she said, getting out of the car and sounding more confident than she felt. "I wouldn't give him the satisfaction."

"You did what?"

A vein jutted out in Abe Stephenson's temple as he took in what his wife was saying.

They were in the cattle shed bedding the pedigrees and he was glad that one of the heifers had just roared and blurred the tone of his question.

He cleared his throat to speak again.

"You called in on . . . ?"

"Jim Casey's granddaughter, Hannah. She seemed a bit nervous at first but she relaxed after a while," his wife said as she spronged straw around Knocklannon Gem's pen. "I like her. She has a good head on her shoulders, I'd say."

Abe tried to sound casual.

"When was this?"

Stay calm.

"Friday – on the way home from town. I thought we might have seen her in church yesterday, actually."

Abe felt the hairs stand up on the back of his neck. What the hell was going on?

"Rathbrandon?"

Florrie explained about Hannah Casey not being reared in her mother's faith.

"Wise woman," his wife was continuing. "If she'd had the child in one of those other awful places, God knows if either of them would have got out."

Fuck!

"So it was just as well."

His wife had now paused from spronging straw.

"She was treated ok, she says, but there's probably a lot she's not saying."

Abe kept his head down, reluctant to speak until he was sure his voice would be steady. Sudden images of hungry, poorly dressed children from television documentary trailers about institutions came into his mind . . . Had she suffered like that? Again he stopped his mind from going to the end of that thought. Get a grip . . . That's what he had to do. Make general conversation.

"How . . ."

He cleared his throat again.

"How long was she in that place?"

"Until she was eighteen. She did her nurse's training in the Adelaide. A friend of hers – someone she was in the home with – was coming down for the weekend."

Florrie was now at Knocklannon Gem's head, patting her neck. "Did you ring Greg about the scanning?"

"Tomorrow at eleven."

"Good. Then we'll know if everything's right with that calf you're having, won't we, girl? She's doing a great job on the cottage – Hannah – new furniture and everything."

Abe pretended to bend down to tie one of his laces. Shit! She *was* moving in!

"Oh?"

"She was hardly going to hang onto what was in it – fit for the tip, most of it, I'm sure. Jim wouldn't have spent much on style."

Abe forced himself to keep calm, concentrating hard now on tidying up the stray silage in the aisle of the shed.

"You'd wonder at her coming to a place like this."

"It's a link, I suppose. Roots – what always pulls people back, especially as they get older. She didn't know about the cottage until a few weeks ago, from what I can gather, so you can't blame her for being curious. And it's not every day you inherit a house, is it?"

"Is that what she said?"

Florrie was closing the gate of the pen.

"No. It's just me reading between the lines. We hit it off though. It was an odd sort of experience but good – like we'd met before but we haven't. Sometimes you just click with another person, I suppose."

Abe Stephenson spat into the straw.

"I hope she settles," his wife was going on. "She could do with a bit of stability in her life."

"Have you not got enough friends without bothering with the likes of her?"

"Nonsense. The world is too full of interesting people. Why should I put limits on myself like that?"

His wife had now stopped scratching Gem's head and was staring at him.

"You think I shouldn't be bothering with her because she's only Jim Casey's granddaughter – is that it? I thought that kind of snobbery was gone. For God's sake!"

Abe didn't answer, just made a big show of checking the water troughs. Let her think what she likes.

He left the shed, rubbing his hands on his trouser legs to wipe the sweat off them. Fuck! He should have said nothing at all.

No, he reassured himself. He hadn't acted any differently than he would normally act when a piece of local gossip came up.

His left hip hurt as he got into the jeep to go check the cattle on the outfarm. Children's homes . . . Awful dives . . . The thought of them and of her turning up in church! Think of something else – that's what he had to do. Keep your mind on farm tasks . . . He'd have to bring the cattle in earlier than planned if this bad weather continued. That'd mean more work, more fodder and less profit at the end of it.

"Maybe she doesn't have a clue about me," he said to himself, his mind reverting again. Lil had sworn she'd never tell, hadn't she? What was he worrying about? He just had to stay calm . . . The image of her – the child – standing behind the hearse, tall and striking-looking came back to him . . . He wouldn't be able to gauge what she knew until he saw her face to face, though, he decided. He would know by the eyes.

He wished now he'd got more information out of his wife. Had the subject of a father come up in the conversation? He suddenly felt sick as he changed the jeep into four-wheel drive to tackle the mucky gapway.

As he walked through the stock looking for signs of illness or injury, head bent against the rain, he couldn't get the images of her out of his head. Think of something else . . . that's all he had to do.

Royle . . . That was the name of the place. Lil had told him the day she met him at Lar Finnegan's funeral. What year was that? He tried to remember. 1967? '68?

He remembered not answering except to make some comment about the weather and the size of the crowd at the burial. His chest now felt tight again. What if she looked like him? What if Florrie had noticed a similarity? He'd always imagined her favouring Lil, being pasty-faced and running to fat as she got older. Lord! Think of something else . . . The co-op – he needed some piping to fix the water supply to the lower shed. His heart pounded as he headed back towards the village and Wexford town.

He glanced in quickly as he passed the cottage in Drumcadden. No smoke. No car. She wasn't there. Relief . . . Maybe she'd cleared out . . .

As he drove along Wexford's quays, he worked it out in his head. If Lil had told her she'd have been on his doorstep straight away, wouldn't she, he thought, or she'd have written to him, setting up a meeting.

And those silent phone calls could have been someone else. He had just let his imagination run away with him, that's all. And wasted good money on a solicitor.

Heading out the Rosslare road he tried to think of some sort of pacifier to bring back to his wife. He needed her in good form when he told her about the building plans. And he'd need her help sometimes when the development started. She was a good organizer – he'd give her that. An electric shower – yes, that would do. She had been talking about getting the one in the downstairs bathroom replaced for a long time. He'd get one in Wexford Co-op.

Arriving home at lunchtime he knew something was wrong the minute he stepped into the kitchen.

His wife was sitting at the kitchen table, her laptop in front of her, a hard edge to her face.

"How could you?"

Fuck! She knew!

"How could I what?"

"How could you not tell me?"

He threw the box containing the shower down on a chair.

"Tell you what, woman?"

"As if you can't guess! I've just had to listen to your sister on the phone crowing over the fact that I knew absolutely nothing about your building plans!"

Abe felt the relief flood through him. This he could cope with.

"I've been meaning to tell you."

"After I've heard it from someone else!"

"Whist, will you and listen! She only knew a few days ago. I had to tell her first because we needed her four-acre field as well as our three for it to work at all."

"Our!"

"It'd have gone nowhere if she didn't want to be in on it. What use is a development with only four houses in it?"

"And you couldn't discuss any of this with me?"

"Ah, will you stop . . . I had to tell her first and now I've told you why. You're making a mountain out of a fucking molehill as usual!"

His wife was shutting down her computer, white-faced with anger but looking straight at him.

"And your language is offensive!"

Abe searched for something to say. Appealing to her "bottom line" mentality might have worked with Vera but it wouldn't work with Florrie. He would have to try another tack.

"Wouldn't we be doing the community a service, for God's sake, letting off a bit of land for housing? You're always saying there's local people crying out for houses and how they should be able to build in their own locality. Those two fields are a stone's throw from the village – they're the right ones to sell if we were ever going to sell anything."

"We! It's a bit late for that! And for your new-found social conscience! Lining your own pockets, more like."

Still, her face had softened a bit . . .

"What was the point in bothering your head about all this until we were ready to apply for planning permission?"

"So I could read it in the paper, is that it?"

"Christ Almighty! That housing scheme will bring in a lot of money, just like every other risk I've ever taken has – success you've warmed your arse on too!"

"Don't be so crude!"

She was now throwing her notebooks into a plastic box as she spoke.

"What's all this pursuit of money for? Tell me that! You can only eat so much, wear so much, do so much at this house. You want to stack the notes up on their edges, is that it? It's not as if we . . ."

His wife was now silent.

He was tempted to say "whose fault is that" but that would antagonize her for days.

"I'm not dead yet," he said, eventually, forcing himself to speak calmly. "If I die killing myself trying to finish this project, so be it – at least I'll have died working, not lying over a gate whinging about farming going to the dogs like some around here are doing. At least I won't have run up the white flag."

She was looking even less sure of herself now.

"You have all the answers, don't you?" she said before taking the box out of the room.

Abe sank back in his chair, exhausted. Let her come after him like she used to.

Two hours later she still wasn't talking.

"All picture and no sound – is that how it's going to be?"

"Until I make sense of all this, yes," she said. "You should try it sometime – having change imposed on you with no say whatsoever. Imagine I got involved in some project that was going to take over your life as well as my own and I didn't even consult you – you'd have something to say about it too."

Shit! He hadn't expected her to speak up for herself like that. She was doing that more and more now. It was working in that day care centre that was doing it. Freedom, the worst thing you could give women. Made them uppity. He could remember a time when she'd do his bidding quick enough. Even in bed now, though, she was calling the tune, turning away from him if it suited her, or tolerating him entering her sometimes, as if it was just something she had to do, some part of a bargain she had to honour to keep him quiet. Sometimes it was as if she was taking him instead. Once he had ordered her to be more enthusiastic when they were making love. She'd laughed.

"Love?" she said. "I feel like a piece of meat."

Women!

Abe grabbed his cap. Let her sulk. He could do what he liked with his own land.

He was in the yard power washing the combine harvester an hour later when Leo rang, asking if he could borrow some welding rods.

"Yeah, there's plenty. Come on over."

Cleaning the combine was a job he liked. Maintain your machines properly, fix them before they break – that way they won't let you down when you're busy and under pressure. He would soon have it clean and greased and ready for storage for the winter.

Within minutes Leo was there, Max growling at him as he came in the shed door.

"Shut the hell up!" Abe shouted.

"I'll do a bit. Give it here."

Abe was glad to be able to get off the ladder. He envied his nephew's speed as he took his place.

"Did you check the riddle? It sounded a bit dodgy on the last field," Leo asked.

The remark irritated Abe.

"I wasn't born yesterday."

"Right."

Leo continued the work in silence.

He was heading out the door with the half box of rods when he spoke.

"I met yer one the other night."

"Who?"

"Ms Casey – in the Corner Inn."

Damn him to hell!

"Oh?" he said, pulling a wad of straw out of the prongs on the header.

"I wouldn't kick her out of the bed either."

Abe shut his eyes, holding on tightly to a steel bar . . .

"She's a nurse, no less. Must have had more brains than her ma."

Abe felt the hairs rise on the back of his neck. Leo fancying her!

"Hardly your type."

Leo smirked as he leaned against the doorframe.

"I don't know about that. She's a classier bit than I thought she'd be. Fire in her too. She wasn't saying what her plans were, unless she said more to himself, of course."

"Who?"

"The lad. He was all cosy with herself and her friend when I walked in."

Abe felt his stomach heave. His two nephews interested in her – Christ!

"There's better fish in the sea," he said, eventually.

Leo was grinning now.

"I don't know – it mightn't be such a bad option. If I set my cap at her, the planning permission mightn't be such a problem."

"That's enough!"

He could see the shock on his nephew's face and softened his tone immediately.

"Mixing business with pleasure – it never works," he said, turning back to the header.

"Right."

Abe picked up the grease gun and put it back on its hook on the wall. He had to think . . .

"She won't be long around here. I'm getting Flynn to make her a better offer – one that she won't say no to."

Leo looked surprised.

"How much?"

"That's for me to know."

"Right."

His nephew was getting into his van.

"Well, let us know how Flynn gets on. She'll hardly turn down a lump of money like that."

"Aye."

Abe now sat down on a five-gallon drum near the bench as Leo left the yard. His heart was thumping in his chest. Take it more slowly – that's all he had to do. Leo had met her . . . And the way he talked about her! Stay calm, he told himself . . . You have to think straight.

"To him, she's just a new bit of skirt in the area, that's all. His reaction was totally normal."

And he had to act normal too – that's all he had to do.

The upped offer for the cottage would have to be made anonymously, though. Flynn would have to keep his lip zipped.

If she knew about him and got an inkling that he was the buyer she might dig her heels in. A bit of fire in her – that's what Leo had said . . . What made him think that?

No, don't start imagining her face . . . He squeezed his eyes shut again then took out his mobile phone to ring the auctioneer. If Flynn handled things properly he'd have killed two birds with one stone – bought the cottage and got shut of a ghost.

Chapter
FIVE

Hannah was driving to Waterford when her mobile phone rang.

"Who the hell . . . "

She pulled in on the hard shoulder past Ballinaboola and checked the number on the screen. No, it wasn't his number . . .

"Hello – is that Hannah?"

"Yes."

It was Ernie Flynn of Flynn's Auctioneers in Wexford, the voice said.

"We've spoken before in relation to your mother's – sorry, your property, in Drumcadden."

"Yes?"

"Is this a good time to talk?"

"Not really."

"Sorry. You're busy – what about if I call out to you for a chat sometime soon?"

"Why? The cottage is off the market – I told you."

"Yes, of course – absolutely – but perhaps we could still have a chat?"

"I'm away for a few days. It would have to be after that."

"Right."

"Could you not just tell me what this is about now?"

"I'd prefer to speak to you in person, if you don't mind."

Hannah turned the wipers on to a faster setting.

"Ok. I'll be back on Monday morning, November 1st."

"Fine. Would eleven o'clock suit?"

"As good a time as any."

"Thanks. That's great. I'll call at the cottage at that time."

What on earth was all that about, Hannah wondered as she hit the "off" button? Did he or someone else want to buy the cottage? Why else would he be contacting her?

"Either that or he's trying to sell me something," she said to herself. "Maybe he sees me as a potential buyer for some new

147

development property – as an up-sizer," she thought. "Wasn't everyone doing it these days? Or some timeshare maybe."

All the estate agents were trying to flog property abroad nowadays.

"Well, he'll be wasting his time," she said to herself. "A holiday home in the Costa del anywhere isn't on my mind at the moment."

Right now she just wanted to be home in Waterford, tucked up in front of the fire with a glass of wine or three.

The last few days had been lonely. With Beryl gone the cottage had seemed so empty. Somehow she couldn't summon up the enthusiasm to do more painting. A visit to the cinema the day before had made her even more restless. She sat through *Bridget Jones: The Edge of Reason* and thought increasingly of Matt. One of the male characters in the film reminded her of him. She felt lonelier than she had in a long time but was she missing Matt or missing sex, she wondered?

Before she left the cinema she had sent him a text. "Hi. Wl b back in Wtrfrd 4 few days". No promise of meeting, no suggestion, no asking – just letting him know. Would he read between the lines and respond, or would he leave her text unanswered as she had done with so many of his?

"Serve me right if he does. Why should he jump when I click my fingers? I'm the one that ended it."

Past New Ross now and heading for Waterford city, Hannah couldn't help thinking of him.

Children – that was the rock they'd perished on in the end. Him wanting them had come as a shock to her. She thought he'd be too old for all that broody stuff. It had been quite obvious from the time they'd visited a teaching colleague of his who'd just become a father. Matt had held the child, at ease with the tiny person, rocking it to sleep.

"He's a natural," Tim, Matt's friend said to Hannah. "You'd better watch out."

Hannah had refused to hold the baby.

"I'm no good at that sort of thing," she said, staying well away from the bottles and nappies and mess.

The relationship had gone downhill after that and she had eventually ended it. The following few months were a bit hazy – too many hangovers . . . too much stuff surfacing about her childhood and Nanna dying and feeling bereft . . . Looking back now, she knew she was lucky she wasn't suspended from work with the way she was going on. Maybe her real mother getting sick had given her something to focus on . . . How long ago was it since the funeral? Nearly three weeks. Right now it seemed like an eternity ago.

Beryl wasn't there when Hannah arrived but there was a note on the table saying she'd be back by six.

Hannah filled the kettle, glad to be home. If Abraham Stephenson was trying to contact her he would have to wait until she returned . . .

Telling herself that she wasn't in Waterford to avoid him, she checked her mobile phone again. Maybe he would ring her. His wife would have told him by now about calling in on her. The past few days had been weird on that front – every time she heard a car slowing on the road outside she thought he was going to drive in.

It wouldn't be a big job for him to get her mobile number from directory enquiries, though. It had been easy enough to get his. She had saved it to her SIM card under AS, resisting the temptation to key in "asshole"– that's what a father who didn't acknowledge his child was, wasn't it?

She had showered, changed and eaten dinner with Beryl when the text came in from Matt.

"Will be in Rafferty's tomorrow night at 7 p.m." He was never one for text-speak. Brutalization of the English language, he called it.

"Matt?"

Beryl sounded surprised when she told her who the text was from.

"Yes."

"Did you text him?"

"I just told him I'd be here for a few days."

"Right . . ."

"What's with the tone? It's my business who I text or don't text."

Hannah was shocked by the look on her friend's face.

"Ok! Ok! Let's change the subject," she said.

Beryl got up to put the plates in the dishwasher while Hannah helped herself to another glass of wine.

"I'm going to bed," she said. "Maybe I'll wake up less of a grump. There's just so much stuff going on in my head at the moment that I don't know whether I'm coming or going."

"Yeah . . ."

Hannah turned when she got to the bottom of the stairs and called back to Beryl.

"You know when we were talking about going to Bethany Home with Nanna to collect babies when we were at Royle?" she asked.

Beryl came to the kitchen door carrying a tea cloth.

"Yes."

"The way we'd get two buses there and then a taxi to bring the baby back. I keep wondering who collected me when I was a baby – and if my mother was staring out the window when I was going…"

Hannah sat down on a step, still holding her glass.

"That's why midwifery wasn't for me – did I ever tell you that? Remember how I used to give out about the training? It was all those babies – and me jealous of those who had mothers and fathers and upset for those who didn't. Either way I couldn't win."

"You're overtired. Maybe you should have that early night."

Hannah stood up and toasted the air again.

"Good old fatigue – that's right, let's put everything down to that – never to a screwed up life, eh?"

"You're drunk."

"So I am – hallelujah!"

She made up her mind early the following day to meet Matt in Rafferty's.

She tried not to think about what Beryl's reaction would be. She wouldn't want her playing him for a fool.

"Maybe she's just jealous," she said to herself as the hairdresser washed her hair.

"I wish she had a man in her life, though. The sooner she has a man of her own the better. Maybe then she'd get off my back a bit."

In a boutique in the shopping centre Hannah treated herself to a new pair of jeans and some new lingerie. Expensive, but what about it? Matt had always counted her bottom as one of her best features. The world could be divided into breast men or bums and legs men, he said one time. He was definitely a bums and legs man.

Wearing a cerise cowl-necked jumper and the new jeans stuck into her black high-heeled boots she felt she would pass for thirty as she eventually headed for the pub.

Rafferty's was busy, but then it was Thursday – payday.

It wasn't one of their favourite haunts. Matt probably didn't want to risk meeting anyone they knew and having to counter awkward comments like "I thought you two had split up". Fair enough, neither did she.

She glanced at the clock over the bar. Two minutes to seven. She had considered being late but decided against it. It wouldn't be fair.

He arrived at seven fifteen and nodded when he spotted her in the corner.

"I wasn't sure if this was a good idea," he said, after ordering from the floor waiter.

"Me neither."

"So – how have you been since . . . ?"

He was a good listener. She'd forgotten that. She told him about going to Drumcadden and about the improvements to make it more homely.

"Do you want to make it 'home'?"

"Depends . . ."

He was sitting opposite her, looking at her with those eyes she'd loved so much, traces of chalk on his corduroy trousers as usual, relics of a day's teaching.

She almost put her hand out to brush them away.

"I know who my father is."

"Oh!"

He listened without interrupting until she eventually stopped talking.

"You're living a mile down the road from him?"

"Yes."

"And how do you feel about that?" he asked over and over again as she relayed each detail.

His concern and the wine were going to her head.

She ran her finger round the rim of her wine glass.

"I feel like I'm near the edge of something – a big hole, maybe. Does that make sense? It's like I can't help going towards it, but I don't know whether if I fall in I'll break my neck or have a soft landing. All I know is that I'm being drawn to the hole."

"At least you're aware of where you're at. Maybe it'd be better not to force things too much . . . There's a lot to be said for letting things unfold in their own time . . ."

"Matt the mentor! Maybe. Anyway, what about you? Any new teacher swept you off your feet this term?"

"No."

"Right ."

He was staring at her now.

"You look well . . ."

"Thanks," she said, feeling a flicker of desire in her groin. He'd been a tender lover – gentle.

"You look good too. Would you like another drink?"

"No, I should be going. Correcting to do."

"Of course. I should head as well."

The taxi rank was a couple of hundred yards down the street. As she put up her umbrella, his hand covered hers.

"Where to?" the driver asked.

Matt gave him his own address then Hannah's.

As they got into the back of the car their legs touched. He didn't pull away.

"You ok?"

"Fine."

The taxi turned right, into the estate where Matt lived.

Now his hand was on hers.

"Coffee?"

"Why not?"

She saw the taxi man smile as Matt gave him a substantial tip.

"Have a good night," he leered, before driving away.

The house was warmer and tidier than she remembered it. Matt shared with another male teacher, the younger guy paying rent that helped Matt pay his mortgage.

"I'll put the kettle on."

"Leave it . . ."

She put her arms around his neck as his slid round her body, his face buried in her hair.

"I told myself I wasn't going to ask you in."

"And I told myself I wasn't going to turn up, but hey . . ."

"For old times' sake . . ."

Then they were kissing – soft, single kisses at first then longer, deeper ones, their arms wrapped round one another, bodies touching all the way down.

"I've missed you," he said into her hair, her neck, his hands under her jumper now, touching her bare flesh.

In bed he brought her to orgasm twice, knowing where to touch her, to titillate her, knowledge that had come with years of practice and knowledge of her body.

She knew what he liked too – the pace to set, the slower then faster movements, the writhing that would make him thrust harder, deeper, pumping himself into her until eventually their bodies arched and the sensations peaked.

Him wanting to hold her for a long time afterwards irritated her and she pulled away.

"You're not sorry?" he said.

"No. You?"

"No. It was wonderful."

She glanced at the digital clock on the locker.

"God, I'd better be going."

She got out of bed and fumbled for her underwear.

"Why? Where's the fire?"

"Beryl'll be wondering where I am."

"She'll think you're a loose woman, is that it?"

"She worries."

Hannah cursed, realizing she'd put her jumper on inside out.

"So – you've just got what you wanted and now you're going?"

She stood up to pull on her pants and jeans and made a face.

"Ah, don't be like that! It suited both of us, didn't it, so what's the big deal? We're both adults!"

She pulled on her left boot.

"I see. Don't let me delay you," he said, getting out of bed.

"Now you're being stupid – you wanted it as much as me."

She ran a comb through her hair and grabbed her jacket before calling a taxi.

Matt was putting his shoes on by the time she'd made the call.

"In relation to your father – where do you stand legally – do you know?"

Hannah shrugged as she grabbed her jacket.

"I have the same rights as any legitimate child. It's the law."

She thought of the framed *Irish Times* cutting that she'd kept since 1988 – about the Status of Children Act becoming law in Ireland. June 14th. *The end of the term 'illegitimacy'* . . .

She had held an impromptu party that night, for as many Roylers as she could round up.

She remembered wondering at the time was her father, whoever he was, shaking in his shoes knowing that she – a bye child – might some day come after him or make a claim on his estate? At the time she'd imagined him, faceless, beads of sweat appearing on his forehead as he watched the six o'clock news on RTE. Now she could put a face and a name on that man – Abraham Stephenson. She shuddered. Would she have the nerve to meet him?

"Mightn't do any harm to have a chat with a solicitor, though – unless, of course, you're not interested in the inheritance side of things?"

Hannah looked at him.

"Why are you asking me that? When it comes to it I'm his flesh and blood, aren't I, whether he likes it or not? What's wrong with thinking he should face up to the fact he has a daughter – and that he hasn't treated me right?"

"So that's what this is all about?"

"I don't have to justify anything to you."

Hannah grabbed her bag.

"No, but you should at least be honest with yourself about why you're doing it . . ."

Hannah turned round.

"Look, all I want – would like – is a father who'd love me – does love me – the other stuff is by the way, but it's normal stuff if you're someone's child. Am I supposed to apologize for that? Now I've got to go."

In the taxi home Hannah didn't speak to the driver. Instead she stared out at the wet streets and the neon signs. Feck Matt! She was glad she hadn't married him. He had lasted longer than the rest of them, she thought, as the taxi headed out the Cork road. He'd been nearer her own age than most of the others, too.

How many older men had she been with? Brian, a physiotherapist at the hospital, twenty years her senior, was the first. She'd gone out with him for two years then left him when he started getting too serious. Then there'd been David, the bank official, with beautiful hands and a balding head and a taste for fine restaurants, who talked to her of archaeology and history and how she should improve her mind.

Her appetite for him telling her he loved her had been insatiable at first, but she bored of him eventually too. What was wrong with her? Was she capable of sustaining a long-term relationship at all? No, she mustn't think like that. Of course she was worthy of being loved – it was just a question of finding the right man.

The lights were on in the house. Beryl was home. She would go straight to bed. That way she wouldn't have to talk . . . Turning the key in the lock it suddenly felt as if this house or this city wasn't home anymore. She thought of the cottage in Drumcadden. Right now she wanted to be back there. Close to the answers.

Fuck her anyway! Leo Kemp spat the words out.

"I thought Flynn wouldn't take no for an answer! Find out how much she wants, you said, and give it to her!"

"Keep your voice down, lad! He tried."

"Not hard enough!"

His Uncle Abe had sat into the passenger seat of the van after pulling up beside Leo in the village.

"Twenty thousand more than the market value – that was the offer," he said.

"What? Why the fuck wouldn't she sell then? She'd have change out of a place in Spain for that! It'd have to be better than living in that hole. What reason did she give for not selling?"

His uncle was looking out the side window.

"Some sentimental shite about wanting to live in her mother's house."

"Fuck!"

Leo hit the steering wheel, blowing the horn unintentionally.

"Get a grip on yourself! Do you want the whole place gawking at you?"

Leo was sweating. What was he going to do now? He'd ordered a new four-by-four from Bolands garage on the strength of the building development starting. '05 . . . How could he go back on that? Shit!

Ms Hannah Casey was getting seriously up his nose.

"So what now? Sit around and wait until she gets tired playing babby-house? Did you ask Kinsella again about putting an entrance somewhere else?"

"Yes."

"And?"

"The answer's the same as before."

"We can't just sit here and do nothing!"

"We have no choice for the moment."

"Well, she can think again! She'll sell – one way or another."

"What's that supposed to mean?"

"That a little persuading mightn't do any harm."

His uncle grabbed his arm.

"Stay away from her, do you hear? This is my business and we'll do it my way, or not at all. She'll get fed up in the place eventually. Flynn is going to keep sending her out stuff about other properties coming on the market. Sooner or later something else will take her fancy – you'll see."

"I hope you're right."

Leo felt irritated by his uncle's "softly softly" approach. A blow-in like Hannah Casey wasn't going to dictate to him like that. All he needed was a plan.

His uncle was about to get out of the van.

"You never told me what that quack said after," Leo said.

"Who?"

His uncle was having trouble finding the door handle.

"The doctor you went to see a few weeks back – the day I got the loader."

His uncle had finally got the door open.

"Nothing a few tablets won't sort out."

"You're ok so. Did you tell Ma?"

"No! And you say nothing to her either!"

The sharpness of his uncle's tone surprised him.

"Whatever you say."

Odd that his uncle was so touchy . . . Was there something up? Maybe he'd got bad news and was trying to keep it quiet . . .

Driving off, the thought of his uncle being unwell excited Leo. Not that he wished him ill or anything but it was only natural to look forward to what was coming to him. Knocklannon would be his and he'd have his due after all the years of helping out and working cheap and curbing his tongue when his uncle was giving him orders and him long past the age of taking them. Right now, though, he had to get on with everyday stuff . . . Hitting button number nine on his mobile, he waited for Eileen Miller to answer. As usual it didn't take her long.

"Hi." Her voice was warm, seductive. He felt turned on already.

"Tonight's no go, I'm afraid."

"Aw! You said Monday night was fine!"

"I know. I forgot. I have a meeting to go to."

"I could come over and warm up the place for you later."

"Maybe. I'll text you if it finishes early."

"See you then, lover boy."

"Shut up, for fuck's sake! Anyone could be listening!" he hissed, knowing she was at work.

"There's no one near and anyway how would they know who I'm talking to?"

"Yeah, right, look . . . I'll text you later."

"Ok."

That's what he liked about her – no strings, no humours, no hissy fits – not like most of his friends' girlfriends and wives who were always bitching and calling the shots.

Out of the shower half an hour later, Leo looked at himself in the mirror. He liked what he saw. Farm work kept him fit – his upper torso was well defined from a life of lifting bales and buckets. His hair getting thin on top annoyed him a bit, but there was nothing he could do about that. He rooted a new pair of Calvin Klein underpants out of the wardrobe now. You never know, he thought, he might get lucky with Ms Hannah Casey. It paid to be prepared.

He was glad of the silence in the bungalow. No mother grating his ear . . . There was a lot of "snagging" still to do on the house but it would be all done eventually. He'd finish it in style once the development money started flowing in – Jacuzzi bath, classy tiles, one of those forty-two inch televisions and Sky and black leather sofas with the reclining chairs.

He'd be on the pig's back, money wise, with his foreman's cut. A chick trap – that's what this place would be.

He splashed some expensive aftershave lotion on his face. His mother would blow a fuse if she knew how much the bottle had cost him and how much he spent on clothes and drink or that he had Eileen Miller staying over regularly. That would get up her nose the most. He always got Eileen to park round the back, where the car couldn't be seen if his mother did happen to be passing up or down the lane. He'd designed the house that way. Eileen Miller wasn't his mother's idea of marriage material – too much of a track record and didn't dig with the right foot. A decent girl, that's what he was supposed to be looking for. Decent meant Protestant.

"She could have square eyes and three tits as long as she was that," he said to himself.

His mother wouldn't approve of what he was going to do right now, either – pay Hannah Casey a visit. Roy Boy wouldn't be too happy either.

"The dope hasn't a hope," he said to himself as he checked his image again in the mirror.

At seven thirty he arrived at the cottage. Good, only one car there. She hadn't got company.

Eventually he heard the bolt being drawn back on the door.

"Yes?"

"You'll have to get that outside light fixed," Leo said, "so's you can see who's at the door. It's Leo – Leo Kemp – we met last week in the pub."

She was standing there, her hair wet, a zip up fleece on over her pyjamas.

"I remember."

"It's freezing out here – are you not going to ask me in?"

"It's manners to wait to be asked," she said as she held the door open. "This really isn't a good time. What is it you want?"

Leo was looking around.

"Just being neighbourly – calling in to see how you are. I'm impressed. You're done a good job on this place," he said, standing with his back to the Rayburn, hands in pockets. "Better than the kip it was anyway."

Leo saw her flinch. Take it easy . . . Don't get her back up . . .

"Jim – your grandad kept it tidy enough when he was younger, of course. It slid a bit in the last few years with him not being well, but that's the way it goes, I suppose . . ."

Hannah Casey still had her hand on the door.

"Was there something in particular you wanted?

Leo grinned.

"No, just dropping in, as I say . . . I didn't see the car for a few days. You must have been away."

"Yes, I was."

"Back seeing the boyfriend, I suppose."

"I don't think it's any of your business where I was. Now, if you don't mind, I've things to do."

Leo put his hands up.

"You're right, it isn't . . . I was only saying, but are you settling in ok really?"

"I'm fine."

"Have you got to know many yet – apart from the brother, that is?"

"Roy is a nice man."

Leo laughed.

"Nice! That about sums up our Roy all right."

"He's a gentleman. How long has he had the stammer?"

"The st-st-st-tutter? I dunno. As long as I can remember."

"Has he ever had help with it?"

"There was a few bob spent on speech therapy all right. Ma packed it in as a bad job in the end."

"That doesn't mean he couldn't get help now."

"True. I'll tell him Nurse Casey says so."

"I can speak for myself, thank you."

"Whoa! Course you can."

Leo was now running his hand down the partly-sanded banister.

"Good wood in that all the same. They didn't do a bad job on these houses really. Is that the plan? Do up the whole gaffe?"

"I'm taking things day by day."

"As long as it's not money down the drain . . . why not, I suppose?"

"How do you mean?"

"I dunno. It's just that it's a bit of a bog hole – this site – marly ground. Damp could be a major problem . . ."

"My mother never mentioned anything . . ."

"No? Then you've nothing to worry about . . ."

He saw a shadow of uncertainty in her face now, though. Good!

"Not to worry. Your home's your castle, isn't that right? And what's a bit of damp here or there as long as your lungs are good?"

He glanced at her chest.

"And I'd say you've a good pair of lungs . . ."

Hannah Casey was holding the door open, her face like stone. Fuck! He should have toned it down a bit.

"Goodbye."

Still, faint heart . . .

He stopped as he was halfway out.

"I don't suppose you fancy going out some night? Hitting the local hot spots . . ."

"I'll pass, thank you."

"Fair enough, but it's your loss!"

"I don't think so. Goodnight."

"Well, if you change your mind let me know . . ."

In the car Leo cursed as he put the key in the ignition. Frigid bitch!

No, he'd handled it wrong, that's all.

"I shouldn't have been so cocky," he thought as he drove out. Still maybe he hadn't messed up altogether. He'd planted doubt about the condition of the house – it was a start. The fact that she wouldn't go out with him annoyed him though. Probably got some long-term fella. Still, anything worth having was worth chasing. He wasn't about to give up on his idea of getting a night out of Hannah Casey yet.

He pulled in now at a gateway of one of his uncle's beet fields to send a text to Eileen Miller.

"Ten o'clock. My place."

The night wouldn't be wasted after all . . .

As he moved off again he spied a rat ahead of him by the side of the road. It was feeding on a sugar beet that had fallen off a loaded trailer.

He put his foot down on the instant. The rat bolted across the road right into his path. Thump!

"Gotcha!" he said, pleased at the noise. One less pest in the world . . . If Eileen had been in the car she'd have freaked, he thought. She hated mice, never mind rats. There'd been a mouse in the bungalow one night and she'd screeched like a lunatic until he caught it.

Women! He checked his rearview mirror. The rat he'd hit was now white belly up on the muddy road. Women frightened of rodents? Leo smiled as the dead rat gave him an idea. Supposing there just happened to be a rat problem around Hannah Casey's cottage? Country life mightn't be quite so exciting for her then . . .

Yes!

"There's always more than one way to skin a cat," he said to himself, grinning as he put down his foot again and sent beet muck flying up from the wheels.

No painting anything today. Not in this weather, Hannah decided. She would go to the village and get some groceries instead. The outing might clear her head.

The last couple of days had been irritating. First she'd had that auctioneer, Ernie Flynn, calling the minute she returned on Monday and then Leo Kemp turning up unexpectedly last night. Leo had some neck – not to mention frightening the life out of her by making her think it was Abe Stephenson coming to the door.

The amount the auctioneer was offering on Monday had taken her by surprise, even though she was aware that house prices were increasing rapidly all over the country. Still, she wasn't selling. He could do what he liked . . .

And Leo Kemp – he had made her skin crawl.

"Peg's right – he thinks he's God's gift!" she said to herself.

Maybe he had some redeeming characteristics but right now she couldn't see them. Look for the best in people, Nanna used to say, and you'll find it eventually. No, with Leo Kemp, she doubted that there would be much point in quarrying. The smile wouldn't be long disappearing off his face if he knew who she really was, she thought. If he got up her nose much more she'd be tempted to tell him.

"What am I thinking? That'd be stupid. First things first."

She hadn't even encountered her father yet. Nerves twitched in her stomach again. A lot would have to happen before Leo Kemp was any the wiser . . . What he said about the cottage being damp worried her a bit, though. Was it true? Maybe she should get an engineer's report. If there was a problem maybe she'd be a fool not to sell for what was offered . . . No, forget it, she'd only inherited the cottage a few weeks. She wasn't going to moider her head thinking about selling it already.

The village looked unusually busy for a Wednesday morning.

"Is there something on?" she asked shop-owner Tom Carthy. "A funeral maybe?"

"No, thanks be to God," he said, laughing as he registered her purchases on the till. He nodded at a homemade poster stuck on the wall behind him.

"Bring and buy sale. Rathbrandon parish fundraiser. In the Corner Inn."

Tom was grinning.

"You can't beat a Protestant for making a cake," he said.

"I don't know – I wouldn't say baking was one of my strong points."

The shop-owner's face dropped.

"I'm sorry. No offence! That'll teach me not to jump to conclusions but it's a compliment really. If there was a sale like that in the village every day I'd be out of business."

Hannah looked at the poster. Eleven o'clock start, it said. She checked her watch. It was twenty past now.

"Perhaps I'll drop over," she said.

"You might as well. Meet more of the natives."

The lounge was packed when she entered, winter sun shining in through the stained glass windows and door. Fintan Doyle was at the counter pouring tea. All the seats were taken, mostly by women. Tables full of home produce of all kinds were lined up round the walls of the bar at the far side. There was a table where people were queuing up to buy raffle prizes. Hannah suddenly felt very nervous. She shouldn't have come . . .

"Hannah, love, over here!"

It was Peg Travers, calling her from a seat in the corner.

"Come on over and have a cup of tea."

At least she knew someone . . .

"Thank you."

Peg introduced her to everyone at the table.

"Shove up in the pew there, girls, and make room for a new neighbour."

Hannah saw the women's faces light up. Obviously Peg had filled them all in.

"Thanks."

She liked the women. They were chatty and down to earth and talked to her of her mother and her grandparents. It was obviously an ecumenical event, Hannah decided. That pleased her – better than the cliquishness she'd seen so often as a child.

"We never miss one of these," Peg was saying. "I'll be putting a few things in the freezer for Christmas. The mince pies here are second to none."

Hannah looked around. How many times had she been at events like these, most of them to raise money for Royle? Hundreds of people had come to them, even the mothers of children Hannah and the others went to school with. They'd be holding on to their offspring's hands, though, children who, because they were with their mothers now, didn't stick out their tongues at the Royle kids or call them scabby arses like they did at school.

"Coffee or tea?" Fintan Doyle shouted over.

"Coffee please."

The women were now discussing what was being charged for Madeira cakes and the benefits of dearer flour compared to the cheaper variety. Hannah was half-listening, her eyes scanning the room. A woman waved at her from the jam and preserve table at the far side. It was Florrie Stephenson.

Hannah waved back.

"You've met Florrie then?" Peg said.

"Yes, she called in one day last week."

"Told you she was a good sort."

"Yes. Yes, she is."

Heart beginning to thump, Hannah scanned the crowd for a male face that might be Abe Stephenson's.

"Do the men help out at these things?" she asked.

"Very few, unless they're retired," Peg said. "They set up the tables and help with the clearing up – heavier stuff like that. The rest is left to the women but sure, what else is new, isn't that right?"

"I suppose," said Hannah.

Would Abe Stephenson be back to help with the heavy stuff when the sale was over? Her knees suddenly felt weak.

"It has to happen sometime. Cop on to yourself!" And she had as much right to be here as anyone else, hadn't she?

When she finished her coffee she walked to the bar where the stalls were, buying a loaf of brown bread, a tiny bag of potatoes, six handmade Christmas cards and a crocheted toilet roll cover in the shape of a ballerina.

She left Florrie's jam stall till last.

"It's good to see you," Florrie said. "How are you?"

"Fine, thank you. And you?"

"Glad this is nearly over. My feet are killing me from all the cooking and the standing but it's for a good cause, so I'm not complaining."

"My mother used to make apple chutney," Hannah said, picking up one of the jars. "Did you make this?"

"Yes. It's one of my specialities. My mother's recipe."

Hannah tried to imagine Florrie at the kitchen table chopping and sorting, stirring and watching the saucepan like her mother had been that day when she'd called to the flat in Dún Laoghaire unexpectedly.

It had been unusual to see her mother engaged in some domestic activity. Usually every meeting was stiff and formal and Sunday-like. Her mother's face that day was flustered red with the heat of the kitchen and the surprise of Hannah calling without prior arrangement, and every so often she'd brush wisps of hair from around her face with the back of her hand. Hannah could still remember the smell of vinegar and apples and ginger and the tray of glistening jam pots waiting to be filled.

"I'll take two pots of this and one each of the raspberry jam and the lemon curd," Hannah said.

"Thank you and I hope you enjoy them."

"I'm sure I will. What time is the sale over?"

"Half past twelve or so. I told Abe – that's my husband – that I'd give him a ring when the raffle started and he could come down for the tables then. It's handy enough with the jeep and trailer."

Hannah felt her heart lurch.

"Right . . . I should get some raffle tickets before they finish up . . . Excuse me . . ."

"Good luck! It was good to see you again."

"You too."

"I meant to ask . . . did your friend like the cottage? You were waiting for her to arrive the day I was there."

"Beryl? Yes, she loved it. It was great having her. I brought her here one night for a meal, actually."

"That must have caused a bit of a stir! It's not every day they see a new face around here."

"Possibly. We met your nephew, I think – Roy?"

Florrie's face lit up.

"Roy? He often heads down here on a Saturday night, all right. What did you think?"

"I liked him. Sound, like you said. Peg said something about his father dying when he was very young. That must have been awful."

"Yes. A terrible time . . ."

Hannah could see the sadness in Florrie's eyes.

"Right, I'd better get some of this money over to the treasurer . . . You should introduce yourself to Reverend Mundy – John – he'll be glad to hear he has a new parishioner in his midst."

"I wouldn't want to get his hopes up – I'm more of a fair weather follower than a regular churchgoer."

"No matter! I'm sure he'd like to meet you all the same. He's very approachable, you'll see."

She was right. John Mundy was in his fifties and welcoming.

"Do you sing at all?" he asked after they'd talked about who she was and where she was living.

"Sometimes."

"Marvellous. We're looking for carol singers. Any chance you'd join us?" He went on to explain that an ecumenical group of singers raised money for Barnardos every Christmas by singing in town and in a few local venues.

"Peg Travers mentioned something about it. Why not? It'll give me something to do."

"Great. If you let me have your phone number I'll pass it on to the organizer."

He lowered his voice, smiling.

"Her name is Vera Kemp. She keeps us all in line but we need it sometimes. She's not here today as she has a cold, I believe, but she'll be in touch once she gets your name, I'm sure."

Hannah swallowed hard. Vera Kemp . . . Vera Stephenson . . . Roy and Leo's mother . . .

She made two mistakes before writing her mobile number correctly on the back of a beer mat to give the rector.

Hannah now jumped as a spoon was suddenly rapped off a biscuit tin lid.

"Raffle tickets everyone!" someone was shouting. "We're going to have the draw."

163

As Reverend Mundy made his way to the raffle table, heads dived into handbags and hands into pockets for tickets that might mean a prize of a bottle of whiskey or a box of chocolates or a voucher at the local hairdresser's.

Hannah could see Florrie Stephenson take out her mobile phone and dial a number. How long would it take him to get here, Hannah wondered, as she felt adrenalin rush into her veins again. Ten minutes? Fifteen?

Hannah won nothing. Neither did anyone at Peg's table.

"I wouldn't win an argument," Peg said, "but what the hell, hadn't I a good morning out?"

She gave Hannah the contact details of a handyman she knew who could help with the heavier work at the cottage.

"Thanks a million. I started sanding the stairs myself, but it's hard going."

"Well, he's your man. Look after yourself, love, and don't leave it too long till you call."

Now the tables were being cleared and leftover items packed away in boxes that women were carrying out to their cars.

Hannah went to the Ladies and ran cold water over her wrists for a long time . . .

Back in the lounge she approached Florrie Stephenson.

"Do you need a hand with anything . . .?"

"That's very good of you. Whatever's on my stall has to go out to the jeep. There's Abe now . . ."

It was him, closing the stained glass lounge door behind him! He was taller than she'd imagined and very slightly stooped. He wore a tweed hat, a sports jacket and beige trousers. He was greeting the bar owner and some of the sale-goers who were going in and out.

Hannah felt rooted to the spot. Jesus, don't stare . . .

Florrie was now handing her a box as Abe Stephenson approached.

"Good, you're here. Hannah is giving us a hand. Hannah, this is my husband, Abe Stephenson."

They made eye contact. Was it shock registered in his? Trying to stay calm Hannah held out her hand.

"How do you do?"

He ignored her gesture and her greeting, distracting himself instead with picking up several folded up card tables.

"All these have to go out?"

"Hannah's our new neighbour. You remember – Lil Casey's daughter."

"Aye."

He was heading for the door now.

164

"Sorry about that," Florrie said. "It's one of his grumpy days. Probably out of sorts because he had to leave whatever he was doing to come here, but don't mind him . . . You take that box out – he'll tell you where to put it."

Heart in her mouth, she followed him out.

He was at the far side of the pub car park, putting the tables in the trailer.

"I'll leave these here, shall I?" she said, when she reached him.

He stopped what he was doing for a second but didn't look round. She heard a grunt as he continued to straighten up the tables.

Her heart was thumping but she forced herself to speak.

"It's good to finally meet you," she said.

"And why would that be?"

Hannah swallowed hard.

"My mother told me she knew you."

"Like half the country. What about it?"

Hannah forced herself to keep talking.

"I think you knew her better than that."

He straightened up and turned to stare at her. His eyes were like steel.

"What's that supposed to mean?"

Hannah struggled to hold his stare.

"I don't know. You tell me."

"I don't know what you're intimating, girl, but if I were you I'd be very careful what I was saying."

Hannah tightened the belt on her coat but she didn't look away.

"We have things to talk about, don't you think?"

"We do in my arse! Go on about your business before I have you thrown out of the place! Go on!"

In shock, Hannah forced herself to hold her head high as she walked across the road to her car, parked by the service station. How could he treat her like that?

She glanced over at him as she put the key in the ignition. He turned away on the second. Fecker! This wasn't the way she'd imagined it would be. How could he be so heartless? Still in shock, Hannah had to concentrate hard as she drove back to the cottage. Once there, she slammed the door behind her and wiped her face. Whatever hope she'd had now turned to anger. No! She wouldn't waste tears on him – he wasn't worth it! Who did he think he was, treating her like that? No, it'd only be a matter of time before he'd have to face up to the truth.

"He won't have any choice," she told herself. "And the truth always catches up with people – sooner or later."

Chapter
SIX

Beryl Nash was tired by the time she reached the cottage in Wexford.

Another fire brigade trip after Hannah had sounded strange on the phone . . .

How many times had that happened over the years – crisis or breakup or the latest drama where Hannah needed a shoulder to cry on or someone to pick up the pieces?

Getting time off from the hotel hadn't been easy either. She'd had to go out on a limb to get Clare Deegan to stand in on her day off, which meant she'd be in her debt in the future. She hated being under compliment to colleagues.

Did Hannah ever think about how she put people out sometimes, Beryl wondered. She wouldn't even say exactly what had happened over the phone – just "please come if you can – please . . ."

Seeing post sticking out of the letterbox by the cottage gate, Beryl removed it after parking by the door. Why hadn't Hannah been out and collected it herself? Now she felt panicky . . . Hannah had sounded very low on the phone . . . What if she'd done something stupid? Jesus!

The door was finally unlocked.

"Hannah!"

Beryl Nash was shocked at the mess her friend was in.

Hannah looked terrible – greasy hair, hung-over, standing there now shielding her eyes from the light and wearing a grubby dressing gown and pyjamas.

The kitchen was like a tip – curtains closed, surfaces cluttered, empty wine bottles on the ground, half eaten sandwiches discarded by the sink . . .

"I don't need this right now . . ." Beryl thought. "What's going on? Come on – out with it!"

"Sssh . . ." Her friend was holding her head.

Beryl decided that the mess would have to wait. Coffee – and lots of it – that's what was needed.

Within minutes she had a strong cup of coffee plonked down in front of her friend.

"Drink that and tell me what's up – come on!"

"I'm sorry for dragging you all this way . . ."

An apology! At least it was something . . .

"I thought it wouldn't affect me so much . . . I met him . . . on Wednesday."

"Your father! Where? When? What happened? Why didn't you say, for God's sake?"

Beryl listened to all the detail about the bring-and-buy sale, about meeting Florrie, then Abe Stephenson coming in. About what she'd said and he said and how he'd been abusive and the shock of it all.

"Feck!"

Beryl took her friend's hand. No wonder she was in bits.

"I've thought about it over and over," Hannah was saying. "He is my father. I know he is. If he wasn't he'd have been totally confused by what I was saying and the conversation would have gone on a lot longer but the shutters came down on the minute, I'm telling you . . . So much for fairytale endings."

Beryl struggled to find something to cheer Hannah up.

"Maybe you just caught him on the hop. He wasn't expecting you to be there – nor for his wife to introduce you. He was probably terrified she was going to come out any minute, so he was trying to get rid of you. Maybe if you'd met him somewhere else on his own he'd have acted differently. You took him by surprise, that's all."

"He looked like he hated me . . ."

Beryl gave her friend a hug.

"You don't know that. Who can ever say what another person is thinking?"

Hannah looked very pale. How long since she had eaten anything or slept properly? She was tearless and controlled, though her eyelids were swollen.

"Do you remember all the times we talked about meeting our fathers?" she said. "How they'd be bowled over when they met us, how they'd be kind and friendly and funny and sorry for not having found us and how it was all a big mistake that they'd lost touch and how they'd want to make it all up to us?"

"We were kids."

"I know, but down deep, didn't you really hope it would happen?" said Hannah.

"I suppose."

"That's the trouble with dreams – they're hard to give up. This one's been nailed to the cross, good and proper!"

"Ssh! Where to from here?"

"Good question!"

"You can't avoid seeing him if you stay around here . . ."

"And go carol-singing with my aunty! She has my number by now. The clergyman was going to give it to her. What do you think of that? He'd get a right land if he knew!"

Beryl heard Hannah explain about the rector and the carol singing. Everything was getting knotted up . . . What Hannah needed was a good meal, a shower and a lot of sleep. Until she had that she wouldn't be able to think straight.

"Miss Practical, as always," her friend said. "What would I do without you?"

"Come on – you'll feel better when you're cleaned up. And we'll throw those clothes in the washing machine."

"Right."

Beryl had sausages and rashers under the grill when Hannah eventually came out of the bathroom. She looked clean and pale but brighter-eyed than before.

"Where did you get these?" she said, picking up the three letters that Beryl had left on the counter.

"In the postbox outside. I saw one of them sticking out. You didn't collect it . . ."

"I never heard the postman . . . who could be writing to me here?"

Hannah was flicking through the post.

"Circular – supermarket bumph . . . one addressed to Mr James Casey – an advertising flyer for a vintage machinery magazine in the UK."

"They mustn't know he's dead . . ."

Hannah was turning the third envelope over and over in her hand.

"It's addressed to me. Posted in Wexford."

Beryl turned back to the grill to give her friend privacy.

"It's from him!"

Beryl nearly dropped the grill tray.

"What?"

Hannah held out the letter – if you could call it that. There was just one sentence on an otherwise blank A4 page.

Miss Casey

I will be in the car park on Mount Leinster next Sunday morning at 10 a.m.

A.S.

"Mount Leinster? Where's that?"

She could see Hannah's hand shake.

"Near Bunclody. You can drive up. We were there on a school tour years ago — remember? We were all screeching thinking the bus'd fall over the side."

Hannah took the page from her and read it again.

"He doesn't even say meet! He's going to be there and that's it – take it or leave it."

Beryl felt disgusted. The letter was so cold.

"He's mad!" she said.

"No, there's method in it. He doesn't want to be seen – what else? If it was a hotel in Wexford anyone could walk in. Up there the chances of someone being there that he knows or knows him are slim."

"I don't like the sound of it – what if he wants to push you over the edge – literally!"

"He's not going to murder me. Threaten me or try to buy me off, maybe, but he wouldn't be that much of a fool, would he?"

"God, let's stop thinking about this – it's too scary. What are you going to do?"

She could hear the excitement in her friend's voice.

"Go, of course! Maybe it's like you said – maybe the last day he couldn't talk but this time it'll be different . . . If I don't go I'll never know, will I?"

Beryl still felt frightened.

"No, but you're not going on your own!"

"I won't be on my own. There'll be lots of people there, hill walkers and that."

"I don't care – I'm going with you or following after you. You have to have some kind of back-up."

Hannah hugged her.

"You're a good friend."

"And first class eejit."

"No. Good."

Beryl watched the determination creep into her friend's face again.

"Maybe he'll own up. I'm entitled to the truth, amn't I, no matter what anyone says? Maybe he's had a re-think. I just caught him on the hop, like you said . . ."

Beryl watched her friend stuff the letter into her clean jeans pocket.

"Maybe . . ."

Beryl felt Hannah shake her awake at 6.30 on Sunday morning.

"It's time. Come on."

Hannah was at the wardrobe deciding what to wear.

"What do you think?"

"Whatever you like. Be yourself. Anyway, you could wear a sack and you'd still look good."

Hannah had pulled a black jacket out of the wardrobe and was holding it up against her.

"It's weird. I want to look well when I'm going to meet him – stupid or what?"

"It's only natural. We're all complicated human beings. Who knows – maybe he got such a shock that he couldn't talk to you the other day . . . Wear whatever you feel good in – be yourself."

Hannah now pulled out a red three-quarter-length coat that she'd had for years.

"At least he'll see me coming in this."

"You'll look great. Anybody'd be proud to call you their daughter."

She could see tears well up in her friend's eyes again.

"We'll see. Thanks for saying you'd follow me up."

"I'm hardly going to let you go on your own. I'll park a bit away so it doesn't look like I know you but I'll be there if you need me."

"Thanks!"

"Breakfast – you should eat something."

"I couldn't stomach it, honest."

"Me neither. After, maybe."

"A lot could happen between this and then."

Hannah was now sticking her jeans into her black boots.

"I'd love to make him wait," Hannah said, brushing her hair. "Give him a taste of what it feels like."

By eight thirty Beryl had her car keys in her hand. She would leave a few minutes ahead of Hannah and park on Bunclody street near the church, where she would wait until she saw Abe Stephenson's car or jeep pass by.

Hannah had given her the colour of the Mercedes and the jeep so that she'd recognize him passing but what if he used a different vehicle altogether, so no one would identify him? Then she wouldn't see him pass and wouldn't know that he was on his way and wouldn't follow at the right time. Would Hannah be in danger? What if she was too late getting there?

173

Beryl's heart was thumping. No, she had to concentrate and keep calm. She checked her phone – yes, she had the telephone number of the Bunclody Gardaí saved on her mobile phone just in case.

"Good luck," she said to Hannah at the car door.

"Your phone is charged? You're sure?"

"Yes, don't worry."

"I won't be far away."

"Thanks."

"Good luck . . ."

Hannah Casey's legs felt like jelly as she drove up the steep and narrow road to the top of Mount Leinster.

She turned up the heater as the temperature in the car dropped.

It was the sort of a drive that she would normally love – one that gave her car a good run, but right now her mind wasn't on nifty drives. She actually felt a bit sick. Maybe she should have eaten something . . .

She took a sharp left, the last turn to the foggy summit.

Would he be there? What if he didn't turn up? What if he'd hired a hit man to do her in? Stop! This was rural Ireland, not New York. She should think positive. You never know – maybe he'd be there with yellow ribbons tied around the old oak tree . . .

His car wasn't even there. The jeep neither. She was too early. She checked her watch. 9.48 a.m. There were two other cars in the parking area – one with a couple beside it putting on their walking boots and another man in his forties, she guessed, opening the boot of his hatchback to let out a black Labrador.

She wished the fog would lift a bit. It wouldn't look so spooky then. What if he didn't turn up? She sent a text to Beryl to say she was here and that there was no sign of him yet.

It was ten to ten. She turned on the radio. It was tuned to RTE Radio 1 and *Sunday Miscellany* was just over . . .

She glanced at the roadway again and her adrenalin began to flow when she spotted a wine-coloured four-by-four coming up the hill. It had to be him!

She sent a one-word text to Beryl. Hopefully Beryl was a short distance behind him. The thought gave her comfort.

Relax . . . She flexed her fingers in an attempt to get the tension out of them.

What should she do now? Stay in the car or get out? She braced herself for getting out. Opening the door it was as if everything was now going in slow motion. She didn't look towards him or his jeep. Instead she tied the belt of her coat tighter and put up her collar against the November cold. She pulled on her black leather gloves and walked round to the front of the car looking down on the foggy glen in front of her. She couldn't even see any sheep.

She listened for the sound of him getting out of the jeep, which had pulled up a few parking spaces further up.

She knew from the delay in him getting out of the jeep that he was stiff from sitting in the one position for a long time. She listened to the footsteps approach – fast, purposeful for a man his age . . .

She kept staring ahead of her.

"You like a bit of power . . ." he said.

The statement threw her.

"What?"

"The car. Turbo, isn't it?"

She turned to see him looking at her vehicle.

"Yes."

"They're good little cars."

He was talking about cars — God!

"At least you've a few horses under the bonnet when you need them," he went on, not looking at her. "A lot of women drive boxes on wheels."

What was he doing? Complimenting her taste? Worrying about her safety? Just saying the first thing that came into his head?

"Some people can't afford anything else," she said. The words had come out sharply. She didn't care. She forced herself to look at him for the first time. God, she had the same shaped nose as him! She felt the hairs stand up on the back of her neck.

"It's good to get a chance to talk," she said.

He seemed to be smiling as he stared out over the foggy glen.

"Humph! You've made allegations, girl – you think I'm going to roll over and let anyone spread lies about me?"

"I've made *allegations* to no one but you."

"And it had better stay that way."

Hannah stuffed her hands into her pockets.

"Your wife is a nice woman – we got on well."

"You'll stay away from her, do you hear?"

"Are you threatening me?"

"Advising you."

Hannah looked out into the fog again and spoke as slowly as she could.

"Did you know my mother – Elizabeth – Lil Casey?"

"Of course I did. She lived up the road."

"Did she work in your home when she was in her teens?"

"Like a lot of others – so what? Caseys have worked in Knocklannon for generations."

"Did you go out with her?"

She heard him snort again.

"I don't see what's so funny," she said.

She saw him kick a squashed plastic bottle from under the fence. It disappeared into the fog.

"Is that what she told you?"

"She told me more than that – that you're my father."

"Lies!"

"My mother wasn't a liar."

"She had a great imagination then."

"Why would she make up something like that?"

"Because she was gone in the head, because she had some kind of grudge – how the hell do I know? Because she was looking for someone's name to ruin when she got herself up the duff."

Feeling stunned at his ignorance, Hannah clenched her fists and forced herself to keep talking.

"I was born on February fifth, 1965, forty weeks after the RDS Spring Show of 1964. You turned up at her door on your last night there. Your cow had won reserve champion. You came to the door with a bottle of whiskey."

"You're talking through your hat!"

"Am I?"

"You've no proof."

"Your name isn't on the birth certificate but that doesn't mean anything."

"Anyone could be your father. God knows how many fellas she took up with in Dublin."

The words were out before she could stop them.

"You bastard!"

She saw him smile.

"Keep a civil tongue in your head. I don't know you and I had nothing to do with your mother and if you as much as hint at this to anyone else I'll have you in court so fast you won't know what's hit you!"

Hannah watched him walk away.

She found herself walking after him.

"You paid for her stay in the mother and baby home, didn't you? You organized it too, didn't you! And the money you gave her – she never spent a penny of it – did you know that? I'll bet you didn't. She put it in an account for me, you hear! She gave it to me a few days before she died."

Hannah kept talking, unable to stop now.

"It should come in handy for fighting you in court."

She was at the window of the jeep. He was struggling to start the vehicle.

"Get out of my way!"

"My name is Hannah," she said, holding onto the window. "She called me after your grandmother."

Had he flinched?

"You're gone in the head!"

Hannah didn't know where she got the strength to continue speaking.

"My mother might have let you away with all this, but I'm not afraid of you!"

He was muttering now. The jeep still wouldn't start. "Get out of my way! I know your sort! After what you can get. You heard your mother talking about where she was from and who was who and who had what and you thought you'd squeeze some money out of me. Well, you can forget it! You should take the offer for the house and get to hell out of here."

Hannah felt rooted to the spot.

"How do you know I've had an offer for the cottage?"

She watched him turn away, red faced with anger.

She pulled her hand away quickly as the jeep went suddenly into reverse.

"It's you – isn't it?" she called out. "You want to buy the cottage? You thought you'd get an auctioneer to sweet talk me into selling so you'd be rid of me! Well, tough! I'll never sell to you! Do you hear?"

Chippings flew up from the wheels as he drove out of the car park area at speed. Hannah eventually made her way back to her car, knees like jelly and shaking like a leaf.

Within seconds of him going out of sight, Beryl had pulled up beside Hannah and jumped into the passenger seat.

"What happened?"

Hannah stared ahead of her.

"Disaster. Absolute disaster."

Hannah put her head in her hands. It would be a long while before the adrenalin would stop flowing, before she'd recover her composure enough to be fit to drive. Even to talk.

Driving to the day care centre in Rathbrandon Florrie Stephenson found it difficult to shake off her anger. This building development business was getting to her more than she liked.

She took a few deep breaths, trying to let go the resentment. What was the point of letting it fester? All it would do was sap her energy. Better to let it go.

"Easier said than done," she said to herself. Still she knew she was dealing with stress a lot better than she used to. And that is a miracle in itself. Tears had been a part of her pattern in years gone by – and blaming and feeling hard done-by.

At least she had set her boundaries around this development business in her own mind. She would not be his go-for or his bookkeeper in the building enterprise. If it happened that such a person was needed for those tasks she would, perhaps, find a suitable candidate, but she would not be taking on such commitments herself. She would make that quite clear. If her husband wanted to kill himself in pursuit of money at his age that was his choice. She didn't have to follow suit.

Rain – did it ever stop? She hated the way it greyed the world – and her mood.

She tried to figure out exactly what was upsetting her. It wasn't just the development plans.

Abe's moodiness wasn't helping either. He was cranky – disconnected. Usually when he had a new project on the boil he was in great form, but not this time.

His colour wasn't good either.

She had asked him if he was ill and he had told her to stop annoying him.

It was the disconnection that was unsettling her. Old fears were surfacing, try as she might to banish them.

The times when she had sensed disconnection had always scared her – particularly after she knew it was her fault they couldn't have children. In her gut she feared the switch-off had been because he'd taken up with some other woman.

The one time she had dared to mention this fear to him he had told her to stop moidering him or he *would* think of taking up with someone else. At least then he mightn't have to listen to this bullshit, he said.

The fear had lessened as they got older, triggered only sometimes when he flirted with other women when they were out. It had helped her to think of it as men's normal way of acting – always on the lookout or just him trying to inflate his own ego.

While it had been difficult to ignore his behaviour her hard-practiced indifference had worked eventually and the frequency of his flirtations had decreased – perhaps because he saw it was having no effect.

Sunday morning was a worry, though. Where had he been?

He hadn't gone to church with her, yet he had headed off somewhere early in the jeep. Was it something to do with the building plans? She doubted it. He had never done business on a Sunday in his life, so where was he?

"There was probably a simple explanation," she told herself.

Yes, she must leave the worry down. Detach. That was the way to survive. She'd learned that much. What was the point in letting her imagination run away with itself?

Initially her detachment had made him angrier, though. He'd call her names when she stopped reacting to his criticism and ask her had she turned into a dimwit or what.

In the end she had told him, very calmly one day, that she would accept his verbal abuse no longer. She would not be the butt of his anger about the weather or cattle prices or whatever it was that was annoying him, and she would also be treated as an equal. She would fulfil her duties to him as a wife and equal in a respectful way, and she would expect him to do the same.

It was the tape recording that had made him really see the light, though. Hearing one of his rants played back to him in the kitchen at full volume as he ate his dinner had shocked him into silence. At first she thought he might hit her, but then he had gone very quiet. The tape had never been mentioned to this day, but his anger had never been so bad since.

Good, there was a parking space . . . A young mother was pulling out of it, outside the community hall. There was a baby about a year old in the seat in the back. Even now, Florrie couldn't help looking at the child until the car went out of sight. At least the dreaming of babies had stopped though, she thought, as she reversed into the space. That made things easier. And menopause, too, had stopped the hormones creating a want in her womb.

As she picked up her notebooks and digital recorder from the passenger seat, painful memories surfaced despite her attempts to stop them. Memories of 1984, when her heart had gone out to Anne Lovett, the teenager who died in a grotto giving birth to a child. As bad as it was, listening to the radio coverage of the story that day had been a turning point in her life. She knew that now.

Abe had come home to find her sitting on the floor of their bedroom hugging the christening shawl that she had hidden for almost twenty years in a bottom drawer.

She could still see him standing at the door.

He had said nothing apart from, "You'll catch your death sitting there". When she didn't answer he had pulled a bedspread off the bed and put it round her shoulders. That evening their clergyman, Frank, had arrived. Abe had telephoned him, he said, and she had sobbed and talked and prayed with him for two hours and out of it had come the decision to have professional help to come to terms with never having a child . . .

It had taken two years of talk and thinking before the cloud had lifted, but it had been worth it. And Abe had signed the cheque each week without question. Florrie blew her nose and checked her eyes in the car mirror before she got out of the car.

"That's all in the past," she said to herself, "and today is a new day, full of promise."

Being at the day care centre in Rathbrandon always gave her a lift. It had been a lifesaver from the first time she helped out with a senior citizens' party to now when she was doing the reminiscence project to mark the twentieth anniversary of the opening.

New friends and focusing on others – that's what had helped in the long run.

Umbrella up, she hurried now to the main door of the community hall.

Ten past eleven. With a bit of luck some of the patrons would be in the humour for talking today.

She mentally checked her list – Maimie Breen was the last person that she needed some life story detail from.

Still, with Maimie showing signs of early-stage dementia, Florrie knew that she would have to tread gently with her. Some days the eighty-nine year old was lucid and communicative and others she wasn't. All the same it would be important to have some detail of Maimie to go in the book, even if it was only something short. Everyone needed to be represented.

"How are you all today?" she asked the group of people in the armchairs in the reflection area off the main hall.

"Still breathing," Jimmy Fitzgerald said, "so we're on the pig's back."

Jimmy had an ulcerated leg and lived on his own and loved coming to the centre even though he wouldn't admit it.

"My sciatica is killing me," Nancy Hore said. "And they had no ginger nuts today – how is anyone supposed to dunk a custard cream – that's what I want to know."

Florrie chatted away, making small talk and trying to placate them as best she could before she began reading them a few of the poems they'd learned in school. The poems helped to trigger memories and once they started talking she would jot down some notes. Maimie Breen was dozing in her chair.

"You won't get much out of her," Jimmy was saying. "Away with the fairies half the time."

"Ssh . . ."

Jimmy gave one of his rumbling coughs that lasted half a minute.

Florrie raised her voice a bit to get Maimie's attention.

"Do you know this poem, Maimie? *The Old Woman of the Roads?* Did you learn it in school?"

Maimie looked up, a bit more alert now, so Florrie continued.

"Did you like school, Maimie?"

The elderly woman with the watery eyes considered for a minute.

"No."

"Course she didn't! Fucking jails the lot of them!" Jimmy said.

Florrie started reciting.

Oh to have a little house
To own the hearth and stool and all
The heaped up sods upon the fire . . .

Nancy and Jimmy now joined in . . .

The pile of turf against the wall . . .
To have a clock with weights and chains
And pendulum swinging up and down

Maimie's mouth was now moving. At last . . .

A dresser filled with shining delph
Speckled and white and blue and brown . . .

Maimie had now gone silent again, but it was a start . . . Maybe she could talk to her on her own next time she was in and say the poem again. She should have realized that having the others around wouldn't give Maimie a proper chance to talk.

When lunch was over Florrie prepared to leave. She had helped out with the serving and enjoyed the chat with all the helpers. Roy had sent a text, she saw, as she checked her mobile phone. Wanting her to call over. It was always good to hear from him. She didn't feel like going home yet, and anyway she wanted to ask him to help her put up the Christmas lights in the garden for the carols at Knocklannon.

"Bye everybody."

Florrie touched Maimie's hand. She was looking a bit more awake after her lunch.

"I'll be back again soon, Maimie, and we'll talk then. Take care."

Maimie grabbed her arm.

"What are you called again?" she said.

"My name? Florrie . . . Florrie Stephenson. You see me here a couple of times a week."

"Stephenson?"

The older woman looked confused, as if she was trying to catch hold of some elusive thought that she couldn't quite grasp.

"Yes, that's right. You were cook for my mother-in-law a long time ago, I think . . ."

Maimie looked as if she was about to say something, then her fingers began to fidget with the edge of the blanket that covered her knees. No, it wasn't one of her good days.

"I'll see you on Friday, Maimie. Goodbye now."

It was raining heavily again as she left the centre. Did it ever stop? Such flooding in town – a lot of businesses had suffered because of the heavy rain and the high tides.

She hurried to the car, glad she had a hood on her coat.

It was 2.15 p.m. Roy must be working on something exciting if he asked her to call out.

Roy had come a long way with his sculpting, she knew.

Funny the way things happen, she said to herself, remembering how, as a small boy, Roy had been fascinated the day in the 1960s that the rocks in the stony field in Knocklannon were being blasted as part of Abe's land reclamation.

What age was he then – eight? Nine? He had spent ages after the contractors had finished the blasting walking among the bits of shattered rock, touching one jagged piece after another before the field was cleared by Abe and Jim Casey working flat out for days with a horse and drag.

Leo was near the turnip house door as she drove in. What was he taking out of the back of his van? Cages of some sort?

Was there a mink problem? She'd have to make sure her henhouse was secure if there was, though Abe hadn't mentioned anything about it. Still, she'd better be careful – mink could wipe out a henhouse in minutes just for the sport of it.

She parked outside Roy's workshop – one of the old stables on the farm. He appeared at the door the minute he heard the car.

"He is so like his father," she said to herself. Roy had Harry Kemp's kind face, and it was becoming more obvious as he got older.

"Good to see you."

"Y-y-you too.

"You've a heater out here – good. You'd be frozen otherwise," she said, glad to get in out of the rain.

"H-h-have to k-k-keep these working," he said, holding up his hands.

"Absolutely. And tell me – did you sign up for the course? I was thinking about it earlier."

"N-n-no b-b-but I will. D-d-don't worry . . ."

"That's great," she said, squeezing his arm.

Florrie felt relieved – and delighted. She felt certain he would make the call. It would have taken a lot for him to tell her of his decision to do the course in the first place and he wouldn't be about to go back on it now.

"Now what was it you wanted to show me?"

"O-Over h-h-here. You could put it by the h-h-h-hebes – on the patio."

She watched him pull off the piece of clean silage plastic that covered the large object in the corner of the shed.

Florrie stared. It was an S-shaped stone love seat.

"I saw a p-p-p-icture of one in a b-b-book. The V-V-Victorians had them so's m-men and women couldn't t-t-t-touch one another when they were c-c-c-ourting."

Florrie choked back tears as she stood staring at the granite masterpiece.

"It's wonderful! There are no other words for it!"

Roy had blushed.

"I-I-It's for you – you can c-c-call it your g-g-godmother seat."

Florrie ran her hand along the stone again.

"No! I couldn't accept this! All the hours of work!"

"It's yours."

"Nonsense. It's part of your – what do you call it – portfolio. Has your mother seen it?"

"N-n-not yet."

Florrie stood well back to look at it again.

"Well, she should. It's marvellous. Where did you get the stone?"

Roy told her about pulling it from the briars on the headland of one of the fields, as Florrie touched the granite again.

"It's a treasure and I know what you'll do – bring it over to Knocklannon just for the carols night. And maybe a couple of your smaller pieces, then it'll be like an exhibition of your work. Everyone'll see it. You never know what it could lead to."

"I d-d-don't know . . ."

"But that's what it's about – making a name for yourself – getting your work out there . . ."

There was a noise at the door.

"I thought I heard a car."

It was Vera, standing in the doorway.

"Vera. I just dropped in to have a look at Roy's work. Isn't it marvellous?"

Vera came over and looked at the seat.

Florrie explained, as Vera walked around it.

"So this is what you've been chipping away at, every hour God sends."

"And worth every minute of it. Isn't it great?"

Roy was silent.

"For them that has the time, I suppose."

Florrie felt like throttling her sister-in-law. Did she ever encourage anyone?

"You've a talented son – one of these days the world is going to see that. Starting with the carols."

"How do you mean?"

Florrie explained about her idea of exhibiting the work.

"It could be a lot of trouble for nothing."

Vera was looking at the chair again.

"It's a classic piece – you know it is."

"You'd want to get a lot out of it for all the work that's gone into it . . ."

Vera was looking at the smaller pieces, standing stones with celtic symbols carved into them.

"And at least it has some sort of use . . ."

God, did Vera ever see further than her nose . . . Florrie changed the subject rather than have her dragging Roy down anymore.

"How are the rehearsals going?"

"They start next week – three practices'll have to do."

"I'm sure it'll be ample. If you want me to play just let me know."

"What'd be the point in that when they'll be singing unaccompanied when they're out? The rector'll give them their notes same as always."

"Whatever you say. Anyway, I'd better be going. Roy, maybe you'd pop over when you can to help me with the lights, as usual? And maybe we could put a special light over or beneath your seat to show it off."

Roy winked at her.

"N-n-no bother."

Vera was already at the door.

"Abe isn't in great form these days whatever you're doing to him," she said.

"What makes you say that?"

"He's very sharp. I asked him if he was coming in for a cup of tea the other day and he nearly cut the face off me."

Florrie pulled the hood of her anorak up.

"He's tired. He's been busy at beet, not to mention this development business. As if he hadn't enough to do . . ."

"Why wouldn't he be looking to something else with the backside falling out of farming? There's young lads don't have half the energy he has."

Vera was still standing in her way at the door.

"It could be the Casey one that's annoying him, of course . . ."

Florrie was taken aback.

"Who? Hannah? How do you mean?"

"Probably thinks she can screw more money out of him. As if what she was offered wasn't enough for a place like that . . ."

"I've lost you. What are you talking about?"

Florrie saw Vera smirk.

"About them not having a hope of getting planning permission unless they can get the cottage land as a site entrance, of course."

Anger surged through Florrie's veins again. Abe hadn't even told her he had made Hannah an offer for the cottage, and now Vera was rubbing her nose in it . . .

Florrie headed for the car.

"If Hannah doesn't want to sell, that's her business," she called back.

"You two seem very pally . . ."

Vera had followed her and was standing by the car window.

"I've just met her a couple of times, but she strikes me as someone who knows her own mind. No one will walk over her. That house is the only connection she has with the past. You can't blame her for wanting to hang onto it."

"It's trying to forget her background you'd think she'd be, instead of broadcasting it to the world the way she's doing by coming back here."

Roy was outside now.

"I-I-It's no f-f-fault of hers."

"Hmph!"

Florrie saw Vera give her son a withering look.

"Exactly," Florrie said. "The plans'll have to be ditched now – maybe it's for the best."

Vera was getting soaked but Florrie felt no sympathy for her from inside the car.

"You wouldn't say that if you'd paid an architect a small fortune already – those fellas don't work cheap. And me supposed to contact the Casey one about the carol-singing, according to the rector – probably can't sing to save her life."

"H-h-her name is H-H-Hannah."

His mother's response was fast.

"And how would you know what her name is?"

Florrie saw Roy turn and go back into the workshop.

"He could do worse," she said to Vera, as she rolled up the window and drove off.

In the car on the way home, Florrie felt angry again. Abe making a huge offer on the cottage and never even mentioning it? More secrets . . . It explained a lot though, she thought – how he was so snappy with her when she told him she'd called in at the cottage – and why he was so rude to Hannah at the bring and buy sale.

That's probably where he was on Sunday morning – trying to persuade her to sell. It would certainly explain his bad humour.

Florrie took a few deep breaths as she drove down the avenue to Knocklannon, her anger easing. She felt relieved in a way. Her old fears were groundless. It was business, pure and simple. Still, she'd have trouble being civil to him for a while – him and his secrets – and always playing his cards close to his chest.

The persistent knocking woke Hannah. She had fallen asleep on the couch again. Picking up her mobile phone, she saw that there were seven missed calls and four texts on it – all from Matt.

She got up unsteadily, blinking as she turned on the light.

What time was it?

The knocking came again – and this time it was more insistent. Her heart pounded as she went to the door. What if *he* was outside?

"Who is it?"

"Hannah? It's Matt. I've been ringing and ringing! Thank God you're in there."

She clunked the bolt back with difficulty.

"Jesus – you look terrible!" he said when she let him in.

"I had the phone on silent. What are you doing here?"

"I was worried about you for one thing . . ."

"I can look after myself."

She could see him take in the state of the place in one glance.

"Yeah?"

Angry now, Hannah opened the door and held it open.

"Go then, if you've come to preach! Having Beryl on the phone ten times a day checking up on me is enough. It's not a crime to want a bit of peace in my own house, is it?"

"No, but drinking yourself to death is. Jesus, Hannah!"

Hannah looked round. Bottles . . . Dirty glasses . . . After a while she'd run out of glasses . . .

"I'll tidy up in a minute. Did Beryl send you?"

"No. Well, yes – but I was coming anyway."

"I'm all right."

Hannah smelled the sleeve of her dressing gown. God, how many days had she been wearing this?

"What date's today?" she asked.

"It's Saturday. Saturday the thirteenth of November. It's 5.46 p.m. What day did you think it was?"

Six days since the mountain. And him.

"Look, I'll get myself cleaned up and then I'll tackle all this. Chill out, for God's sake!"

She could see him opening the door.

"Where are you going?"

"Into town. To get us a take away. I'm starving and I doubt you've eaten anything decent for days."

Clearing away all the rubbish in the kitchen now Hannah tried to remember what had happened in the last few days.

It was all a bit of a fog after Beryl left on Monday – apart from driving to the nearest off licence, that is.

"You having a party?" the assistant had said as she checked out the box of wine.

"Yes. That's it."

"Lucky you!"

Hannah hadn't answered her.

Back at the cottage she had parked the car round the back of the house so that it wouldn't be easily seen from the road. Peg Travers had called but she hadn't answered the door. She would have to catch up with her soon . . .

At night she had gone to bed early, using as little light as possible, falling into a drunken sleep and waking in the morning to a television set that had been left on all night . . .

God, she needed a shower right now . . .

The takeaway eaten, Hannah made tea for them both after taking two Solpadeine for her headache.

"So – are you going to tell me what happened?" he said eventually.

Hannah wrapped her wool cardigan more tightly around her.

"He doesn't care," she said. "He'll deny me till the day he dies."

"You don't know that."

Hannah closed her eyes and laid her head back against the sofa.

"Please! The last thing I need now is anyone pumping me full of false hope. I've learned my lesson about that . . . I thought when he'd meet me – talk to me – that he'd be, I don't know, bowled over by some sudden marvellous paternal feeling. Jesus, was I thick!"

"It's understandable to hope for that . . ."

"And stupid! He was so . . .businesslike!"

"He's probably repressing a lot. People did that years ago."

"My mother . . ."

"Your mother . . . Him . . . Lots of people. Times were so different. It's probably self-protection . . ."

"And living a lie? Never admitting I existed . . . A fine pair of upstanding people they were!"

"It was society . . ."

"Yeah, well, feck society! Feck it to hell!"

Hannah hated herself for sounding so coarse, but she couldn't help it.

Matt tried to hold her hand but she pulled away.

"What did he say exactly?"

"He thinks I'm after his money. He implied that my mother named him because of some grudge she had against him. I hit a nerve when I threw in the bit about the Spring Show, though – I could tell. That and me telling him I was called after his grandmother. I thought he was going to burst a blood vessel."

"I see."

Hannah couldn't taste the last of her tea.

"I did find out one interesting fact, though."

"What's that?"

She explained how he'd disclosed that he was trying to buy the cottage.

"It had to be him if he knew that much. Talk about crafty! He was probably trying to buy it off my mother too, if I only knew! Me taking it off the market must have been a right slap in the face for him!"

Hannah's laugh sounded weird, even to herself.

"To have to up the price *and* buy it off his worst nightmare – me!"

Matt had gone quiet now. She could see him glance around the kitchen.

"You really want to stay here?"

"I should clear out and stay quiet forevermore – is that it?"

"I didn't say that."

"Yeah, well, you're implying it."

"I'm just saying it's not exactly the hub of the universe, is it?"

Hannah got up and put her mug in the sink.

"It's the hub of my universe at the moment, and I don't see why I should let anyone drive me out of it . . ."

"I'm not saying you should. What about work, though? Are you going to get a job nearer here?"

"I don't know yet. I'll think about it after Christmas. Right now this is me time."

Matt was rinsing his own mug.

"There could be another option . . . until you figure out what you want, that is . . ."

They both jumped as Hannah's mobile phone rang.

Taking it out of her pocket she stared at the screen. It was a local landline number. Her heart was thumping as she answered.

"Hello . . ."

Hannah listened as the woman on the other end of the line asked if she was Hannah Casey.

"That's right."

"Reverend Mundy gave me your number," the voice said. "I'm ringing you about the carol-singing. He said you might like to join us."

"The carol singing? Yes, I remember. Who is this?"

Vera Kemp . . .

Hannah listened while the sharp, mature female voice told her that rehearsals would be held in Rathbrandon community hall for the next three Wednesdays at eight o'clock.

"You'll need to be there for all three or you won't be allowed to take part."

"Ok! I'll be there. Thanks for letting me know."

Hannah's hand shook as she rang off.

"That was his sister!"

"What?"

Hannah told him about the carol singing and how Florrie Stephenson had suggested she join.

"And you're going to?"

"Why shouldn't I? It's a free country."

"What if he's in the choir too?"

Hannah shrugged even though she felt terrified.

"So?"

"A moth to a flame . . ."

Hannah was livid.

"How dare you! None of this is any of your business . . ."

Matt was picking up his coat.

"It's time I was going."

"Ok, look – I'm sorry. I don't want to be fighting with you. My head's all over the place . . ."

He had his hand on the door.

"You have your plans made. You wouldn't want what I came to suggest."

"What was that?"

Jesus! He was hardly going to propose marriage!

"You needn't worry. I'm not getting carried away," he said, as if reading her mind.

Hannah felt awkward now.

"I was actually coming to see you before Beryl told me anything about the last few days, but it's not relevant anymore."

"What isn't? You hardly drove all this way for nothing!"

"I'm taking a year out from teaching."

"To do what?"

"Voluntary work overseas. Malawi."

"What?"

"I've mentioned it before."

"Yes but I didn't think you were really serious."

"Maybe you never really listened . . ."

He had been tiring of teaching for a long time, he said.

"But you can't just go like that – what about language? Culture shock? Your job? You can't just up sticks and clear out."

"I signed the contract yesterday."

Hannah felt shocked.

"God! You're definitely going? You came here to tell me that?"

"That and . . ."

"What?"

"To ask if you'd consider coming too. No strings attached – don't worry. Maybe it's what you need. To get away from everything for a while. You used to talk about wanting to make a difference when I met you first. You could out there. Nurses are needed even worse than teachers."

"No."

"You're sure?"

Hannah nodded, her head heavy.

"I couldn't even imagine doing something like that at the moment. I know it's worthy and all that but it's not for me – at least not right now."

He was zipping up his anorak.

"Not to worry. It was just a thought. Maybe you'd tell Beryl I called."

"I will."

The silence in the cottage weighed heavily after he had gone.

Part of her wanted him to stay for the company but more of her was glad he had gone. Like he said, what was the point? Whatever there was between them was over. And she wasn't going anywhere! The thought of aeroplanes, heat, flies and strangeness didn't appeal to her right now. This was her house and she had the right to live in it and in this community if she wanted to.

She put on a classical CD and turned the volume up – it would energize her as she cleaned up the place properly.

Seeing Matt had helped her focus, she decided. He was right – the way she was carrying on made it look like she couldn't look after herself. Why had she let herself get into this mess? The last few days had been a total waste. Wallowing in self-pity – that's what she'd been doing. Well, it was time to stop that. No one ever got anywhere in the world by going off the rails. From now on she was going to be strong. She had plenty of backbone and that's all the world would see. She'd licked her wounds for long enough.

She would go ahead with her plans to do up the cottage. She would sing carols. She would go out and about as other people did. After Christmas would be time enough for making decisions about work. And a lot could happen between this and then . . .

Going upstairs she searched in a box that she had brought from Waterford.

There it was – the framed newspaper cutting about the passing of the Status of Children Act.

Dusting the glass with the sleeve of her cardigan she walked over to the bed and hung the framed cutting on a nail where her mother's Sacred Heart picture had been.

The end of the term illegitimacy . . .

She stood back now, staring at it. Good, it was straight on the wall. Having it there, she knew, would somehow keep her strong.

The twinge of pain made Abe Stephenson ease up walking.

Fucking indigestion! He shouldn't have eaten that fry for breakfast.

He rubbed his chest but it didn't make any difference – the discomfort continued. That was it – he'd have to cut out the frying pan and go for smaller meals. Wasn't that the way they said to avoid this sort of indigestion torment? A wave of tight pain came again, and he leaned over a gate on one of the cattle sheds on the outfarm in Newtown.

Fuck! He had some Rennies somewhere . . . A search of his pockets produced a tiny pack with three left in it. Tearing off the paper he put the three of them in his mouth together and chomped on them to get them into his stomach quicker. That should do it . . .

After a few minutes he belched and felt a bit better.

Stress wasn't helping him either. He was gulping his food without really tasting it and sleeping badly since Sunday, dreams of children wearing red coats and pigtails and calling him "Daddy".

"Here, lad," he called to Max, trying to push the thoughts away.

His feet felt like lead as he walked back to the Land Cruiser. No, he'd be all right in a minute. And he'd have a lie down when he got home. A bit of a rest and he'd be right as rain. And Florrie wouldn't be there. Good. She'd be at the centre all morning, she said . . .

He woke at 12.45 p.m. He had slept for an hour in his reclining office chair, his coat pulled over him and he felt the better of it. His chest area still felt a bit tender after the pain but it was ok. He'd be careful what he ate for the rest of the day. Maybe he should have listened to Florrie when she told him he'd have to ease up on fries.

He went up to the kitchen and put the kettle on. He had too much on his mind – that was all. The meeting on Mount Leinster had taken a lot out of him. Who did she think she was, talking to him like that? She had no proof and she'd never have it. Her knowing about the show and the dates had unnerved him, though. Lil had told her too much. What had she said anything for? Hadn't he kept his part of the deal, paying up where others mightn't have?

He felt the sweat build up on his brow again. No. She had no proof. It would be her word against his, but it would never come to that. She wouldn't be stupid enough to go blabbing after he had warned her off.

Florrie was watching him, though. Saying nothing, of course, but he knew she was picking up on his mood. No, act normal – that's all he had to do and it would all pass over.

Abe thought again of the name. Hannah! Lil shouldn't have called her that. He should have asked early on but he'd never felt able to. No names, no faces – that's how he'd survive, he had told himself.

He was plugging in the kettle to make himself tea when he heard Leo's voice in the back kitchen.

"Anyone home?"

"In here."

Leo stuck his head around the door.

"I was here earlier but the door was locked."

"What?"

"You wanted me to weld the chain on the cleaner loader. I called over about twelve but there was no answer."

Jesus, had he slept that heavily?

"I was up the land."

"Right. I can do it now if you want."

Abe stayed sitting in the chair.

"There's no rush on it. There was a breakdown at the depot so everyone's delivery dockets are put back three days. No more'll be going till Wednesday."

"Right. I'll do it Monday or Tuesday then. I was supposed to get the last of ours out of the Pound field tomorrow but it's like shite."

Leo was looking out the kitchen window at the rain.

"Fecking diseased weather!"

"Aye," said Abe.

Leo was still at the door.

"No news, I suppose, on the cottage?"

Abe concentrated on the paper.

"No."

"Right. Still, there's no point in getting into a twist about it like you say. She'll get bored quick enough. That's if she hasn't upped sticks before then, of course . . ."

Abe sat up straight.

"What?"

"Nothing. We'll see what happens."

What was Leo hinting at? By the snigger at the corner of his mouth there was something going on. Abe forced himself not to think about it. Or to ask. That way he'd only be drawing attention to himself.

He was on his second cup of tea when he heard Florrie's car drive in.

"Did you not eat anything?"

She had noticed in seconds that there was no plate on the table.

"I didn't feel like it."

"Waiting for me to come back and get something ready for you, I suppose."

Her voice was icy.

"I'll get something later," he said, yet made no attempt to move. Better she think that he was waiting to be served than for her to know that he didn't feel well enough to prepare himself anything.

She was standing at the table looking at him.

"You could have told me."

"Told you what?"

"That you were trying to buy the cottage from Hannah Casey."

Vera again! Did his sister ever know when to shut up?

"Buying property's not a crime. I've bought lots before and you've never said a word about it."

"Yes, when you were younger – farmland, not buying stuff because of some hare-brained development plans. And once again not even discussing with me!"

Abe took up the *Farmers Journal* again.

"Well, Hannah Casey is not selling," Florrie was going on. "So that'll put a stop to your gallop."

Shit!

He cleared his throat before speaking.

"She said that?"

"As good as. That house is very important to her. What else has she got to hang on to? Even if she doesn't settle down around here she'll keep it as a holiday home – you'll see."

She was making noise now. Clatter, clatter . . .

"So – would you not give up this building notion altogether?"

"Ah will you whisht!"

He got up from the chair as smoothly as he could manage and grabbed his hat.

He heard her call after him as he went to the door.

"I'm having the carols here on December 5th. Are you ok with that or am I supposed to whisht about that too?"

"Amn't I ok with it every year?"

"I'll take that as a yes then."

He had his hand on the door handle when she spoke again.

"Roy is going to bring some of his stonework over. It's about time people saw his talent."

What was she twittering on about now?

"Roy! His sculpting," she said. "He's bringing some pieces over here as a kind of exhibition the night of the carols."

"Fat lot of good that stuff'll do him."

"He may never make a fortune out of it but you never know. There's a lot of money splashing around these days for art. He could surprise you – and Vera. And in the meantime money isn't his god. He does what he does because he enjoys it. And there has to be a reason behind that sort of gift."

He closed the door behind him. Getting into the jeep he opened the door for the dog to hop in.

He drove back to the outfarm at Newtown. His chest area still felt a bit sore after the pain. He would sleep for a while in the jeep and no one would see him. Maybe he should go to the doctor, he thought. If Florrie got wind of the indigestion pain she'd nag him until he went.

She was always telling him not to eat so fast and so much – that he wasn't as active as he used to be and that he didn't need all that food.

He felt like telling her wouldn't she be all right – she'd come into a fortune if he popped his clogs. The thoughts of her being a wealthy widow agitated him. There'd be plenty eyeing her up with that kind of money behind her. And she wasn't that bad looking either when she was done up . . . He tried to shake off the thought of Florrie in bed with another man. She'd always been loyal to him, but then he'd never given her the space to be anything else.

He'd kept her at home where he could keep an eye on her, not like some farmers, whose wives had jobs and too much freedom.

"Foal at foot and half time gone" – that's what he'd heard his father say once about how women should be kept. He hadn't said it when his mother was within earshot, though . . . She'd have cut the ground from under him if he had.

What would his father have said if he'd lived long enough to know that his son's marriage had produced no children, though? Abe tried to switch his mind off. He was thinking too much.

He opened a window in the Land Cruiser to let more air in.

Max, the dog, was wondering why he wasn't getting out.

"Lie down. Good dog."

Abe lay his head back against the headrest, pulled the car rug over his knees and closed his eyes. His mind still raced. Her . . . Hannah. If he'd gone to Mount Leinster thinking she was a pushover he'd left knowing differently. She had backbone. A thorn in his side, that's what she'd said she'd be to him . . .

Abe Stephenson wiped the sweat off his forehead. He had warned her off, though, hadn't he, telling her to stay away from everyone belonging to him? It was all bluff with her.

He would have to tread very carefully, but he would survive this.

Could she take him to court to demand a DNA test, he wondered?

The solicitor had said she could, hadn't she? He cursed technology. A lot of men had got out of being fathers in the past because nobody could prove they were . . . Abe turned his head to try to sleep, but the thoughts kept coming. Going looking for Lil Casey's house that day had been a mistake. What was he thinking of? He remembered how he felt, though – wanting sex and saying it'd be ok, that he could control himself but as the pleasure built the desire to climax had been overpowering. It was like all orgasms – when he thought he was in heaven, how could he pull back?

Besides, he knew he didn't really want to stop. Not when he had something to prove. Now he closed his eyes to block out the eyes of the child – the woman – and the red coat . . .

"Am I nervous? Yes. I've never met an aunt before, so it's a bit freaky all right."

It was Beryl on the phone again. Hannah was getting ready to go to the carol practice. Phone in her left hand, she brushed some blusher along her cheekbones with her right. No point in looking like death warmed up for the big occasion . . .

"I don't know how I'll react until I see her," Hannah said.

Beryl was looking on the bright side as usual.

"Maybe she's ok, like his wife."

"I don't know. She sounded very cut and dried on the phone."

Meeting Vera Kemp would be weird, putting a face to the voice, knowing they were related.

"I'll ring you afterwards."

"Ok. Talk to you later."

Hannah had thought of telling Beryl about Matt asking her to go abroad with him but she had stopped herself. She would tell her next time she saw her. It was all too complicated.

A couple of times she had regretted not saying yes. It would have been escape in a way, if she'd signed up for Malawi. She could forget about all this – the cottage, her father, the lot . . . No – that would just be running away.

DNA tests had been on her mind for days – could she insist on him doing one? Would she have the courage to insist? She would ask her mother's solicitor in Dún Laoghaire when she went to see her on Friday. The test would prove it once and for all, wouldn't it? Maybe then he'd admit it. He'd have to get to know her then, wouldn't he?

There were fifteen or so people in the community hall foyer when she arrived. The bottled gas heater smell hit her as soon she walked into the place.

It instantly reminded her of Royle and Nanna's parlour where if you were lucky and if you were close to being grown up, you could have a cup of tea there and a posh biscuit, as Nanna called them, from a box bought separately from Bolands, where Nanna drove every so often to buy the broken ones cheap.

"It's good to see you," Reverend Mundy said, extending his hand.

"Thank you."

Hannah responded to the smiles around the room, including Peg's.

"This is Hannah. She's a new recruit, so don't frighten her off – we need every voice we can get!"

Hannah could feel the eyes of one sharp-faced woman, standing there with sheets of music, watching her intently.

"And this is Vera – Vera Kemp – our organizer. She keeps us all in line."

"Pleased to meet you," Hannah said, shaking Vera's hand. It was limp and cold.

Vera handed her a hymn sheet.

"Soprano? Alto?"

"Soprano."

"Music to our ears," said the clergyman. "Will we make a start?"

Hannah had just taken her place with the other sopranos when the door opened and a man came in. It was Roy Kemp.

Catching his eye, she smiled at him. For a second she wondered what he was doing there, but of course he could sing. Hadn't Peg said? She knew other people with stammers who could sing, too.

"Right – shall we start with a few scales? Would you like to run through a few on your own, Hannah, so we get an idea of your range?"

"Sure."

Hannah knew she was being listened to intently as she sang.

The rector now had a broad smile on his face as he shook her hand.

"You'll be an asset to the choir. You've sung in choirs before?"

"In secondary school. Church. A lot of us did – in the children's home."

She saw the curiosity in a lot of the faces but she had passed muster, she felt, even with Vera Kemp.

"Right, *O Come All Ye Faithful*, everybody . . ."

Glancing round she could see Peg Travers giving her the thumbs up from the alto line.

The rehearsal had gone well. Hannah had met most of the singers during the interval – teachers, shop workers, office workers, civil servants, a pharmacist . . .

Those who knew her mother and her grandfather spoke well of them. It was good to hear.

They would be having a good chinwag about her afterwards, though, she guessed but what of it – people talk – that's just the way it is.

She spoke briefly to Roy, who seemed a bit uneasy with his mother's eagle eye on him.

Had he actually blushed when she said hello?

He had asked her if she was enjoying it then moved on as if to speak to someone else. Hannah looked at Vera Kemp again. For the third time she caught Vera looking at her and returned her tight little smile.

"I don't take after her, thank God!" she said to herself.

Vera was stick thin, probably had lost some height through osteoporosis, Hannah guessed, and she had hardness to her face that Hannah didn't like. Thank goodness she inherited her mother's softness and good skin.

"Ok, everyone, back to work – *Away in a Manager* next. This'll be a doddle, but let's try thinking about the actual words this time as if it's the first time we've sung them. Hannah would you like to sing the first verse for us?"

"Solo?"

"Yes."

"Sure."

Hannah listened for the note then opened her mouth to sing. The notes came out clear and sweet.

"*Away in a manger, no crib for a bed . . .*"

A child born against the odds – the carol had always appealed to her. The baby Jesus had a bum start in life too.

The rehearsal was finally over and Roy Kemp was switching off the gas heaters.

The rector was speaking again.

"Our next rehearsal is this night week. Then another on the 31st and that's it. The plan is that we sing four times for charity – the 5th, 8th, Saturday the 18th and Sunday the 19th – about two hours each time. Is everyone all right with that?"

Women all round her took diaries out of substantial handbags. Hannah keyed the dates in on her mobile phone calendar.

"Where will we be singing?"

"On the main street of Wexford on the Saturday and Sunday."

"What about the 5th?"

"That's the good news. We've been very kindly invited to sing at Knocklannon house again. For anyone who hasn't been here before, it's the home of Florrie and Abe Stephenson. It's always a great evening, and there will be mulled wine and mince pies to fortify our spirits, I've heard, so we can all look forward to that. And each of you can bring along a friend or two to support the event as well, so we should have a great crowd and raise a good few bob for Barnardos."

A shiver ran down Hannah's spine. Knocklannon House – Abraham Stephenson. She'd be in his house . . .

Vera Kemp looked older than her brother, Hannah thought, as she got into her car.

She tried to ring Beryl to give her the lowdown on the rehearsal, but it rang out. She'd catch her later . . .

The phone rang as she drove in through the cottage gateway on dimmed headlights. Hannah screamed as she pressed the answer button, as she spotted five or six rats scurrying around the shed and stick house in the yard. Jesus!

She closed her eyes as she stopped the car, hoping she'd been seeing things. She opened them again. No, she was right – she'd just seen two tails disappearing behind the shed. Feck! She eventually answered the mobile.

"Hannah? HANNAH! Are you ok?" Beryl was saying when she finally put the phone to her ear. "Say something for God's sake?"

"Rats! The place is crawling with them. I've just driven in to the yard."

"Oh my God!"

"I feel sick."

"I don't blame you! Have you seen any before?"

"Never."

"Maybe it's the time of year or something," Beryl was saying. And there are always rats in the country, aren't there?"

"Well they can piss off somewhere else! How am I going to get out of the car?"

"They're probably as terrified as you are. Can you see any now?"

"No, they're gone."

"Just bang the door hard before you get out of the car – that'll frighten them off. And keep making noise. You'll be in the house in a minute."

Hannah did as Beryl had suggested but it took three attempts to get the door key into the lock because her hand was shaking so much.

"I'm in. My skin is crawling. I hate rats! Remember we had that one in the attic in Royle once – I can still hear him scurrying across the ceiling – yuk!"

"I know but you're in now."

A terrible thought struck Hannah.

"What if there's one in the house? The thoughts of it!"

"Don't start imagining things. The house is sound and you've seen no signs of a mouse, never mind anything bigger. Just ring a pest control crowd in the morning and they'll sort it out."

"You're right," Hannah said, feeling a bit calmer now as she took off her coat.

She shouldn't panic. She would sort it out. The thoughts of them, though . . . She looked out the window. She could see nothing in the darkness.

"Think of something else," Beryl was saying. "How did the rehearsal go?"

Hannah told Beryl about who was there and about Vera being a cold fish and about Roy being there too.

"He has a very good voice, too – baritone. The more I meet him the more I like him – not that he was saying much with his mammy breathing down his neck."

"He's nice all right."

"Oh? Do I detect interest? Does Beryl fancy my new cousin?"

"Will you stop! Can I not say something without you acting like a juvenile? He's nice – so what? There are enough jerks in the world."

"You're right – the world needs more like him. He is a good sort – not like that brother of his. I know where he got that sharp puss now anyway."

Beryl said she had to rush.

"This place is like a madhouse tonight," she was saying. "What is it with Christmas that everyone starts partying before November is even over?"

"Because the country is awash with money, though I wish some of it would come my way. Hang on a minute – Beryl!"

"What?"

Hannah told her about the carol singers being invited to Knocklannon.

Beryl sounded anxious.

"You're joking! Will you go?"

"I suppose . . . I'll be part of the group . . ."

"Is it a good idea, though? Going into his lair, so to speak . . . Promise me you'll think about it . . ."

Remembering the rats again, Hannah went back to the window. She could see nothing this time either. No, she wasn't imagining it – there had been half a dozen of them out there, at least.

She wished she had an outside light – she would have left it on all night if she had.

She was ready to make the phone call at nine o'clock on the dot the following morning.

At last . . .

The guy on the other end of the line would be there late this evening, he said. She felt relieved after making the call. It would cost money, but no matter – she had to get it sorted before it freaked her out.

"Where on earth did they come from?" she wondered. It wasn't as if she had left food waste out. She tried to think what her mother would do in a situation like this. Or her grandfather. Buy a few traps and catch them themselves – that's what.

People years ago didn't have money to spend on pest control officers. Still, the thoughts of taking dead rats out of traps and disposing of them . . . No thanks!

Thank goodness she was going to Dublin tomorrow. By the time she came back on Monday the rodents would be dead, either in traps or after eating the fast-acting bait that the guy on the phone said he'd use.

She took out her notebook to check her mother's solicitor's number. She would call to see her just to check that all was going well. She had given her her mother's savings book and bank details. There wouldn't be much to get. After paying for the funeral maybe nothing at all.

She thought of the post office book in her name with the forty thousand in it. The money was safely in her bank account now. What would she do with it? Go on a world cruise? No. Right now she felt no inclination to use the money. It was tainted because of where it had come from. Silence money . . . No, it would stay where it was for the moment. And maybe she *would* need it to fight him in court . . . Court . . . The thought petrified her . . . What if she really had to go that far?

She would get by until after Christmas. Then she'd have to decide about going back to work.

The rest of the day was spent packing and cleaning. She felt the urge to disinfect everything. God, the rats were really getting to her.

"Grow up, girl," she said to herself, then stopped in shock. Girl. That's what he'd called her . . .

The pest control guy arrived in a van, thankfully with no name plastered over it so that the whole locality would know she had problems.

He spent an hour in the place. He had seen droppings but no sign of a nest, but he'd laid three traps and a serious amount of quick-acting bait.

"I'll come back on Monday to check on progress. Don't go near the traps. That should sort them out."

"Thanks."

Still feeling uneasy when he had gone, Hannah decided she didn't feel like staying in the house and waiting until tomorrow to go to Dún Laoghaire. She would go now. Why not? It would be extra B&B costs, but so what? She would stay in that cheap place she had stayed when her mother was in hospital. And she would go see Kit.

Traffic in Dún Laoghaire was heavy, but then it was rush hour and it was Thursday and payday. Lots of people stopped off to shop before going home. After she had put her bags in the B&B she rang Kit Bermingham, her mother's friend.

"You're looking great, love," Kit said when they met in the shopping centre café. "I was just thinking of you today. And of Lil. I've been out to the grave a couple of times. The girls at work have been very good. They do a whip round when I'm going out so I get a bunch of flowers."

"That's very good of you all."

"Least we can do. Lil worked with us for a long time. I think of her too every time I sit down on that sofa you gave me."

"That's nice. Did you get your garden room done?"

"We did and we don't know ourselves, honest to God. When the going gets tough we retreat out there for a bit of peace and quiet. Jesus, it's great!"

"I'm glad."

When they were on their second cup of coffee Hannah asked Kit if her mother had every mentioned men in her life.

"You must have had those kinds of conversations . . .you know – about men."

"We did at work sometimes, of course – about how men are mostly a pain in the arse," Kit said, laughing.

"Did my mother join in?"

"No, not really. When we'd pressure her for information she'd say she's better off on her own. More trouble than they're worth – that's the kind of thing she'd say. Or she'd say her cat was better than any man – at least he didn't give her grief."

Kit took another bite out of her muffin.

"She was quiet, though one day during tea break. Trish – one of the other cleaners – started teasing her, saying she couldn't be that much of a Holy Mary, that she must have put a few men through her hands in her time. I still remember it – your mother standing up from the table and saying she didn't have time for all this blather and that she was going back to work."

"She was upset?"

"She got out of there very quick whatever it was. Trish can be a bit of a bitch sometimes, of course, but I can still see her stubbing out her cigarette and saying, 'That one's hiding something, I'd put money on it'."

"God! But when you were on holiday with her – you know sometimes you get to talk to someone on a deeper level when you're away out of your normal environment with them – did she ever say much then?"

"I wish I could say she did, but some sort of shutter always came down. She'd listen to me rabbiting on about meeting Jimmy in the Top Hat ballroom and the stress we used to be under trying to wait for the wedding night – it was desperate. She was looking out at the Twelve Bens when we got out of the bus to stretch our legs and she says, 'I don't know what all the fuss about this . . . this intercourse is' – that's what she called it. I remember thinking if she had ever done it she mustn't have had any pleasure out of it. Jesus, I'm sorry – I didn't mean to say anything hurtful."

"It's ok. Lots of women didn't get much out of sex years ago, I'd say."

Still, it saddened Hannah. Had her mother never experienced orgasm? Had she felt no pleasure the night she was conceived? No physical pleasure to at least look back on when she was going through the torment of an unplanned pregnancy . . .

"I should have kept me mouth shut," Kit was saying. "I yap too much for my own good sometimes."

"It's all right. I want to know. There's so much I want to know."

"I did ask her one time why she never got married. I was at her flat and we were washing up. 'It's a wonder you never got married,' I said. 'You must have been a fine-looking woman in your day.' 'No one ever asked me,' she said, making a clatter as she put away the saucepans – I can see her still."

Getting into bed at the B&B later Hannah came close to crying. Her mother had had a rotten life – all because of her.

Beryl, on the phone later, told her to stop loading blame on herself.

"It's not your fault you were born."

"I know, but she did suffer because of me."

"She suffered because she had a child outside marriage at a time when everyone suffered for that. It was just the times she lived in – there's no point in beating yourself up about it."

Beryl was right. She wasn't to blame for being born into the world. They had to stop thinking like that. It was negative thinking – thinking that dragged you down. She'd stopped doing that in her twenties – eager to move on with her life and now here she was at it again, worse than ever.

Her mother just hadn't had sex often enough, that was all. She just hadn't had it with the right man. First times were never great anyway. She remembered her first time with Jack Delaney, her first real boyfriend, when she was in nursing training.

He was a garda recruit based in Dublin. The first time had been rushed, meaningless for her, more about pleasing him than pleasing herself. The second time had been different, though. She had demanded time and stimulation, not let him just grunt and thrust until his pleasure peaked. She was born in a different age to her mother, though, one where there was a Well Woman centre down the road, even if you did look over your shoulder before you went down the steps to the place.

Her mother had never been proposed to . . . She tried to imagine Abe Stephenson's post-coital conversation. There was probably none, just an "I have to be going". Back to his hotel in Ballsbridge. Back to his wife. To Florrie . . . How could her mother even have considered having anything to do with a married man, Hannah thought? She had tried before now to convince herself that her mother wouldn't have known, but she knew that was a lie after living in Drumcadden. Abe's wedding would have been the talk of the locality. Her mother couldn't not have known . . . Hannah switched off the bedside light, trying not to think of "if onlys" and rats and hoping sleep would come.

The solicitor's office smelled of age and furniture polish.

It would be a year or so before her mother's estate would be settled, the female solicitor said.

Would what was left even cover the cost of the funeral and a decent headstone? Just about.

"Is there anything else I can help you with?" the solicitor asked.

"Yes, actually there may be," she said.

Briefly she outlined the position with her father and asked if she could take him to court to get a DNA test done.

Her solicitor sat forward in her chair.

"You could. Is that what you want to do?"

Hannah shrugged.

"Maybe. I don't know yet."

"Is your . . . alleged father a man of substance? Financially, I mean?"

"He has a farm."

"And there are no other offspring – within marriage or outside?"

"None that I know of."

Her father having other children outside marriage – she couldn't even go there in her head . . .

"I see. Well, if you decide to pursue the court route just let me know. You could also make a claim on his estate after his death, of course, but that would depend on what evidence you have."

"I have my mother's word. That's enough for me."

"And he has denied it?"

"Yes."

"In that case it's evidence you'll need. Hard evidence. And even if you do want to go to court for the DNA test he may not comply."

"The mother and baby home I was born in – would I be able to get records from there – accounts – something that would show that he had paid for my mother's stay there?"

"That would imply that he'd taken responsibility all right but it's unlikely there are records and if there are there may be a time lock on them."

Hannah was glad to get out into the street. She needed fresh air to clear her head. So many decisions to make . . . Why hadn't he just owned up when she confronted him, like she'd hoped he would? Damn him! Instantly she felt sorry for saying it. Nanna would be shocked. That kind of language dignified no one . . .

She tried to think of something to do to take her mind off things. Would she go to the cinema? Go shopping? No, she would go to Rathgar, to the mother and baby home she was born in – Bethany Home. She knew it had been a nursing home for years now. It would hardly be that hard to find, would it?

She would recognize the building when she saw it from being there several times with Nanna . . .

She had to buzz to be answered at the door. The nurse who answered said, "Yes?"

"I'm sorry . . ."

Why had she said that? Why should she be sorry?

She started again.

"I'm looking for some information. I was born here – when this place was a home for unmarried mothers."

"Oh!"

"I'm trying to find records."

The nurse took a business card from a shelf beside the door and handed it to Hannah.

It was for an organization called PACT.

"They deal with all the records from here and from a lot of children's homes. It's probably what you need."

Hannah looked at the card again.

"Ok. Thank you. I'll try that."

She heard the door close and lock behind her as she went down the steps.

How had her mother felt going into this place when she was four months pregnant? Terrified? Like she was going into jail? She hadn't left until she had weaned Hannah at six months.

Was it like leaving jail when she got out, or was her heart breaking leaving her baby?

Hannah's mind tried to back away from thinking of that.

She knew she couldn't remember anything from so young an age. She remembered very little until she was about eight. Even then she wasn't sure was it remembered or was it stuff people had told her.

Was that because it was better not to remember? Repressed memory – it was a survival mechanism – she'd learned about that in nursing training. There was lots of stuff even in Royle that she didn't want to remember – Nanna and her tempers, kids crying, the rod not being spared . . .

She pushed it out of her mind as she hurried back to where she had parked her car. It was pain from the past – best to leave it there. It was the way she'd held herself together all her life.

Right now she wanted to put distance between herself and this place.

Her hands felt jittery as she drove back towards Dún Laoghaire, deciding in Blackrock that she would go to see her mother's grave. It would only take a few minutes.

Her mother's grave had flowers on it. Kit had been there like she said. Hannah squatted now to remove blades of grass that had pushed up through the clay in the two months since Lil was buried. Was she right to pluck them out? Weren't they life-affirming? Proof that life – and growth – goes on even in the midst of death?

She felt empty. Like there was a hollow where her heart was. Like she hadn't a clue who she really was. All she wanted to do was get out of the place.

She would be glad to be back at the B&B – a hot bath, read, anything to distract herself. Maybe she would go to see a film after all – a comedy, that's what she needed – a rollicking good laugh, but one with no particularly happy ever after ending. Realistic endings were better. The others just fecked up your mind.

Rats. They were the first thing she thought of as she approached the cottage next day. The pest control guy, Dave, had telephoned to check she would be there.

His van was already in the yard when she arrived, parked near the shed.

She could see him now thoroughly searching the trench in front of the boundary ditch. He looked very serious . . .

"Any luck?" she asked.

"Some good, some bad."

"Tell me."

"I've caught six in the traps."

"Fuck! And the bad news?"

"There's something you should see. Otherwise you might think I was making it up."

The man pointed at several places along the top of the ditch. What was it?

"It's corn – barley. Someone's thrown it there deliberately, in my opinion."

Hannah felt sick.

"You mean, someone has been throwing grain there to *attract* rats?"

"It looks that way."

"My God! Somebody came onto my property?"

"Or threw the stuff from the other side of the ditch. I've never come across anything like it before, to be honest."

Abe Stephenson's land . . .

"Does someone have a grudge against you or anything? Or like playing mean tricks on you? Sorry, I didn't mean to pry . . ."

Hannah felt the hairs stand up on the back of her neck again.

"I don't know."

Hannah looked again at the grain. Had he done it? Her own father?

She tried to think straight. Should she ring the Gardaí?

"Can you remove what's here, please, so it'll stop attracting them?"

"I'll do my best."

"Thanks. And can you re-set the traps and put down more poison in case more come along?"

"Of course. I can come back in another few days to check them if you like."

"That would be great, thanks . . ."

The man was looking at the back of the house.

"A few sensor lights around the place mightn't be a bad idea."

"I know. They're on my list of things to do."

"You live on your own?"

"Most of the time."

"Right . . ."

What was he not saying – that he thought she was in danger? That she was foolish to live on her own if things like this were happening?

When he left she poured herself a stiff vodka. Who else but Abe Stephenson would have done it? It was his land.

The more she thought about it the sicker she felt.

"He won't get away with this," she thought.

She would be a thorn in his side, like she told him that day on the mountain. 5th December . . . If she had had any doubts about going to Knocklannon for the carols she had none whatsoever now. She would find the courage somewhere to invade his space.

Making the phone call had taken a lot out of Roy Kemp. He had put it off for days. Several times he'd rang the number then got cold feet when the call was answered. The words just wouldn't come out. He wished he'd been able to text the Voice Power number. That way he wouldn't have to speak – and stammer.

Work wise he'd always found it easier to text farmers to let them know when he'd be there to cut their hedges. He was always glad when they texted back. Even if some of his older clients didn't, it was somehow easier to answer a call than make one.

Right now he decided what to do. He would pretend he was ringing the course number for a friend who had a stammer. That way he wouldn't block as much and he'd get the information he needed.

He pressed the buttons to ring the number again. No. No good.

"Lighten up," he told himself. "It's no big deal. The people answering the phone will be used to people like me ringing up . . ."

He sat down on one of the stones in his workshop and took a few deep breaths.

At least no one would interrupt him. His mother was up at the church doing her cleaning rota and Leo had gone to the parts supplier in Enniscorthy to get diesel filters for the tractors and wouldn't be back for three quarters of an hour at least – probably longer.

"Feck it, I'm a grown man, not a child!" he said to himself as he rang the number again.

This time he let it ring.

"Hello, Voice Power, Audrey speaking . . ."

It seemed an eternity before he could answer.

"H-h-h-h-hello."

"Hello there. And how can I help you today?"

Roy slowly got the words out.

"A f-f-f-friend of mine wants t-t-t-to sign up for the c-c-c-c-c-course."

"That's wonderful. Why don't I tell you a bit more about it so you can tell your friend?"

"Th-th-thankyou."

The relief at getting the words out was immense.

The warmth of Audrey's voice helped relax him too. She sounded nice. Not impatient with him or anything. He listened as she told him that she was a speech therapist and one of the Voice Power course directors. The other director, she said, was a man who had a stammer but who had learned to control it with special breathing techniques. There would be an assessment meeting to decide whether his "friend" was suitable for the course or not, though.

"Wh-y-y is that?" Roy asked.

Audrey explained that the course was a live-in, week-long course and unless the person was ready in their own mind it wouldn't work.

"Do you think your friend is really serious about controlling his stammer?"

"Y-y-es."

"That's great. I'll tell you how you – your friend – can apply."

Roy listened as Audrey told him that his friend needed to make an appointment for the assessment. Did he know if December 11th at 2 p.m. would suit his friend?"

Feck! Roy decided to own up. Pretending he was ringing for someone else was a stupid thing to do anyway.

"I-I-It's me ac-ac-actually – R-r-r-r-r-oy K-k-k-k-k-Kemp."

"That's great, Roy, and it's good to talk to you. We'll be delighted to see you on that day if it suits, and if you give me your address I'll get all the details and the directions out to you straight away."

When he ended the call Roy took several deep breaths to relax. He'd done it! He wished now he hadn't made an eejit of himself at first, but she had probably come across it before.

And he cursed for blocking so badly on his name. He closed his eyes, trying to suppress the memory that trying to say his name brought up. Primary school . . . Secondary school . . . Secondary was worse. Ryekemp, they nicknamed him, because of the burst of words that finally came out – that's when they weren't mimicking him or calling him "stutter box".

Relief flooded through him again as he realized that he had made the call.

The course would be held in a hotel in Waterford. At least it wasn't too far away. Not that he'd be able to go back and forth from home, even if there was some crisis. Live-in for the week, they said. You had to be prepared to do that for the course to work . . .

What it would be like being with ten other people with a stammer, Roy wondered? Like boarding school? He hoped not. He'd hated boarding school. All he'd wanted was to go to the local tech and do woodwork and metalwork instead of languages and subjects like physics. His mother wouldn't hear of it, though. He would go where everyone else from the Church of Ireland primary school in Rathbrandon had gone – to boarding school in Kilkenny or Waterford – some even to Dublin.

It had meant having very few friends in the locality. His mother had never encouraged it. If he hung round with any of the local lads he usually ended up getting in trouble.

His mother had come down hard on him that time he had gone apple stealing with the Doyle twins when he was ten.

"What the hell were you playing at?" she had shouted at him. "Haven't you tons of apples in your own backyard without stealing them from a man who has never been anything but polite to you and this family! I'm ashamed of you."

And he had stood there, not knowing why he'd done it and why he had laughed with the twins about old Symes never missing the apples and how it'd be great craic to rob the orchard and how you were chicken if you wouldn't do a little thing like that.

"Lie down with dogs and you'll rise up with fleas," his mother had said as she smacked him across the legs after Mr Symes rang up and told her what had happened . . .

Roy sorted his hammers and chisels, to be ready for when he would have spare time for sculpting again.

His mother . . . What was he doing living at home with his mother at his age? He should have made a home for himself somewhere else years ago . . .

"And I might have only for this s-s-tammer . . ."

He hoped the course would give him more confidence to talk to women. Lots talked to him all right, but very few wanted to go out with him . . . The right woman just hadn't come along, his Aunt Florrie said. Well, he wished she would – pronto. He was sick of sleeping on his own.

His mother had made the whole girlfriend thing worse by putting restrictions on who he could go out with. He wouldn't dare look at anyone local. Anyway he never went to social events that they'd be at. Instead, he had to confine himself to dreaming about girls in boarding school.

Leo had more girlfriends in first year than he had his whole time there, because he was better looking and had no shortage of words.

Even when Roy did manage to get as far as talking to a girl at a hop she bored of his slow talk, or she got teased by her girlfriends for dancing with someone that most people made fun of.

He was allowed to go to church socials when he learned to drive and Leo got old enough, travelling miles to parish halls where the segregated dances were held.

Going to any kind of dance had been a nightmare for him. Sometimes he sought Dutch courage in Danish beer, and the alcohol made conversation easier for a while, but if he did manage to ask a girl if he could walk her to the car he found himself awkward in action as well as in speech.

Either he couldn't pick up the courage to kiss her at all and she thought he didn't fancy her or the drink made him grab at her crudely, almost eating the face off her, frightening her off when it was the last thing he meant to do. Jesus, he was an eejit sometimes . . .

In the last few years he had started going to the pub in the village more often but had seldom had the guts to make a move on any woman he saw there.

"Effin spastic," Leo had said once, when he saw him go almost up to a woman in the Corner Inn to ask her to dance then falter at the last minute.

"No balls," Leo had said to him, grinning as he went off to ask the same woman to dance himself.

The sound of a vehicle in the yard signalled Leo's return.

"Are you going to flog this stuff or what?" Leo asked as he looked round at the finished stonework.

"Maybe."

Leo laughed.

He was looking at the small stone with the celtic swirl chipped into it.

"Fools and their money, what?"

Bollocks!

Roy concentrated on his sorting, trying to deafen himself to his brother's jibes.

His mother wasn't much better.

"She'll probably wait until she sees how other people react to it," he thought. "And if they like it she'll accept the praise as if she did it herself."

"Taking after your father," she'd said, the first time she saw him working away with the hammer and chisel . . .

"He spent hours in sheds too – whittling or foostering – anything to get away from the things that needed to be done."

Why couldn't she leave the dead alone? Roy wished his father was still around. How much different would his life have been if he'd lived longer? He resembled his father a lot – he could see that from photographs. His Aunt Florrie always spoke well of Harry Kemp – that meant a lot to him.

"One of nature's gentlemen," she'd say to him sometimes when she was minding him as a child. "And you're the same."

Too soft for his mother's liking though . . .

As Leo left the shed to go change the oil in one of the tractors Roy looked at the love seat. It would look well in the garden in Knocklannon.

He could see his Aunt Florrie sitting in it reading on a summer's day, her wide-brimmed hat on and a book perched on her knee.

The assessment for the Voice Power course would be a few days after the carols. He hoped he wouldn't flunk it. No, think positive. He'd be ok. He was ready – he knew it in a way he'd never known it before. 2005 would be the year that he'd get a life.

"What's he going to say when he sees you in his own house?"

Beryl had arrived at the cottage on the day of the carols at Knocklannon.

"Not much with a crowd around. He'd hardly want to make a scene, would he?" Hannah said.

"What if he does freak out?"

Hannah took a deep breath as she tried not to imagine such a scene.

"I'll cross that bridge if I come to it, but he's more likely to act normal because he'd only be drawing attention to himself if he makes a fuss. That's the last thing he'll want."

"I suppose. God, talk about going into the eye of the storm . . ."

"I didn't plan this or anything – you know I didn't. I just joined the carol singers – that's hardly a crime."

"I know."

"And he'll know it too. You have to come with me – for moral support – please!"

"I don't know . . ."

"Please!"

"It doesn't feel right . . . It's like you're pushing your luck or something . . ."

"No, I'm not! I'm just going where the group's been invited. You can't cop out now – just when I need you – please?"

"Ok! Ok! But I'm not hanging around if anything kicks off – and neither are you . . ."

Hannah hugged her friend, relieved.

"Thanks!"

After Beryl had gone upstairs to change, Hannah wondered if she was pushing her luck . . . Would she have the guts to go to Knocklannon? No, she told herself, you have to have backbone in this world . . . Still, was she in danger of obsessing, like Matt had implied?

She glanced outside at the yard. There was no more rat activity, thank God. How could he have done such a thing? Only for Beryl stopping her she would have driven up to his door to confront her father. Beryl had been shocked all the same, though, when she told her what the pest control guy had said about grain being planted there.

"You don't know for sure it was him that did it?"

"Who else could it be?" she'd asked. "He wants me out. He wants to buy this place . . ."

Now Beryl was pushing her food round on her plate.

"Hannah . . ."

"What?"

"Did you ever think that maybe you'd be better leaving things be . . . I mean, maybe he isn't the sort to be vexing . . . Your life's not that bad, really is it? You've got a home, a good life, a family – all of us from Royle and friends and stuff. It doesn't have to be all about wanting him to accept you . . ."

Hannah stopped eating.

"I know I've all those things but why shouldn't he accept me? I'm more his flesh and blood than his two nephews."

"I know but . . ."

"But what?"

"Did you ever think that maybe he'll . . . never accept you? It's a possibility you have to face."

Hannah felt ill.

"Yeah, maybe, but me being here means he'll know that I exist, at least. He's been able to pretend I wasn't born for long enough and that isn't right."

"And his wife?"

Hannah put down her knife, breathing slowly to stay calm.

"Why shouldn't she know – eventually anyway, when the time is right? I like her, I know, but it's not a crime to be sick of secrets, is it? She'll have to know what kind of husband she has some day. Wouldn't she be better knowing? Why should I always have to be the one to stay quiet?"

Hannah knew she was raising her voice but couldn't stop herself.

"We're all like that from Royle – mice – the whole lot of us. You know we are! Don't go asking questions, don't go looking up your family, don't go making a nuisance of yourself, don't go stirring things up! Nanna preached that at us all the time. Yeah, well, maybe I can't do that anymore!"

"Maybe she was trying to protect us."

"From the truth? Weren't we entitled to it, whatever it was? Jesus, we're human beings – we've the right to know who we are and where we come from! Often times I wonder who did she think she was to do that – God?"

"Maybe sometimes things are better left . . ."

"Oh yeah – what you don't know won't hurt you. But it will hurt you, *is* hurting us – can you not see that?! It's eating away at us, day after day, making us think and dream and fantasize and hate and feel like second class citizens! She wasn't doing us any favours rearing us like wimps."

"You were never a wimp."

"Yeah, well, that was the way she wanted us to be – submissive, passive . . ."

"She did her best – you know she did!"

"She was a good Christian, yes. She gave her life looking after us – society's forgotten children but did you ever think of the way she reared us: dependent on her, pandering to her, afraid of her, afraid to leave the fold because she needed us and we'd be letting her down by going, when all the time she needed help minding all the other kids . . . Jesus, wake up and smell the roses – half us were institutionalized!"

Beryl was covering her ears.

"You can't even listen to the truth!"

Beryl was ashen-faced.

"You were her favourite – how could you say that?"

"Why was I her favourite, though – because I was pretty – because I was strong – because she depended on me to stand up for the rest of you in school? Because I was stupid enough to help her trying to control the younger ones when she couldn't anymore? Maybe that's not the right reason for being a favourite?"

"The rest of us envied you – resented you, even . . ."

Hannah looked at her friend. God what had she said? Why had she shouted?

"I'm sorry, I know you did, but I didn't want it to be like that . . .you know I didn't. I didn't play on it, did I? I hope I didn't anyway . . ."

Beryl was silent for too long.

"You couldn't help the fact that she liked you."

"God . . ."

"We used to think it was because your mother came with money."

Hannah sat down, her head in her hands.

"I'm sorry. Jesus, I shouldn't have said all those things. Stuff festers away, that's all. It's like it's all just under the surface waiting to get out . . ."

Hannah gave her friend a hug. It was several seconds before Beryl returned it.

"I'm sorry – you came here for a break – not to listen to all this."

"I'm ok."

Beryl was blowing her nose now.

"You're right. We've all kept our heads down too long. If you want me to go, I'll go. Whatever happens, happens. We'll cope with it as we go like we have with everything else we've been through."

The hug was warmer this time.

"Thank you."

"Now where's that makeup bag till we repair our faces? We must look a sight."

Hannah indicated right to enter the gateway at Knocklannon.

"It's a beautiful place," Beryl said, looking round. "All the trees. And the drive up to it."

"Yes."

It was a cold, crisp afternoon, frost still lying on the grass where the winter sun hadn't reached it. There were ten or twelve cars in the yard already. Peg Travers was getting out of her blue Punto. She waved as Hannah drove up.

"Peg, this is my friend, Beryl Nash. Beryl – Peg Travers."

The two women exchanged greeting before Peg led the way.

"We're all to go in the front door – hostess's instructions," she said.

"Lead on."

Hannah shivered involuntarily as they approached the door. This felt weird . . .

"There's Roy!"

Roy Kemp had driven up close to the front door.

"He's still smiling anyway," Beryl said.

"Maybe he's smiling because you're here . . ." Hannah said, grabbing her friend's elbow.

Beryl laughed, but she looked pleased.

They waited for Roy to catch up with them.

Hannah was glad to have Roy and Peg to walk into Knocklannon House with.

Florrie was at the door, smiling.

"More of our singers . . . You're all very welcome. Come in, please."

Hannah introduced Beryl, asking Roy at the same time if he remembered Beryl from the pub weeks before.

"Y-y-yes."

"Roy – will you show our singers where to hang their coats? Vera is handing out mulled wine in that corner and we'll have mince pies shortly – they're just coming out of the oven."

"You've gone to a lot of trouble," Beryl was saying, covering up for Hannah's sudden silence.

She suddenly felt overwhelmed by where she was – in the hallway of the house she'd liked to have been reared in.

"You've a lovely home," she said, looking at the mahogany stairs, the ancient paintings on the wall, the stick basket under the stairs and the grandfather clock in the corner.

"Thank you. It's a bit of a barracks sometimes, but it's lovely on days like this when it's full of people – and music."

"Yes."

"Get yourselves a glass of wine and go through to the conservatory."

Hannah glanced at Beryl as they followed Florrie's instructions.

"Is he here?" Beryl whispered.

Hannah glanced quickly around the room.

"No."

"Phew!"

Hannah shivered suddenly. What had she done? Why hadn't she just made her excuses and stayed away? Right now she felt scared.

"Some mulled wine?" Vera Kemp, tray in hand, was in front of them.

"Yes please. It smells lovely."

"It's the cinnamon. No use without it."

"Yes. This is my friend Beryl. Beryl, Vera Kemp, the choir organizer."

"Nice to meet you."

Hannah could see Vera look Beryl up and down.

"Yes."

After greeting other choir members, Hannah made her way out to the conservatory. A patio opened off it. Florrie had an outdoor gas heater lit. Several people, including Peg Travers, were walking around looking at stone objects. Hannah and Beryl followed them out.

"What do you think of Roy's work? Isn't he gifted?"

"Roy did this? It's beautiful."

Hannah was looking at the unusual granite seat.

Beryl was equally impressed.

"The patience it must have taken – and the skill . . ."

Florrie was beside them, smiling.

"He doesn't even know how talented he is – that's the wonderful thing about him."

Florrie was calling Roy over.

"See – other people are impressed, like I knew they would be . . ." she said, linking his arm.

"You're an artist – no doubt about it," Hannah said.

"It's really great work," said Beryl. "It must have taken hundreds of hours to do that."

Roy's face had reddened with pleasure and embarrassment.

"I-I-It k-k-keeps m-m-me out of m-m-m-ischief."

"Modest – what did I tell you . . ." Florrie was saying.

Hannah thought Florrie looked like a proud mother.

"Now, excuse me while I check the oven or we'll all be having burnt mince pies . . ."

"What does your brother think?" Hannah asked Roy.

"S-s-says I-I'm an e-e-eejit."

"Shows what he knows."

"He should be proud of you," Beryl said. "That chair looks like it's grown there."

Roy explained about it being a love seat.

"It's marvellous."

Behind them a gong now sounded. Florrie was speaking.

"Ladies and gentlemen, if you'd like to make your way back in to the hall and dining room we'll ask our carol singers to entertain us for a while. Don't forget that all today's proceeds are for charity so we'd ask that you give whatever you can afford. Thank you very much and, as always, I think we're in for a real treat."

"Talk later," Hannah said to Beryl.

"No sign?"

Hannah looked around again, feeling uneasy.

"Maybe he's away. Or maybe he knew I'd be coming and has steered clear."

"See you in a while. You'd better take your place."

Take her place . . .

Hannah headed for the stairs where the rector was positioning the choir to sing.

Forcing herself not to think of her father, she stood in the front beside the other sopranos.

By the second carol they were beginning to warm up. *Good King Wenceslas*. So far, so good . . .

They were on the last verse when she saw him appear at the drawing room door, Florrie handing him a glass of wine as he arrived.

Hannah kept singing, though she had no knowledge of whether or not any words were coming out.

She glanced at Beryl, who knew from the way she looked that he was there.

She glanced at him again. He had seen her. He looked momentarily stunned. Now he was looking away and raising his wine glass hurriedly to his lips. What was he thinking, she wondered?

She glanced at him again as the applause started. He was clapping but was it because it would look strange if he didn't? She could see him glance back as if to make his way out of the room, but she saw Florrie tug at his sleeve. Was she telling him to stay where he was?

The rector had his baton in the air again.

Away in a manger.

Hannah felt a lump in her throat. She had forgotten she was supposed to sing the first verse solo.

She had a bum start as a frog settled in her throat. Feck! Why couldn't she have done it perfectly?

"It's ok, Hannah. We'll try again."

The conductor gave her the note a second time.

This time she concentrated on breathing properly and the opening line came out sweetly and clearly . . .

"Away in a manger, no crib for a bed . . ."

Concentrate – that's all she had to do . . .

She was glad when the others joined in on the second verse. She looked straight ahead until the carol was over and the applause came again.

He was gone. Someone else had taken his place in the front. Where was he now? Alone in the kitchen, further back behind others, where he wouldn't have to look at her, or gone out to the yard, effin and blinding about the goddamned cheek of her coming here?

Beryl looked uneasy when she caught her eye.

It was all right. She would be ok. She had done nothing wrong . . . If he was feeling bad this minute wasn't it his own guilt that was affecting him . . .

After the carol singing, more wine was handed out.

"Where has Abe disappeared to? That fire needs stoking," Hannah could hear Vera ask Florrie.

"He was here a while ago. I'll find him. He can't be far."

Hannah felt Florrie touch her sleeve.

"You have a lovely voice, Hannah – really beautiful. It was a pleasure listening to you."

"Thank you. I'm glad you think so."

"Husbands! Never there when they're wanted, are they? Help yourselves to more refreshments . . ."

"We will. Thanks."

Beryl was beside her now, handing her another glass of wine.

"You ok?"

"Sort of," Hannah said. "He's disappeared."

"I saw. Do you want to go? Just say when . . ."

"Soon," Hannah said, as Peg Travers came over to them.

"It's official – we're a success. And you're the star of the show."

"After messing up the start . . ."

"Nonsense – you were grand."

Peg lowered her voice.

"Well – what do you think?"

"Of?"

"This place. Fine house, isn't it?"

"Yes."

"You have to hand it to Florrie – she's a great hostess."

"Very gracious. I like her," Beryl said.

"Makes up for Mr Grumpy anyway, I always say. You never know where you are with him. Civil one day, wouldn't see you the next."

Now Peg had raised her voice again.

"Anyway, I'm off and I've made a wish in Roy's chair – for a toy boy to sit in it with me. Wouldn't it be grand, sitting in that of a summer's evening and a fine fella gazing into your eyes?"

Hannah and Beryl laughed.

"You never know what can happen."

"Never say die," Peg said. "Do you hear me – an ould one like me! I'll see you both soon again, I hope."

Ten minutes later Hannah decided to leave. After asking Roy to thank Florrie for them, they headed out to the car.

"Strange the things you don't know about people – a lot of people were obviously surprised that Roy could do stuff like that," Beryl was saying.

"I know, but it was good seeing the shock on their faces."

They were nearly at the car when a van drove into the yard at speed.

It was Leo Kemp.

"Don't tell me I've missed it?" he said, getting out.

"The carols are over. There are lots of people in there still though."

"Fuck! I knew I got the time wrong! I heard you'd joined up. And now I've missed the whole shebang – fuck!"

"You'll live, I'm sure."

Beryl was in the car. Leo hadn't even recognized her presence.

"You reckon? So how are you anyway? Did I hear that you've been having a spot of trouble with rats? Sore dose that!"

"It's sorted."

"You should have given me a ring. I'd have shot the bastards for you."

Hannah felt sick.

"Like I said, it's sorted. Now if you'll excuse me."

Leo moved out of the way, hands in pockets now.

"I see you've got sensor lights put up – good idea. Security is important when you live in the country."

"How did you know that?"

Leo tapped the side of his nose.

"Not much gets done in this neck of the woods without someone knowing. I saw Peter Conway up on the ladder the other day."

"Right."

"We'd better go," Hannah said, getting into the car with Beryl.

He was leaning on the car roof, head bent to talk to her through the window.

"Ok, but any time you need a knight in shining tractor to come to your rescue, just give me a ring . . ."

Beryl didn't speak until they had reached the end of the driveway.

"Sleazeball."

"I know," Hannah said, stopping the car. She rested her head on the steering wheel.

"You ok?"

"I just have to stop for a minute. My legs are like jelly."

"It's just shock. With all that's happening."

Hannah tried to control her voice but couldn't.

"He couldn't even stay in the same room as me . . ."

"He got a fright, that's all."

"You should have seen the look on his face . . ."

"I did, but it's useless trying to read anyone's mind. Who knows what he's thinking. Maybe his heart was breaking for all you know."

Hannah shook her head.

"I thought he was going to order me out of the house."

"It's ok. You're out of there now."

"Why am I letting him affect me this much – I swore I wouldn't."

"You're a bit overwhelmed, that's all. It's been a big day. Do you want me to drive? We'd better get out of here in case someone else needs to get by."

"No, you're all right."

Hannah put the car in first gear and eased out onto the road after checking for passing traffic.

"He's not well," she said when they'd gone half a mile.

"Who?"

"My father."

"How do you mean?"

"He has heart trouble. I'd put money on it. He's a bad colour."

Hannah drove home, a hollow feeling still in her stomach. She parked beside the cottage.

"My whole family was there today," she said.

"Yes . . ."

They were all there and I was outside the circle . . .

"Leo!" Leo heard his Aunt Florrie calling him from the kitchen door.

"Have a look for Abe, would you? He's disappeared somewhere instead of staying to talk to people. I don't know what's got into him."

Leo glanced round the yard.

"The jeep's here – he can't be far. I'll have a look."

"Thanks."

Leo headed for the cattle sheds first – all that was left there now were the pedigrees. That's where his uncle spent a lot of his time, watching, looking, judging . . .

Did the pressure of Aunt Florrie's "soirée" get to him or what? He wouldn't fancy it himself – some of those ould biddies would bore him senseless.

The Casey one was another story, though – he'd missed out badly by turning up late. He grinned to himself as he thought of how he'd mentioned the rats. Maybe he should drop off another few. It'd be nice to have her leaning on his shoulder or eating out of his hand with gratitude . . .

The pedigree Hereford heifers stared back at him from the shed when he slid back the door. No sign of his uncle.

Round the back the pedigree Hererford bull roared in the bull-house.

Leo jumped down off the gate as a thought struck him. His uncle hadn't tried to handle the bull for any reason himself, had he? No, he wouldn't be that stupid. Fuck! He ran round to the pen, but no sign. Phew!

"Where the hell has he got to?"

Normally he was there at one of Florrie's do's, being "mein host", pouring drinks and enjoying showing off his home.

Leo grinned. If he had what his Uncle Able had he'd want to show it off too.

Feck! What if his uncle wasn't well? What if he'd taken ill and was lying in a heap somewhere begging for help?

He hadn't been to see a specialist for nothing. Perhaps his ticker had given out. Leo walked faster, heading for the back lane. There he was! Coming round the bend, stick in hand and dog at his heels.

Seeing him, Leo stood still until his uncle reached him.

"What's up?"

"She was wondering where you'd got to."

His uncle kept walking. Leo followed him.

"Can I not piss without someone looking for me!" Abe said. "I thought I'd left a gate open."

"Right," Leo said, keeping up with his uncle. "Better to be sure than sorry."

His uncle walked on.

"Are they gone yet?"

"Most of them by now. You all right?"

"Never better."

"Good."

They were at the yard gates now. Leo opened the main one to let them through.

"The heifers look good. You'll have a winner next summer."

"Which one?"

It was a test. Leo knew it. They walked over to the shed. Leo got up on the gate and pointed.

"That one – nearest the trough."

Had his uncle smiled?

"Aye."

He was on a roll . . .

"I met the Casey one as she was leaving."

"Aye?"

"Sorry I missed her – singing sweetly in the choir."

"Get down off that gate, for fuck's sake. It's hard enough to keep them hanging without you jumping up and down on them."

His uncle now looked unusually flustered.

"One of the bars is dodgy. It needs welding," he muttered.

Leo got down off the gate, seeing no need for weld. Christ! Talking to him like that! Maybe he could get back into his good books by mentioning the rodents. At least he was trying to get shut of her.

"My ploy didn't work."

"What ploy?"

Leo explained where he'd put the rats.

"You did what?"

"Outside."

"Keep your voice down!"

Leo spoke lower. "I was only trying to get her to sell, like you wanted."

"What did she say?"

"That she had it sorted."

His uncle now looked white in the face.

"No more, do you hear? If she gets wind that you did it she'll have the law on you."

"And what about the planning permission? How are we going to get that with her stuck there?"

His uncle was heading back for the house.

"Stay away from her – you hear?"

Leo shrugged. What was up with him? A sickening thought occurred to Leo. Maybe he fancied her himself. Dirty fecker! He'd always had an eye for the women, hadn't he? Well, he could whistle . . .

Leo laughed as he followed his uncle into the house. Fair dues to him all the same. He hoped that when he hit seventy his willie would still be stirring.

The last of the visitors were leaving. He could see his mother waving the rector off, arse licking again in the hopes of getting into heaven. If there was a big fella up there he wouldn't keep her long, though – she'd be trying to run the operation for him.

His mother was drinking tea.

"Where have yous been?"

"Fixing a gate," Leo said, before his uncle could speak. Now Abe would owe him one.

"Right."

"How did it go?"

"Three hundred and fifty-euro – not bad for an afternoon," Vera said.

Florrie was coming into the kitchen with another tray of wine glasses for the dishwasher.

"Open that, will you?"

His uncle obliged.

"I thought you'd disappeared off the planet."

"I had things to do."

Throwing her eyes up to heaven, Florrie left the kitchen.

Roy came in then, carrying another full tray.

"You'll make someone a great wife someday."

"F-f-feck off!"

"Leave him alone," his mother said. Leo couldn't believe she was siding with his brother.

"He got a lot of compliments today – for the stonework."

"My brother, the sculptor, what?" Leo said, mimicking. "Next thing you'll know he'll be growing a ponytail and wearing a beret."

"Hmph! He'll never make a fortune out of it," Abe said.

Leo put two salad sandwiches in his mouth at the same time.

His uncle was sitting in his chair by the cooker now, looking knackered. He was slowing down – that much was obvious.

He'd better not pop his clogs before the building development starts, he thought.

That's why sorting the Hannah Casey problem was important. He would do it all right. And get her into bed too – see if he didn't. She wouldn't be the first unwilling filly he'd tamed. All he needed was time.

"Roy Boy is welcome to his chisel and his compliments. Chip off the mad block, if you ask me."

Abe Stephenson woke in the spare room. He had gone there at 2 a.m., after twisting and turning for several hours, unable to sleep.

His dreams had frightened him into it. Not the ones he had but the ones he was afraid he would have. What if he said the child's name out loud – hers or her mother's – after sleep left him without control?

He'd told Florrie he had a sick stomach. He looked at his watch. It was now 6 a.m. and he felt as if he had been pulled through a sceach hedge backwards. Needing to go to the toilet, he got out of bed slowly.

His legs felt a bit wobbly from lack of sleep and his joints ached. Old age was a curse!

He struggled to find the light switch in the room he wasn't used to. When had he slept there last? When Florrie had that bad chest infection and he couldn't sleep with her coughing? Probably.

He headed for the bathroom, walking quietly so as not to wake his wife.

By the time he got to the bathroom he had to hold onto the washbasin for support. He felt dizzy, as a wave of fear came over him.

He lowered himself down onto the toilet seat as beads of sweat came out on his forehead. He sat still. Good, the dizziness had passed.

He urinated – slowly. That was another problem – his waterworks weren't working as good as they used to. Prostate probably. What the feck else was wrong with him? He felt like an old machine starting to rust out in the haggard.

He would sit on the toilet until he dared get up again. He wished he'd put on a pair of pyjamas instead of the old shirt he had worn to bed. It didn't hold much heat.

Eventually he stood up, holding the wash hand basin as he did so. He was all right . . . Grabbing a dressing gown from the back of the door he left the bathroom as quietly as he could. He hoped Florrie wasn't listening to him. She'd be out fussing and firing questions at him. He passed their bedroom door. No sound. Good . . .

In his study chair downstairs Abe breathed deeply. At least he'd had no pain. The tightness he'd felt in his chest last night was probably just fear. He would shake it off. He couldn't let her get to him. *Away in a manger* . . . Still, the words haunted him . . . her voice . . . Had she had a crib or cot of her own as a baby or was she jammed into God knows what and left crying for hours . . . No! He couldn't think about those things . . . He'd get sleeping tablets from the doctor if necessary.

Within seconds, he had decided what he would do. He needed to rest for a day or so. He would tell Florrie he was coming down with something – a flu or cold and that he'd stay in bed to stop it getting any worse.

It wouldn't be like him, of course, but hopefully she'd think he'd finally got a bit of sense.

Six twenty . . . He would ring Aidan at eight o'clock and ask him to do the yard work. It wouldn't take too long now that there were fewer cattle. He'd ask Leo to check the bullocks in Newtown.

Lying back in the chair he closed his eyes hoping sleep would come, but the words of the carol came back again, making him angry this time . . .

"Trying to provoke a reaction, that's all she was trying to do – catch me out," he said, trying to compose himself. "Well, it's not happening."

She'd seen him arrive too. Looked straight at him, brazen as you like.

Stay calm . . . that's what he had to do . . .

He had got out of the house as quickly as he could and headed up the back lane to the upper fields.

"A farmer's work is never done, what?" Tom Carthy had said, late coming for the carols and seeing him hurry off.

"Aye."

It had taken half an hour of walking for him to settle a bit. The nerve of her . . . Carol singing, my arse! She joined up just to get the chance to get into his house!

He took several deep breaths. No, he mustn't let her get to him. That's what she wanted – for him to crack, for him to lose it in front of everybody, so that the secret would be out . . .

Up the lane he had stood looking out on his farm, land farmed by Stephensons for generations. They'd come over as planters with the Wentworths in the seventeenth century, showed the natives how to farm, planted trees, built houses, lived like civilized human beings, not next thing to animals.

Standing up now, he looked again at one after another of the aerial photographs of the farm that were hung around the walls in sequence – the earliest one dated from his father's time, but the rest from his . . .

"Are you all right?"

His wife was at the door.

"I heard you coming downstairs."

"I've a dose of some sort," he said. "Couldn't sleep. I was going to make a hot whiskey then go back to bed."

"I'll take your temperature . . ."

"I'm all right – a day's rest and I'll be fine."

"Do you want a cup of tea? Water? You should be drinking plenty of fluids if you've a bug."

"Whatever."

"I'll get some now."

When she came back, it was on the tip of his tongue to ask about how she – the Casey one – had got there, but he stopped himself and made a comment about there being a fair few singers there yesterday . . .

"It was great. Especially seeing a new face or two. Hannah has a lovely voice. She should have had it trained."

"Huh! Who got her involved?"

He listened while his wife explained about suggesting to Reverend Mundy that Hannah might like to join the choir ages ago. So she hadn't orchestrated it, just to be invited here . . .

"I could see Roy watching her, grinning like a Cheshire cat. If you ask me he's fond of her – or her friend, I'm not sure which. He'll be too shy to do anything about it probably, but it's nice to see him taking an interest."

Fuck!

"Who's the friend?"

"Beryl. They were reared in the children's home together, like sisters really, but it's good they have each other."

So she hadn't joined the carol singers just to be invited here. That was something. Still, she could have stayed away, made some excuse. Instead, she'd walked straight in, knowing she'd unsettle him . . .

"I'll let Max out and get you that tea."

"Right."

Abe sat back down in the chair, his knees weak. Panic flooded his body again. He had to decide what to do. No, he'd never acknowledge her! Even if she accused him in public, he would deny everything. That way she'd never win. And he'd never agree to a DNA test. Without that she'd have no proof.

If he stood his ground it would all blow over. He wasn't going to be an eejit like that farmer in the next parish, Walter Fox. He'd thought he had the small farm he owned all to himself after his single brother, Charlie, died but the brother had had a son years before who'd turned up and made a claim on the place. The farm had to be sold to give Walter's nephew half the money. He, Abe, had bought the land . . .

Abe headed back up the stairs to bed.

As long as she couldn't prove any connection between them he was safe and everything belonging to him was safe.

Right now all he had to do was take things a bit easier. He'd even go to the doctor for a checkup. If his blood pressure was up he could get medication for it. And a few days away – in a hotel in Cork, maybe. That'd be a good idea. Rest and relaxation, lots of sleep and eat properly for a week. It would help clear his head and build up his strength. Keep his wits about him. That's all he had to do and everything would be all right.

Chapter
SEVEN

Vera Kemp woke at 6.30 a.m. No, she wouldn't be shaking a bucket with the carol singers today on the streets of Wexford. Roy neither. She had got notice of a sheep inspection late the night before so there was too much to do. Goddamned bureaucracy! Europe gives you a bit of money but the piper has to be paid for it in terms of paperwork and torment.

Reverend Mundy would understand. God knows, she did enough for charity and for the parish, she thought, as she swung her legs out of bed. The farm had to come first.

And she had to go to Knocklannon to get the keys from Abe before he and Florrie left for their break in Cork. She, Leo and Roy would have to keep an eye on the place in their absence. The winter break must have been Florrie's idea. Abe had never gone away at this time of year in his life, so it had to be one of her notions.

She opened her bedroom window to get the gist of the weather. Dark clouds hovered and an east wind cut at her face when she stuck her head out. She hated an east wind. It went right through you regardless of how many layers of clothing you wore. It was a day for the fire, not facing the elements.

Just as well the sheep were close to the house. Some of the ewes were already housed in preparation for lambing. She had stayed up until one o'clock making sure all the records were up to date – the register and the vet book that listed what medication they'd had. Traceability – trace the meat back to the farm it came from, that was the tune the EU piper was singing now. It was a good idea in principle, Vera knew, as the consumer would know where their leg of lamb had come from, but it did mean extra bookwork. Still, it was up-to-date now and the Department of Agriculture inspector wouldn't find anything wrong with her records.

She put on a second vest and a pair of tights under her acrylic trousers, trying not to look in the mirror at her ageing body. It was no day for sorting sheep or standing on the street in Wexford singing *Tis the season to be jolly* for that matter.

All this Christmas lark had got out of hand – a pagan festival, she thought sometimes – spend, spend, spend . . . She would be glad when Christmas Day was over. She didn't like crowds in town. All her life she had tried to avoid them. Her Fridays in town had always meant early starts. She was in town before 9.30 a.m. That way she could park easily and be in the bank when it opened and have most of her business done before the town really woke up.

Then she'd drive to Pettitt's supermarket in St Aidan's Crescent to do the grocery shopping. Local shops were only for the paper and odd items that she might have forgotten or for doing the Lotto. She did that religiously, playing the same numbers each draw. What she would do with the money if she won she didn't know, but she would enjoy having it. It had been the Sweepstakes when she was younger.

"I'll get you a pony when I win the Sweep," she used to tell Roy when he was pleading for one. She didn't mention that she'd have left his father and bought a farm somewhere else and been her own boss for the first time in her life.

Her mother had encouraged Harry Kemp's attentions. She'd known it the second time he had called to the house unexpectedly. He had a pretext, of course, like wanting to know how the cattle prices had gone at the mart when Vera's mother had sold cattle the day before.

"What's that fucker doing here?" Abe, her brother, had said, as Harry arrived just as they finished their dinner. "He seems to be haunting the place these days."

Her mother hadn't paused in her work of clearing the table.

"I think he has set his cap at Vera."

Abe had looked at his sister.

"So what if he has?" Vera had said. That was all that was said.

She was twenty-nine and she could do worse. Working in an auctioneer's firm until she wizened into old age wasn't her idea of a future. Boyfriends had always been a problem for her. Ever since boarding school, her mother would make regular enquiries about who was showing interest in her. If any of the local lads came sniffing around, her mother's antennae were up straight away. Suddenly an invitation would materialise for Vera to spend time in Wicklow with her aunt and uncle, or maybe Dublin to her mother's first cousin. When she came back there would be no sight of the boy who had once been given work beet-weeding or potato-picking.

She had gone out with Bill Watson for all of six months, her longest courtship ever, but her mother hadn't encouraged it.

"No prospects," she said.

Prospects meant property. She'd finished with him eventually, after hearing Bill and one of his acquaintances laughing on a Sunday evening drive to Courtown about Bill having "done well for himself hooking up with the Stephensons – a right few bob there, wha' . . ."

She had seen Bill's face flush with pleasure at what his acquaintance was saying. So, he did think he was doing well for himself. From that moment on she couldn't be sure that it was her or her name that he liked. She hadn't cried over him either.

Roy and Leo were already in the kitchen when she went downstairs, both silent and sleepy looking, Roy as he ate Weetabix and Leo as he made tea in a cup.

Vera was glad to see him having his breakfast here. He might sleep in his newfangled bungalow, but this was home. If he came here for meals most of the time because it was handier, what of it? She was glad to see him. She would persuade him to get a tenant in the bungalow soon enough. All she had to do was keep her ear to the ground and find the right person. That'd put a stop to him bringing women over there. He might think she didn't know about his nocturnal activities, but she wasn't stupid. She knew enough about men to know what needs they had – even her own sons. This morning he was post-coital, she knew. Tired but at ease, like a physical need had been met. As long as he didn't make any commitment to the women he hung around with that was all right.

"T-t-t-toast?"

"One slice. Thanks."

Roy was always the one to be thoughtful – and to make a pot of tea rather than a cup for himself.

"You'd need to have the ewes in the collecting yard before half-eight," Vera said as she put sugar in her tea.

"We know that."

"And watch the rams – the Texel'll kill that young ram if he gets anywhere near him . . ."

Leo plonked his mug down on the table.

"Jesus – will you stop? We're not eejits. We can organise a few fucking sheep."

Vera bit off a piece of toast.

"Language! I'm only reminding you in case you forget."

"W-w-w-we'll h-h-handle it."

"I'll give you a hand getting them in."

She saw Leo grimace. He didn't want her fussing around the yard, shouting at him when any animal looked as if it was ready to bolt, she knew, but he could put up with it. He wasn't cock of the walk yet.

"I thought yous were supposed to be off singing today – isn't it the eighth of December?" Leo was saying.

"I'm going l-l-later."

Vera saw Leo smirk.

"Of course you are, you being the arty type – lah-di-dah. Maybe they'll want a sculpture of you to stick up on the main street yet."

"Sh-sh-shut up!"

"That's enough, the pair of you! We'll all have enough to do without you squabbling when your uncle is away."

"Very sudden, that. He must be losing it. He usually has to be prised away from the place," Leo said, putting his cup in the already cluttered sink.

"He's entitled to a break if he wants one. You just be glad he's asked you to look after the place."

"I-I-Is Aunt Florrie going?"

Leo laughed.

"No, he's leaving her here to look after you. Suck, suck."

"Stop that! Of course she's going. Maybe it's her idea – I don't know. She is always looking for diversion. If she had her way, they'd be going on holiday twice a year and then some."

"W-w-what's wrong with that?"

"Waste of effin time, that's what. And money."

"Why shouldn't he go on holiday when there's you two to look after the place as well as myself while they're away? We can take turns sleeping there at night so the house isn't empty. You never know who might get wind of them being away and raid the place."

"Th-th-hey have an alarm system."

"Huh! That's not the same as having a human keeping an eye. They're going at three o'clock and I'm going over then to get the keys and see them off. I'll sleep there tonight."

Leo laughed.

"Don't forget the shotgun under your pillow."

"Rinse off that cup and plate – I'm not your slave," she said. "I've enough to do without picking up after grown men."

Roy already had put his away and was getting his boots on.

"And don't forget that mad ewe – she'll go for you in the pen if you don't keep an eye on her."

"She'd better not or she'll get the fucking chop."

It was odd seeing her brother in his Sunday clothes on a Wednesday afternoon and looking a bit peaky. Maybe he did need a rest after the flu he was complaining of.

"How did the inspection go?" he asked.

"All right," Vera said, after arriving in the yard at Knocklannon. "Apart from being half an hour late. Where exactly are you off to?"

"She's booked somewhere in Kinsale. It's far enough."

"Sounds good. How are you feeling now?"

"All right."

"Flu takes a lot out of anyone, so you'd want to mind yourself."

Vera saw her brother nod towards upstairs.

"Herself wants a few days away. It'll keep her quiet."

Just as she suspected – it was Florrie's idea.

"Did you talk to the lads?"

"Aye. I left a list there on the table of things that need to be looked at and phone numbers they might want, but there's nothing sick at the moment so it should be all right. I'll give Leo a ring every day to see how things are going. And if he can't reach on anything I've told him to ring Aidan and I'll fix up with him when I get back."

"Right."

Vera was pleased that Leo would be the one that her brother would ring. He had always favoured him over Roy.

Florrie was downstairs now, pulling a large suitcase on wheels behind her.

"We're going for a week, not a month," Abe said.

"Well, unless you want us to go naked for the week we have to have something to wear. Are you ready? And thanks for coming over, Vera. I've made a list out with the alarm code on it and Max's food directions and anything else I thought was important. The oil lorry is supposed to come tomorrow with a fill for the house, but I've left a cheque wrapped up in a plastic bag under the tank for him so you needn't worry about being here for that."

"Ok."

Typical Florrie – to trust an oil delivery man. Vera wouldn't trust one as far as she'd throw him. One had tried to cod her one time, giving her less than she ordered, but she had caught him out by reading the gauge on the lorry. It was the last time that oil lorry was in her yard and every one after that was stood over.

"Have you got everything then?"

"Yes. Money . . . mobile . . . medication."

"Medication?" Vera was all ears.

"The doctor has put him on water tablets. For blood pressure."

"Bastardin' yokes. They'd have you pissing for Ireland."

"Do you have to be so crude?" Florrie said.

"At least you're a man – you can stop at a gap on the road."

"It's a man's world," Florrie said. "Ok. Are we all set?"

Vera took the bunch of keys that Florrie handed her.

"I've labelled them so's you'll know which is which. And the electric blanket's switched on in the spare room. You needn't bother to switch it off. It's only on low, so it'll be grand until you're going to bed."

The spare room – her old bedroom. Even after all these years it still rankled to hear it called that.

"Safe journey."

They were gone, the navy Mercedes freshly washed, disappearing round the bend of the yard.

Max, the sheepdog, barked and barked, unable to understand why his master had gone without him.

"Whisht!"

The dog went silent, tail between his legs.

Back in the house Vera stood in the kitchen for several minutes. It had changed a lot since she left to get married, Abe's prosperity showing in the quality of the fitted kitchen and the finish of the place.

She opened cupboard doors. Her mother used to keep all the baking ingredients in there – the baking powder, cherries, sultanas. The cupboard was still used for that. In the drawing room now she ran her finger along the piano, looking for dust. There was none.

It wasn't the piano she'd had lessons on as a child. No, that one wouldn't do her sister-in-law.

Sitting down on the stool she played a verse of *The Lord's my Shepherd*. It was the first hymn she'd learned.

"We'll make an organist out of you yet," her father had said the first time he heard her play it.

"At least you're getting some return for your money," Abe had said, then thirteen.

Her father had chuckled and repeated the story over and over to friends. Her playing the tune well had been forgotten in the middle of her brother's cute business comment. Eventually she had tired of piano lessons, deciding her fingers weren't cut out for it, and practising was a nuisance and she could never quite get the rhythm of a piece right. Not like Florrie who seemed to have it instinctively even at the age she'd started.

Vera wondered now if the plans for the building development were lying around anywhere. The study probably . . . Walking down the hall she tried the door – locked. Well, it made sense to keep it locked, in case the place was broken into, or did Florrie know she'd be trying to snoop?

It still galled her that everything had come to a full stop just over Casey's cottage, though.

Why wouldn't that Hannah one sell? All the roots talk was rubbish. What roots did she have? How bad she'd be, a couple of hundred thousand euro in her pocket for a place not worth two thirds of it? Couldn't she buy herself a house somewhere else? Timbuktu preferably. That'd get her away from here.

Vera didn't want her staying around. Her two sons were eyeing her up, but Roy was more of a worry than Leo. Leo would just get a night or two out of her and that would be that, but Roy hadn't a tither of sense. He'd think he was in love if any woman as much as batted their eyelids at him. Love! It'd take more than that to make a sound future. He'd bring someone she didn't like into her house over her dead body.

Vera checked that the patio doors were locked.

They were.

Roy's stone seat looked well outside — the granite bright after the wash of rain.

Lots of people had been impressed by the sculptures on Sunday. Maybe he was on to something. Maybe he had an alternative enterprise idea – the buzz phrase in farming now. She hated the phrase though. Alternative enterprise. It was surrender talk. She wouldn't be giving up. She'd been through bad times in farming before, and if she knew one thing it was that things go round in circles – those who had the backbone to stick it out through the bad times would profit again in time to come.

Vera looked round the drawing room, already decorated for Christmas. The last time she had been there was three days earlier at the carols.

Vera brushed up the cold ashes around the fireplace.

"She could at least have cleaned out the grate," she thought.

Abe didn't seem to enjoy the carol singing as much as usual, judging by how short a time he hung around.

"Probably couldn't stomach the Casey one being here, seeing as she is so uncooperative about the cottage," she thought. She had a cheek, really, turning up at all, knowing she'd refused his offer for the cottage, but then her sort were never backwards in coming forwards.

She ran her fingers over the huge polished dining room table that dominated the length of the room. In boarding school she'd always bragged about how big it was and how it was mahogany and must be worth a fortune.

Lil Casey had often polished it when she'd worked here.

"If she was alive she'd have thought it a great coup for the daughter to be in the same room as a guest as where her mother had worked as a domestic servant," she thought.

Lots of times Vera had been practising her piano pieces while Lil polished and polished until the table shone. If she didn't do it right she had to do it again after her mother inspected it.

"Elbow grease, girl! I've told you before."

And Lil had worked harder.

Vera had always hated having staff in the house. Yes, they cleaned the place and cooked, but she never relaxed until they were gone home and it was just the four of them left. Maimie Breen, the cook, had her nose in everything, but Vera's mother had always warned her staff that if she ever heard any detail of the Stephenson household repeated in the village they would be sacked immediately and not alone that there would be legal repercussions.

Still, someone had to work in a house the size of this and so many workmen to feed in the kitchen.

Lil hadn't been there that long, though. What age was she when she got that job in Dublin? Fifteen? Sixteen? Lil was a year younger than Vera. She'd known nothing about Lil leaving until she came home from boarding school one Easter holidays and she was gone.

"Did Mother sack her?" she'd asked Abe.

"Not that I know of," he said, but she sensed some discomfort. Her mother had been tight-lipped too.

"She found a position in Dublin," she said. "Full time work, so what would she stay around here for?"

Florrie never had anyone to help her in Knocklannon – why would she when she had nothing else to do? No children to rear, not like her. No, a few hens and helping out with the cattle and the odd bit of paperwork. She had the life of Reilly really.

Vera lifted the Aga hot plate lid now in the kitchen. She'd make herself a cup of tea. She opened a cake tin on the counter. A freshly-made coffee cake.

"If she made less of this sort of thing she mightn't be as plump," she said to herself at the same time as she cut herself a slice, while she waited for the kettle to boil.

How many times had she seen her mother stand at the cooker? She'd been a good cook, a good housekeeper. Her word was law. She'd been widowed young, just like her. Women like them had to be tough. It had been a bond between them in her mother's final years.

"You'll find strengths you didn't know you had," her mother told her. "And you'll be your own boss."

She was right. No deferring to anyone. There had been satisfaction in it.

Finger-stabbing the last crumbs of the cake on her plate, Vera Kemp's mind went back to the problem in hand – how to get rid of Hannah Casey.

What if she made her an offer herself or through a different auctioneer? It'd be worth a try. What woman like her couldn't be bought if the price was high enough? Everyone had their price. Would ten thousand over what Abe had offered swing it? Abe would pay her back, no bother, if she succeeded.

The thought of being the one to sort the problem gave her pleasure. Abe would owe her one. That'd be a good feeling.

Perhaps she would talk to her at the weekend when the carol singers were doing the pub rounds.

That's presuming that Beryl friend of hers wasn't with her. She's there a lot, Vera said to herself.

"Maybe they are a pair of . . . lesbians. It'd solve a lot of problems if they are," she thought, knowing her sons would be wasting their time then.

Carols! Hannah was tired of them.

"Why did I ever say I'd get involved in this?" she asked herself as she drove into the Corner Inn car park. The plan was to call to three pubs in the locality then finish up in the village. Hannah couldn't wait. She had never felt so miserable in her whole life but she would never give him – Abe Stephenson – the satisfaction of seeing that. It was six days since she had been in his house. His reaction still smarted.

She had seen shock in his eyes, then hatred, was it, when he had spotted her? It had affected her more than she let on to Beryl who had gone back to Waterford the following morning.

"Chin up," she said as she got into her car.

She had filled the cottage with sound, to take the emptiness out of it, switching on the radio upstairs, the CD player downstairs, even turning the television on with no sound so that at least she had the images of people in the room, even if they weren't real.

She had worked hard that day, scraping pink flaking paint off her bedroom walls. She would speak to handyman Peter Conway about treating those areas for damp or should she dry line the whole room? It would make the room smaller but would it be a plus if she was selling it?

Where had that thought come from? Was she weakening, wanting to escape from the locality now that she had continuing evidence of Abe Stephenson's aversion to her? She didn't even call him her father. He was "he" or "him" – Abe Stephenson. That was all. What was the point of the word anyway unless it encompassed the full meaning – parent, nurturer, protector, teacher – Abe Stephenson had been none of those things to her.

The mini-bus was already in the car park when she arrived. Shit! Was she late? No, thank God she wasn't the last one to arrive. Not that a few minutes would matter one way or another – the pubs wouldn't have filled up enough until at least nine-thirty, and they needed a good crowd to fill the buckets.

Peg Travers drove into the car park behind her. Hannah waited at her car while Peg parked so that the two of them could get on the minibus together.

"Jesus – it's windy – what possessed me to leave my warm fire on a night like this I'll never know."

Peg was pulling on her sheepskin gloves.

"Because you've got a big heart and you want to do your bit for the community," Hannah said.

"Yeah, that or I'm half cracked!" Peg was looking around the car park.

"Lady Kemp is here, I see. I didn't think she would be."

"Why?"

"Her brother Abe – where we were last Sunday – he and Florrie are gone away on a sudden holiday from what I hear. Not well, or so the story goes. I didn't think he looked great last Sunday myself – a bit flushed and that. Still, staying still for a few days'll go hard on him. He was never a great one for holidays unless it was to some cattle show or other. He'd travel for that all right – the two of them would. Vera is head bottle-washer, I'm sure, when they're away. That's why I'm surprised she's here."

Hannah tried to cover her interest.

"You think there's something more serious wrong with him?" she said, as casually as she could.

"There's the nurse coming out in you! Supposed to be the flu or him doing too much but, between you and me, I'd say it's his heart. His father died a lot younger than he did with it."

"Oh?"

Hannah felt weak as she got into the minibus behind Peg. Had she driven him over the edge? She tried not to think about it . . .

Roy Kemp put his hand up in greeting. His mother was in the seat behind. She gave a tight little smile.

"He can't be too bad if they're here," Hannah said to herself as she sat down.

She heard very little of Peg's prattle on the way to the town pubs. Though she had said to Beryl last Sunday that she didn't think Abe Stephenson was a well man, it was still a shock to find out that it could actually be the case and that heart problems ran in the family.

Had she triggered a "turn"?

She took out her mobile phone to text Beryl, angling it so Peg couldn't read what she was writing.

She wished she could talk to Beryl right now but that would have to wait. She couldn't trust the walls of ladies' toilets – not in a small place like this, where someone could put two and two together very quickly.

Vera Kemp seemed friendlier than before for some reason, asking her how she was and was she enjoying the carol singing and small talk like that.

"Use the hymn sheets if you have to," the rector was saying. "Better to look at them than fade in and out because you forget a verse."

"Have you all got your red scarves and Santa hats?"

There was a chorus of yeses.

"Right! Off we go, so!"

Hannah turned to Vera.

"Peg was telling me that your brother wasn't feeling the best."

Vera sniffed as she glanced at Peg, who was cracking some joke with another caroller.

"He's fine, thank you. Hardy as a snipe."

"That's great. I must have misheard."

When they reached the first country pub, the rector stood up at the front of the bus again.

"Right, all in single file as we walk in, ringing the bells. That'll get everyone's attention. Then we stand in the agreed positions and sing at least four carols – that should be enough. Are our collectors all here?"

"Yes."

"Hannah . . ."

Hannah turned as she felt the tug at her sleeve.

It was Vera again, actually smiling this time.

"Could we have a little chat later on when we get back to the Corner Inn?"

"Certainly . . . if you want . . ."

What was going on? What did Vera Kemp want to talk to her about?

For an instant, she thought Abe Stephenson had told his sister about her and now she was wanting to get to know her better . . .

"In my dreams!" she said to herself. Vera would be far from smiling if she knew . . .

Peg Travers was beside her now as they got off the bus.

"What did Lady K want?"

"I'm not sure."

"Keep your wits about you if she's asking for little chats. That one seldom does anything without a motive but, listen to me, I should be minding my own business."

"That's ok."

The bells were rung as they walked into the pub then there was a general cough as everyone cleared their throats before opening with *God Rest You Merry Gentlemen*.

Hannah was on automatic pilot in the first pub. She could hear the sound of her own voice but her mind was on Abe Stephenson and his being ill. What if her being around had sent him off his rocker?

As long as he was alive there was hope that he would have a change of heart and accept her. Maybe the shock of seeing her in his house was too much for him? Hannah's mind kept racing.

"Or maybe seeing me has upset him so much that he was considering admitting that I'm his daughter and he just got over-excited because of the emotional trauma of making that decision . . ."

Roy Kemp was behind her, his voice adding depth to the harmony.

She talked to him on the way to the second pub.

He told her he had booked the Voice Power course that was being held in Waterford.

"That's splendid. I'm really pleased for you. When do you start?"

"Eighth of January."

"That's great. I know someone who did it and it changed his life."

Hannah wondered should she mention that the courses were often held in the hotel that Beryl worked in. Best not! It might put him off thinking there'd be someone there he knew. Or make him want to go more . . . It was probably best to say nothing.

"Roy!"

It was Vera Kemp calling her son.

"We'd better hurry. Your mother is cracking the whip!"

"Wh-wh-what else is new?"

Peg was beside her again.

"I wonder is herself afraid you're going to sweep Roy off his feet! Can't you see it now – her as a future mother-in-law?"

"I don't think so."

Hannah changed the subject, irritated now by Peg. Roy was only feet away and Peg mightn't know it but her voice did carry.

"Only one pub left, thank goodness."

"Just as well. I'm knackered."

The Corner Inn was packed when they arrived back. Some of the faces she recognised – the shop owner Tom Carthy, handyman Peter Conway . . .

Leo Kemp was on a bar stool at the counter. He inclined his head in recognition when she glanced at him. At least he'd be on his best behaviour tonight with his mother there.

There was rowdy applause when they finished singing.

Several drinkers shouted "More! More!"

Leo Kemp had obviously been there a while for he sang loudly from his stool, lifting his arm and glass in a flourish as the final line was sung – *What a laugh it would have been if Daddy had only seen . . . Mammy kissing Santa Claus l-last night.*

Was it her he had winked at? She felt repulsed. Her own cousin! Still, he didn't know. To him she was just another piece of fluff, a new female in the area to try to score with.

How would she ever accept the likes of him as her cousin? She genuinely liked Roy but Leo – no thanks. She would keep as far away as possible from him.

Vera Kemp was now nodding at her from over her Britvic orange, signalling Hannah to come over to her table.

Vera pulled over an extra stool when she reached her.

"I'm not sorry all this carol-singing is over. It's all right for you young ones."

"Nonsense. You'd probably run rings around me," Hannah said. "All the farm work – keeps you fit, I'm sure."

"I don't know about that. Wouldn't be much different than nursing, I'd say. You'd be on your feet a lot with that too."

"Never a dull moment."

"You must be enjoying your rest from it all the same."

"I am – after twenty years it's good to get a break."

"Yes, still there's not many can afford to take a few months off work. Did you have to take a break?"

Hannah bristled as she watched Vera take a sip of her drink and wait. Cow!

"My mother died. I got compassionate leave. I just extended it a bit, that's all."

"Of course. Your mother passing away so quickly must have been a shock all right."

"You said you wanted a chat . . ."

Vera Kemp took another sip of her Britvic orange then pursed her lips.

"That's right."

Hannah saw Vera glance around as if she feared being overheard.

"I was wondering what your plans are . . ."

"My plans?"

"In relation to the cottage?"

"How do you mean?"

"Well, how long you intend staying in Drumcadden?"

"I don't think that's any of your business."

"No, of course it's not, of course, but you have a house in Waterford, I believe."

"Yes."

"Must be difficult going between two houses, though. Of course I know you don't have a mortgage to pay on the cottage. Must be nice to have inherited a bit of property like that. Gives you a lot of freedom."

"How do you mean?"

"Well, if you sold it you could have your pick of apartments in Spain, say. I believe that's all the rage now – holiday homes in Spain or Portugal or Croatia – isn't everyone doing it?"

"I don't know anyone."

"Or you could give up working altogether for a few years – tour the world."

"I travel enough in my holiday time."

"Of course you do, but if you're a bit of a home bird you could always buy a bigger house in Waterford. There's nothing like a bit of space, is there and why not before house prices go through the roof altogether? You could make a big profit in three years' time."

"Who said I was selling?"

"No one. Sure that's your own business. And you never know, with all the work you're doing on it the cottage'll be worth more."

"I'd better go back and join the others."

Vera Kemp took a piece of torn-up Corn Flakes box from her handbag and a pen.

"That's what the cottage might fetch – if the right buyer came along."

Hannah looked at what Vera Kemp had written. It was thousands more than what Abe Stephenson had offered her.

"You? You want to buy it?"

"Maybe. Maybe not. I'm a business woman, same as you. Why shouldn't I make an honest offer? I have the money. The cottage would make a good investment property, I could rent it out and you'd have financial security for a long time. I'm sure your mother would like it to go to someone local."

The nerve! Hannah could hardly bear to look at her.

"Are you wanting to buy this for yourself or for someone else?" Vera pretended surprise.

"For myself, of course."

Hannah stood up from the table, taking her drink with her. Vera was lucky she didn't get it over her head.

"I'm not selling, and next time, tell your brother to do his own dirty work."

"My brother has nothing to do with this."

"Really? Isn't it odd then that he's been trying to buy it too? Or get it for half nothing off my mother if he'd been able."

Hannah shoved the piece of cardboard back across the table.

"No thanks."

"You're a foolish girl."

"I'll take my chances."

"Well, if you ever change your mind, you know where I am. I'm sure if your grandfather or your mother were still alive they'd see the sense of it. They were always very practical people – they weren't the sort to get caught up in their emotions . . ."

"Excuse me!"

Hannah left her drink down on another table and went to the Ladies.

She stared at herself in the mirror for several minutes. The nerve of the woman! Peg Travers was right. Vera Kemp was the sort to have a reason for everything she did. Why did she want to buy the cottage, just like her brother did? Investment property, my eye!

Hannah had a serious think – the land the cottage was on joined Stephenson's land. Some of Vera's land backed onto it, according to Peg . . . What were they planning? Something fishy was going on here if there was so much interest in her small cottage . . . What was it? Some kind of housing development?

"Close to the village . . ." Land around villages was bringing a fortune now from developers.

But why did they want the cottage? She didn't know exactly but her instinct told her she was on the right track. Maybe she should pay a visit to the county council planning office . . . If there was an application in for outline permission she would know about it.

Not that that was going to make her sell. It would make her dig her heels in even more. It would hurt Mr Abe Stephenson in the pocket if he couldn't do what he wanted to do. The thought pleased her. Hadn't she been hurt long enough and in worse ways than that? Now, at last the boot was on the other foot. When she came out of the Ladies she glanced at the bar. Vera was there talking to Leo. Talking at him would be more precise. He looked irritated. Meeting his gaze she looked away as she returned to Peg.

Hannah suddenly felt exhausted. It had been an emotionally draining day. All she wanted right now was to be back in the cottage in her own bed.

"Not clearing out already, are you? I thought you'd be a party animal."

It was Leo Kemp. He was beside her now as she put the key in her car door lock.

"It's been a long day."

"Fair enough, but if you fancy being rocked to sleep I'm your man."

"You're drunk."

He was holding the door, preventing her from getting into the car.

"A few drinks – what harm is there in that? Unless you're one of those holy Marys who keeps a padlock on her knickers."

"Let go of my door – now!"

"Ouch! You're a real vixen when you're riled, aren't you?"

"Get out of my way!"

Suddenly Roy was there shouting at Leo.

"Le-leave her alone!"

"Piss off!"

"Mam is l-looking for you. She's coming out . . ."

As Leo loosened his hold on the door Hannah got into the car and slammed it, her legs shaking as she put the key into the ignition.

Leo was stepping backwards unsteadily.

"Goodnight Sweetheart," she heard him sing as she drove away.

She was grateful to Roy for coming out when he did.

She was sorry she hadn't kneed Leo in the groin, like she'd done once on that holiday in Greece when one of the natives had come on to her too strongly.

Leaving the car park, she could see Vera Kemp getting into her car, a face on her that would stop a clock. Had she seen Leo follow her out? Then Roy? God knows what she was thinking.

In bed at the cottage now she phoned Beryl.

"What's happened?"

Beryl sounded drowsy but concerned.

Hannah told her friend about the night's events, starting with the news that Abe Stephenson wasn't well and about Vera wanting to buy the cottage.

"Maybe he's not really on holiday," Hannah surmised to her friend. "Maybe he's having tests somewhere and just doesn't want anyone to know."

"Could be. Hannah, are you ok?"

"I don't know. So much of this feels weird. Part of me hates him, part of me wants to love him, if he'd just give me a bit of encouragement."

"You're bound to feel mixed up."

"Screwed up, more like. A father who won't acknowledge me, an aunt who hasn't a clue and a gobshite cousin who keeps coming on to me . . ."

"It'll all come out sooner or later."

"Yeah but when? Do I just go up to Vera Kemp and say 'you don't know this but I'm actually your niece, yeah, a blood relation' or 'You can't come on to me, letch, because I'm your cousin' – God!"

"Just take it easy – promise me – don't force stuff . . ."

"No – just let it do my head in! I'm so addled I can't even think about Christmas plans."

"Do you want me to have Christmas here instead? I don't mind cooking. Rita and Ivy and Noel could just as easily come here as the cottage."

"No, I'll have it here. I've said I will and why shouldn't I? This is my house. No one is going to run me out."

"Hannah . . ."

"What?"

"You will be careful, won't you? Sometimes . . ."

"Sometimes what?"

She heard the sharpness in her own voice and softened it.

"What?"

"I'm just saying – sometimes you . . ."

"Sometimes I what? Go on – spit it out!"

"Sometimes you go a bit bull-headed at things."

"I do not! The truth has to come out some day, doesn't it, and right now I'm just so sick of staying quiet."

"I know that and I'm not trying to get at you . . . Why don't I come down tomorrow? I'll be off Monday and we can talk then. And try not to worry . . ."

"Easier said than done. God, my head is spinning with it all. You know what? It'd probably suit him if I ended up in the mental. Then he'd really be able to say I was making it up, that no one should believe a word I'm saying."

"You're not going to crack up!"

"Not if I can help it. I wouldn't give him the satisfaction. Look, go back to sleep and stop worrying. This is stuff I'll have to sort out myself. What happens, happens."

There was silence on the other end of the line for a few seconds.

"Hannah . . . you will mind yourself, won't you?"

Getting out of the house for a couple of hours to do the shopping in town would be a relief, Florrie thought. Every since she and Abe had come back from holidays he had been unbearable to live with.

On the holiday even, he had been sulky, withdrawn, taking no real joy in anything.

As crooked as the hind leg of a dog would have been her father's description . . .

"Are you in pain – is that it? Do you need a doctor and you just won't admit it?" she'd said to him.

He had just told her to stop annoying him and in the end she had. What point was there in trying to get him to do anything he didn't want to do? She had to stop trying to control things. She had learned that in counselling. She didn't have to humour him either. She had learned a lot about people pleasing in counselling too and how she'd done too much of it all of her life.

She had tried to enjoy herself on holiday in Cork in spite of him, going for walks, looking round the shops, reading . . . Live in the moment – that was the way to do it. Stop looking back and don't look too far forward – there was no point. And stop trying to change people. You won't succeed. The only one you can change is yourself.

Now they were eight days back and it was as if they hadn't had a holiday at all.

That hadn't stopped her telling everyone that, yes, they'd enjoyed themselves, yes, the hotel was fine and, yes, the weather hadn't been too bad. At least nothing had gone wrong on the farm while they'd been away. She'd checked on Knocklannon Gem the minute she got back to the yard. Although she had a while to go yet before calving, she was anxious that she was ok but she needn't have worried – Roy had done well looking after the pedigrees. And she had appreciated the regular texts from him.

Abe had been on the phone to Leo several times. It had been the only time Florrie had seen her husband animated – the rest of the time he seemed to be just putting in time.

There was little sign that anyone stayed in the house, thank goodness.

Vera had stripped the spare beds on the last day and put the linen in the wash basket in the utility room.

"I didn't switch the machine on because I didn't know how. Mine doesn't have all those fancy digital displays."

That was Vera putting the boot in.

"Will you be here today?"

It was Abe, shouting her from the kitchen.

"I'm going to the centre. Then I've shopping to do. Why?"

"The ID card for that heifer that's going to the factory – I can't find it."

He was fussing in the office.

"It should be with the others," she said. Why did men always say they couldn't find things? It's a code for "I couldn't be bothered looking. You find it for me since you've nothing better to do".

"There." Today she wouldn't fight about it. There was no point. Breathe it out . . . She handed him the card.

He didn't say thank you, just enquired what time she'd be back.

"Four or so. I've the groceries to get for Christmas Day. Vera and the lads are coming over for dinner. There's no sign of an invitation in the other direction anyway."

Not that Florrie would want to go to Vera's for Christmas dinner – packet gravy and dry turkey, no thanks very much.

Florrie left the office to go write her shopping list. Being organized – that's all it took to ensure everything went well on Christmas Day. She never really tasted Christmas dinner, though. Not once in all the years she'd been married. Each year there were guests. First Abe's mother who would overlook all the good things about a meal that she didn't have to lift a hand for and home in on something small.

"You must like your carrots on the hard side . . ."

And back then Florrie would have resolved to cook the vegetables more the next year.

Now she wished she'd said that, yes, she did like her carrots al dente – they were also better for you that way. She'd do a lot of things differently in hindsight.

Vera's husband, Harry, had died before her mother-in-law, so every Christmas since then Vera and the boys had come to Knocklannon for Christmas dinner. Not once had Vera suggested they go there instead. It was as if it was her due each year – a Christmas dinner in the place where she was reared.

Florrie wished she didn't have to go to the day care centre today, as she had so much to do, but she would make time. She had Maimie Breen's reminiscences to record, after all, if Maimie was in form for saying anything. With a bit of luck she'd be lucid today, but you never could tell with Maimie. One minute she'd talk sensibly about what sort of day it was, the next she'd be shouting "Dan, let out the calves!"

Dan was her brother that she had lived with on a few acres, Maimie supplementing their meagre income by working as a domestic in places like Stephenson's.

"With a bit of luck, I'll get it done," Florrie said to herself.

After the centre she would do the grocery shopping.

She double-checked that she had bought presents for everybody she wanted to buy presents for.

Luckily she had started early. Now they were all labelled and packaged under the tree. She had been very practical with Abe's present – he needed a new coat, so she got him a voucher for a shop in town.

She would persuade him to go with her the first day of the sales. It wouldn't be too difficult. While Abe mightn't spend a lot on himself other than diesel for the jeep and tobacco for his pipe, he had always bought quality when it came to clothes, even workwear. She couldn't deny that he looked well when he was dressed up – even still. Presence – that's what he had, being so tall as well. People still looked up when he entered a room. And his measurements hadn't changed that much over the years.

"Not like me, with clothes three different sizes in the wardrobe."

Food, she was too fond of it . . . Every so often she went on a slimming drive and she'd lose a bit.

Once she had lost a lot of weight, but it had only taken a comment from Abe about her breasts now being flaccid to make her start eating again. Her breasts were a major part of his attraction to her – she knew that. She'd prefer to think it was her enquiring mind or her personality that he'd been drawn to, but she was more of a realist than that.

Getting into the car now she felt foolish as she remembered suspecting that Abe was having a relationship with another woman. She'd been stupid to even think it. He wasn't feeling well and this building business wasn't going to his liking – that's why he was so disconnected and grumpy.

Yes, she had everything – her recorder, extra batteries and a notebook for the centre and her bags and list for the shopping later on.

"Roll on half past four," Peg Travers said as Florrie hung up her coat.

"They're all wound up with Santy coming this morning. Mattie Dillon got a copy of Dolly Parton's new CD and Dec Hannigan went into a sulk because he only got one of Charlie Landsborough's and he can't stand him. Once an adult, twice a child – nothing surer than that! How's Abe?"

"Fine, thanks."

"You enjoyed the holiday?"

"Yes, thank you. It's always nice to get away for a while. How is Maimie today?"

"A bit erratic. She was humming *Rudolph the Red Nosed Reindeer* a bit earlier on, so you might get something out of her."

"With a bit of luck. It'd be great to get all the interviews finished."

"I'll tell her you're here."

Maimie was in her wheelchair near the top of the room. "She ate most of her dinner," Peg was saying, as she tucked the blanket round Maimie's legs. "You're a good girl, aren't you, Maimie?"

"Girl?" Maimie looked confused.

"You know Florrie Stephenson, Maimie? Florrie wants to talk to you for the book. Remember everyone at the centre telling their stories . . ."

"Book," Maimie said.

"That's right," Florrie said, pushing Maimie's wheelchair towards the retreat room. She'd try for half an hour – maybe all she'd come out with would be gibberish, but she had to try.

When Maimie was settled close to the guarded fire and the door had been closed on the noise and confusion, Florrie switched on the CD player. *Favourite Melodies of Ireland.* Maybe it'd work like the last time when she'd remembered the old woman poem. With a bit of luck she'd hit on some tune that Maimie liked and it would trigger some memories.

Florrie took a bunch of old magazines from her bag. Sometimes photographs in magazines could be triggers too.

"Did you dress like the woman in the photograph when you were younger, Maimie?" she'd ask, and the person would respond with what they had worn.

"Do you like the music, Maimie?" she asked after another while.

"Yes."

"It's Slievenamon. That's the name of a mountain in Tipperary. Tell me about where you live Maimie? Are there mountains – rivers, or is it flat?"

"Hills," Maimie said. "Hill of Croagh and Rathbrandon between us and the world. Us and the world."

"Was that something your mother or father used to say?"

Maimie seemed far away, and Florrie waited for an answer.

"Father."

Florrie was delighted. It would make a good quote for the book.

Florrie had to take it very slowly – what about school, what had that been like . . .?

"The master has a big stick," she said, suddenly looking afraid. Florrie stroked her hand and tried to bring the conversation back to more pleasant things.

"Had you lots of friends in school, Maimie? Who was your best friend, can you tell me?"

Eventually Maimie mentioned a couple of names. Florrie waved at two of the other patients who were gazing in through the glass panels of the retreat room. Hopefully they wouldn't decide to come in and interrupt. Great, Peg was guiding them away to play bingo for the last half hour.

"Maimie – are you awake?"

Maimie's eyes opened again.

"What's your name?" she said.

"Florrie – Florrie Stephenson."

"Stephenson . . ."

"Yes, you used to work in Knocklannon, didn't you? When you were younger? Did you cook mostly? What kinds of dishes did you like cooking best?"

Maimie suddenly clutched her sleeve.

"Can't tell . . ." she said, now agitated. "Mistress wouldn't like it."

Mistress? Was she talking about Abe's mother? Her mother-in-law? What was Maimie talking about?

A cold shiver ran down Florrie's back.

"What would the mistress not like, Maimie?"

Maimie clutched the sleeve of Florrie's jumper again.

"Lil?"

"No, Maimie, I'm Florrie. Florrie Stephenson, married to Abe, Abraham Stephenson. You'd have known him when he was young when you worked in Knocklannon."

"Young? Lil?"

"No, I'm . . ."

Maimie now put her finger to her lips, still grabbing Florrie's arm.

"Ssh, you mustn't tell. About them in the henhouse . . ."

Florrie sat stock still.

"What about the henhouse, Maimie?"

"You know! Me and the mistress going to clean out the henhouse and there yous were – him chewing the face off you and one hand up your dress and the mistress roaring at yous . . ."

Maimie Breen was now covering her ears and looking fearful.

"Don't tell, she said, not a word, she said!"

Florrie felt numb. Was it Abe's father that Maimie was talking about who'd been with Lil?

"Who was *he*, Maimie?"

Maimie laughed now.

"Cock of the hoop – Master Abraham. I told ye to stay away from him, but ye couldn't, could ye? Out where he was every chance you got . . ."

Florrie felt ill.

"Was it Lil that the young master was with? In the henhouse?"

"Yes. Back to school next day with a big red face on him after all the shouting . . ."

Florrie felt sick. She switched off the recorder, glad her back was to the glass panels. Her hands were shaking.

Abe and Lil . . . She tried to stay calm. Maimie said Abe went back to school. He was a teenager then. She tried not to get upset. Teenagers do things, hormones bubble up. And Lil had obviously fancied him or she wouldn't have kept following him round like Maimie said. What age would she have been? The same age or thereabouts. She could understand her mother-in-law being upset, shocked, but these things happened when children were growing up and had no sense.

"We'll leave it there for today, Maimie," she heard herself say. Go through the motions. Stay calm, say goodbye to everyone, thankfully no one else had heard it. Anyway, it was no big deal.

"Everything ok?"

It was Peg at the door.

"Yes. Yes thanks. All done."

"Did she tell you anything of any use?"

Florrie swallowed, busying herself with putting her things in a bag.

"Yes. A few bits."

"Great. Well done, Maimie! You're a great girl."

"Girl," Maimie repeated.

"Now we have to get you ready to go home. The big bus will be coming."

"Big bus."

"I'll head off," Florrie heard herself say. "I've shopping to do."

"Of course. You have a good Christmas, won't you? And I'll see you back here on the seventh of January, please God, if not before."

"Yes. And happy Christmas to you too."

In the car, Florrie sat still for several minutes, her feet unable to move. Why was she so upset? For God's sake, Abe was a teenager at the time. What did it matter that he had been caught kissing one of the servants? These things happen . . .

Maimie had been told not to tell, though – she seemed afraid somehow. Why was that – had something worse happened? Was it that they'd had full sex?

No, she had to stop thinking about it. It was unfortunate that she had heard it, but it was best to scrub it out of her mind. It was in the past and it had nothing to do with her.

As soon as she reached town she wished she hadn't gone, though. Unable to find a parking space she drove to St Aidan's Crescent Shopping Centre instead. She would get a cup of strong tea in the little café in the supermarket after she'd finished the shopping.

Maybe buy a magazine in the newsagents too – anything to get her mind back on what she was supposed to be doing.

She took a few deep breaths. She tried to isolate exactly what she was feeling. Jealousy?

"That's stupid – everyone has a past. Everyone was young one time. She'd been young herself, though her opportunities for associating with boys were limited. There were no young men working on the farm full-time and at busy times when there were her mother gave her no opportunity for fraternising.

Still, somehow Maimie's talk had hurt. Lil Casey was a good-looking girl in her day – someone had told her that. Not the bloated, unwell looking woman she had shaken hands with at Jim's funeral. She had kind eyes — she remembered that. Abe had shaken hands with her to sympathise too. What had been going on in his head at the time, she wondered? Lil's head?

Chestnut purée – that's what she needed. Now she was searching the shelves. She always made a special chocolate log, Buche de Noel. An aunt of hers had given her the recipe years before and it had stuck with her – chocolate Swiss roll with cream and chestnut purée, shaped and decorated like a log.

"This'll put the inches on all right," Vera always said before helping herself to some nevertheless. If she'd paid her a direct compliment it would have been better.

Florrie felt flustered as she tried to find her list again. Where had she put it? Right now she wished she hadn't come to town at all – or gone to the centre.

"No, don't be silly, you've just been listening to the ramblings of a woman with early dementia . . ."

What she said mightn't be true at all . . . Put it out of her mind – that's what she had to do . . .

Queuing at the checkout took ages. Florrie didn't know if she had all the things she needed. Right this minute she didn't care.

"Florrie! Mrs Stephenson!"

She turned to see Hannah Casey smiling at her.

"Hannah! Hello."

Hannah had a trolley with a lot of alcohol in it.

"Just stocking up for Christmas."

"I have some to get too. I usually get the table wine. Abe buys the rest himself."

"Right. Are you in a rush or do you have time for a cup of tea?"

"No. Well, yes . . . if you're having one . . ."

"I'm going to treat you – to thank you for the gift that time you called and the carols."

Florrie felt a bit jittery as they parked their trolleys near their table at the door of the café. Hannah was Lil Casey's daughter. At least Lil had had some man in her life in Dublin. No one she could depend on, though, if Hannah had to be reared in an orphanage. Men! They always left women holding the baby.

"Oasis in the midst of chaos," Hannah said, as she put down the tray with two cappuccinos and two scones on it.

"Yes."

"Are you all right – you look a little . . . stressed?"

Florrie forced herself to make eye contact with her neighbour.

"I'm grand. It's all this Christmas shopping – it has me worn out. It's always a relief when Christmas is over, really."

"Yes."

"It won't be easy for you either – without your mother."

Hannah was spooning froth off her coffee.

"I never saw much of her at Christmas, actually – she usually went to a friend of hers for Christmas Day. We'd meet up over the New Year usually."

"She didn't go to stay with you – or you with her?"

"No. It wasn't that sort of a relationship. Bit strange, I know . . ."

"Relationships are never perfect, are they? My mother and I didn't always see eye to eye either."

Maimie Breen's words suddenly came back to Florrie and she felt her face flush.

"You ok?"

"Yes."

There was concern in Hannah Casey's eyes. Had Hannah been a wild teenager like her mother, Florrie wondered.

"Your mother used to work in Knocklannon – I remember you telling me that. Before my time."

"Yes."

Why did her coffee companion suddenly look uneasy? It was fleeting, but there.

"I'm sure she was a hard worker. Did she ever mention it – where she worked?"

"No. She wasn't exactly forthcoming with information."

"She can't have been very old when she went to Dublin."

"Fifteen or sixteen, I think. She didn't talk much about it – about anything, really. That's probably where I envied school friends the most – the way they knew this little story about this aunt and that aunt and how they could trace their family back for generations. My mind was just full of blanks."

"She never mentioned Knocklannon at all?"

Florrie struggled to keep the tremor out of her voice as she asked.

"No."

"I'm sure my mother-in-law worked her hard."

"What was she like – your mother-in-law – Mrs Stephenson senior?"

Florrie tried to laugh.

"Tough going. Oh, she worked hard, but she didn't suffer fools gladly, but then I suppose she had to be tough. She was widowed relatively young. Had to finish rearing the children by herself."

"What age was he – your husband – when his father died?"

"Thirteen, I think."

"Did you get on well with her? It must have been difficult moving in with someone like that who was used to ruling the roost."

"That was the way it was then. There was no building bungalows and having your own space then. You moved in – that was it – whatever the personal cost."

"Would you do it over again?"

"Hard to say. I was the way I was at the time – quiet, shy, too eager to please. I remember being so worried that the first loaf of bread I made in the house wouldn't turn out right. It was like every single thing I did was being tested for a long time – whether it was making dinners or making beds."

"I'm glad I haven't got married so. I'd be no good at that sort of thing."

"And the world has changed, thank God. Be yourself – that's what everyone should have the courage to be. Don't care what people think."

Florrie saw Hannah Casey give a wry smile.

"I was born too early for that. My life would've been a lot different if my mother hadn't cared what people thought."

"Probably."

Florrie suddenly felt shock run through her. What if Lil had been packed off to Dublin because she was pregnant? That's why Maimie could have been sworn to silence.

"Are you feeling ok?"

There was concern again in Hannah Casey's face.

"I'm fine. A bit overtired. I always find Christmases hard, to be honest, but I'll be grand. I should be going," Florrie said, fussing with her handbag.

No, Hannah would be forty next birthday, so she was born years after the henhouse incident. If there had been a pregnancy that child would be in his or her fifties now, wouldn't he or she? Lord, her mind was running away with her now . . .

"I probably should be going myself. Beryl is coming down tomorrow. I'm cooking Christmas dinner in Drumcadden. Some of the others from Royle are coming too."

"That's great. You'll enjoy that. Help to keep your mind off things."

They parted company in the car park.

"Happy Christmas, then."

"You too."

Florrie felt as if Hannah was going to hug her for a minute then drew back.

"Right. I'll see you then."

"Yes."

Hannah Casey was still standing there.

"Are you sure you're ok?"

"Yes. Yes, thank you."

"You do know you'd have been a great mother, don't you?" she said.

Florrie felt a lump rise in her throat.

"Thank you."

After driving half a mile down the road she drove into a housing estate she didn't know and stopped the car. What was she crying for? Lost love? Never known children? For her husband's boyhood intimacy with someone else? What had gotten into her? It was half past four. She had told Abe that she'd be back by four.

"Get a grip," she said to herself.

Best to put all the Maimie talk out of her mind. Abe didn't care for Lil. He hadn't even gone to her funeral. Florrie tried to remember exactly when Lil had been buried? The middle of October – wasn't it the 13th Hannah had said? 13th October – wasn't that the day she'd gone to Kilkenny with the centre? She felt sick again.

"I was away all day . . . He could have been at the funeral for all I know."

"You're becoming neurotic," she said to herself, switching on the ignition. No, her mind wouldn't go there. Lil Casey had moved out of the area years ago. She'd had a child with someone in Dublin when she was nearly thirty years of age. It had nothing to do with her. Now she was dead. What threat could a dead woman be? And what was the point in letting what a woman not right in her head had said get to her?

Taking several deep breaths, Florrie let off the handbrake, turned around and headed home.

"Why would she ask all those questions if she doesn't suspect something? She was tense – I'm telling you! And sad-looking," Hannah said to Beryl as they peeled potatoes on Christmas Eve in the cottage at Drumcadden.

"I don't know. Who knows what goes on in someone's mind?"

"She asked if Mam had ever talked about working in Knocklannon."

"What did you tell her?"

"What could I tell her? What did my mother ever say about back here? I was sitting there saying, no, she never said anything, and all the time wondering if the next thing she was going to ask was 'Is my husband your father?'"

Hannah took another gulp of her red wine.

"It'll be all gone for tomorrow if you keep knocking it back like that."

Hannah drank some more.

"It's Christmas."

"What if she'd asked you straight out? What would you have said?"

"I don't know . . . told her – what choice would I have had? She'd have known by my face anyway. What good would lying to her do? She'd only think less of me for it when the truth does come out."

"You want her to like you, don't you?" Beryl said, running another potato under the tap.

"I suppose so. I liked her from the start. I don't know – we just clicked somehow."

"Are you sure you're not thinking of her as some kind of mother substitute?"

"What?"

"Maybe not mother substitute as such but . . ."

"I like her – so what?"

"And talking to her gives you some kind of access to him . . ."

"No, Miss Amateur Psychologist, I'm not using her!"

"Sometimes we do things for a mixture of reasons."

"I only had a cup of coffee with her, for God's sake. Why shouldn't I?"

"Who suggested it?"

"I did. What about it?"

"I'm not criticizing you."

"Sounds like it to me."

"I'm not. God! You're so defensive!"

Hannah was silent as she topped and tailed the carrots. There would be four for dinner tomorrow – her and Beryl, Rita and Noel – who were reared in Royle.

Neither of them were married and they usually met up with other "siblings" on bank holidays and festive seasons.

"I know it's going to come out sooner or later," Beryl was saying. "You'll just need to be strong for when it does happen."

"I will be, don't worry!"

Hannah left the carrots, took her glass and the wine bottle to sit on the couch.

Beryl joined her.

"Have you thought about how you'll feel when it is out in the open?"

Hannah shrugged her shoulders.

"Relief . . . Terror . . . Who knows, but anything has to be better than this limbo."

"Is that why you're drinking so much?"

"Jesus, will you drop it? I can drink if I want!"

" Ok . . . Ok . . ."

Hannah put one leg up under her on the sofa.

"I went to Dean's Grange yesterday."

"You never said . . ."

"I wanted to put a wreath on her grave for Christmas . . ."

"That's nice."

"I couldn't even find the grave! I thought I remembered where it was, but I didn't – I was rows out. Eventually I had to go to the office and ask – how bad is that? I couldn't even remember!"

"It's a big cemetery."

"The funeral flowers were dead – it looked awful."

"At least you put fresh ones on."

"I have dreams about her, you know, where I'm shouting and screeching at her and she's on her death bed and I'm shaking her and cursing her for not telling me who my father was years ago and I'm telling her I hate her . . ."

"It's anger – that's all . . . Who knows – maybe things'll work out ok."

"Who knows is right! He could go to his grave denying me. You didn't see him that day on the mountain . . ."

"Maybe he was in shock. Maybe when he's had time to think about it . . ."

Hannah held up her glass to salute the air.

"To Beryl. The optimist!"

"I'm only trying to help . . . You're imagining the worst."

Hannah wrapped her arms around her knees.

"Because that way you get ready for the worst, see? Every little good thing that happens after that then is a bonus."

"Maybe. Anyway, it's Christmas Eve. Rita and Noel will be here tomorrow, so promise you won't let all this spoil Christmas for us. You've done marvels with this place. Why not try to enjoy it – there's lots of people'd give their right arm for what you have."

"That's me told. Yeah, I know, I do have a lot to be thankful for. God, I sound like Nanna now."

Hannah was glad when they decided to call it a night. The vegetables were all ready and the stuffing made. All that would have to be done in the morning was to put the turkey in the oven.

"Good night."

Hannah was glad Beryl had a room to herself this time. Peter, the handyman, had dry lined what was her grandfather's room. It had taken three days, but Hannah was delighted with the finished product – new bed and curtains, walls painted white and the wooden floor sanded and varnished.

At least Beryl wouldn't know how badly she was sleeping. How many times had she woken last night? Four? Five? More? After meeting Florrie her mind had been working overtime.

"I'm getting too wound up about all this," she said to herself.

The visit to the County Council planning office a few days before had revealed nothing about any planning application either. So much for the theory that Abe Stephenson and his sister were both up to something . . .

When she thought about it Leo had, in his own way, tried to persuade her out of it as well, talking about the damp.

Still, no application . . . Maybe they all just wanted her out. Maybe there was gold under the foundation, or they were just all land-grabbers and a cottage adjoining their land was just another asset to acquire.

Hannah thought of Florrie and the stressed look on her face at the supermarket. Was Beryl right? That she was "courting" Florrie as a way of getting information about her father? Was that what she was doing – like that time in secondary school where she had deliberately made friends with Gladys Stotesbury because she had a brother in fourth year that she fancied? So what if she did? Sometimes you had to go after what you wanted in this life, didn't you? No one else was going to get it for you.

"What's it going to do to her to know that her husband was having it off with someone else while they were married?"

Hannah took out the standby bottle of wine she had in the locker, handling it gently so that Beryl wouldn't hear her in the next room. She took two gulps of it before putting it back.

Lord! What was she coming to – she had seldom drunk much before Nanna died. Nanna didn't approve of drinking or smoking. Then once Nanna died it was like she didn't have to pretend to be something she wasn't. She could drink if she wanted to. In the last two years it had been a de-stressor.

She'd come off a week of night duty and drink herself silly. It didn't seem wrong. Lots of nurses did it – worked hard, played hard. They needed it after that kind of stress – people dying or near dying all the time.

"You're great," relatives of patients would say to her. "You stay so calm."

What would they have said if they'd seen her after her last shift knocking back double vodkas as fast as she could and dancing on top of a table because she was too drunk to know what she was doing?

In the past year or so she'd started buying more drink to bring home. The first time she did that still loomed large in her mind. She'd nearly lost it on the ward that day, overtired, overstretched and a patient's relative being obnoxious and demanding. She knew she'd come close to hitting her. Only a door banging had made her pull back . . .

Hannah lay back in bed, trying to stop herself thinking. She had a tough streak in her, even if she didn't like admitting it. Did she get it from her father? Sometimes she could be bossy and short-tempered but it was over quickly, wasn't it? What if anger built up to such an extent that it exploded some day, though, with serious consequences? Maybe she needed counselling to help her make sense of all this and of herself. Beryl was as good as hinting at it.

No – she was ok . . .

Going to switch off her bedside lamp, she saw the church times list that the rector had given her at one of the carol singing events.

She looked at the times of the services for Rathbrandon church on Christmas Day. 9.30 a.m. Holy Communion.

Would she go?

It was Abe Stephenson's parish church. He would surely be there along with his wife and the Kemps. Most people made an effort to go to church on Christmas Day, even if they didn't go other days.

"Once a year Christians" Nanna used to call them.

Why shouldn't she go to church in the morning? She felt scared yet excited at the thought of it.

Turning off the light Hannah closed her eyes. She would decide in the morning – that's if she slept at all.

The clock said 8.15. Hannah sank back into her pillow. She had woken several times in the night from bad dreams, good dreams, dreams that left her anxious and wanting to wake up. What was the worst one? Florrie Stephenson calling her the spawn of the devil, throwing groceries at her in the supermarket car park and ramming her with her trolley . . .

Hannah pushed back the bedclothes and her feet found her slippers. She moved about as quietly as possible. Beryl was very tired. She had worked seven days on the trot before driving to Drumcadden after finishing work in the hotel at noon. She wouldn't wake her if she could help it.

She would go to church. Anything was better than this vacuum . . . Why should she stay away from church on Christmas Day just to convenience him?

After taking several deep breaths to ease the fear in her chest, she scribbled a note for Beryl then drank some orange juice. Why had she drunk so much wine last night? Checking her image in the bathroom mirror she thought she looked tired and drawn but makeup would cover up most of it.

She put on her red coat over her jeans and a black jumper. He wouldn't be able to miss her in the church . . .

So much for a white Christmas! Outside the air was cold and damp.

There were at least twenty cars parked on either side of the laneway that led down to Rathbrandon parish church.

She said hello to other parishioners as she walked down to the gate. Instinctively she looked toward the Stephenson graves that she had found when she first came to Drumcadden.

She swallowed hard – Abe Stephenson and his wife were putting holly wreaths on them.

"At least he remembers his dead," she said to herself, walking straight into the church and accepting the hymnal and prayer book handed to her by the churchwarden.

Where would she sit? Towards the back?

Roy Kemp was already in a seat further up. Where was Leo? She doubted if he went very often. Vera looked away after glancing down at her. Roy smiled when he looked round.

Now she saw Abe Stephenson and Florrie walk up the aisle, Florrie heading for the organ. He walked up to their pew on the left side of the church without looking round.

"Stephensons have probably sat in that same seat for generations. Maybe even owned it," she said to herself.

Did Florrie look paler than usual? Maybe she was just cold . . .

"To begin our service of worship on this Christmas Day, we will sing our first hymn . . . *The holly and the ivy . . .*"

There was a clatter as everyone got to their feet.

They were singing the final verse when Hannah felt someone stand into the pew beside her. Rough hands flicked through a hymn book. Hannah's nostrils twitched. What was the smell? Cow dung? Sheep shit? She could see a spatter on the back of the man's hands. God – could whoever he was not wash himself before coming to church?

She glanced sideways as the hymn ended and she sat down. It was Leo Kemp. He winked at her. His wink repulsed her. Why did he have to sit beside her? With only about sixty people in the church there was lots of room elsewhere.

She could see Vera Kemp turn and scan the congregation to see who the newcomer was. She didn't look best pleased.

"*Almighty God . . .from whom no secrets are hidden . . .*"

Hannah tried to concentrate on the words. What was her father thinking as the clergyman read those words? How could he pretend to be a pillar of the parish when all the time he was denying his own flesh and blood?

Her heart began to pound when the clergyman summoned them to the altar for communion. *Draw near with faith.*

Abe and Florrie Stephenson were among the first to receive, being at the top of the church.

She watched them from her seat, looking dignified, reverential. It shocked her that she was impressed by the look of him – physically he was still handsome. Bearing, that's what he had.

When it came to the turn of those in the seats near her, she stood up to go up for communion. Leo, beside her, stood up too, standing back to let her and the two other people in the pew walk up ahead of him. At least he had some manners. She didn't look sideways as she approached the altar.

The wine tasted like paint stripper. Where did they get the stuff? *Receive the body and blood of Christ . . .*

Getting up from the communion rails, she turned to walk back down the aisle looking straight ahead.

Was he looking at her? She felt scared again. No, if he was, so be it . . . She had as much right to be here as he had, didn't she?

The next hymn was the collection one. She heard Florrie fumble over a few notes, but she got over it.

Christmas must be difficult for her at the best of times . . . Today she seemed pale and distracted as she sat at the organ.

The rector was full of good cheer as he shook hands with each member of the congregation as they left the church.

"Hannah – I thought I could hear a good voice. A very happy Christmas."

"The same to you."

Leo was behind her as she stepped out of the church.

"I didn't know you dug with this foot . . ."

"Well, life is full of surprises."

"Hello, Hannah."

It was a couple that had been carol singers – the Malones – greeting her. Hannah tried to make small talk with them, keeping one eye on the door at the same time.

Leo had stood to one side and was now lighting up a cigarette.

Eventually Florrie Stephenson emerged from the doorway, carrying her music bag. He was following behind, talking to another parishioner as he walked.

Hannah stood on the gravel near the door.

He looked straight past her.

Florrie was pale but friendly.

"Happy Christmas, Hannah."

"And to you."

Abe had moved away to talk to Leo. Hannah felt hurt but what was she expecting – that just because it was Christmas Day he would throw his arms around her and shout "This is my beloved daughter!" at the top of his voice. Dream on . . .

Florrie seemed uneasy as she stopped to speak to her.

"Hannah, you know the day of your mother's burial – did many locals go?"

"Not that I know of. No one made themselves known to me if there was. Why do you ask?"

"No reason, really. I was just thinking that it's sad more didn't go, really, but I suppose with her being out of the area so long . . ."

"Yes. Are you ok?"

"Yes, thank you. Don't mind me. I ramble on sometimes. I hope you have a good Christmas."

"You too. Fingers crossed there won't be any rodents around."

"Sorry . . .?"

Hannah explained about the rats infesting the place and how she'd had to get rid of them.

"It's as if someone wants me out," she said. "But sure, they're gone now and there's no point on dwelling on it."

Florrie looked shocked and even more uneasy now.

"That's dreadful. Yes, I hope that's an end of it. No one should endure that type of harassment."

Hannah saw Abe pass by, still deep in conversation with another man.

"Hannah – wait up!"

It was Leo Kemp, running, his left hand holding his coat closed as he ran.

Hannah glanced up the lane at Abe, who was looking back at Leo and getting into the Mercedes, his face like thunder.

Florrie said a quick goodbye before Leo reached them.

"Happy Christmas, Hannah – excuse me . . ."

"Your uncle doesn't look very happy about you talking to me," she said when Leo reached them.

"He's all right. He's only jealous he's not young enough to be chatting up women anymore himself."

"Is that what you're doing?"

"Maybe. God loves a trier, like they say."

Hannah watched the Mercedes roar up the laneway.

"Sorry about the smell of sheep. I went to look at them before I left the yard and one was having trouble yeaning, so I got delayed."

Hannah felt sorry for the ewe.

"Actually I wanted to ask you to a party – New Year's Eve. Few beers, bit of craic . . . at my place – the bungalow."

"I didn't think you were the party organizing type."

"There's always a first time. So – how are you fixed?"

"I don't know. I'll have to see what Beryl's plans are."

"Bring her along. The more the merrier, as they say. Nine o'clock."

Hannah opened her car door, waving at Roy as she did so.

"Is Roy going?"

"I suppose. That right, brother – New Year's Eve, the piss-up?"

"M-m-m-maybe."

"There."

"I'll see," Hannah said as she started the engine.

It was 10.45 a.m. by the time she got back to the cottage. Beryl was at the door looking anxious.

"You put the turkey on – great! It smells good."

"You never woke me . . ."

"You needed a rest. I just thought I'd go on my own – to church."

Her friend looked concerned.

"Was he there?"

"Yes."

Hannah stood in front of the cooker to heat up, glad to be back in the security of the cottage.

"He blanked me the whole time," she said quietly, trying to keep her voice steady. "Florrie spoke though. She seemed a bit out of sorts. She asked me if there were any locals at Mam's funeral. Why would she ask that?"

"Maybe she suspects him of going . . ."

"You think? God, I'd love to get inside her head – and his for that matter. Stop looking at me like that . . ."

"I'm not!"

"Yes you are! Like I'm losing it or something . . ."

"You're sailing so close to the wind . . ."

"So what? Isn't it about time something happened?" Hannah poured herself a glass of wine from the fridge. "And please – just stop gawking at me – you're not my mother."

"Whatever you say . . ."

"Anyway – guess what – we've been invited to a party."

Beryl looked shocked when Hannah told her where it was.

"You're not going, surely?"

"Why shouldn't I? It's a free country. You're asked too. You never know – it mightn't be so bad."

"Hannah . . ."

"Why shouldn't we go? It's rude to turn down an invitation. Besides, Roy is going – we can talk to him. You see – now you're interested!"

"I am not! What if everyone's there? What are you going to do – play happy families?"

"I doubt he'll have old fogies there – not by the way he was talking . . ."

Beryl stood up to clear the table.

"Can we just stop talking about all this? It's freaking me out. Let's just get Christmas Day over first. The others should be here any minute. I'm going to get dressed."

"Right."

Beryl shoved a piece of paper towards her. It was a cooking schedule.

"And I'm not doing all the cooking on my own . . ." she said, looking at Hannah's glass.

God, did she have to be such a holy Joe?

"I'm stuffed," Noel said as he plonked himself down on the sofa.

Rita was too.

"That was some dinner – cheers Beryl!"

"Just as well Noel is driving back," Rita said. "This wine is great, Hannah."

"She should know," Beryl said.

Bitch!

"Come on, cheer up – tis the season to be jolly or to stuff the turkey's hole with holly or something like that . . ."

Noel was looking at her, a bit amazed.

"Whatever happened to holy Hannah? You'll have to be careful or you'll set us a bad example. Nanna used to hold you up as a model of good behaviour. If we did something wrong she'd say, 'What would Hannah say if she knew how you were behaving?' You were Little Miss Perfect."

Hannah dropped a plate that she was attempting to dry.

"I should buy a dishwasher," she said, staggering as she tried to pick up the pieces. "Bloody ridiculous drying up all these dishes. Life's too short."

"Sit down before you break something else. The rest of us will finish up."

Hannah felt the tea cloth being taken out of her hands by Beryl.

Rita had asked about the progress with her father over dinner. Everyone from Royle was interested in what was happening to her. Noel had never known his parents or anything about himself. Rita had tried to find her mother, but it had not gone well.

"So what do you do if he keeps denying you?" Noel asked.

Hannah held up her glass.

"Expose him for the liar he is."

"Hannah . . ."

Beryl was at it again.

"Hannah what? Come on, Hannah what? I can do what I like and say how I feel, can't I? If I want to call my own father a liar, I can. I could call him worse."

"You're angry . . ." Rita said.

"Bloody right I'm angry . . ."

"Maybe you should calm down a bit . . ."

"Oh great, it's three against one now, is it? Go on, Noel, tell us what you think."

"I'm saying nothing."

"About right. Not one of you here can point a finger at anyone. You're all as bitter as hell in your own way, you just cover it up most of the time, that's all. Yeah, well, I'm tired of covering it up. At least I have some target for my anger – it's more than the lot of you have."

"Hannah . . ."

"Why shouldn't we be bitter? I'm sick of all this 'keep your head down and let it go and move on' shite. Let them all off the hook – is that what you want to do – the parents who bonked away good-o then threw the lot of us nuisance babies into homes!"

"You don't mean that – you can't wish you were never born," Rita was saying. "We're all part of God's plan."

"My eye! We're the result of human beings' mistakes – dirty secrets, the lot of us. We were hated when we were in our mother's wombs because we were tragedies and inconveniences. Fear of shame – that's why we were shut away – to keep the fornicators looking like saints."

"Now you're being crude!"

"Oh dear – have I offended Beryly Weryley's sensibilities? Aw!"

Her friend was standing up now, her face redder than she'd ever seen it.

"Would you be pursuing him as much if he was an on-the-dole-alcoholic living in a kip – answer me that? You've been eyeing up what he has from the minute you first heard about him, so have a good look at your own motives!"

Hannah threw her glass hard against the cupboard.

"I'm his daughter and I'm entitled to what I'm entitled to, and don't you dare say anything else!"

Hannah could see her friends all staring at her. Now she felt light-headed.

"This is some Christmas . . ." she could hear Rita say.

Hannah felt more anger surge through her.

"Well, I'm sorry! Speak a few home truths around here and you get criticized, is that it? *Home* truths. I've a good mind to give someone a few home truths . . . and he's only up the road . . ."

Hannah grabbed the car keys from the windowsill, but Beryl was now wrenching them out of her hand.

"You can't drive! For God's sake!"

"Jesus, Hannah!"

Hannah heard the shouts of the others as they tried to pull her back from the door. Beryl was trying to take the keys out of her hand.

"I'm going to tell him what I think of him – you hear? Do you know he infested this place with rats just to get rid of me? That he says it's my mother's word against his that I'm his daughter and that I'm to crawl back in under whatever rock I came from – my own father – saying that to me!"

She felt Beryl and Noel now guide her back to the sofa.

"Black coffee – now!"

"Just put her to bed. She'd be better just sleeping it off."

"You're right."

Hannah felt weak now and ready to bawl.

Beryl and Rita were helping her upstairs.

"I'm sorry, I've messed up the day for you. I'm a feckin' eejit . . ."

She was vaguely aware of being plonked down on her bed and a duvet being thrown over her. Someone was pulling off her boots.

"I'm like a cowboy in a Western – yahoo! Too much firewater – that's what the Indians called wine, you know – or was it whiskey . . ?"

Beryl and Rita were rolling her over on her side and tucking in the duvet.

"Go to sleep!"

"Hark the herald angel sing . . ."

"Ssh! Just go to sleep!"

" Ok, right. . . whatever you say . . . you're all a shower of bossy boots . . ."

Chapter
EIGHT

As he foddered the cattle before dinner on Christmas Day Abe Stephenson was remembering. It was the autumn of 1949; he was thirteen and he'd caught Tim Leary's pucán.

Stolen him really, but he preferred to call it temporary relocation – relocation that would mean that his services couldn't be availed of.

People who owned goats for a radius of ten miles brought their nanny goats to Learys to get them impregnated by Tim Leary's pucán.

Abe had bought his own pucán, though, with hard saved money and now had him corralled in the orchard. He had put an ad up in several shops and the pub and in the local paper to let people know that "Puck" was available. There hadn't been much response, however, because of Tim Leary's longer-standing enterprise.

"We'll see," he said.

When very few people arrived at Knocklannon with their goats. Abe decided that he had to do something and soon. The plan was to make Tim Leary's pucán disappear until the goat-mating season was over.

The farm dog, Nell, as good a cowdog as you could get, had helped, as well as a good blackthorn stick and the ropes – one to slow him by getting round a horn and another to tie to a back leg so that he could be driven where Abe needed him to go. He had gone prepared and his research done. Tim Leary spent every Saturday evening in the pub, so the coast was clear at nightfall. Tim Leary kept his pucán along with a few sheep on the rosses – bogland to one side of his cottage – land that Abe knew like the back of his hand from lamping rabbits there for years. He smelled the he goat before he saw him. Pucáns always stank during the mating season – a desperate smell, like something had died . . .

The sweat ran down Abe's back as he kept the dog on alert, running the pucán and the sheep into the pen that Tim Leary used for visiting goats. Under threat, the pucán ran at the dog repeatedly, keeping his eye on him rather than Abe – just what Abe needed him to do. Eventually he got the noose onto one of the pucán's horns, pulling tight and dancing out of the goat's way in case he struck him. Now he had some control . . . He tied the rope to the fence, the pucán all the time struggling to get free and watching Nell, the dog, who was snarling and ready to pounce. All he had to do now was get a long rope round one of the pucán's back legs and he'd be able to drive him wherever he wanted to go. The noose made, he bided his time until the rope was under a foot, then pulled. He had him!

Opening the gate, he whistled orders to steady the dog and keep him driving the pucán ahead of them, fifteen foot between him and its white rear end.

Eventually he drove the goat out of Leary's rosses, across the river at its lowest point into Holohan's lower field, along their boundary ditch and up the hill into the forestry.

He got a bit afraid that someone might see him but no, he was all right – there wasn't a sinner to be seen. At least three miles from where he had caught the pucán he cut the rope as close up as he could get, then let go. Deafening him with the unmerciful cry that pucáns make when they're cornered, the pucán eventually realized he was free and took off at speed into the forestry. Abe shone the flashlight after him. He was gone . . . He'd run for miles. Abe grinned. It would be weeks before anyone would find him. The way was now clear for his own pucán – and for him to make money.

It was three weeks before the letter arrived at the house. His father opened it at the dinner table after Fred Rooney, the postman, had cycled into the yard.

Saying nothing, he passed the letter to his wife, who turned red when she read it.

It was from Tim Leary demanding the return of the pucan which had "mysteriously" disappeared. He had a witness, he said, who had seen their son, Abe, leading the goat through Holohan's land. Abe doubted it. He had seen no one. Tim Leary had just put two and two together and got four.

His mother was horrified at his behaviour and brooked no objection when his father said serious punishment was necessary.

"I'll deal with this," his father said. "Out to the barn!"

"How could he shame us like this?" his mother was crying as Vera, his older sister, sat mute and ashen-faced.

In the barn George Stephenson closed the door.

"Get ready to bawl," he said.

Abe shook, anticipating the pain but what was going on? His father was laughing!

"Best fecking story I ever heard! You hid the pucán?"

"Yes."

"So's you'd do Tim Leary's pucán out of business?"

"Yes."

His father laughed again.

"That beats all!" And he took to laugh again.

"You caught him all by yourself?"

"Yes."

And he told his father how he had done it like a cowboy in one of those books he read.

"That beats all," his father said, tears rolling down his cheeks now. "You're a plucky fucker. You'll go far."

"But Mammy is cross," Abe said.

"I know and so she should be. No son of ours should steal."

"I wasn't stealing. I was going to take him back in a few weeks."

"I know that and you know that, but justice will have to be seen to be done."

His father took off his belt as he stood up, and Abe almost wet himself in fear.

His father wrapped the buckle part of the belt around his hand.

"Now, every time I hit that stick horse you let out a roar. And make it sound real. The workmen'll be watching and listening and word of this will go back to Tim Leary – that and a letter of apology, but never let a word of what I've said here escape your lips. Now, yell!"

Abe Stephenson could hear his father's laugh again as he tipped the loader bucket full of silage into the side feeders in the shed. Lord, his mind was all over the place.

His father had died a year or so after, when he was only fifty-two years old.

"At least I've lived longer than he did," Abe said to himself. He had worried about that sometimes in his fifties but the fear had eased as he passed sixty, and at sixty five it ceased concerning him.

He must have his mother's genes – the Johnsons were all hardy as snipes and only gave in to death when old age had worn them out.

Stopping the tractor he heard a car drive into the yard. It would be Vera and the boys arriving for Christmas dinner.

Going into the house the atmosphere was a bit strained. Florrie was in a strange humour and seeing her – the child – at church earlier had unsettled him, too. There she was, as bold as brass, in his face, chatting to his wife outside the church.

The gravy had been lumpy and the turkey overcooked – the first time that had ever happened in his married life.

"Did you get out the wrong side of the bed this morning?" Leo had made the mistake of asking Florrie.

"If I did at least I wasn't harming anyone else."

"What's that supposed to mean?" Abe had growled. What the hell had got into her? Then she mentioned the rats. The ones someone let out at the cottage. He glanced at Leo.

Florrie had put down her fork and knife and was speaking very quietly.

"Someone did it. Someone whose land joins the cottage. Someone who was trying to get the owner of that cottage out of it."

"What are you talking about?" Vera said. "Who are you accusing?"

"Someone round this table did it. I'd put money on it."

Her voice was icy. It was a Florrie he didn't know.

Abe swallowed hard. "I didn't do it."

Leo was busy eating. Roy looked shocked.

"You'd want to be careful what you're saying . . ." Leo said eventually.

"What is going on? Are you saying that Leo did?"

His sister was almost screeching.

"Leo wouldn't do the likes of that, and I won't have you accusing my son!"

"Maybe he can deny it then," Florrie said quietly.

"Tell her you had nothing to do with it," Abe told his nephew.

"Course I didn't. Why the hell would I do a stupid thing like that?"

Florrie's voice was still quiet.

"To run her out of the place."

"You're mad!"

Vera was now on her feet.

"I won't stand for having my son accused in the wrong."

"Then what was he doing with rat cages the day I went over to see Roy's sculptures? They were being taken out of the back of the van . . ."

"Leo?"

His sister's voice was even shriller.

"You're off your rocker. You saw nothing," Leo said, standing up. "And you can keep your Christmas dinner."

"Leo!"

His mother went after him.

Abe saw Roy rise as well. Florrie was looking at him.

"I'm sorry. It had to be said . . ."

Roy just nodded.

"What are you at?" he shouted at Florrie when the others had left.

"I saw him with the cages. I know he did it. I'm asking you again, did you tell him to do it?"

Florrie was still sitting at the table, moving the food around on her plate.

Abe pushed his plate half way down the table.

"I'm not listening to this!"

"Well, perhaps you can answer another question . . ."

There was ice in her voice again.

"What?"

"Was there something between you and Lil Casey?"

Jesus! She knew! Abe kept his back to his wife as he spoke.

"What are you talking about now? You're off your head!"

What did she know? How much did she know?

"I was at the day care centre the day before yesterday talking to Maimie Breen. The reminiscence project . . ."

"What about it?"

"Maimie used to work here. As cook."

"That one wouldn't work to heat herself. What about it?"

Abe listened as Florrie recounted what she had said. Relief flooded through him as she finished.

"Is that all you're fussing about? A bit of a fumble when I was a chap and had no sense?"

"You were seventeen – eighteen?"

"So what? And you never did anything stupid, I suppose? She's as daft as a brush and you're blowing this bullshit out of proportion."

"Why would she seem uneasy then? Like she was supposed to keep a secret . . ."

"How the hell do I know? Because her brain's not working right – that's why. You're losing it."

"Belittling me is not going to change anything."

"Well, you're letting your imagination run away with you then. You should have more sense than letting anything that one says get inside your head. The whole parish knows she's going loopy."

Abe could feel the sweat dampening his underarms. He forced himself to stare his wife down. Eye contact, he had to hold that, whatever else.

Florrie was still looking at him, saying nothing.

The waste of the food on the table angered him now.

"Are you happy now? The whole day destroyed. Some fucking Christmas this is!"

Florrie was still staring at him.

"Did you go to her funeral?"

"What?"

His stomach sank again.

"She was buried on the thirteenth of October – the day I went to Kilkenny."

"No, I didn't and what the fuck has that to do with anything?"

"I wondered . . ."

"Well you can stop your fucking wondering," he said grabbing his hat. "I'm going to Newtown."

In the jeep he felt numb with relief. His wife's mind was only working overtime – that was all. It was the same as years ago, after being told she couldn't have children. She'd get upset if he as much as looked at another woman.

What if Maimie Breen knew more – the ould bitch? What if Lil had told her she'd had a child – in a weak moment, telling her who the father was too. Jesus Christ!

He slept badly that night, images of Maimie Breen and Lil Casey and a child with no face filling his nightmares.

He was glad Florrie was sleeping in the spare room. God knows what he said in his sleep.

St Stephen's Day – another bloody bank holiday! He went downstairs and put the kettle on, cursing his body for its stiffness. He switched on the television to banish the silence.

The newsflash told of the tsunami in Indonesia. He stood there in the kitchen looking at the images of devastation, wrecked houses, a landscape utterly demolished. The images made panic rise in his chest. It was nature out of control, the world out of control. If Hannah Casey opened her mouth about who she was, a tsunami would hit Knocklannon.

Sweating again, he switched off the television. He didn't want to look at it now. It had been a dreadful twenty-four hours. There was still silence upstairs. He debated whether or not he would do the yard work. No, he couldn't face it yet. Instead he took his mug of tea with him to his study. It would ward off conversation if Florrie did come down.

He had to stay calm, in control. He glanced up at the aerial photographs of the farm – by God, no one would take it from him!

He had to think clearly. The housing development could be put on hold for the moment – he could bide his time with that. Better to back off and tell Leo to do the same. He had gone too far with the rats – or had been stupid enough to leave it obvious that corn had been thrown over the ditch. What was more worrying was that Leo had the hots for her. What could he tell his nephew that would put him off? That she wasn't worth messing with, imply that she had some kind of colourful history, that he expected Leo to go for someone better? He doubted, though, that Leo wanted to do more than get into her knickers.

His stomach heaved as thoughts of Leo having sex with . . . her . . . . came to his mind. No! It wouldn't happen. She wouldn't let it happen. She knew he was her cousin, for God's sake, with the accusation she was making.

So, she thought he was responsible for the rats. She was almost right. She had the balls to tell Florrie too – she was sending him a message, there was no doubt about it. She had backbone, he'd give her that.

He tried to think of a strategy. Planning – that's how he'd always succeeded at anything he'd tried to do. Florrie had to be kept away from her from now on – that was important. They would go to church somewhere else for a while, if necessary. He would go with his wife when she was shopping too, just by the way. That way he'd know who she spoke to.

She wouldn't be going to the day care centre again either, even if he had to take the distributor cap off the car to stop her.

The pucán incident came back to him again. He hadn't thought of that for years. It had been a secret between him and his father and gone to the grave with him when he died.

Abe's life had changed so much after that. He had so much work to do and he was expected to step into his father's shoes but yet his mother kept control. She had become a tyrant and seemed to relish the power she had. He got a wage every week – a meagre one at that, and it was only through building up his stock that he gradually began to have more money.

"Easy come, easy go. If you don't work for it, you won't appreciate it," she said.

Every Friday he drove her to town and sat in the car while she went to the bank and to the shops. She wrote out the cheques and lodged all the money. The fifties were hard and most of the sixties. She had made half the farm over to him in 1962, when he got married – begrudgingly, but he had insisted, after threatening to clear out if she didn't. He was tired of being told what to do. He was thirty years of age then and entitled to something.

She had caved in, though there were still joint names on the cheque book. All correspondence came to the farm in the names of Mrs Mabel and Mr Abraham Stephenson, as if they were man and wife, not mother and son. Florrie used to hate it, the way it made her feel excluded.

The tea was helping him to feel calmer. Good. There was still silence upstairs. She must be asleep. It would be all right. She would probably be sorry when she came down, the way she usually was after a row, and it would all settle down eventually.

Right now he felt exhausted and he didn't like it. It made him vulnerable. Tsunami. He thought of the images he had just seen on the television screen – big waves coming in unexpectedly and destroying everything, washing lives and property away . . . He lay back in his leather chair and closed his eyes to block out the fear.

Beryl Nash felt a bit sick at the thought of going to Leo Kemp's New Year's Eve party that evening.

"You're not really wanting to go, are you?" she said to Hannah who was going through the sales racks in one of Wexford's boutiques.

"Why shouldn't I? It's rude to turn down an invitation. Besides, you'll have a chance to see Roy, won't you? Could be just what you need . . ."

"I don't need you matchmaking for me, thanks very much . . ."

Hannah was now holding up a low-cut sequinned top and viewing herself in the mirror. Beryl felt panicky.

"You're not going to wear that to Leo Kemp's party?"

"Why not? I'm thirty-nine, not ninety-nine."

More like nineteen in the last few days. Hannah had gone home to Waterford on the twenty-seventh of December and met up with nursing colleagues four nights in a row, drinking heavily.

"It's Christmas. Give me a break," Hannah told her now. "Since when are you the morality police?" she'd said when Beryl got irritated by the noise of her coming in late and her crankiness as she recovered from hangovers.

Hannah was unbearable when she was like this. Even when she was sober she was sour now. Beryl had never seen her in such a state – not even when she was breaking up with Matt, not even after Nanna died. Hannah was spending too much money too, given that she wasn't working. She had used her credit card five times already that day and had snapped when Beryl got on to her.

"Retail therapy – you can't beat it and, besides, Peg put me in touch with a nursing home near Drumcadden – I'll be doing a few nights' work there, cash in hand, so what about it?"

Beryl knew she was no expert, but it was like Hannah was only grieving her mother now.

A suggestion of bereavement counselling had been thrown back in her face.

"Get off my case! God!"

In a restaurant now, Hannah had ordered a hot chocolate. When there were no marshmallows floating on top of it she was smart with the waitress.

"No marshmallows?" She cut the ground from under her with a look.

"No, sorry."

"Christ! Call this a restaurant!"

It had been like that all week – Hannah got cross about little things. When the car wouldn't start first time she cursed it. When she couldn't find a parking space she'd shouted, "What sort of a town is this?" When she'd laddered her tights she had put her fingers into the nylon, pulling an even bigger hole in them with frustration.

Now Hannah was still disconnected, hard.

"I don't need counselling."

Beryl felt hurt. Why did she bother?

"Maybe you want to go home," Hannah was saying. "It doesn't matter to me. I can get a taxi back to the cottage. Maybe we need a bit of space from one another . . ."

Beryl felt angry now.

"You know what? You could be right. So much for trying to help you!"

"I don't need a babysitter."

"No? And what if you get drunk and you don't know what you're doing or saying . . ."

"God, will you stop! Just butt out, ok?"

Trying to concentrate on her lunch Beryl bit her lip. This was a nightmare. Hannah was in the mood for making trouble. Beryl remembered her getting like that sometimes in Royle. Aggravation would build up in her over days and then she'd explode over something small. Maybe slap one of the younger children for very little. At those times Nanna would step in and slip Hannah a few bob to go into town for a few hours to get away, knowing that she'd have cooled down when she came back and be nice to everyone again. The damage would have been done, though. The younger children had learned that when Hannah was in good form she was great fun, but when she wasn't it was best to stay out of her way. Like now . . . Say nothing and her humour would pass eventually.

"Let's go."

The streets of Wexford were packed, the pubs already busy even though it was only three o'clock.

Beryl would be glad when New Year was over. She would go on a diet like she did every year. Right now she was looking forward to the self-denial, the control after all the excess of Christmas.

Maybe 2005 would be the year to get her weight problem sorted once and for all.

"Any resolutions?" she asked Hannah, more to break the tension than anything else.

"Drink more, start smoking, give up men and make bastards pay – that enough?"

"Nanna wouldn't like to hear you talking like that."

"Nanna's pushing up daisies so she won't be listening."

Beryl indicated right after the railway bridge. This Hannah frightened her. Since Abe Stephenson had cut her dead at church on Christmas Day, it was like someone had thrown a switch in her.

"You used to say she was with you in spirit . . ."

Hannah was staring out the side window, watching the sceachs go by.

"Yeah, well, that was then. I'm on my own, you're on your own – anything else is bullshit! Anyway, which of us were our real selves when Nanna was alive – did you ever think that? She terrified us into behaving, that's when she wasn't humiliating us to control us. She wasn't so perfect herself, though . . ."

"You usedn't to hate her like this . . ."

"Wake up and smell the roses! All that money she collected – that wasn't hers, but she acted like it was. Money rolled into Royle in the last few years and she kept most of it for herself . . ."

"You don't know that."

"Yes I do. You didn't hear the argument that day with the trustees. They wanted accounts kept, but she was having none of it."

Beryl felt tears running down her cheeks as Hannah ranted on.

"She loved us . . ."

"No, she didn't. She possessed us, more like. She had so much power it was wrong and you know it. Did you ever wonder why so few got adopted? Because she wanted to keep us. And the ones that did get adopted – how do we know that was all even legal? And did you ever wonder why some got treated better than others – because their mothers were giving her money, that's why! You got that right!"

"She was a good person . . ."

"Maybe I'd have been better off with adoptive parents."

"Maybe your mother wouldn't allow it."

"Thinking of herself as usual."

Beryl changed down a gear as she approached a bad bend.

"What's the point in talking about 'what ifs?'"

"Because it takes the pain out of 'right nows', that's why."

Back at the cottage two hours later, Beryl wished Hannah would get out of the bath.

She put her hand on the hot water cylinder. It was lukewarm. It would take ages to heat up again with Hannah topping up the bath so often. Typical Hannah – as long as she's all right, everyone else can whistle.

Right now Beryl wished she was back in Waterford.

Maybe I'd be better buying a house on my own, she thought. Maybe we should have gone our separate ways a long time ago, Beryl said to herself as she resisted the temptation to pick up the boots that Hannah had just left thrown on the floor.

She would prefer just to stay at home on New Year's Eve. She'd hated New Year's Eves since she was eighteen and she'd been in a pub singing *Auld Lang Syne* and everyone kissing everyone and then an old man had grabbed her and kissed her on the mouth, forcing his tongue between her teeth. He has smelled and tasted of Guinness and spit and she had cried and washed out her mouth and gargled with salt over and over again when she got home.

The man had laughed when she pushed him away, saying, "but I thought ye'd like it."

"Sicko," Hannah had shouted, seeing what happened, then taken her home as quickly as she could.

Hannah was putting on her makeup now at the kitchen table, using a hand-mirror. She had her tartan dressing gown on. She looked well, even at the age of 39, even without makeup, Beryl thought. It had always been that way – no matter where they went, men always looked at her first.

Hannah nodded when she said she would drive tonight.

"You don't have to come, but thanks . . ."

Beryl got up to go upstairs and get ready.

"No, I don't, but that way I'll know you're safe."

Hannah put down her mascara.

"Ber – look, I don't want to be rowing with you. I know I can be horrible sometimes . . . Friends?"

"I suppose . . ."

Upstairs, Beryl tried to think positive. Maybe the party at Leo's would be ok. Maybe it would be packed and they wouldn't have to talk to him very much. Who knows – it could be a good night. And Roy would be there . . . Who knows, maybe they'd get a chance to talk . . .

Besides, Beryl thought, everyone goes out on New Year's Eve and she was thirty-six, almost four years younger than Hannah – too young to be stuck at home by the fire . . .

She opened her suitcase, trying to decide what to wear.

She took out a black trousers and the pink top she'd bought for Christmas. She had a black bolero to go over it – that way she wouldn't be as conscious of her fat arms or her bust.

It had always been big, her bust, bursting out of her pinafore, even at the age of twelve. Her first bra had been one that had been donated to the home by a woman named Miss Pritchard – a big, white, sensible cotton one and a size 36C. She had never seen her in church after that in her fur coat and hat, red lipsticked lips and horn-rimmed glasses without thinking of how her breasts and Miss Pritchards were the same size.

There were about a dozen cars outside Leo's bungalow.

"At least he's having a crowd," Beryl said, as she tried to find a parking place where they wouldn't be blocked in.

Beryl saw Hannah looking at the vehicles. There was no Mercedes, no wine-coloured Land Cruiser. Beryl felt relieved.

The bungalow was basic in shape but with pillars at either side of the front door that looked a bit over the top for a house that size. The back of the house was still rough ground with building waste thrown here and there – bits of cement blocks, breeze blocks, laths, a section of radon barrier. Gravel had been lain around the house and all the way to the gate.

"It'll be ok when it's properly finished," Hannah said, looking round. She had a bottle of spirits and a bottle of wine in her hand.

"Come on, I'm freezing."

The music was loud. Bruce Springsteen . . . *Born in the USA* . . .

Hannah was singing along. Beryl suspected that she'd downed several shots before she left the cottage.

Roy answered the door. He looked a bit unsure, but smiled.

"C-C-come in."

"Thanks."

"H-h-appy new year."

"Same to you."

Hannah handed Roy the bottles as Leo appeared from the sitting room.

"Yeah! You found your way! Great! Roy'll put the bottles in the kitchen, won't you, Roy Boy? Come on and get a drink."

Leo's attention was totally focused on Hannah. Beryl felt as if she might as well not have been there.

The disco-lit sitting room was practically full of people, a few dancing, most standing or sitting around, drinking bottled beer. Beryl could see all the men's eyes giving them the once-over and lingering, as usual, on Hannah.

Leo shouted.

"This is Hannah . . . and . . ."

"Beryl."

"Bery-l the per-il, what?"

Women outnumbered men so far – another Leo plan?

They found seats on the windowsill. With the radiator on underneath, it helped them to heat up.

Roy brought them drinks as the tune ended. Beryl was glad he had stayed standing beside them.

"So, any strange?" Leo was asking as he stood in front of them.

One too many of his shirt buttons was open and he smelled as if he'd fallen into a bottle of aftershave.

"Cigarette?"

Leo was offering.

"No, thanks."

"No vices – is that it?"

"Bad for the lungs," Hannah said.

"Ah sure – we'll be dead long enough. How was Christmas?"

"Ok. And you?"

"Shite."

"Oh?

"Never mind. Dance?"

Leo had his hand out towards Hannah.

Several couples were on the wooden floor, dancing to Abba's *Waterloo.*

Beryl wished Roy would ask her to dance too, but he seemed uncomfortable and had gone back out into the hall.

Beryl thought he looked well, though – less conservative with his new clothes. Whenever she caught his eye he smiled then looked away.

By eleven thirty Beryl had a splitting headache. Anyone that had asked her to dance had had too much to drink and she couldn't hear a word they were saying because the music was too loud. A couple of times she had thought Roy was going to approach, but each time he held back.

"Probably too self conscious with everyone he knows around," she thought.

Now she could hardly see round the room with the smoke. She made her way through the hall to go to the bathroom, hoping to find Hannah on the way. Twice she was groped as she tried to get through.

"Ber-yl wants a wee-wee!" someone said and laughs broke out. God, some people were so ignorant!

Coming out of the bathroom she still couldn't find Hannah. She remembered her dancing most of the night, arms wrapped around the neck of whoever she was dancing with, showing off her figure. Every man in the place had been looking at her – even the ones half her age.

God, her head hurt. Where was Hannah? In one of the bedrooms? She'd hardly paired off with one of the men, had she? Maybe she was in the kitchen?

Beryl's heart started to pound. She'd hardly gone somewhere with Leo, had she? Not her own cousin! She wasn't that drunk, was she? Jesus!

Beryl felt terrified. She'd had enough. The music was doing her head in, *Brown-eyed Girl*, at high volume. In the hall again she asked Roy if he'd seen Hannah and he just shrugged.

They were interrupted by banging on the front door.

Roy moved to open it, with difficulty as a couple were sitting on the floor in front of it, snogging.

It was Abe Stephenson, beetroot red.

"Where's Leo?" he shouted over the music.

"Leo!"

The front door was still open. Beryl saw Vera Kemp coming after her brother, face pinched and nearly out of breath. What was going on?

"Wh-what's wrong?"

"Find that brother of yours," his uncle barked.

Beryl felt terrified as she followed the three of them through the hall towards the kitchen door. Good God – what if Hannah *was* with Leo?

Roy was knocking loudly on the door before trying to open it.

"S-s-something's b-behind it . . ."

"Get out of the way!"

Beryl saw Abe Stephenson now put his shoulder to it. The kitchen door burst open. Beryl could see Hannah pinned against the kitchen units by Leo, his hands up her skirt . . .

Beryl could see shock register on both their faces when they realised Abe Stephenson was in the room. And his sister.

Hannah looked confused – and very drunk as she attempted to straighten her clothes.

"Get . . . her . . . out of here!" Abe shouted, grabbing Leo by the shoulders and pulling him away. "You fucking eejit!"

Beryl was terrified as she watched Leo stagger and knock bottles off the table.

"Hannah – let's go!"

This was a nightmare. Her friend's eyes looked glazed and her mascara was running as she struggled to put on her jacket.

"Get out of here – now, you trollop!" Abe shouted.

"Aye. Same as her mother."

Hannah was staring.

"How dare you call me names? Call your nephew names! He's here as well. I told him to back off but he wasn't getting the message . . ."

Leo was picking himself up off the floor.

"You were well up for it . . . don't listen to her."

Beryl felt sick with fear.

"Hannah – please, let's go!"

"You and your parties – this is where they get you! And fraternizing with the likes of her!"

Vera Kemp was shouting at her son.

Abe Stephenson was pointing his finger at Leo.

"I told you to stay away from her but you couldn't, could you?"

Leo's voice was slurred.

"Keep your hair on . . ."

Beryl saw Hannah start to laugh now.

"Hannah . . . please . . . come on!"

"Why did you come here?" she was asking Abe Stephenson. "Go on, tell us! You heard I was here, is that it? That's what made you come running."

"Shut up!"

"What's she talking about?"

Beryl could see Vera Kemp look from Hannah to her brother to her son . . .

Roy had closed the kitchen door on the noise and other people's curiosity.

"C-C-C-alm d-d-down, f-f-for G-G-God's sake . . .

Beryl felt as if everything was going in slow motion.

She could barely hear her own voice as she tried to pull Hannah towards the door.

"Let's go!"

Hannah wrenched her arm free.

"I'm not going anywhere!"

Hannah's voice was slurred.

"Go on – tell them, Mr High and Mighty Stephenson – tell them why you burst in here . . ."

There was a dangerous glint in Hannah's eye.

"Shut up!"

Everyone looked confused. Beryl felt terrified.

"What's she talking about?"

"What?

"She's drunk!" Abe said. "Get her out of here – now!"

"Hannah – come on!"

Again she wrenched her friend's arm away.

"I'm not so drunk that I don't know my own name. Does anybody want to know what my name is? My real name? No? Well, I'll tell you . . ."

"Hannah, no!"

"I'm his daughter! His and Lil Casey's."

There was silence for two seconds before Vera and Leo started to shout.

"You liar!"

"How dare you!"

"She's drunk out of her skull. Mad!" Abe Stephenson said.

"Hannah – let's go – NOW!"

Beryl grabbed her friend, now looking a bit stunned and confused, pulling her as best she could towards the door.

"The fifth of February 1965. That's when I was born. Ask him! He knows!"

Leo was holding his fist up.

"Shut your mouth!"

His mother was behind him.

"She's making it up!"

"She's deranged, you hear? She's got some sort of grudge and she's come up with a cock and bull story. Don't listen to her!"

"Come on!" Beryl had never felt as frightened in her life. They had to get out of there fast.

She shouted at the couple in front of the door to get up, then wrenched open the door, still holding onto Hannah's arm with her other hand.

Beryl started to run the minute she got out through the door, forcing Hannah to do the same to keep up.

Hannah was half shouting, half sobbing.

"Let me go!"

Beryl unlocked the car, opened one of the back doors and pushed Hannah in on the backseat, still terrified that someone was after them.

She cursed when the car didn't start first time.

Beryl's heart was in her mouth all the way back to the cottage, checking the rearview mirror frequently, terrified that Abe Stephenson was following them. She had to concentrate . . . Hannah was alternating between crying and ranting. What had she done? Now the cat was out of the bag . . .

"He effin well deserved it . . ." she was saying.

"Stay there!" Beryl said when they got to the cottage. "I'm grabbing my stuff and we're getting out of here!"

All she wanted to do now was put distance between herself and Drumcadden – and this mess.

Neither of them was safe. Tomorrow the news would be all around the village. He or they would be liable to do anything. Hannah's disclosure would have turned their worlds upside down. She could still see the shock on Vera's and Leo's face, the bewilderment on Roy's . . .

Beryl stuffed clothes into a holdall, grabbed coats and a duvet off the bed as well. Handbags – everything else didn't matter.

She threw the duvet in on top of Hannah on the back seat.

"Wrap that around you before you get pneumonia."

Beryl's legs were like jelly as she tried to start the car again.

The truth was out but it shouldn't have happened like this! Right now she hated Hannah – the state of her . . .

A few miles down the road Hannah started to mutter.

"Did that just happen?" she said.

"Yes! And you did it! He could have killed you, for God's sake! What were you thinking of?"

Beryl knew she was shrieking now.

"At leasht I told the truth. He can deny it . . . all he wants but he knows it's the truth."

"Do you know what sort of danger you put yourself – and me – in? God knows what could have happened in there. I thought he was going to hit you!"

"Let him try . . ."

"Shut up!" Beryl shouted. She'd had enough. "What were you thinking – going into the kitchen with Leo! Are you totally thick? Can you not imagine what that looked like?"

Beryl was shaking with anger. She was fed up of Hannah, fed up comforting, fed up watching out for, fed up minding, fed up picking up the pieces . . .

Good, they were on the main road to Waterford . . .

Her heart was still pounding.

She could still see Abe Stephenson's face as he came in the front door.

Hannah had been stupid to go there. Beryl had been stupid to let her but how could she have stopped her – by locking her up?

"Gonna be sick . . ."

"Shit!"

Beryl braked and pulled in on the hard shoulder as quickly as she could to let Hannah open the door and vomit onto the grass.

A car drove by on the N25 blowing its horn.

"*Happy New Year*" its occupants shouted through the open windows as they passed.

Beryl put her head down on the steering wheel. Some Happy New Year . . .

"He's doing what?"

Abe Stephenson jumped up off his chair as what his sister said sank in.

"Inviting the Casey one from the cottage to the party he's having – what about it?"

"What? He can't do that!"

His hands shook as he got up from Vera's table.

"Where are you going? What's up with you? What matter who he asks – not that I want him mixing with that one . . ."

Abe tried to hide his shock as he headed for the door. Fucking eejit!

"Who else is invited? Are there more people?"

His sister was following him.

"Yes, Roy's there, Macra people – lots as far as I know. Why? What are you shouting for? So what if he fancies the Casey one? You know him and women. Always looking for one-night stands. Where are you going? What's up with you?"

Abe could hear the music coming from the bungalow as he got into the Land Cruiser.

"Stay here!"

Vera already had the passenger door open.

"I will not. Not until you tell me what you're so riled up about."

Abe tried to think as he drove down the rough roadway that had been made to give Leo quick access from the farmyard to the bungalow.

Shouting at Vera to stay in the jeep, he jumped out and banged on Leo's front door. The music was so loud it was ages before Roy opened it.

"Where's Leo?"

Vera was behind him. Christ, why did she never do what she was told . . .

There was no sign of him, or her, in the sitting room as he pushed his way through the crowd. Damn disco lights – he couldn't see a thing.

The kitchen . . . He tried the door handle. He couldn't open it – there was something behind it. A chair? A table? Why was Leo locking other people out? Jesus! He was with her. She wouldn't . . .

Abe put his shoulder to the door, shouting "Leo" repeatedly.

He stood in shock for a second as his eyes took in the scene.

She was at the counter, clothes half off her, Leo groping her. Fuck!

Abe grabbed Leo by the shoulders to pull him away from her.

"Get . . . her out of here!"

"Abe!"

Vera was pulling at him now. Leo had lurched back in confusion, knocking bottles off the table as he staggered back. Roy was trying to get between the two of them.

"C-C-Calm d-d-down!"

"I told you to stay away from her!"

Leo looked dazed.

"Look at the state of you! And you . . . you hussy! This is where your parties get you . . ."

Abe looked at Hannah. Her hair was dishevelled and her clothes awry.

"She's drunk! Get her out of here – now!"

He saw the hatred in her eyes.

"I'm not going anywhere! Go on, Mr High and Mighty Stephenson – tell them why you burst in here!"

"She's drunk! Get her out of here!"

"Not so drunk that I don't know my own name! Does anybody want to know what my name is – my real name? No? Well I'll tell you!"

"Shut up!"

Her friend was trying to grab her arm, but she was fighting her off.

"Hannah, no!"

"I'm his daughter! His and Lil Casey's!"

Abe thought the blood would burst in his ears. God Almighty . . .

"She's a liar! Don't listen to her!"

"Hannah – please, let's go! Now!"

It was that friend of hers talking again.

"Shut up!"

"What's she talking about?" Vera was saying.

"Hannah – let's go!"

"Go on – tell them why you burst in here!"

"Shut up!"

He heard his sister's voice.

"What are you talking about? What's she talking about, Abe?"

"She's drunk out of her skull! Mad! Don't listen to her, you hear!"

"The fifth of February 1965. That's when I was born. Ask him! He knows!"

"She's deranged, you hear? She's got some kind of grudge and she's making up this cock and bull story."

The one with the glasses was now pulling Hannah towards the door.

"Lying bitch!" Leo shouted after them.

"I'll see you in court!" Abe heard himself say. He could see Roy standing there looking totally bewildered.

"Shut that door," he heard Vera say, as the two women left. Thankfully the noise in the house was loud. Had anyone in the hall heard? He didn't know. He tried to think fast. Attack would be the best form of defence.

"I'll drag her through every court in the land if I have to – she's not going to get away with this kind of slander."

"She's fucking not!" It was Leo, kicking the leg of a chair.

"Such a thing to say!"

"She's not the full shilling."

"Fucking loco!"

He saw his sister's deathly white face.

"What if someone's heard? It'll be round the village in no time."

"What if it is? It's not true. Anyone who has any sense will know that."

"W-w-why w-w-would she say it?"

"How the fuck do I know? She's a liar – that's all there is to it."

"The bitch!"

"Let's go," Abe said, making for the door. He saw several faces in the corridor stare as he and Vera walked out. He stood up straight ignoring the eavesdroppers. Fuck her! Fuck this whole mess!

Vera had gotten into the driver's seat, her hands like white claws around the steering wheel. He got into the passenger's seat rather than argue with her.

"I'm driving you home. You're as white as a sheet after that one's rant. She's lucky you didn't have a heart attack with her vile lies. Such a thing to say!"

Abe tried to think as Vera headed for Knocklannon, grating the gears at every junction. What was he going to do? What was he going to say?

Abe could feel the sweat under his arms. Florrie!

"It's better Florrie knows than hear it from someone else."

Florrie was at the back door before they got to it.

"Vera? What's wrong? What's happened? Is Roy all right?"

"He's ok. It's something different, but we'll put a stop to it, don't worry."

"Come in out of the cold."

Abe tried to stay calm as he watched his wife's face. She was trying to take in what Vera was saying. The accusation. It was all lies . . . How Abe was going to take the Casey one to court for such slander . . . How she mustn't be right in the head.

"She says you're her father?"

"She's a liar."

"And she'll rue this day," his sister was saying. "To think everyone was so nice to her, that butter wouldn't melt and you having her here for the carols and saying how nice she was . . ."

Abe hated the way Florrie kept staring at him. He had to stare her down.

"It's lies."

"Vera, I think you should go – go!"

His wife's voice was strong, cold.

"I'm not going anywhere until I know you're all right," his sister said.

"Go on. I'll get the jeep in the morning."

When Vera left there was total silence. Florrie was still staring at him.

"It's lies – I'm telling you! She'll have a solicitor's letter so fast she won't know what's hit her."

His wife was still staring at him.

"Is she a liar just like Maimie Breen is a liar?"

"Ah, will you whisht, that one's batty, I've told you! That's the way it'll be now, is it? Me being tormented after that one's planted nonsense in your head. That's what the likes of her wants – to make people's lives miserable."

"Hannah's not the sort to tell lies."

"And what would you know? You're soft when it comes to judging people. That's one's off her head."

Florrie was just sitting there now, staring into space.

"I'm going to bed," he said. "By the time I'm finished with that one she won't have a penny to her name."

Florrie's voice was icy quiet.

"She'll be forty in February – she told me."

"I don't care what age she is . . ."

"That'd make it 1965 when she was born so she would have been conceived in May 1964, early May . . ."

"Will you stop! What has that to do with us?"

It was as if his wife was in a world of her own.

"Spring Show time . . ."

Jesus!

"I wasn't near her. You're believing her over me, is that it? Lil Casey could have put her up to it, or Jim – he was always a cute hoor. He probably told her to say it so she'd get money out of me. Do you not see there's scheming behind it?"

"She grew up in a children's home in Greystones, the sort of a place you never wanted me to visit . . ."

"I'm not listening to anymore of this shite. You're mad, woman, you hear . . . If that one has any sense she'll get to hell out of here and never come back. No one around here is going to believe that lies."

His wife seemed to be smiling.

"You think you have that many friends . . ."

"Fuck off!"

Abe headed for his study. He needed time to think. He had denied it – that was what was important.

He had nearly cracked when she mentioned the Spring Show. She didn't know how close to the truth she was. Ridicule her – that's what he'd have to do, brazen it out, make her think she was the one who was in the wrong. He would see O'Connell the minute he opened.

He would just tell him the woman was a liar and order him to sue her for slander.

A sweat broke out on his forehead now, as he thought of her telling him about the money on Mount Leinster – and how she'd use it.

He cursed Lil Casey for opening her mouth. Why couldn't she just go to her grave with it, like she was supposed to?

"Maybe she wanted me to be found out when she wouldn't be around to face the flak . . ."

He sat in his chair for a long time. Eventually he heard his wife go upstairs. He would wait until she was asleep. He heard a door clunk at the far end of the house. She had gone into the spare room. Shit!

Deny it – that's all he had to keep doing. He closed his eyes but couldn't stop the images coming into his head, of her – the child – eyes flashing, looking straight at him, the spit of his grandmother.

The sound of his mobile phone ringing woke Leo. Shit! His head hurt. Squinting to focus on the screen, he saw that it was his mother calling. He pressed the "off" button to cancel it. What time was it? 7.34 a.m.

He sank back into the pillow. His stomach felt sick.

For a few seconds he thought he had woken from a nightmare. He was awake and the nightmare was over, wasn't it? He tried to concentrate but the knot was still in his stomach. No, it wasn't a dream and waking up wouldn't make it go away.

He could see her now shouting that his Uncle Abe was her father . . . Fuck! This wasn't happening.

The bitch!

No, she fucking well wasn't his daughter. No way! It was like his uncle said – she was a liar out to stir up shit for no reason. And he'd told her that, no messing. Hadn't he said he'd get the law on her for her outburst? That'd show every nosey Tom, Dick and Harry who would be revelling in the gossip today . . .

Leo hauled himself out of bed. How many hours' sleep had he had – three? Four?

He pulled on the clothes he'd worn the night before. They stank of beer and sweat. The place was a mess, the corridor strewn with cans and spills all over the floor.

Fuck it – what did he have a party for anyway? All this wouldn't have happened then. She wouldn't have been here, mouthing off like that . . .

He had very little recollection of the New Year dawning. He had staggered to his room after Abe left, shouting at everyone to get out be fucked. He had vague recollections of squaring up to Davey Brosnan and asking him what the hell he was grinning at. Everyone had cleared out after that. So-called friends! Probably dying to get away and spread the news, or had they already sent texts to half the country? It'd be all over the village by now.

He kicked a can of beer as he went into the living room. More mess! Fuck it!

Catching sight of himself in the mirror over the fireplace, he barely recognised himself with eyes sunken back in his head. He splashed cold water in his face at the kitchen sink.

What was he going to do? What if it was true? His uncle and Lil Casey . . . He felt like vomiting.

His mobile rang again. This time he answered it.

"I'll be there in a minute," he said to his mother, and then hit the "off" button.

Putting on his yard boots and grabbing a coat, he headed out into the air to walk up to the yard. Bitch! How could that one come out with lies like that? She was a troublemaker – off her head . . . His uncle had said it over and over again. She wouldn't get away with this either. No one crossed his Uncle Abe and got away with it.

Zipping his coat up against the cold Leo's head pounded. But what if it was true? Shit! He tried to stop the full implications of that possibility seeping into his brain . . . Someone coming between him and Knocklannon . . . what he'd counted on all his life . . . He shoved the idea out of his mind. That wasn't going to happen.

His mother was in her dressing gown, as white as a ghost.

"Could you not answer that phone when I ring you? Driving me out of my mind!"

"Stop, will you – I'm here now."

"I haven't had a wink of sleep. Roy's doing the yard work – at least someone can be counted on."

Leo filled a mug of water and drank it down in one go.

"What happened when you took him home?" he asked.

His mother sat down at the table, like a balloon that the air had gone out of.

"I told Florrie. It was better she know than hear it from someone else."

"What did she say?"

"Hmph! I was told to go, no less! I know by the look of her that she half-believed that one's poison! I tried ringing several times but there's no answer."

"You don't think . . ."

Leo jumped as his mother hit the table hard.

"He isn't! You hear! And he'll sort that one out – you'll see! If she's any sense she'll pack up and go back where she came from. She's a filthy liar! To think she'd come out with such talk . . ."

Leo couldn't even taste the tea he'd made.

He jumped as Roy came in and went to the sink to wash his hands.

"Th-hree lambs. T-t-two dead."

His mother's screech lifted him off his chair.

"Can yous do nothing right? There's little enough to be made out of them without letting them die. Have yous learned nothing at all?"

Leo saw his brother's back stiffen, but he said nothing.

"Shut up! That ewe is ancient and it's lucky there's one alive, so shut up!"

"Don't you tell me what to do!"

"S-s-stop!"

His mother seemed to be talking to herself.

"She'll get what's coming to her – lies like that – God forgive her, because I can't. And people talking about it this morning – feeding on the gossip – she should be hanged, drawn and quartered for what she's done to this family!"

Leo had to get some air. She would calm down eventually, but he wasn't going to listen to her in the meantime.

In the yard he went through the motions of the morning's work, revving the tractor more than normal as he put haylage in the feeders for the sheep and brought straw bales from the hay shed to the sheep shed. Bedding them he cursed when a ewe didn't get out of his way quick enough.

"Get out of it be fucked!"

He'd pay Miss Hannah Casey a visit – that's what he'd do. He'd sort her and her lies out. She wouldn't get away with it. As he stopped the tractor a terrible thought struck him? What if she had proof? What if his uncle's name was on the birth certificate? What if Lil Casey had been gone in the head at the time she had her and had put his uncle's name on the birth certificate out of some kind of spite or revenge? Or what if she'd forged some kind of documentation to prove her claim and the daughter now took it as gospel truth?

He was going to find out right now . . . His mother ran out of the house in her dressing gown when she heard him start the van.

"Don't go near her – do you hear? Do you hear! The law'll deal with her. Keep your head high! Act as if nothing had happened – it's lies, that's all!"

His mother was screeching as she ran toward the van.

"I'm going to clean up the bungalow," he shouted at her, after letting down the window.

"You and your parties and that bungalow! You should never have built that place. Parties! Bringing this trouble down on us . . ."

Leo drove down to the bungalow. Where did his mother get off criticizing him? He was forty years old and listening to this shite. Still, he knew she was off her head with worry.

He had to think what to do. His mother was right – better not go near the cottage – someone might see him and it'd only add to the gossip.

He would bide his time. As he threw cans into a black refuse sack, he planned what he would do. He had to know that she had no evidence and a little conversation with her would help. He would wait till tonight. He would walk across the fields and cross the ditch into her yard – no one would see him or know he was there. If she wasn't there all the better – it would give him a chance to look the place over himself . . .

The cottage was in darkness. Yer one's car was there, though, but her pal's wasn't. Had she gone to bed early? Hardly at half past eight in the evening.

He slipped the first time he tried to get up on the ditch when the tree branch he'd held onto broke under his weight.

He shone the flashlight he'd brought with him at the vegetation so that he could decide on a secure handhold. A sceach. That would take his weight. He had been here before letting out the rats and putting the corn down for them. Why the fuck hadn't she cleared out after that instead of blabbing to Florrie, no less? Or taken what she was offered for the cottage. No one else would have given her near that amount of money . . .

He climbed up, his wiriness making his movements easy.

She could be in bed. Would she answer the door? Leo tried to remember how she had got to the party the night before. That speccy friend of hers was with her – Beryl. She must have driven.

Leo took two plastic lambing gloves out of his pocket and put them on before going to the back door. He flattened himself against the wall as he waited for a car to pass on the road in front of the cottage.

He scanned the ground with his flashlight. Yes, there had been another car there – narrower tyres than the Casey one's.

He knocked on the door, once, twice, three times. No answer. He listened carefully and watched the bedroom windows upstairs. No sound of anyone scurrying to a window, no lights switched on.

The security light was still on. No point in trying to break it – it had a steel mesh around it.

What would he do now? He walked round to the bathroom window. It was small, the frame rotten – he could get in easily enough. There was no sign of a house alarm – if she had one she would have publicised the fact to put burglars off.

He used the hammer he'd brought with him to break the window. There was a crash as the glass shattered. He jumped back to allow it to fall, then put in his hand and moved back the old window latch before pushing up the window frame.

He waited and listened again. Silence.

It was a tight squeeze but he levered himself in, his jacket protecting him from any bits of glass that fell as he pulled himself in.

He listened again. Silence.

He took the flashlight out of his pocket. He would switch no lights on in the house. He scanned the kitchen. It was untidy, like they'd left in a hurry.

Still listening he headed up the stairs for her bedroom making as little noise as he could. The stairs creaked. He stopped and listened. No sound. He moved on up.

He went into the first room, shining the torch around. He opened and closed drawers and wardrobe – nothing! This couldn't be her room. The next room looked more promising. Clothes were strewn around, things thrown on top of the chest of drawers. He rifled through a jewellery box – rubbish, most of it. He was more interested in what was in the drawers. In the second drawer he found two bank statements.

Let's see what she has . . .

The first account had very little in it.

She spent her wages as soon as she got them by the looks of things.

He looked at the second statement – a savings account. Not a bad figure. All paid in in one lump – where had she gotten that? No, it was some kind of inheritance from her mother, that was all.

Shoving the drawer shut his first instinct was to trash the place but he decided against it. He would find what he was looking for. He searched through more envelopes in another drawer – there was nothing that resembled a birth certificate or old letters that could be used as evidence. Fuck! She must have all the stuff like that in Waterford. This was a waste of time . . .

He went over to the bed. There was a pyjamas on the pillow.

"I thought she'd have some bit of a thing," he said to himself, picking it up.

He pointed the flashlight over the bed. What was it? A picture?

It was a framed cutting from a newspaper – an odd thing for someone to have over their bed, he thought.

Leo Kemp removed it from the wall to read it.

It was dated the 13th of June 1988. *The end of the term illegitimacy, the headline read. Tomorrow the term 'illegitimacy' with all its stigmas and awful connotations will be gone legally at last.*

In the calendar of social change tomorrow is a significant day. It marks the coming into effect of the long awaited Status of Children Act . . .

Leo read on . . .

This Act radically alters the law relating to children born outside marriage. Banished forever are the legal discriminations endured by one group of children known as fillius . . . nobody's heir.

The hairs stood up on the back of Leo's neck. Illegitimacy gone . . .Jesus – she meant business. No one would put a thing like that up over their bed unless it was important to them.

He vaguely remembered the act being passed sixteen years before and all the talk about the word illegitimate being banned – no more bastards. He remembered scoffing at the news and his mother saying the whole world has gone cracked and what was the point in getting married at all?

Nobody's heir . . . Somebody's heir . . .

He was sweating now as he continued to stare at the cutting. She was out to get her father – whoever he was.

She must believe his uncle was her father, and if she was studying this kind of legal stuff she would be a force to be reckoned with. For the first time since last night, he began to have real doubts about his uncle. Was he the one telling lies?

He cursed himself for coming here now – he felt worse than he did before. He rubbed his face to banish thoughts of what she looked like – of her face, of similarities . . .

Leo kicked the base of the bed.

His uncle could go on telling lies if that's what he was doing. He would see to it. No way was any bastard child taking what was due to him . . .

Putting the frame back on the wall, he went downstairs quickly. He felt like burning the place to the ground now but she wasn't worth it. He wouldn't get himself locked up because of her.

Time he was out of here. As he stuck his head out the bathroom window he heard a car coming from the village direction.

He pulled his body back in instantly, in case the security sensor light would come on and the car driver would notice.

As soon as the car had passed he climbed out the window. Fuck! He had cut his hand on some of the glass, through the plastic lambing glove.

Damn! Had any blood dripped down inside the house? No, he didn't think so.

His hand throbbed as he scrambled back over the ditch into his uncle's field. At least it was a bright night. He had the van parked in the laneway at the far side of the field. He would drive back to the road without lights in case someone saw him.

The glove now lapped back over his bleeding hand, he eventually reached the bungalow. After going in, he sat down and grabbed one of the bottles of beer left over from the night before. What would he do next? Would he tell anyone what he had seen?

No – then they would know he had broken in.

His Uncle Abe had said he would see his solicitor first thing tomorrow. Leo would make sure he did. His uncle would know how badly he wanted Knocklannon. He took another slug of beer. No one was going to do him out of that. Not now. Not ever. He took a third slug out of the bottle, trying not to remember the flash of fear in his uncle's eyes when yer one had mouthed off. The flash had been followed rapidly by anger, but he had seen it all the same.

Florrie had dreamt of the children. She had been playing in the garden with them in one of the homes she'd visited years ago, three year olds and ten year olds hanging out of her asking, "can I go home with you?"

She woke in the spare room in a sweat. She could see their eyes – all saucered and hopeful . . .

What day was it? The first of January. Why was she sleeping in here?

It was several seconds before she realized what was giving her a black hollow in her stomach.

She could see Vera, her sister-in-law, saying it now – that Hannah Casey had claimed Abe was her father.

A wave of shock passed over her again, and she closed her eyes tight.

Sleep had come late. She had sat watching a silent computer screen for a long time after Abe had gone to bed, unable to move.

He had denied it over and over and in the end become angry at her doubt.

If she believed him everything would be simple, she knew. They could go on with their lives, drawing a line under this unusual and upsetting incident eventually, putting it down to Lil Casey's unstable mind.

But the doubts kept coming to the surface.

"That ceiling needs a fresh coat of paint," she said, looking up. "And that curtain needs a few more hooks to stop it sagging at one end. " Paint . . . curtain hooks . . . Why was she thinking about such things? It was her mind trying to help her, she knew, making her sidestep what she was unwilling to deal with, until she was able to deal with it . . .

She heard a tractor start up in the yard and cattle bawl knowing they were about to get their meal. He was up.

He had denied it. Hannah Casey was the liar. Dead Lil Casey too . . .

Florrie closed her eyes tight again and did the sums in her head.

Hannah would be forty years old next month. That means she was born in 1965. That she was conceived forty weeks before that. May 1964. Florrie's stomach heaved. She was right – Abe would have been in Dublin for the Spring Show. 1964. It was a year she preferred to blank out. The one where he'd told her to go get herself checked out – that she was probably to blame for them not having children.

She tried to reason it out.

Why had he not said that the year before? Was it that now he knew he was capable of fathering a child? That Lil Casey was carrying his child that summer and that winter?

Throwing back the clothes she put her dressing gown on and went downstairs to the study. The photograph of him taken on prize giving day was on the wall. It had been in the *Irish Independent. Wexford farmer Abraham (Abe) Stephenson (left) being presented with the . . .*

Knocklannon Glory, Gem's ancestor, had swept the boards in the Hereford class and against all other breeds. It had been a glorious day . . . And all the time . . .

She felt a wave of nausea pass over her again. He couldn't have done that to her, could he?

She shivered as Maimie Breen's words came back just as they had come back to her several times in the night – Abe and Lil. They had history. Had he been picking up where he left off with her every time he was in Dublin?

Florrie couldn't stop herself painting the pictures – him meeting up with her every time he was away at cattle shows round the country? In hotels . . . beds . . .

Florrie felt nauseous at the thought of such betrayal.

What was she going to do? The word would be out in the locality by now and the rumour would spread like wildfire.

The thought of people talking about them . . . about her. Pitying her . . .

No, best not let that kind of thinking in . . . She had no control over what anyone thought of anything, so why worry about it? She had only to concentrate on what she would do herself.

There would be plenty of people who would revel in the news, she knew. The great Abe Stephenson – how the mighty have fallen, they'd say! Some people would fatten on the news.

No, don't think of those things, she told herself. Stay calm. She had to do that. And tread warily. Innocent until proven guilty . . . She knew she must be careful. If she believed Hannah Casey over him and it turned out not to be true, there would be no going back. Instead, she must bide her time, be sure of her facts. Only then would she know what to do . . .

It surprised her that she wasn't tearful, but she knew it was because she was too full of fear. Tears would come later – if they had to.

She stared at her husband's face in the photograph. He was forty years younger then. Was there a resemblance between him and Hannah? Around the eyes . . .

She went into the drawing room. It was freezing cold. Her teeth chattered as she rooted in boxes of photographs. She found the ones she'd taken at the carols night. There was Hannah in the front row, singing . . .

She stared at the photograph, again searching for resemblance. Hannah. Abe's grandmother was called Hannah. Why had Lil Casey chosen that name, of all names?

Hannah didn't look like a Casey – her height, her figure, her skin tones were different. Why hadn't she seen it before? Was that what had drawn her to Hannah in the first place – some kind of physical appeal based on Stephenson familiarity that she just hadn't seen?

She picked up a photograph of Abe's grandmother. Hannah Jane Stephenson had a kind face. The eyes . . . She held the photo with Hannah up beside it. Was there a resemblance? A lump formed in her throat as the realization sank in that there was.

"No, it's only my imagination," she said to herself. "I'm seeing things that aren't there."

She wrapped her dressing gown round her more tightly. No, it was her imagination. She was getting light-headed from lack of food.

It was 10.45. She needed to eat. She would get a shower, get dressed up and have breakfast. Then she would be ready to face the world – and him. She had learned that over the years – make the effort when you are feeling low to look good and it will help bring you through the day.

No, she told herself, he was telling the truth. He hadn't been unfaithful to her. What happened between him and Lil was years before that and only teenage stuff. She was putting two and two together and getting eight.

Hannah's father was someone in Dublin, like Vera said.

The phone rang downstairs again as she got into the shower. Let it. It would be Vera again.

Florrie practised her deep breathing. In for seven, out for eleven . . . Let go and let God . . . Breathe out the pain. Stop imagining the worst. It seldom happens . . .

She had to keep calm – that's what she had to do. And think carefully how to act. Everyday routine – that would help her survive for the moment. She would act as if everything was normal and the acting as if would help her get through this, until she knew what to do.

It was New Year's Day 2005. Any other year she would have been making resolutions. Lose weight, do more for the community, finish another project . . .

Stay strong – that would be hers right now.

She didn't go down to the kitchen until twelve fifteen.

The thought of being in the same room as him and of making lunch for him appalled her, but innocent until proven guilty . . . She would go through the motions of normality until such time as she knew that normality had really changed.

Again she told herself that if he was telling the truth she would be doing him a great wrong.

When he came in with Max, the dog, at a quarter to one, his comments were on the cattle and the weather and how he'd have to clean up the yard now that the beet season was over.

She heard herself make short answers – a bad night's sleep making her head feel weary and as if she was at a distance from herself.

The sound of a car coming into the yard made her jump. Her husband went to the window to see who it was.

"Roy."

Florrie wished he hadn't come but she knew why he had – to see if she was all right.

"H-H-hello."

Abe was putting on his yard coat to go out again.

"Will you have a cup of tea?"

She noticed that Roy didn't look at his uncle.

"Many lambs last night?"

"S-s-s-six."

"Good. I'm going to Newtown."

Florrie felt as if she was in a surreal world – talk about lambs and checking cattle on the outfarm, as if everything was normal.

Roy was struggling to say something, she could see.

"I-I-I'll be a-a-away f-f-f-f-for a week."

Her husband stopped at the door.

"What? Where?"

Florrie saw Roy's face redden. His speech was always worse when he was talking to his uncle.

Eventually he got what he wanted to say out – he was going to Waterford to do the week long speech therapy course.

"That's wonderful. Really wonderful."

"What about the yard work?"

"L-L-Leo'll do it. A-a-nd A-a-idan will h-h-help if he n-n-needs h-him."

"Right."

Florrie heard her husband whistle Max and the back door close.

Roy was looking at her.

"I'd forgotten you were going today," she said. "I should have remembered. I'm so glad you're doing it. It'll be new life for you . . . Sit down. There's tea . . ."

"Th-anks."

Roy was looking at her anxiously.

"Y-you all right?"

Florrie sat down, afraid that her legs might no longer hold her.

"You were there last night?"

"Y-yes."

"Tell me what happened exactly. You're the only one I can depend on . . . Do you think she was telling the truth?"

"I-I d-don't know."

"He's denying it."

"Y-yeah."

"Right now I'm not sure what's happening, what's true and what's not true, but it will all come clear in time. In the meantime we'll all have to carry on and you mustn't worry about me . . . You must make the most of this course, you hear . . . There'll be gossip, but it'll pass over. You look after yourself."

"I d-d-don't want to go now."

"Yes, you do and you will, you hear? This is not your load to carry. I will be all right . . ." She was hugging Roy now. "What happens, happens. If he's telling the truth, I have to stand by him."

"I-I-f he's n-n-not?"

She was grateful that Roy still had a hold of her.

"I'll cross that bridge when I come to it."

Going to church the following morning was one of the hardest things she ever had to do.

Not going would have drawn more attention. She never missed a Sunday. If she, or they, didn't attend it would be a signal to other parishioners that things were very grave.

Some people seemed a bit uneasy, but Florrie steeled herself for talking to them – superficial conversation about weather, the sermon, the usual things . . .

For a second, as they walked out of church, she felt Abe's hand on her elbow guiding her through the door. She shrunk from his touch.

"Help me through this, Lord," she prayed silently as they headed to the car.

Abe had got ready for church as usual, dressed and ready to leave the house at 10.30 a.m. for the 11.00 a.m. service.

He hadn't even asked her if she was going. He had just presumed she was, as always.

She was silent in the car on the way home. She couldn't get Hannah out of her head – the time she had gone to welcome her to the locality, when they'd talked of private things. Was that when she hatched the plan – seeing the history of her and Abe? No, she found that hard to believe or was she a hopeless judge of character, a gullible eejit like Abe had said?

She thought of the day before Christmas Eve when she'd had coffee with Hannah.

No wonder Hannah had seemed uneasy with her line of questioning after the Maimie incident in the day care centre. Questions about her mother working at Knocklannon . . . Was it on the tip of Hannah's tongue that day to tell her?

Maybe it was Lil that was telling lies. Maybe Hannah was just believing what her mother had told her. Maybe Lil had a fixation with Abe and had said he was the child's father out of some kind of revenge at being spurned? Who knows how a person's mind worked? Perhaps she'd been mentally unstable. Who would have known when she wasn't living in the area?

Florrie thought of Hannah telling her she would have been a great mother, if she'd had the chance – was that genuinely felt or was Hannah Casey winding her up, all the time calculating when and where she would make the accusation?

No, leave it down . . . Stop letting your imagination cause you pain . . .

Abe stopped the car at the service station in the village. Why wouldn't he, she said to herself, it was normal Sunday behaviour for them to get the papers there.

She steeled herself to go into the shop while Abe filled the Mercedes with diesel.

"I'm fine, thanks," she said, when Tom Carthy in the shop asked her how she was. "I'll pay for the diesel as well."

Through the window, she could see her husband replace the nozzle in its place and put the cap back in.

Coming out of the shop she looked neither one way nor another. She would not avoid anyone but she would seek no conversation either.

Her heart was thumping as she got back into the car. So much for thinking she had achieved serenity in her life – that she could accept what it threw at her with equanimity. Right now she felt very fragile.

In the afternoon while Abe slept, head back and snoring in front of the television, she went for a walk down the fields. She did not reply to Vera's phone calls. She was glad Vera wasn't in church.

After checking the cattle, she walked down the fields until she saw Casey's cottage from a distance. She thought of all the housing development plans. She was relieved to think that they might never happen. She felt the urge to walk further but changed her mind and turned back to the house. No, she wasn't strong enough yet.

Vera's car was in the yard. Florrie went into the cattle shed. She would stay there until Vera had gone. Listening to her would only agitate her. Knocklannon Gem was lying down in one of the far pens chewing her cud. She opened the gate of the pen and went in.

The cow, heavily pregnant, didn't move. She stroked the cow's head.

"Good girl . . . Your time is getting close now, isn't it? Good girl."

She checked the cow's teats. Nothing yet, but it would be soon. The udder was firmer.

Abe had high hopes for the calf. He'd imported semen from an internationally renowned bull – one whose offspring had featured in the prizewinners' rings in Tullamore for the last two years running.

She took up the currycomb that was on a shelf over the pen and started to comb the cow's coat as if she was preparing her for a show.

The rhythm of the movement and of the cattle chewing their cuds calmed her. Gem was a fine animal, she would be the mother of a fine calf . . . She had been bred for beef, genetics studied to get the best animal possible by good choice of sire and dam.

She heard Vera's car start up, revving it too much as usual. Burn the clutch. She never learned.

Back in the kitchen, Abe didn't comment on Vera being there. She didn't either.

She went into the drawing room and lit the fire. She couldn't stand to be with him in the kitchen.

She tried to watch television but all the images ran together. Every channel had a family film on. Florrie zapped again as yet another child hugged a parent.

Hannah would have had very few hugs as a child . . .

She sat there in front of the drawing room fire, staring at the flame, praying for guidance about what to do. Again and again the memory of Hannah singing *Away in a Manger* in that room came back into her head. Why was she seeing her face so much? Did it mean that it was Hannah she was meant to talk to?

By nightfall her instinct was still to get in touch with Hannah. Her husband would be livid if he knew, but he didn't need to know. She would organize it on her own and make up her mind then, based on what real information Hannah had.

No, she wouldn't go to the cottage. That was too public.

Getting up from the chair, she went to the landline and rang Directory Enquiries.

Glancing out the window to make sure that Abe was still out checking the yard before he went to bed she asked the operator for phone numbers for Hannah Casey.

No landline nor mobile were available – ex directory.

"Thank you anyway."

Florrie considered what to do now.

Hannah's numbers were withheld. Florrie thought of the two silent calls she'd had. In September? October? Was it Hannah making those calls? Now she was getting paranoid . . . It could have been anybody.

Florrie got out her mobile phone and taking a deep breath rang another number – Peg Travers.

She kept her voice as light as she could. Florrie asked her neighbour for a favour.

"Do you have Hannah Casey's mobile number, I wonder. I thought I had it but I seem to have mislaid it . . ."

There was a brief silence on the other end of the phone.

"Hannah's?"

"Yes."

"I do have it but I'd have to ask her permission to give it out first," she heard Peg say.

"Of course. That's perfectly understandable. Perhaps you'd pass my mobile number on to her then? I'd appreciate it. Thanks. No, no, it's not urgent, just if she'd ring me when she can, thank you."

She could hear Peg asking her if she was all right.

"Yes, yes, of course I am. A Happy New Year to you."

Her hand shook as she put down the phone. Abe was coming in through the door. Had he heard? No, he couldn't have.

Switching off the drawing room light to go to bed in the spare room she felt calmer. It was a good sign. It meant her instinct or God's prompt, if that was what it was, had been right. At least now she had a plan of action. Calm had come, but would it be the calm before the storm . . .?

Hannah felt exhausted as she got off the Waterford bus at Wexford station. Good, there were taxis there. Another twenty minutes and she'd be back at the cottage.

Her car was in Drumcadden since New Year's Eve when Beryl had driven them back to Waterford.

How much sleep had she had in the last five days? Very little and even that hadn't been sound.

By the time the taxi turned off the main Rosslare road relief at being back was turning to fear. What was facing her back at the cottage? What had happened at the Stephenson house? At the Kemp house since Leo's party? Had Florrie been told? What was going to happen? She felt terrified but also excited.

She fumbled in her bag for her keys as they got closer to Drumcadden. Beryl had already gone to work when she was leaving the house in Waterford. She had told her she was going back to Drumcadden. Beryl surprised her by not raising any objections.

"What has it to do with me?" she said. "You've told me that often enough in the last few days."

"I didn't mean . . ."

"You never 'mean'. You just go on doing what you want to do regardless of what anyone says."

"I do not!"

"You don't need me. I have to go."

"I do need you. You're my best friend, for God's sake!"

Beryl had looked back at her from the door as she left.

"Yeah, well, friendship is a two-way street. Right now, you're too high maintenance for me."

"You think I was stupid telling them . . ."

"Yes – when you were drunk!"

"Maybe that's what gave me the guts to do it."

Hannah saw her friend shrug her shoulders.

"I have to go. Maybe we need some space from one another. I'm getting into trouble at work, making mistakes because I'm wrecked tired or agitated after phone calls from you at all hours of the day and night, but you wouldn't want to know my troubles, would you?"

"Beryl . . . I don't want to be messing up your life."

"I have to go. The place is full this week."

"I'll ring you . . ."

"I don't know."

Hannah had been physically shaken after the row. Beryl wanting space, turning her back on her when she was in the middle of the biggest event of her life – how could she? Hannah felt wretched. No Beryl to talk to . . .

The cottage looked bleak and unwelcoming as Hannah paid the taxi driver at the gate.

She had just gone to the toilet when she noticed the broken window. Her heart almost stopped. There'd been a break-in! What if the burglar was still in the house?

She needed something to defend herself with – the poker? It was in the kitchen beside the cooker . . .

She went back into the kitchen, feeling terrified.

"Get a grip," she said.

She pressed the 999 digits on her mobile phone.

"How long before someone will be here?"

The voice at the other end of the phone suggested she ring a neighbour to come stay with her.

"Yes, I will."

Hannah felt petrified. Who would break into her house? Petty thieves seeing there was no one at home? Some local drug addict desperate for goods to sell to buy drugs? Who would she ring? Peg. Peg Travers . . .

She got through on the third attempt, her fingers fumbling with the digits.

"You've rung the guards?"

"They're on their way."

"Good. I'll be there in five minutes. Get into your car and lock yourself in it, just in case there's someone still in the house."

"What's been taken?" Peg asked, as she surveyed the broken bathroom window a few minutes later.

"Nothing in the kitchen. I don't know about upstairs. I haven't gone up there."

"Right, we'll go up together. Maybe nothing's gone . . . Just don't touch anything."

"There's nothing to take."

"Usually it's small valuables they're looking for – jewellery, money," she heard Peg say as she struggled up the stairs behind Hannah, who was wielding the poker.

They went into the spare room first.

"Someone's been in here all right."

The wardrobe door was open and all the drawers.

Hannah's skin crawled – the cottage felt dirty now, contaminated.

The door to her own room was open.

"I'm behind you, don't worry," Peg said.

They walked into the room. Every cupboard was open.

"Someone's been through my letters and stuff – Jesus!"

"God Almighty, isn't that desperate?"

It was then she saw it – the incorrectly replaced frame over her bed. Whoever had broken in had taken it down to read it. Fear gripped her. Her bank statements, the framed article about the Status of Children Act – it was no ordinary burglar that had broken in – it was someone who knew her and wanted to see what she had. A two-legged rat rifling through her papers . . .

Hannah suppressed the urge to tell Peg what she was thinking.

"Could be worse," Peg was saying. "Whoever it was saw there wasn't much worth stealing and cleared out. The guards'll fingerprint the place, don't worry. Come on, there's no point in hanging around here. You can stay with me tonight, and tomorrow we'll come back here, roll up our sleeves and give the place a good clean-up. Peter Conway'll fix that window straight away for you, no bother, but you might think about getting new windows sometime. The double-glazed ones are more secure, not to mention keeping in the heat better . . ."

They stood in the kitchen waiting for the Gardaí to arrive.

"You were back in Waterford for a few days?" Peg asked, as Hannah handed her a mug of tea.

"Yes."

"That's nice," Peg said.

Was Peg using this as a conversation opener? Had word got out from the party on New Year's Eve?

The Gardaí didn't hold out much hope of finding who did it.

"We'll check out the usual suspects, of course, but it was opportunists most likely. At least they didn't wreck the place on you."

"That's what I said," Peg said.

"Could you stay with a friend until you get the window fixed – you look a bit shook."

"She's staying with me. As long as she likes."

She was sitting in Peg's kitchen with a mug of cocoa in her hand before Peg said it.

"I . . . heard about the party."

"Right."

"I called over the other day – Monday – to see if you were ok but you weren't there."

"We went back to Waterford that night. It was a bit tense . . ."

"I can imagine . . ."

"Were you shocked?"

"Yes. You could have knocked me down with a feather actually. To think he's your father . . ."

"He's saying he isn't . . ."

"Bullshit. If your mother said he is he is. I knew your mother well enough to know she wouldn't lie about a thing like that. I wish she had told me about you – about this whole thing . . ."

"She probably couldn't risk anyone knowing."

"Now everyone knows . . ."

"I didn't mean for it to come out the way it did. I just lost it when I saw him standing there, looking at me as if I was on a level with something stuck to his shoe."

"Do you think he knew about you?"

Hannah felt reluctant to go into much detail with Peg.

"It's something I can't discuss too much at the moment – sorry."

"I understand. It's your own business."

"Thanks. I appreciate that."

"He's denying it . . ."

"It's my mother's word against his and she's dead . . . Have you heard anything – about how they're taking it?"

Hannah knew from Peg's face that the news wasn't good.

"It's like you said."

"He's swearing blind he isn't?"

"Yes."

"And?"

Peg looked uneasy.

"He's threatening legal action against you – that's the story that's going round."

"God!"

"He'll probably trying to protect what he has. Who knows what he's thinking. Maybe when he gets over the shock of you finding him . . ."

"And pigs might fly! Who was I codding coming to live here – he'll never acknowledge me."

Hannah suddenly thought of Florrie.

"Have you seen Florrie? She wouldn't have known and she was so nice to me . . ."

"She's a good woman."

"I shouldn't have opened my mouth . . . She doesn't deserve that – not me blabbing it out in front of all and sundry."

"We all do things we regret sometimes."

"I was fed up of being brushed under the carpet . . . it all just burst out."

"I know. Em . . . Florrie was in church with him the next morning . . .or so I heard . . ."

Hannah was shocked.

"What? She knew that and she stood by him?"

"She looked very pale – or so I hear – but she may not have known. You could be accusing her in the wrong . . ."

"But she must have known! Jesus, what sort of woman is she? She probably blames my mother, thinks she was a slut."

"Your mother wasn't a slut. She knew Abe Stephenson since she was a child."

"Did she ever mention him to you – liking him or anything?"

"Not when she was grown up, but she fancied him as a young one – I used to tease her about him. All she'd say was, 'He'd never look at the likes of me.'"

"Well, he must have! Unless he took advantage . . ."

Hannah felt Peg's arm around her.

"Don't go torturing yourself with them sort of thoughts, love. What happened happened and the way you've got to look at it is that the world is a better place for you being in it."

Hannah suddenly felt weary.

"I wish I was certain of that . . ."

"You can be. Nothing's without a reason, even though it might be rocky for a while. You keep your head up – you've done nothing wrong by being born. You've put your truth out there, that's all."

"His sister and Leo won't be happy. They'll think I'm after his money."

"It wouldn't do the pair of them any harm to get their comeuppance. That Leo fella is too sure of himself for his own good."

"What about Roy? Do you think he'd accept me? He seems like a good sort . . ."

"He is. I'm sure he would. His mother'd be a different story. I don't think she's been seen in the locality since."

"I almost feel sorry for her. Her brother falling off his pedestal. She wouldn't have been expecting it."

"You know what they say about the peacocks – they'd die of pride only for their two big ugly feet. Everyone's human when it comes down to it."

Hannah closed her eyes. This was a nightmare!

"No one has contacted you – not even Roy?" Peg asked.

"No."

Peg was getting up with difficulty from the table.

"Come on, let's go back to the cottage and clean it up – you'll feel better when it's back to the way it was."

"Ok but would you stop at the shop – I need to get some disinfectant . . ."

Tom Carthy looked a bit shocked when she walked into the shop but greeted her as normal.

"Hannah. Good weather, isn't it?"

"Yes, yes it is," she said before going down the aisles to find what she wanted.

She felt as if every eye in the place was on her.

"I've had a break-in. Peg is going to help me clean up the place."

Tom Carthy looked shocked and concerned.

"Ah, no! God love you. That's an awful thing to happen. It's happened here once and I wasn't the better of it for days. Did they take much?"

"No. Not much to take."

"A good dog – that's what you need – an Alsatian that'd frighten the bejaysus out of whoever it was. Have these things on the house – it's the least I can do after what you've been through."

"I can't," Hannah said, holding out a twenty-euro note.

Tom Carthy pushed it away.

"It's important to support our neighbours. What would we do without them?"

What was Tom Carthy thinking? Had he heard about her and what she'd said? Better not to think about it. Act normal . . .

Back at the cottage the postman had been. There was a Christmas card, looked like Rita's writing. Must have got lost in the post.

"I'll get started," Peg said. "The immersion will have the water hot in no time. If you light the fire we'll be grand. Hannah . . ."

"Yes?"

Peg was looking uneasy again.

"I was going to tell you earlier but I forgot . . ."

"What?"

"Florrie Stephenson asked for your phone number."

"When was this?"

"Sunday night . . . no, Monday."

"What did you say to her?"

"I told her I'd have to contact you before I could pass it on – that's why I called in the other day, but I've got her mobile number here if you want it. She suggested that. Asked if you'd ring her when you can . . ."

"Thanks."

Hannah stared at the number scribbled on a piece of paper. So Florrie wanted to talk . . .

"I'll leave you to look at your post. Now where's the mop bucket?"

"In the shed."

"Right."

The brown envelope was an unusual shape – very long with the address typed differently than other letters. It looked like a solicitor's letter. It was. From McConnell and Co., Wexford. Sent on behalf of Abraham Stephenson Esq. Telling her he was suing her for slander.

Shock ran through her as she took in the gist of the legalize. Her own father taking legal action against her! How much worse could this get? She felt like going over there and screeching at him, telling him what she thought of him, how much she hated him this very minute . . .

"You're white as a sheet. What's wrong?" Peg asked, coming back in.

Hannah held up the letter.

"He's done it."

"Legal action? Good God! What are you going to do?"

"Talk to my own solicitor. I'll ring her now and see if I can get an appointment this afternoon. It'll mean a drive to Dublin, but what else can I do?"

"Better to find out where you stand straight away. She'll be able to guide you. Maybe it's all bluster and bravado."

Hannah looked at the letter again.

"He's demanding that I don't go near his property or any of his family or he'll – Jesus, get a barring order!"

"He's either a very angry man or a very frightened man. Can you prove that he's your father?"

"No. There's nothing written down as far as I know."

Hannah felt herself start to shake.

"He'd be too cute for that, the same fella . . ."

Hannah looked at the letter again. She took out her telephone and rang her mother's solicitor. At least she'd be on her side. And maybe she held some written evidence that Abe Stephenson was her father that Hannah didn't know about? No, she was probably clutching at straws there . . .

"Hello . . ."

Good. After telling the secretary that this was an emergency she got an appointment for half past five. Hannah picked up another note from the floor. Post. It was from the rector. Wanting her to ring him on his mobile. What was going on? She pressed the digits immediately. He was at Rathbrandon church right now, he said – could she meet him there?

"I'll tidy up here – you go ahead," Peg said.

"Thanks. I hate leaving you here. I can do it when I come back."

"Don't worry about anything. Just go."

Driving to Rathbrandon church, Hannah wished she could ring Beryl. She desperately wanted to tell her what had happened – about the letter and about how frightened she was this minute but she couldn't. Maybe later after she had talked to the solicitor.

Like Peg said, she'd know more about where she stood then . . .

The rector's car was outside the church. The Christmas wreaths were still on the Stephenson graves.

Reverend Mundy came down the church to meet her.

"I'll just close the outside door – keep in the heat."

Hannah was glad she had warm clothes on. Lack of sleep made her feel even colder.

The church wasn't as inviting as on a Sunday morning. There was no heat in the winter sun that shone weakly through the stained glass window behind the altar. Jesus cradling a lamb – *The Lord is my Shepherd/Therefore shall I lack nothing* . . . Lack nothing . . . How many times in her lifetime had she repeated those words?

"It was Nanna's favourite psalm – the Lord's my Shepherd . . . Just saying those words gives me strength on difficult days, she used to say."

"They give us all strength."

"You wanted to see me?"

"Yes."

The clergyman sat on the organist's seat opposite Hannah and appeared uneasy.

"Did he ask you to contact me? Abe Stephenson?"

"No. No, he didn't but I am aware of some concerns the family has. I'm also concerned for you, of course. I'd like to be able to separate out fact from rumour. That's why I thought it best to speak with you . . ."

"And every word will be confidential and not relayed back?"

"If that's what you want . . ."

There was no noise in the church while she spoke, the rector listening intently, nodding sometimes. She told him about Royle, about her mother, about who her mother had said her father was.

"You believed her?"

"Wouldn't you believe your mother? She didn't give that answer easily. The only reason she finally told me was because she was dying and because I pressed her. I told her I had the right to know."

"I see. My concern is that this is denied by Mr Stephenson."

"He told you that?"

Hannah felt anger rise inside her.

"No, but his sister Vera is seriously troubled by all this. It is a weighty allegation."

Vera Kemp – she might have known!

"I can't change the facts. She mightn't want to believe it, but that doesn't mean it isn't true no matter how many solicitor's letters he sends me."

"Oh."

"He is accusing me of slander."

The rector looked very serious.

"The burden of proof then is on you. Do you have any proof – documentation or evidence of a public relationship between your late mother and . . ."

Hannah stood up, feeling very sad.

"Excuse me . . . I don't think there's any point in having this conversation. You don't believe me either."

"I didn't say that."

"You didn't have to. And I don't even know if I can trust you enough to be here talking to you in the first place. Right now, I don't know who to trust. If I tell you anything, how do I know that it won't be repeated – they are your parishioners longer than I am. You don't know me a wet week."

"You have my word. I'm just trying to look at the facts of the situation. Abraham Stephenson is a . . . formidable man."

Hannah tried to control the shake in her voice.

"Yes – who contributes to the uptake of this place – and your salary, no doubt." Hannah forced herself to keep talking. "My mother . . . she was a gentle person – naive in a lot of ways – she'd have been putty in his hands, even as an adult. But I'm not like her. I've spent most of my life having to stand up for myself."

The rector stood up now too.

"Of course. Em . . . there is such a thing as a DNA test – done properly it could establish paternity or exclude with a great degree of reliability . . ."

"I can't see him agreeing to that . . ."

"Has it been suggested to him? It would put an end to the matter."

"The matter? Is that all I am?"

"I didn't mean it that way . . ."

"Huh . . ."

Hannah was heading for the door now, beckoning him to follow her.

"I want to show you something."

The cold breeze ripped at her face as she opened the door. The rector following her, she walked up the grassy bank to the Stephenson burial plot and pointed at the older headstone.

She told him about the name and about how she thought her mother had done it as some kind of connection.

"It would be my name and he couldn't do anything about it, you see."

The rector looked uncomfortable.

"She may have just liked the name . . . perhaps . . ."

"This is a waste of time . . ."

Hannah headed for the gate and her car.

"Hannah, wait . . . please!"

Hannah turned.

"What?"

"Only God has the power to see into everyone's heart. Prayer will bring a resolution in time – there can be forgiveness, reconciliation, even in the most difficult circumstances."

Hannah stood very still.

"I'm not the one telling lies," she said. "And I can look you in the eye when I'm telling you that. Try asking Abe Stephenson – see if he can do the same. Goodbye."

She felt even more hurt by the time she reached Dún Laoghaire. She shouldn't have gone to the church to meet the reverend. What had she imagined he'd be doing – carrying some good news to her, taking on the role of mediator between herself and Abe Stephenson?

Instead he was looking out for Vera Kemp, sussing her out – or maybe frighten her off? Yes, that was it – let the clergyman show her the gravity of her lies then she would back off, clear out, never to be seen again. Vera Kemp could think again!

The solicitor read the letter she handed her after she had filled her in on what happened. What did she think of her, she wondered, with her tale of drunkenness and accusation?

"You have no proof of any kind that he is your father?"

Hannah sighed. Here we go again . . .

"No. Unless there is anything here that my mother left . . ."

"I'm afraid not, but you say your alleged father – Mr Stephenson – made substantial payments towards your keep in the early years of your life?"

She took the post office book out of her pocket and explained how it had been in her mother's possession.

"She only gave it to me before she died."

She watched the solicitor study the book.

"She had no copy of the cheques she was given?"

"There's nothing with his name on it. My mother said he gave her bank drafts."

"No correspondence of any kind?"

"He was married at the time I was conceived. He's hardly going to leave a trail . . ."

The solicitor looked thoughtful as she looked at the entries in the post office book again.

"There are ten lodgements in this book in the first two years – if there were ten corresponding withdrawals from his bank account or drafts written against his account a few days prior to these lodgements you might have some evidence of a connection."

"Not much chance of that. He's hardly going to hand me his forty year old bank statements and say, 'Here.'"

"No. Without a DNA test then, I feel you have very little means of proving you are his daughter."

"He won't agree to any test. So what do I do – about the letter?"

"My advice is to do as he asks – stay away from him. I will acknowledge the letter on your behalf and represent you in court, if you wish."

Court! It was the first time the full implication of the letter had hit her.

"When? How soon?"

"A long time – a year maybe, but let's hope it won't come to that."

"Good God!"

"A lot can change in that time. He may not really want to go to court and we can counter with a DNA test request done through the courts."

"That'll put the wind up him!"

"My guess is that he is trying to frighten you off. It may be that he believes he isn't your father or that he isn't prepared to own up to being your father yet. My advice is to be patient."

Hannah stood up, then remembered about the break-in.

She told her about her bank statements being disturbed, about the frame being moved over the bed.

"No valuables were taken?"

"No. It was either him or Leo Kemp, only I can't prove it."

"Are you living on your own in the cottage?"

"Yes."

What the solicitor said next frightened her.

"Please give due regard to your personal safety. Perhaps stay with friends for a while."

"And let him think he's run me out? No way!"

Hannah was glad to get out of the building. It was a raw night – very few people were on the streets except those locking up shops and driving home.

She walked back to the Marine Road multi-storey car park, the wind cutting her cheeks. What would she do now? She wasn't hungry though she had eaten little all day. What she had eaten she hadn't tasted.

At the bottom of Marine Road she found herself in the left lane rather than the right. Why had she done that? She should have been heading back for Sallynoggin and Wexford.

She passed the railway station, the yacht club, the BIM headquarters.

She saw the wall behind the Georgian terrace where her mother had lived and the green back door that belonged to the basement flat. How many times had her mother unlocked that door and crossed the busy road to the shop for milk or a loaf of bread or to make her way to work?

She indicated left and immediately left again then pulled in in front of the terrace near number three.

She got out of the car and approached the gate. There were several lights on downstairs in what used to be her mother's basement flat. The curtains of the living room were open.

She could see a new carpet, different furniture, a big television at one side. It belonged to new people now. It wasn't her mother's anymore. What was she doing standing here like a weirdo spying on people's lives? There was no going back. Her mother was dead and she was stuck in the middle of this nightmare. God, was she losing it?

Hannah looked at her watch – it was six thirty. She couldn't face the drive back to Wexford just yet. She thought of Kit, Kit Bermingham, her mother's friend. She would go see her.

She had sent her a card at Christmas and Kit had replied saying she was welcome to call anytime, hadn't she? Yes, she remembered the address.

Rashers. She could smell them from the door.

"Hannah!"

Kit was smiling, ushering her in.

"Come in out of that before you freeze. It's good to see you. You just missed Jim. He's gone down to the shop with Jacinta and the little one."

"Your granddaughter . . . How old is she now?"

"Eighteen months. We're all mad about her and to think I was in such a state when Jacinta said she was pregnant but time heals, doesn't it, and aren't we blessed with the little mite? Her stuff takes up a lot of space, though. We're so glad to have the extra room in the garden. Jim has it insulated and the electricity and heat in it. We don't know ourselves. I'll show you when we get a bite to eat."

"I'd love to see it."

"I miss your mam a lot, though. Sometimes I catch myself thinking I must tell Lil this or that and then I stop. It's hard to believe she's gone. And your father – did you find him?"

"Early days," Hannah said, before changing the conversation. "Did the furniture come in handy?"

"It did. We're delighted with it. I have her sofa and the little table you gave me in the summer house."

"I'm glad they came in handy."

Hannah stayed with Kit for an hour. Yes, she liked Wexford, she told her and, no, she hadn't gone back to work in the hospital yet.

"I'm going to do a couple of night shifts a week, though, in a nursing home down the road. A neighbour, Peg, told me they were looking for someone for a few weeks. I don't feel ready to go back to work full-time yet."

"You're right too. Take a break while you can. Life is short. What's the point in killing yourself?"

Driving home, Hannah thought it was all moving too fast. Only now could she think of Florrie Stephenson's request, via Peg, that Hannah phone her.

She pulled in on the hard shoulder near a pub at Jack White's cross. She found the number written in the back of her diary. She keyed in the number and saved it under 'f'. Next she wrote the text.

"Will meet you. Let me know where and when."

She heard the text "pips" as she approached Gorey town. She pulled in on the side of the street to read it.

"Monday 10th," it said. "Granville Hotel foyer. 10 a.m.?"

"Will be there," Hannah texted back, her thumb quivering as she pressed the "send" button.

Vera Kemp couldn't believe what she had just done. She had given a bucket of sheep nuts to the hens.

What had she been thinking? Making work for herself . . .

With no shovel nearby she knelt on the damp ground and clawed as much as she could of the nuts back into the bucket, hens at the same time "pwawcking" in the henhouse, wondering what the delay was with their breakfast.

"Shut up or I'll ring your necks!" she shouted at them.

She glanced around hoping no one had heard. What a sight she must make – on her knees in the muck like a madwoman!

She got up with difficulty then stared down at the state of her yard coat. It'd have to be washed now because of the hen shit. Was she thick or what?

Putting the bucket back in the feed house she cursed the fact that she hadn't been concentrating, but ever since New Year's Eve she had felt like a zombie.

How dare the Casey one come out with such vile lies? Vera hoped she would rot in hell! If she had her this minute it'd be her neck she'd ring . . .

Vera splashed water in her face at the back door tap. She still couldn't believe what had happened – the party, Leo and her in the kitchen, the lies and the mad eyes of her . . . And Abe like a bull at a gap trying to get in there . . .

Vera hadn't been out much since. To think that the whole parish was talking about what happened – laughing at the good of it!

The rector hadn't been much help either. He was supposed to talk sense to her, make her withdraw her allegation, but she was standing over her claim, he said. She was mentally ill, that was it, and didn't know what she was saying! And he could go take a running jump at himself when he was looking for sustentation money at the end of the year.

It was all lies. All they had to do was rise above it and the fuss would die down when it was obvious no one gave it credence. That's what Abe had said – several times.

Going over to Knocklannon hadn't been much use. He always cut her off short, and Florrie was nowhere to be seen. A migraine, he said.

When Florrie did finally answer the phone she sounded distant and refused to be drawn into conversation about the accusation.

"Your brother has denied it. Goodbye."

Yes, he had been to see his solicitor, he said, when she pressed him. He didn't want to hear anymore about it. The solicitor's letter would put an end to it.

There was a pile of Roy's clothes on the kitchen table for ironing. He was going away for a week on that course. Such a time to be going anywhere, with the lambing not over and all this going on . . . Still, like he said, he had to go when the course was on and hadn't he stood in for Leo often enough. He could surely manage by himself for a few days.

She had nearly hit Leo when he asked if there could be any truth in the allegation. God Almighty, what was she coming to . . .

"And there fucking well better not be any truth in it," Leo had said, going out the door.

"There isn't!"

She had said it with such certainty. She knew her brother, didn't she? If he said it was lies, it was, wasn't it?

Plugging in the iron, her mind kept going back over every detail of New Year's Eve . . . A lump came back into the pit of her stomach as she relived it. Her brother and Lil Casey! The liar!

Several times she had thought of ringing the Casey one up. She had even searched for her phone number that the rector had given her for the carols. She wanted to scream at her, terrify her until she took back everything she said, until she left the area and was never seen again. Everyone would know then she was a nutter, that Abe Stephenson was the victim of an unhinged woman.

This iron was useless! She looked at the setting. It was at one. Damn! She moved it to three. Roy would probably do the ironing all over again himself, but right now she needed the distraction of doing something. Maybe the movement of the iron would soothe her mind . . .

In spite of wanting to think of something else, she found herself thinking about the day she had shown Abe Lil's death notice in the paper. Now that she thought of it, he hadn't said much. What exactly had he said? Very little. She had done most of the talking. He had hurried off because he was expecting the vet. But he was expecting the vet, wasn't he? He wasn't trying to make up an excuse to get out of there so he wouldn't have to react, was he? No! Vera tried to push the thought from her head, but others came to join it – like how come the child was reared in a Protestant children's home? It didn't make any sense. Surely Lil'd have ended up in one of those Magdalene laundries and her child sent off to America or somewhere for adoption, like you hear about on the telly?

And the name – how dare Lil Casey call her bastard child a name like Hannah? Notions above her station, that's why, she told herself – and because Granny Stephenson always had a soft spot for her . . . Still, she had no right . . .

The boys were in now from doing the yard work and she hadn't even made the porridge.

Roy told her to leave the ironing – that he would do it himself.

"Y-y-you go have a lie-d-d-down."

"I'm not sick!"

"N-n-no, b-but y-you look tired out."

Leo had Corn Flakes in a bowl.

"What the fuck sort of milk is this?"

"Powdered. We ran out."

Leo threw the bowl into the sink so hard it broke.

"Watch what you're doing!"

"I'm not eating that shite!"

"I haven't been shopping . . ."

Vera sat down at the table.

"I-I-I'll g-g-go to the shop and get a few things."

"Thanks. And if anyone mentions those lies to you, you set them right – you hear?"

Roy said nothing as he left the kitchen.

Leo was right – there wasn't much in the house. She'd hoped he wouldn't notice the milk . . . Maybe if she drove miles out of her way – to Bunclody, maybe, she could shop there and not run into anyone she knew. Yes, that's what she would do . . . She still couldn't face going out, running into people, even though she wanted to. She wanted to be able to hold her head up and carry on regardless but this whole thing had knocked the wind out of her. And now Roy, right at the wrong time was going away on this course . . . It'd probably be money down the drain. She didn't hold out much hope of it helping him. Hadn't he had speech therapy years ago and it didn't make a damn bit of difference. She had talked to the doctor about Roy's stammer once.

"A stammer is a difficult thing to cure," he said. "But if he could accept he had one he would relax more and it wouldn't be as bad," he'd said. "He seems to be very tense sometimes . . ."

"It's a cure I'm looking for, not comment," she'd said.

Alone in the kitchen, the anger at the Casey one welled up in her again. What was she doing coming out with lies like that? She wondered where she was now. She'd have received the solicitor's letter by now, surely. That'd show her!

But what if the solicitor's letter didn't work? Maybe it would take something else to drive her out. Vera had never felt such anger inside herself before. She had to do something, but what? What would drive her out? No one could be allowed to defame a person like that and get away with it. She had to be stopped.

Going to the dresser she took out a pen, writing pad and an envelope.

She printed the address – MISS HANNAH CASEY, DRUMCADDEN . . .

Get out if you know what's good for you. Your sort isn't wanted around here."

Sealing the envelope Vera felt better. She would post it tomorrow.

Chapter
NINE

The drive to the Parklands Hotel was longer than Roy expected. Twice he almost got cold feet and turned back. How could he face it – a roomful of stammerers just like himself? He had pulled in on the side of the road and tried to calm himself.

"Let's hope it won't be a waste of money," his mother had said as he left.

He didn't look at Leo.

"Eejit notion," his brother said, "and I have to pick up the slack."

"Roy'll do your work sometime you're away," his mother had said.

Her statement had angered Roy. How many times had he done Leo's work – getting up to fodder and feed when Leo was hung over? He hadn't done it for Leo, though. He had done it for the stock. He couldn't bear to think of them being left hungry or without proper bedding. Truth was he liked those times when he had the yard to himself, his brother still in bed and he with the run of the place.

How many times had he wished that Leo wasn't interested in farming – that he'd gone to college from boarding school or even wanted to spend his life as a car salesman – anything at all that would get him out of the place but no, Leo was always there . . .

He thought of what Hannah Casey had said. Christ, if that was true it would affect him too . . . If she was his uncle's blood she'd be entitled to Knocklannon. Leo wouldn't fall in for it, like he and their mother were sure he was going to.

He tried not to think it was true but some of his Uncle Abe's behaviour came back to him – like when he'd seen him oogling women lots of times, at shows, at the co-op, at one place or another that Roy had gone to with him, sometimes making comment to whatever man he was talking to about some women being a fine thing or a nice filly . . .

His Uncle Abe didn't deserve the wife he had. He would text his Aunt Florrie later to see if she was ok. She seemed to be coping all right but maybe it was just a front.

She was pleased he was doing the course – knowing that meant a lot to him.

He didn't know what to make of Hannah Casey now. Was she a liar? She didn't seem the type and she'd always seemed genuine to him – and her friend.

He wished now that he'd asked Beryl to dance at the party but he didn't want everyone watching him and teasing him so he'd shied away from her. Twit!

There were several cars already in the car park. Seven days in this place – how was he going to get through it?

He pulled in beside a red Vectra. A man in his fifties was taking a holdall out of the boot.

"H-h-hello."

"H-h-owye."

Was this man booked on the course as well?

The man held up the brochure for the course and smiled.

"A-a-all in the same b-b-boat!"

"Aye."

Roy felt relieved. He wasn't on his own. He felt better walking into the hotel but what if the staff laughed at him stammering? Would he blush to the roots of his hair and block so much he wouldn't get a word out?

There was no one on reception when they got there. His new acquaintance rang the bell.

A familiar figure came through from the inside office. It was Beryl.

She looked momentarily shocked and awkward just like he felt but then she smiled. She had a lovely smile.

"Roy! You're checking in?"

"Y-Y-Y-Yes."

"You're here for the course?"

He nodded.

"That's great."

"J-j-jesus, he knows the staff!" said the other man. "W-w-we're w-w-ell in so! I'm T-t-tom Finnegan."

"R-R-oy Kemp."

He shook hands with Tom Finnegan.

"You're both very welcome," Beryl was saying, putting registration forms in front of them. The course leaders have just checked in. The plan is for everyone to meet in the lounge at five o'clock so you've time to freshen up and get your bearings until then."

"Th-hank you."

Roy was glad to get to the privacy of his room. So much for thinking he'd leave home behind him for a week . . . Still, she was nice and he was glad he hadn't blushed when that Tom fella said that thing about them being well in with the staff . . .

She was a receptionist working in this place – that was all. It needn't interfere with his plans but he couldn't help wondering what she was thinking – was her friend, Hannah, a liar? The speed with which Beryl had tried to get her out of Leo's that night suggested that she was just drunk and shooting her mouth off . . . No, he wasn't going to think of all that stuff. He had to concentrate on what he was here for . . .

Later, in the room assigned to the course, it took thirteen minutes for the eight of them to say their names. Nervousness made them all block badly but they all waited until the person speaking got the words out. If he'd known the instructors were going to film all this he wouldn't have come. Was that what he looked like, sounded like?

Visual acceptance, they called it. It was painful to watch.

"You have to know what you're like in order to accept yourself," the instructor said. He'd gone through this himself, he said, and it was an important first step in recovery.

The group included five men and three women. Most of them seemed embarrassed or ashamed of being the age they were and needing help to talk.

Denis, one of the instructors, had a stammer himself but he had it under control. Listening to him gave Roy hope for himself. Denis talked about how, once upon a time, chairing a meeting like this would have been beyond him and of how, while his stammer was part of him, it didn't mean he was a lesser person for having it . . .

Roy saw Beryl smile at him when the group passed reception on their way to the dining room. He smiled back then looked away. Why had he done that? Why couldn't he just smile back and keep eye contact? Over forty years old and acting like a schoolboy . . .

It was the third day and everyone in the group had relaxed a bit. They were all practising the correct breathing and voluntary stammers – deliberately stammering. That was to take the pain out, Denis said, and to lose the self-consciousness around it.

The first trip to a shop to ask for his favourite sweets had been difficult but he'd got the words out eventually – 'Werther's Originals'. He liked those particular sweets but could never ask for them in Carthy's shop because they were on a display unit behind the checkout which meant asking for them by name.

The sense of achievement he felt now after saying it was tremendous.

"See – I knew you could do it," Denis told him.

After dinner they were free to do what they liked. He wondered if Beryl was still on reception. Usually she finished at seven. He'd seen her drive away in her Toyota. Didn't she live in the city?

He met her going through the fire doors on the second floor landing. She had been delivering a message to a guest.

"Hi. How is it going?"

"F-f-fine."

"You look happier than you did on Sunday anyway. I've seen people coming here for that course and walking out different people a week later."

"T-h-hat's g-good t-t-to hear . . . A-a-a-are you r-r-rushing off?"

"Not really. I usually just go home but . . ."

"I-I was g-g-going . . ."

It took an eternity to get the words out. He was going to walk down the road to a nearby pub just to get out of the hotel and away from everybody else for a while . . .

"I-if you f-f-fancied a d-d-drink?"

"Yes. Why not?"

Relief flooded through him.

Jesus, he'd managed it. He'd asked her out and she'd said yes.

"I'll see you at seven then."

He hardly tasted his dinner. What was he doing, asking Hannah Casey's friend out and all the trouble she had caused the family? No, this had nothing to do with Hannah Casey, he was simply asking Beryl out because he fancied her. She had nice eyes behind those glasses and a gentle voice and a caring ease about her that made her good at her job. She was a bit on the plump side but he was too and she had lovely breasts – at least he imagined she had under the top and jacket that they were trying to burst out of.

The first fifteen minutes were a bit awkward. Eventually he asked her if they could agree not to talk about what happened on New Year's Eve.

"I-I-t isn't our b-b-business r-really . . ."

Beryl looked relieved.

"You're right. It isn't. I don't want to get into what happened either. Hannah was drunk . . . We haven't been on great terms since, to be honest," Beryl said.

"R-r-right . . ."

330

Still, if his mother could see him now, she'd have something to say about it. Fraternising with the enemy . . . or her friends at any rate.

Eventually they talked about Beryl's childhood. No, she had no family. Except those in Royle.

Roy couldn't really imagine it – growing up somewhere like that, all those children, only one person minding them, life without relations and a farm and knowing where you belong . . .

It hadn't been easy – he could read that between the lines but Beryl seemed to have a very positive attitude to it.

"It's the past – best to just let it go sometimes. I'm not sure poking through it does any good . . ."

No, she'd never tried to find her parents. She was happy the way she was . . .

She asked him lots of questions – about school and farming and sculpting and singing and was genuinely interested in his answers. God, it was good to really talk to someone . . .

"Time please!"

"We'd better go before we're put out!" she said, laughing and grabbing her coat. "I didn't realize the time."

"M-m-m-e n-neither . . ."

Together they walked the few hundred yards back to the hotel, Roy accompanying her to her car at the staff section of the car park.

"Well – I'd better go. I'm on at nine o'clock. I'd better go home before it's time to come back again.

"Y-Yeah."

"Thanks for a lovely evening. I enjoyed it."

He felt the softness of her lips on his cheek as she kissed him.

"Goodnight," she said.

His arms were around her before he realized it, hugging her, burying his face in her neck and then they were kissing – soft, gentle kisses giving way to more eager ones, deeper ones. And he didn't want it to stop.

"Wow!"

They were back to hugging now but he didn't want her to get into the car and disappear back to wherever she lived.

"Y-You s-s-smell lovely . . . C-C-christ, could I t-t-think of n-nothing better to say . . ."

"You're all right. It's a compliment."

She was laughing but with him, not against him.

He was amazed at how speech came a bit easier when he was with her and she didn't mind waiting for the words to come.

And their mouths found one another again. No, he didn't want her to go. He wanted her in his bed all night, all week, with him in the daytime, talking to him with that soft voice of hers.

"I'll see you tomorrow."

"T-t-text me so's I'll know you g-got home ok."

She planted a kiss on the top of his nose.

"I will."

He wondered how, tomorrow, he was going to keep his eyes off her, how he was going to keep what had happened from the others in the group. They would slag him unmercifully if they found out .

"Goodnight."

He stood in the car park until she had driven out. What would his mother say if she saw him now? Leo? His Uncle Abe? He didn't care. This was his life and they could all feck off. He wouldn't want to hurt his Aunt Florrie though but she would understand about him liking Beryl. She always understood.

He woke early knowing today wouldn't be easy. They were all to talk about how difficult life had been for them because of their stammers. You had to let the pain out in order to move on, they said. Roy tried not to think about it. Everyone else would be going through the same thing too. He tried to reassure himself with that.

His phone 'blipped'. It was a text from Beryl.

"How are you today?"

He replied immediately.

"Great after last night. C U lt8r."

Tom Finnegan that he had met on the first day of the course copped on to Roy's good humour straight away. Roy felt his eyes on him as the glanced for the forty-fifth time through the glass panels of the dining room out to reception.

"R-r-roy h-hasn't t-t-old us where he was l-last night, lads . . ."

Roy could feel himself blush.

"J-j-jaysus. I think we're on to something!"

He had spotted Roy glancing repeatedly at Beryl on reception.

"It-t-t's not R-roy we should be c-calling this fella – it's R-R-Romeo!"

Right now Roy wanted to get up and leave. One after another members of the group told of the pain and humiliation they'd suffered because of their stammers. One man on a bus unable to tell the driver where he needed to get off and going miles out of his way as a result. A woman saying she'd pretended to be a mute and written the name of the place she wanted to go down at a train station rather than go through the embarrassment of blocking with a whole queue of people behind her. Another man talking about being mimicked in school . . .

Roy sat on his hands, his head down, as his turn got nearer.

"Roy? Would you like to tell us about your experience?"

It was Denis putting the question.

Roy had a lump in his throat.

There was silence in the room while they waited for him to speak.

He told it slowly. About his mother trying to cover her irritation with his impediment, as she called it – of his brother copying him when their mother's back was turned . . . He talked about school and social situations where he had experienced teasing and torment.

"And your father?" Denis asked. "How did he act towards you?"

The question floored Roy. His throat suddenly felt tight then big sobs broke from his chest. It took a long time for him to be able to get a word out.

"I-I d-d-d-didn't s-s-s-stammer until after . . ."

Slowly he began to talk about his father. How he'd taken him fishing and lamping rabbits and let him watch him as he whittled wood in the shed and how he couldn't remember his father, Harry Kemp's face, except from photographs and it upset him that he couldn't do that but he was only seven when . . .

There was silence in the room. Roy could look at no one's face as he talked of how a cow had died of ragwort poisoning and his mother had been berating his father for not having called the vet sooner and how his father had gone out to shoot crows in the evening, like he often did, when they were eating the barley and how Roy had heard the shot from the yard and how Bess, the sheepdog, had run howling down to him and Roy, playing ball, knew there was something badly wrong and how he had run up the lane after the dog as fast as his legs would carry him and how he had seen his father slumped over the ditch of the back lane field, red blood running all down the green grass . . .

Eventually he told of how he'd run back to the house and tried to tell his mother and how he couldn't say a word and how she had said 'What's up with you? Talk, for God's sake!' but he could only run up the haggard with her after him shouting that if he was trick acting he'd be sorry and then she heard Bess keening and finally saw . . .

"Harry!"

Roy couldn't say anymore.

Roy felt someone's hand on his back. It was one of the other members of the group handing him a tissue.

Eventually he told them all how he hadn't spoken a word for a month after that. Shock, the doctor said.

Roy couldn't face going down for dinner. At least in his hotel room he could pull himself together. He tried to tell himself that the others were no different. It was normal, Denis said, but tomorrow would be a whole lot better.

He hadn't been able to look at Beryl on his way up. All he had wanted was sanctuary.

The text had followed soon after.

"You ok?"

It took him half an hour to text back.

"Yes. Very tired. Tough day. Text you later."

She wouldn't want to see him like this – as white as a ghost after talking about things he'd never, ever said to a soul before. Right now last night seemed a long time ago. Beryl knew what the course involved though, didn't she? Hadn't she said as much last night about how sometimes boils have to burst for healing to begin . . .

Had his 'boil' burst? He didn't know how long ago it was that he had let himself think about the day his father died. He woke to hear gentle knocking on his hotel room door. He picked up his mobile phone to check the time. 7.30 p.m. Who was it? One of the group? There was a text message symbol on the screen.

He looked at it.

"I'm outside the door," it said.

Beryl looked a bit anxious when he finally opened the door.

"You all right?"

"Yes."

"I was worried about you . . ."

Then their arms were round one another.

"You'll be ok. The worst is over . . ."

He could feel Beryl's breasts through her uniform blouse.

They were kissing now, lying on top of his bed.

"I've never done this but . . ."

"M-m-e neither . . ."

And they had found one another's lips again . . . Under the sheets now he could think of nothing but the softness of her skin, the smell of her perfume, the taste of her nipples stiff under his tongue, her hands touching him all over.

He had never felt such physical pleasure. . . .

Eventually, their pleasure peaked, they lay back, arms still tight around one another.

"Are you all right?"

He felt her stroke his face.

"Never better."

"I'm exhausted!"

And they laughed until they had to cover their heads with the blankets to muffle the noise.

When they had tidied themselves up, Roy lay there, her head on his shoulder.

"Y-you're not s-sorry?" he said. "Was it all r-right – f-f-or a first time?"

She was kissing him on the lips again.

"It was great! Now I know what all the fuss is about. I wouldn't have done it with just anyone, you know that . . ."

"M-me ne-ither."

He tightened his arms around her and she cuddled closer before speaking again.

"You know what you were asking – about it being ok for a first time and that?"

"Y-Yes."

"Maybe we should do it again – just to make sure we don't forget how."

"M-m-my pl-leasure," he said, his arms tightening round her again.

Hannah cursed. She'd hit Waterford just at the time of the bridge lift. Why hadn't she thought of that? God knows she knew the city well enough. Now she would be late.

Sitting in her car in the waiting traffic she fumbled for Florrie's number on her mobile phone. Eventually she brought up the new message screen and sent the text.

"Stuck on bridge. Be there asap."

She was relieved to see the envelope icon float off the screen and the 'message sent' information coming up. She should have left half an hour earlier but she had slept badly. Peg had helped her to tidy and disinfect the cottage but she still felt uncomfortable in it.

She wished she had slept better.

How on earth was she going to nurse all night in the Springtown nursing home? She wished now she hadn't agreed to do the stand-in work . . . At the time it had seemed like a good idea – diversion, a few extra bob so she wouldn't be eating into her resources but a lot had happened since then. Beryl still hadn't been in touch. It was weird. She really must be pissed off with her.

She couldn't go see her today either even though she was in Waterford. By the time she had talked to Florrie it would be time to return home and get some sleep before starting work at seven p.m. like she'd agreed – an hour early to get the run of the place.

Maybe she had taken Beryl for granted – a bit anyway. Maybe Beryl was right and she always wanted to take centre stage. Still it hurt to hear her friend say it.

Beryl didn't have much of a life – that was probably why she was lashing out, Hannah thought.

Hannah wished she'd meet someone nice. Beryl had never had sex – Hannah was sure of it. Still she had the right to hold on to her virginity if she wanted to. She'd know, she said, when the right man came along but until then she was saving herself.

"You'll never marry a man if you give yourself too easy," Nanna used to tell them. "Why should he buy a cow when he can get free milk?"

They, as girls, had often laughed at this statement, Hannah retorting that she didn't want marriage to be a goal that you trapped men into, using sex as the prize . . .

At last! The bridge was down again.

It was twenty-past ten. The inside of the hotel was old world, full of paintings and nooks. Where would Florrie be?

Eventually she spotted her in a far corner, sipping tea, her face pale and drawn.

"I'm sorry I'm late."

"That's all right."

Hannah suddenly felt awkward and shaky. Florrie looked fragile too.

"Can I get you more tea?" Hannah asked.

"No thanks."

The waiter took her order. Espresso. Double.

"I was praying you wouldn't have got up and left."

Florrie spoke quietly.

"What answers would I get then?"

"He told you?"

"Vera did."

"He . . . ?"

"He denies it."

Hannah's hand shook as she looked straight at Florrie.

"I'm telling the truth. But the last thing I wanted to do was hurt you . . ."

"You came into my home. Were you laughing behind my back?"

"Never! You've been so kind."

Hannah tried to explain how it had all come out the wrong way, at the wrong time.

"It wasn't the way to do it – I know that – but I'd tried talking to him in November . . ."

She saw that Florrie Stephenson looked shocked.

"You had already discussed this with him?"

"One Sunday morning last month. Mount Leinster . . ."

"You met him there?"

"Yes. By arrangement. God! This must be hard for you. He hasn't told you . . ."

Had Florrie just smiled?

"He told me to get lost, basically – that I was making it up. That I was a gold digger, if you don't mind! For your sake I wish it was all a lie, or that it hadn't happened within your marriage but I can't change that. You can't blame me for believing my own mother, can you?"

"No."

"The night of the party I just flipped. Suddenly he was there and it all came out . . ."

Hannah looked again at the frail sixty-something year old woman beside her.

"It's a shock for you, I know. I can understand if you don't believe me. Why would you . . . He was so aggressive that day . . . cold . . . And then the solicitor's letter on Thursday. I couldn't believe he'd do that . . ."

"To his own daughter?"

"Yes. I know you don't believe me but . . ."

"I never said I didn't believe you."

Hannah was dumb-founded.

"You know he is?"

"I don't know yet – but I want to know why you think he is. As you can imagine, there's a lot at stake here for me and I have to be right about my facts. Until I am I can't decide what to do . . ."

She knew Florrie was shocked when she took the newspaper cutting out of her bag – the one of him at the Spring Show.

Florrie's hand was shaking as she looked at it.

"This was in the Independent. He'd have preferred it in the Times, he said. I told him he shouldn't be so ungrateful."

Florrie seemed to be in another world.

"Knocklannon Glory – our first champion. Two years after we got married."

"My mother had the cutting in her bag. It was the only photo she had of him."

Hannah stopped herself.

"I'm sorry – this must be dreadful for you."

"It's not for you to be sorry."

"My mother was a good person. He's probably saying she wasn't but she never had any other man in her life that I know of. She paid a high price but she never turned her back on me. Well, not totally.

At least I knew I had a mother. Most in the home didn't but I told you that before . . ."

Florrie Stephenson's voice was barely audible.

"Your birth certificate . . ."

"She didn't put his name down but he gave her money . . ."

Hannah took out the post office book and handed it to Florrie.

Florrie looked at it for a very long time as Hannah spoke.

"My mother said the payments came from him for years – particularly the first two – after I was born. She said he found the mother and baby home for her to go to because she hadn't a clue what to do or where to go."

"She told you all this?"

"I had to keep asking. Only that I said I had a right to know I think she'd have gone to her grave with it. You probably feel it'd have been better for you if she had – you wouldn't be here now with your life turned upside down . . ."

Florrie had picked up the newspaper cutting again.

"He was away for a week in May every year. His mother was sick and I could only go up for the day of the prize-giving even though I wanted to stay the whole time . . ."

"This is very hard for you . . ."

"I told you I couldn't have children. 1964 – that was the year he told me to get myself checked out – that it was me the problem was with, not him."

"You think . . ."

"That he now knew the problem wasn't with him."

"God!"

Hannah felt like crying. Florrie believed her over her husband! A terrible thought ran through Hannah's mind now, though.

"He wouldn't hurt you, if he found out you'd been here talking to me?"

"I don't think so."

"Thank goodness. What will you do?"

Florrie picked up her bag. Her tea sat cold and unfinished in its cup.

"I don't know yet."

Hannah stood up too.

"Thank you for meeting me. It means a lot. Are you ok to drive home?"

"I'm getting the bus. I left the car in Wexford."

"Right."

"Goodbye then. Please text me or ring me – if you want. I can't contact you – the solicitor's letter . . ."

"I know."

Florrie Stephenson was tucking her scarf inside the collar of her coat.

"A DNA test – what would that involve?"

"I asked him to have one taken . . . that day on the mountain but he laughed at me."

Hannah explained as well as she could about the swab from the inside of the cheek or the hair sample with the follicle intact.

"There's a lot of information on the internet but it has to be done by a doctor to stand up in court."

"I see."

Hannah watched Florrie leave. She looked older than sixty-three today. God, what had she done to her, telling her all this? Still, if she was in her position she'd prefer to know, wouldn't she?

It was one o'clock when Hannah got back to Drumcadden. She didn't remember half the journey back. She hoped Florrie had got home safely. What would Florrie do now? She'd just have to wait and see.

She was forcing herself to eat a sandwich when a text came through from Beryl – the first one for days.

"Roy K at hotel. On course," it read.

"Good God!"

Roy – her cousin – in the same place as Beryl worked. How awkward was that? She wished she knew what he was thinking, who he believed.

She couldn't ask Beryl to get talking to him, to suss out how he felt. The old Hannah might do that but no, she had learned her lesson – Beryl didn't want to be bothered with her life all the time. She'd only think she was using her.

Roy would probably steer totally clear of Beryl. He'd be even more tongue-tied than usual. He had seemed to like her though, when they'd met those few times.

"God knows what he thinks of me now – Hannah from Hell, probably. He's probably not even looking at Beryl because of her association with me."

She would text back later and keep it light . . .

Her heart raced suddenly as she heard a car pulling up at the gateway. She stood up to look out the window. Who was she afraid it was – him? It was the postman. Who was writing to her now?

She didn't recognise the writing on the envelope. Her name was written in big block capitals.

A shiver went up her spine as she read what was written on the single page.

"*Get out if you know what's good for you. Your sort's not wanted here.*"

Hannah's knuckles went white. No signature. My God! Who had sent it? She looked at the envelope again. Miss Hannah Casey. Miss. Not Ms. Who had sent her this poison pen letter? Her hand shook. She felt terrified standing in her own kitchen.

She checked the postmark. Wexford. Anyone could have sent it.

Instinctively Hannah locked the back door. She ran to close the windows that she'd opened to air the place, even the upstairs ones.

She was glad she wouldn't be in the house tonight. She would be somewhere safe – on duty in the nursing home where there would be lots of people.

She resisted the temptation to throw the letter in the fire. What would she do? Who would she ring – Peg again? No, she couldn't be running to her all the time. She had to get a grip.

She looked at the wording again. Who hated her that much? Was it another of her father's tactics to run her out of the area? No, he'd spent money on solicitor's letters – he'd hardly stoop to ordinary letters as well. A local crank had probably sent it. The use of 'Miss' suggested someone older.

She rang the Gardai. She asked for the garda she'd dealt with before about the break-in – Kevin Doyle. He remembered her. She explained about the letter.

"You think it could be connected to the break in?"

"Yes."

"Is there any reason why someone would have a grudge against you?"

"Yes, but I don't want to discuss it over the phone. I could call to the station before I go to work this evening."

It was organised. At least it would give her something to do, get her away from this place. She desperately wanted to ring Beryl, just to talk to her but how could she help – she was fifty miles away and had her own life to get on with.

No, she'd have to deal with this herself. Stuffing the letter into her bag she tried to put it out of her mind, tried to sleep for a few hours before her visit to the garda station and work.

She had locked the doors – yes, she had. God, she was getting paranoid. If she got herself wound up about the letter she would be playing into the sender's hands. She was staying put. It was her house and if she chose to live there no one could run her out of it.

"You think this is a campaign of harassment?" the garda said after she told him about the frame being disturbed on the wall.

His description frightened her.

"I hope not. I hope that's an end to it."

"It could just be some crank, someone unstable . . ."

"That's all I need!"

Hannah left the station ten minutes later feeling worse than she had when she'd gone in.

They could do nothing to help her – they had no leads on the robbery, all they could say was that if she received another poison pen letter to let them know immediately. Big help! Another one – Jesus, the thoughts of it!"

After getting something to eat she drove to Springtown nursing home.

Madge Daly, the owner, was a motherly type – big-busted and welcoming. Being shown round the rooms Hannah could see she was well liked.

The nursing home seemed to be run well. There would be a nurse on with her so she wouldn't have any major responsibility. That was the way she wanted it.

Trying to put the day's events out of her head she tried to concentrate on her work. She would need seriously strong coffee to keep her awake and a few blasts of night air every so often.

"Where do you live?"

"Drumcadden – near Rathbrandon."

"Drumcadden? That sounds familiar. There's someone from that locality here. Maimie – that's it. Maimie Breen, though you might have trouble getting any sense out of her. She comes and goes – in her head, I mean. One minute she's making sense and the next she'd lift you out of it with a screech."

"I'll remember that."

Dementia – she'd seen it before.

The old woman was a recent arrival.

"Health board bed. She was lucky to get it. That's her. Room 16. She'll settle down once she gets her medication. Come on – I'll introduce you."

"Maimie – this is Nurse Casey – she'll be looking after you tonight. She's from your neck of the woods, Maimie – Drumcadden."

Maimie's face wrinkled even more as she stared at Hannah.

"Casey?"

"My mother was Lil Casey. Jim Casey's daughter."

Maimie's hand came out and pulled the cover over her head.

Hannah was a bit taken aback. The other nurse rolled her eyes to heaven.

"It's one of those nights. Maimie, it's all right, nobody's going to touch you. Nurse Casey is great for looking after people."

"Wash the dishes, feed the hens, keep your mouth shut . . ."

Hannah couldn't make sense of what she was saying.

"Don't even try to figure it out!" the other nurse said.

"Casey, Lacey, Lil, wash the dishes . . ."

"She knew my mother."

Hannah was certain of it.

"Maybe or maybe it's just gibberish. You can never tell with her. Let it flow over you. It's the only way you'll survive in this place."

Hannah tried to think. Her mother had never mentioned a Maimie Breen but then she had never talked about any of her neighbours. Not even her schoolfriend Peg.

"We'll be getting you ready for bed soon, Maimie. You be a good girl now and we'll get you a nice cup of tea – all right?"

"Tea."

"It's a full time job humouring them – must be a change from coronary care. When are you going back?"

"Soon."

"Wouldn't fancy it myself but everyone to their own."

When Hannah arrived home the following morning at half past eight she was utterly exhausted. She would sleep all day. She stood in the kitchen looking around, fearful that someone had broken in again.

Thankfully there was no sign of disturbance. Quickly she riddled and re-filled the cooker. Even if she slept for hours the kitchen would still be warm. The electric radiator in her bedroom would keep the chill out of the air.

Without eating breakfast she undressed and crawled into bed. The first night of night duty was always the worst as your body got into the pattern of it.

The blaring radio woke her half an hour later. The noise was deafening. Some station blasting out pop music. She sat up in bed terrified. Was there someone in the house? She grabbed the poker that she'd brought up with her from the kitchen for protection. No, the sound was coming from behind the house. Trying to stay calm she looked out her bedroom window onto the field behind. The noise was coming from the tractor parked there with nobody near it. It was Leo Kemp's tractor. He was doing this deliberately. It was definitely his tractor – she'd seen him on the road with it several times, getting into it outside the pub the night he had annoyed her. The sound was deafening, even with the windows closed. What was she going to do? She couldn't sleep like this.

She had difficulty hearing the number the operator gave her. Her hand shook as she wrote it down. Leo Kemp. Mobile. She tried to think straight. If she rang him he would have her number and she didn't want that. She would set her phone to 'private'.

She dialled the number.

A male voice answered.

"Turn that radio off, do you hear? This minute!"

She could hear him laugh.

"It's broken. I can't turn it off."

"Switch it off now or I'm calling the guards. I'll have you locked up, you hear!"

After putting the phone down Hannah shook for a good five minutes. She was terrified, angry. Her eardrums felt like they'd burst. Thump! Thump! Thump! She covered her ears with the pillow. God, where was this all going to end?

Abe Stephenson ended the call on his mobile phone. The rector. Wanting to call out. That's all he needed . . .

Florrie was in the kitchen cooking, back from wherever she'd been in the car that morning, her back turned to him like it often was these days.

"Did you ask Mundy to come out?"

"No."

Her voice was cold, unemotional, unlike her. He'd prefer her to be a blubbering mess – at least he knew where he was with that. She had been like that for years – over-sensitive, dissolving into tears at the drop of a hat but she had only spoken to him in monosyllables in the past ten days. If that's the way she wanted it so be it. It made it easier for him. He had been ready to shout her down whenever she brought up the subject of Hannah Casey but the need hadn't arisen.

He just had to keep denying it if she did confront him, stay calm until the dust had settled. Christ – would he be able to manage it? He could feel the sweat coming out on his forehead just thinking about it. There was no answer from her solicitor yet. Maybe he'd hear no more about it. There had been no stir near the cottage for four or five days either. He'd checked several times using the binoculars from the far field.

He'd heard in the village that her house was broken into. Probably some opportunist who saw the place was quiet . . .

There was no bread on the table. Florrie was eating her lunch in silence. As she didn't move he got up and got the bread board himself.

"You want some?"

"No."

"Did Roy get away?"

"Yes."

"He could be throwing money down the drain."

Florrie just looked at him but didn't answer. She would defend Roy to the last. His wife was very pale.

"Gem isn't far off calving. Four or five days maybe."

"Yes."

"I'll have the vet on stand-by for a Caesarean but with a bit of luck it'll come normal. How do you think she is?"

He watched his wife put her plates in the dishwasher.

"Fine."

He knew she was in and out to the shed a lot these days – to get away from him probably.

Abe was glad of the silence when his wife had gone upstairs.

He was tired and the heat of the Aga was making him sleepy. The tablets could be doing it too. God knows what's in the things they prescribe only his doctor insisted he needed them.

"You should think about taking it easier, Abraham. The chest pain you've been having is a signal that something is wrong. You'd be foolish to ignore it."

He had refused to be referred for an ECG.

"I've never been in hospital a day in my life and I'm not starting now . . ."

The twinges of pain after the rumpus at Leo's had unsettled him though . . .

He nodded off in the chair, only to wake an hour later because of Max's barking. He was glad to wake up. He'd dreamt of her singing in the drawing room, calling him Daddy . . .

He got up with difficulty to look out the window. It was the postman's van.

Bills – co-op, ESB, vet – did they ever end?

He knew it was a solicitor's letter the minute he saw it. Fuck! She didn't waste any time. He opened it, his hands shaking. His letter had been acknowledged . . . He read on, his heart thumping louder as he did so. She'd see him in court – that was the bottom line. Fuck! Court! He leaned against the jeep to settle himself. Did that mean she had proof? What proof? He felt light-headed as he tried to remember if he had signed anything, any letter, any note? He couldn't remember only he knew he would have been careful – very careful. A wave of panic went ran through him again. She wasn't backing down!

He spat in the yard as he tried to decide on his next move. Damn! It was the rector's car!

The clergyman had no collar on. He was dressed in jeans and anorak as if on his day off.

"This isn't an official visit?"

"A chat between friends, I hope. How is Florrie? I missed her at church yesterday."

"She slept in."

"Happens to us all sometimes – as long as she's well . . ."

Abe took off walking across the yard.

"I've a heifer to check on. She's close to calving."

"I'll go along with you . . . It's the time of year for it, isn't it? Lots of new calves . . ."

"Aye."

Abe grinned thinking of the rector with his shiny shoes picking his way over muck and silage near the shed door.

"They certainly look like fine cattle," the clergyman said. "They're a credit to you both. Florrie is pleased they're doing so well, I'm sure. I know the cattle are very important to her . . ."

"Whatever it is you've got to say, Reverend, spit it out. I'm a busy man."

"Direct as always. Well, it's these rumours that are going round – they must be upsetting for you – for Florrie . . ."

Abe concentrated on Knocklannon Gem. She was still eating well. Time enough yet to isolate her in a calving pen . . .

"I hadn't you down as the sort to set store by gossip . . ."

"You and Florrie and Vera are my parishioners but so also is Hannah Casey."

"Hmph!"

"I can only judge character in the best way I can. She seems to believe she is telling the truth."

Abe tried to cover his shock.

"You've talked to her?"

"Your sister was very upset. I thought it my duty to help in any way I could . . ."

"Duty!"

"Mediation can help sometimes. I am just calling out of concern . . ."

"You've had an idle journey so."

The rector coughed.

"Perhaps but what I wanted to say is that . . . a DNA test would put an end to all this. It would set the record straight, put an end to the accusation . . ."

Abe hit the bar of the gate with vexation. The cattle were spooked for a second or two by the sudden bang.

"I think, Reverend, it's time you took yourself and your suggestions out of here."

"I was only trying . . . I will say one last thing . . ."

He heard the clergyman clear his throat.

" . . . not doing the test could be interpreted as being afraid of it . . . perhaps."

"I'm afraid of nothing and no one. Goodbye, rector."

As the clergyman's car left the yard Abe spotted Florrie watching from an upstairs window. Damn! Had she heard? He slammed the back door behind him as he entered the house.

At the sink in the back kitchen he splashed cold water over his face several times.

Fuck! Asking for a test . . . Why hadn't he said something different, reacted more calmly – justified not wanting the test, explained his position . . .

The rector would now think he was the father. Let him think what he liked – he'd admit nothing. It would blow over in a while, wouldn't it? Why was he feeling so scared then?

Heart pounding he listened in the hallway for noise of his wife's presence upstairs. What was she doing up there all this time?

In his study he slumped down into his armchair and took the letter out of his pocket again.

She didn't care if he was going to sue her for slander . . . She was taking a paternity suit against him . . . Beads of sweat broke out on his forehead again. What was he going to do? He tried to blank it out of his brain . . . the letter, the image of her as a child with no face, her singing that carol . . .

Half an hour later he could stand it no longer – he had to distract himself doing something. He would go see Leo – see what he was at, see if he wanted a hand with anything. He would stay away from Vera, though. Why wouldn't she just keep her nose out?

He stood at the bottom of the stairs now to shout up to Florrie.

"I'm going to Leo's."

A distant 'yes' came from the spare room.

"I'll be back in a couple of hours."

Driving into his sister's yard he could see no sign of Leo's van at first so he drove round to the sheep shed. Leo was there, scraping the yard where the loads of sugar beet had been tipped over the past couple of months.

Abe rubbed his hands together to heat them up. At least the sheep shed was warm. He walked up and down the aisle now, hands in his coat pockets, his eye assessing the quality of the sheep in the pens on each side of the shed.

His eye stopped on one of the weaker looking ones. Prolapsed vagina.

"You may cull that one."

"She's already on the list," his nephew answered now that he was out of the tractor.

There was silence as Leo swung his leg over one of the pens to grab a ewe and let an orphan lamb suck her.

"I suppose you've heard . . ."

"Heard what?"

"That yer one's got a job in Springtown . . ."

"In the nursing home?"

"Yep. Starting tonight. So I heard."

Abe tried to think straight.

"I thought she had a job."

"She has but she seems to want to hang around here . . ."

"She should go back where she belongs."

His nephew was staring at him oddly as he jumped off the pen back into the aisle of the shed.

"Maybe she thinks she belongs around here . . ."

"What are you talking about?"

"Maybe she thinks she has the right . . . She's big into rights . . ."

"How do you mean?"

Leo was staring again.

"That's if what she has over her bed is anything to go by . . ."

Before he realized what he was doing Abe had grabbed his nephew and pushed him up against the bars of a sheep pen.

"Get off me!"

Abe backed off. Christ! What was he thinking of . . .

"I'm sorry . . . I shouldn't have . . ."

Leo was staring at him, with what looked like hatred in his eyes.

"Know the enemy – isn't that what you always preach. Know who you're going up against and you've a better chance of winning . . . I paid her house a little visit."

Abe was shocked.

"You? You broke in?"

Abe felt the blood vessel in his temple pound.

He saw Leo smirk.

"I'm not having any bitch spread lies like that and think she can get away with it . . ."

"What if someone saw you . . . ?"

"No one saw me. I just nipped in there for a few minutes and had a look round. What's over the bed might interest you though."

Abe panicked. What? What was it – a picture of him, one of him and Lil Casey? No such photograph existed unless she'd somehow got one made up.

He tried to keep eye contact with Leo who was now watching him like a hawk.

He listened while Leo explained about the newspaper cutting, what it said – about illegitimate children being entitled to property same as legitimate ones . . .

Jesus! Stay calm . . . Think!

"I've told you before. She has nothing on me."

"That's good. Still, I pity whoever is her father. She's going after him, whoever he is."

"She's off her head!"

Leo was still staring.

"She's not short of a bob or two either."

"What? You went through her papers . . ."

Leo's eyes were like steel.

"A nice lump sum to fight a court case, say . . ."

"You steer clear of her – she's off her trolley. Don't let her get to you . . . She'll back off . . . that letter means nothing."

"What letter?"

Abe was sweating. He was floundering now and he knew his nephew knew it.

"From her solicitor," he said.

"What?"

Leo was shouting.

"She'll go to court."

"The bitch!"

Sheep ran around the pens panicked at Leo's shout.

"She's trying to call my bluff, that's all. She hasn't a leg to stand on . . ."

"A court case! And the whole country laughing at the good of it! She needs to be taught a lesson!"

Abe shouted after Leo who was heading out of the shed.

"Stay away from her – you hear! She has nothing on me. It'll all blow over! She'll clear out and everything will go back to normal, you'll see. She's a liar!"

Abe was glad there was such certainty in his voice.

"Aye!" Leo said, spitting on the ground.

Abe watched his nephew go back to his work, grating gears loudly as he resumed scraping the yard. What would he do?

Abe Stephenson stood in his sister's yard, the engine sounds pounding in his ears.

Florrie Stephenson stopped the car in the farmyard and sat there for several minutes. Her legs felt numb but at least she'd gotten home safe. She remembered little of the journey from Waterford to Wexford, her mind instead trying to process what Hannah Casey had said.

Stephenson – that was what she should be called if what Hannah was saying was correct.

The yard was quiet. Abe's jeep wasn't there. She was glad. Her skin crawled at the thought of seeing him right now.

Her instinct was to run but where would she run to? Until she knew for definite she would do nothing – time enough then to make a decision.

She took several deep breaths to steady herself. One thing at a time, isn't that the way she had learned to cope with life, that would get her through . . . She was glad she hadn't broken down in front of Hannah. Wasn't it only natural to not want another person to see one's fragility?

Florrie wished she hadn't told Hannah about not being able to have children. Did she ever think . . . Abe was right – she nattered too much.

"She was probably pitying me, knowing what she knows . . ."

She shivered. Time to go into the house. No, she couldn't face it yet. Getting out of the car she headed for the cattle shed.

She wanted to see Gem. Knocklannon Gem out of Knocklannon Pride. Her husband had chosen the name for Gem's mother. Pride – there was too much of that in Knocklannon – pride, arrogance, superiority.

"And pride cometh before a fall . . ." she said to herself as she slid back the heavy galvanized iron door just enough to get into the shed.

The warmth hit her as she stepped in – that and the smell of cattle, of dung. It was a smell she had always loved.

Several pairs of big eyes watched her as she walked down the aisle between the two rows of pens, the two cows that already had their calves at foot wary, watchful.

Florrie walked to the far pen to see Knocklannon Gem. She was lying down in the clean straw, content and at ease still, her body swollen with impending motherhood.

"Hello girl."

The cow looked at her and struggled up from her straw bed.

Florrie thought of Lil Casey, her belly full with her husband's child. Did anyone ask her how she was? Did Abe?

She felt nauseous again as the image came into her mind.

"Lord, help me, give me strength . . .

She stroked the cow for several minutes to calm herself, gently talking to the animal . . .

"You'll be ok, girl, don't you worry . . ."

Proof – that's what she needed. She needed to find out if what Hannah was saying was true. She couldn't take any action unless she was sure. If she rushed in too quickly and accused him in the wrong that would be the end of her marriage, of life as she knew it in this place and where else had she to go?

Swallowing hard she tried to decide what to do. She had told Hannah that only she could decide what to do. That she had to have proof in order to know what to do.

Think . . . . The bank statements – it was worth a try. She'd stared at the dates of the lodgements in the post office book for a long time in order to remember them. Payments had been made particularly in the two years after she was born – a few times each year.

Could she find any evidence of money matching those sums going out of the farm at those times?

1964 – it had been a dreadful year. She had functioned rather than lived as she went from month to month, devastated at the sight of menstrual blood each time. The old accounts boxes – they were in the attic. She had organized them over the years, putting them in boxes, neatly labelled as her secretarial training had taught her. It hadn't been difficult though – the Stephenson's had always kept accounts and diaries of farm work going back generations.

Knocklannon Gem moved around, uneasy now. Was she picking up on her distress?

No sign of labour yet . . . Florrie's trained eye looked for signs. No bones down yet. No water bag out. It would be days.

Walking back to the house Florrie shock ran through her as she thought of the dates she'd seen – October, January, June . . . They were farmers' times for paying bills – after the harvest, after new-born bull calves were sold, after fat animals had been sold in the mart.

A lump had now lodged in her throat. What if he had paid it all in cash to cover his tracks? If that was the case she might find nothing . . . The jeep . . . He was coming back . . . She must stay calm.

"Where were you?"

"Waterford. Shoes."

"Hmph! You went far enough anyway."

"I didn't want to meet people."

Let him make what he liked of that. Why shouldn't he know she was hurting, embarrassed by the rumours?

Upstairs later she sat for a long time on the spare bed, feeling as if cold had settled into her bones.

How long would she have to wait for him to go so that she could go up to the attic?

It wasn't a place she liked going at her age. Normally Roy did it if there were Christmas decorations to take down or unwanted items to put up there. In latter years she had always asked Roy. Roy . . . She wondered how he was getting on. No, she wouldn't have asked him to go up to the attic on this occasion . . .

Was that a car in the yard? She didn't care. She wasn't going downstairs to talk to anyone. Abe could tell the visitor whatever he liked . . .

She heard the back door slam. Abe had gone out to talk to whoever it was. Probably Leo – he was in the yard a lot these days.

Now she heard a raised voice outside but she couldn't make out what was being said. She went to the window. Reverend Mundy . . . Had Abe been shouting at him? Dear Lord!

Florrie felt herself flush with anger and shame at the thought of the rumours having reached the rector's ears. Now the rector was in his car, driving away.

She heard Abe shout from the bottom of the stairs that he was going to Leo's. Let him . . .

Florrie picked up the mat beside the spare bed and carried it out to the landing so that there would be no signs on the carpet that she had been up in the attic.

Using the special rod, she pulled the stairs down and opened it out. It had been Abe's idea to get a proper ladder fitted. It was like everything else around the yard. He liked gates hung properly, doors hinged properly. He couldn't abide slip-shoddiness.

She went up the stairs slowly. She didn't like heights but . . .

It was years since she'd been up there. The attic smelled of dust and she could hear the loud sound of the cold water tank filling up.

She searched among the rows of boxes. The old ones would be at the back . . .

1969 . . . 1968 . . . 1967 . . . 1964 and 1965 . . .

Her heart pounding she lifted out the two cardboard boxes and removed the string that secured them.

The papers in them had yellowed with time and some of the writing had faded but it was all legible. It was all there – sales at the mart, at the merchants, at the meat factory, invoices for purchases at the co-op, at the hardware shop . . . The old cheque books, with only stubs remaining, for each year were all there, kept together by rubber bands. There were envelopes full of used cheques, too, that in those days came back to you at the end of each month.

Concentrate . . . Florrie sat down on a trunk that had belonged to long-dead Stephensons.

She quickly looked through the entries on some of the cheque stubbs – there was nothing unusual about any of them. Was she mad or what? Did she really think that, if he was guilty, he was going to write 'mother and baby home' on the cheque stub?

Rushing now in case Abe came back she moved the cardboard boxes to the attic entrance. She would have to be careful lifting the two boxes down . . .

Bank statements and the cash books – those were what would give her clues, if anything did . . . She had to look for money received for cattle or crops that didn't show up in the bank records . . .

In the spare room, attic stairs back up and the mat removed she opened the boxes again after pausing to listen for sounds in the yard.

She must concentrate . . . Sales figures had to match up with lodgements, more or less. Abe had never been the sort to keep cash under the bed. Anyway in the early sixties, he had loans to develop the yard and buy land – everything went through the books so that he could prove what he was taking in if the bank manager was reluctant to lend. 1965. Sold 8 bullocks to mart. 421 pounds . . . Wheat 306, oats, sold 66 ton, kept five. She ran her finger over the dates in the statement. Usually there was a lodgement within three or four days of him selling something – usually the Friday after.

She continued to examine the pages, looking for what wasn't written there. Reading between the lines – that's what she was trying to do. What was that? The cashbook entry showed that 8 heifers had been sold to a butcher for a substantial price yet only a third of it was lodged. He must have withdrawn the balance – two hundred pounds – in cash. That was a lot of money in 1965. What was he paying for that he needed a draft?

Her heart almost stopped. There had been a payment of two hundred pounds into Hannah's post office book four days later . . .

Her fingers stumbled over the statement pages.

The cash book told her what had come in . . .so many animals at so much . . . When she did the calculation in her head, however, what was lodged on the day was always a lot less than what her husband had been paid . . . Where had the rest of the money gone?

Her heart was thumping. A lot of the dates of money disappearing coincided with the dates in the post office book.

Her husband had been paying someone off . . .

Any glimmer of hope she'd had of being wrong in her suspicions was now gone . . . the evidence was stacking up against him . . .

Florrie had a sudden vision of him in bed with Lil Casey, rolling off her when it was over. She felt nauseous again. How could he?

Again she prayed for strength. *Lord, show me how to cope with this* . . .

She looked again at the documentation. What was she going to do now? If she showed him the accounts and told him her suspicions he would argue his way out of the accusations. She needed incontrovertible evidence. A DNA test would be the only way to be absolutely sure.

She shivered at the thought of what she had to do. She would need a sample from her husband and from Hannah. A hair with the follicle intact – she knew that. Or a swab from the inside of a person's cheek . . .

She felt stronger now, knowing what she had to do. She tried not to look too far ahead. One thing at a time. .

She took out her computer and found a company on the internet that provided home-testing DNA kits.

She telephoned to check that the kit could be sent by return of post. She would pay a bit extra if it could. Yes.

After dressing and applying make-up carefully and calmly she took her bag and headed for her car.

She would send the money off today, going to the main post office in Wexford, Anne Street, just to be sure. She'd have it back by Wednesday, Thursday at the latest. That's when she'd have to find the strength to do another difficult thing – to sleep with him again so that she could pull a hair out of his head or get a swab from his cheek while his mouth hung open wide and snoring.

Leo Kemp felt irritated by how his mother ate. She pecked at the plate with her knife and fork making too much noise each time. And ate feck all after.

"Your uncle didn't come in . . ."

"He was in a hurry."

"Did he say what he wanted?"

God, did she ever stop asking questions . . .

"To know if I needed a hand at anything with the lad away."

"And what did you say?"

"That I didn't."

"At least he offered. How did he seem?"

Leo shrugged.

"Hard to tell."

His mother was silent, eating the last piece of her rasher.

"I left a message on Roy's phone. You'd think he'd have a minute to ring. It's always switched off. Maybe he has to leave it off."

"So they can brainwash him into talking properly."

"Don't be so smart. With the help of God it'll do him some good."

Leo shoved his empty plate away and stood up. He'd have to check the ewes again. Eighty down, twenty-two more to yean. He was sick of it. Give him tractor work any day – down the lane and away, your head to yourself as you got on with ploughing or sowing or pulling beet. Being stuck around the yard all the time was like being in jail. The sooner Roy Boy was back and the Spring came the better.

Outside the wind cut through him.

His uncle's comment about the old ewe annoyed him.

He wasn't born yesterday – he knew what sheep had to go, for God's sake . . .

His uncle was lying – Leo was sure of it. Sure, he was pretending to be all bluff and bluster but it wasn't ringing true. And the way he reacted when he told him what was over her bed . . .

Leo spat as he slid the heavy door of the shed closed. If his uncle was Hannah Casey's father he had better keep his trap shut about it – now and forever.

The cold still cut at his face as he went back into the house. He would come back out in half an hour to check on the ewes again.

He had no regrets about the break-in. Cutting his hand had been unfortunate but the rain would have washed any blood away.

His mother looked up from the television.

"You may as well stay here tonight. That house of yours'll be freezing."

"Yeah . . ."

Why wouldn't she say straight out that she wanted him to stay tonight – that she was afraid in the house without someone else there?

"I'll put the electric blanket on for you."

Leo threw himself into the ancient leather chair that had been his father's. The low ceiling felt oppressive to him. If he had his way he'd bulldoze this house out of it altogether . . .

He flicked through the television stations, unable to concentrate on anything.

His mother was wetting tea at half past nine when she finally asked.

"Did he say if he'd had a response to the letter?"

"Yes."

"And?"

"She'll see him in court."

"What?"

"Jesus, will you watch before you scald yourself!"

His mother had almost dropped the teapot. He jumped up and grabbed it from her.

"Sit down for fuck's sake!"

"She can't . . . it's all a pack of lies . . ."

His mother sounded bewildered.

"He said she'd run a mile from the solicitor's letter . . ." she went on. "Isn't that what he said? You were there . . ."

"Yes."

"She's mad – that's it – not the full shilling! How dare she come around here spreading filth and lies, dragging the name of a man like your uncle through the muck and tormenting the whole lot of us . . . She's working up the road in that nursing home at nights now," his mother said. "Peg Travers told me. Took delight in it . . ."

Leo put three spoons of sugar and a lot of milk in his mother's tea and handed it to her.

Her stirring it grated on his brain.

"God Almighty, she can't get away with this. She can't be let . . ."

He had never seen his mother look as agitated before. And all because of that Casey bitch . . . If he had her this minute he'd kill her. No, don't be stupid, he told himself, all you have to do is make her life miserable and she'll clear out. And glancing at the radio, he had an idea . . .

Next morning he was in his tractor in his uncle's lower field behind the cottage by half past eight. It was still dark.

If his uncle asked what he was doing he would say someone had told him cattle had broken in and he was checking it out.

Putting one finger in his ear he turned the radio up to maximum volume then jumped out of the tractor, taking the keys with him.

He was in the sheep shed when his phone rang. Private number.

A female voice screeched at him.

"Switch that radio off now!"

Leo laughed.

"The knob's broken."

"No, it's not. You're doing this deliberately! You won't get away with this, you hear?"

"Ah, go suckle your pups!"

Leo switched off the phone after telling Hannah Casey to fuck off. He'd rattled her cage all right. He'd give it half an hour then he'd walk back and switch it off.

He'd do it again every morning for as long as it took to make living there unbearable for her . . ..

The squad car arriving in the yard at three o'clock that afternoon took him by surprise. The bitch!

"Leo!"

He could see his mother coming out of the house, face like a ghost.

"Go back in. I'll deal with this."

"Andrew." He greeted the local sergeant and the younger guard who stood a few feet behind him.

"Leo."

Leo tried to think fast. Stay calm . . .

"Have I forgotten to renew my gun licence?"

"No, no problem with that but we've had a complaint. From a Miss Hannah Casey – she says you've been harassing her."

"I have not!"

"So it wasn't you that left a radio on full blast behind her house this morning?"

"Is that what she told you! I told her the volume was stuck. I went home to get something to disconnect it but she wouldn't listen to a word I was saying. Went on ranting like a madwoman. I don't know what you're wasting your time investigating something like this for – she's paranoid if you ask me."

He saw the sergeant take a sheet of paper from his pocket.

"And this? Do you know anything about this letter received by Miss Casey yesterday?"

Leo read it. Fuck!

"I know nothing about this! I've more to be doing than writing anonymous letters. Whatever I have to say to anyone I'll say it to their face and she'd better be careful who she's accusing."

"Yourself and Miss Casey don't seem to get along very well . . ."

"I've nothing to do with her."

Leo could see his mother at the kitchen window.

Eye contact – that's what he had to keep with the sergeant now.

"You're barking up the wrong tree. I told you about the radio. I sorted the problem as soon as I could – what more could I do?"

"Right."

Now it was the younger garda's turn.

"There was a break-in at Miss Casey's house over New Year . . ."

"Really?"

"You didn't know?" the Sergeant said. "News like that usually travels fast in an area like this."

"I don't pay any mind to gossip."

"A window was broken at the back of the house. Shame that Miss Casey was away so the break-in wasn't discovered for days. If we'd known sooner we might have been able to get a lead on who did it . . ."

"What are you telling me all this for?" Leo asked, folding his arms and lying back against the squad car.

Leo held the Sergeant's gaze.

"Just in case you might hear something. You'd want to help us out if you knew anything, wouldn't you?"

"Of course I would. I've always been an upstanding citizen."

"Aye. Well, we'll be off so. It was good to have this little chat."

"No problem."

The young garda got back into the car. The Sergeant stayed standing a while longer.

"There wouldn't be any 'baggage' between you and Miss Casey, would there?"

"No."

"That's good . . .because we take a dim view of any one being harassed or intimidated. That sort of activity could land the perpetrator in a lot of trouble."

"I'm sure it could."

"We all have to respect the law of the land. How's your mother keeping?"

"Fine, thanks."

"And Roy?"

"He's down the country. On holiday."

"Is that a fact? A holiday does us all good sometimes."

"Yep."

"I see you cut your hand . . ."

"It's nothing. Barbed wire. Hazard of the job . . ."

"Right. I'll see you then. Take care."

Leo's heart was thumping. Fuck!

She'd called the guards – the bitch! And she was blaming him for writing poison pen letters! Who the hell had sent that? His uncle? His aunt . . . ?

His mother was at the door.

"What did they want?"

"To find a letter writer."

His mother looked away. Fuck! She'd sent it . . . That's what she meant by doing something . . .

Leo walked over to the dresser and took a writing pad out of the drawer. Basildon Bond – blue lined sheets, just like the page the sergeant had given him to read.

"Leave that alone! Those are my private things!" she said, grabbing it from his hand.

"They think I did it," Leo said, omitting to tell her about the radio complaint and the inference about the break-in.

"Thousands of people use that kind of paper. It could have been anyone. There's lots of people in this area upset by what that one's been saying. Now she's bringing the guards down on us – God damn her to hell!"

His mother's language unnerved him.

"She's deluded – evil, you hear."

"Or very sure of her facts . . ."

He didn't see the slap coming. Only the shock of what had happened stopped him from hitting her back.

"He's not her father, you hear! He's not!"

He watched his mother sit down, her head in her hands.

"God, what she's driven us to . . ."

The side of Leo's face stung. It was time his mother woke up.

"What if she can prove he's her father," he said.

His mother just shook her head, tears rolling down her cheeks.

"No . . ."

"What if she can demand a DNA test? The stuff you hear about on the telly . . ."

"He'd never agree . . ."

"He fucking well better not!"

"She's lying. He's had nothing to do with Lil Casey."

Leo walked round the room, trying to think. Eventually he spoke, slowly and deliberately.

"Him and Aunt Florrie – when did you first hear they couldn't have children?"

"What are you talking about?"

His mother looked confused.

"Think back – when exactly?"

He knew he was shouting now.

"They were a few years married. I don't know – 1964, '65 maybe. Lots of people don't have children for a while. What are you getting at?"

"Was he agitated about it? Were people getting on to him? To the two of them?"

"I don't know, they could have been. Your Granny was a bit concerned all right but then Florrie went to the doctor and we knew it was her fault. It wasn't his fault at all. What are you asking all these questions for?"

Leo concentrated hard.

"What if he didn't know that he wasn't to blame before that? What if he wanted to find out by . . ."

"God Almighty!"

"It's a possibility and you know it! If he got someone else up the duff he'd know he wasn't shooting blanks."

"No! I won't have that sort of talk in this house. Your uncle has no children and you are going to inherit Knocklannon. He's made a will, I'm sure he has . . ."

" . . . that won't be worth a tuppenny damn if she is his daughter."

"Lord save us! He can't admit it . . . !"

"He won't!"

Leo felt calmer now. His mother was behind him. All he had to do was let his uncle know where he stood. If it took a threat so be it.

That if he ever admitted to being Hannah Casey's father his sister Vera would kill herself because of the shame . . .

Florrie Stephenson glanced again at the yard gate. How much longer now before the postman came? Half an hour? Less? Return of post, that's what the guy on the phone had said . . .

"I'm going to the co-op. I need some angle-grinder discs."

"Right."

She watched her husband get into the jeep, Max hopping in beside him. Several times she had wanted to confront him, scream at him, tell him the game was up, that he was a liar and an adulterer but she had stopped herself. The accounts evidence wasn't enough to confront him with. Better to bide her time until she was totally sure.

At least he wouldn't be there when the postman came. Not that he'd ever ask her exactly what post she got. No, he'd be more indirect than that, enquiring was there much in the post? Waiting for her to say what it was exactly.

She cleared the table of dinner dishes as if on automatic pilot.

Now she jumped. The postman had arrived. Drying her hands quickly she went to the back door and out to where Fergus was sorting through his bundle of letters.

"Mrs Stephenson. Miserable day, isn't it?"

"Yes, indeed. Thank you."

Her fingers trembled as she opened the brown envelope in the drawing-room. All she needed was there – plastic bags with numbers on, instructions . . . Would she have the nerve to go through with it? She would give one test to Hannah so that she could provide a sample as well. Done on the sly, Abe's test would not stand up in court but she would know and he would know that she knew. She suddenly felt very nervous.

"My marriage is on the line doing this."

What marriage, though, she asked herself, if all it's built on is lies and deceit? She had no intention of walking away from what was half hers. Married to Abe she owned half this place. She'd put years of work into it. If she left of her own accord she'd be signing away her rights.

Maybe that's what he'd been trying to force her to do in the early years after he knew she couldn't have children, when he'd been ignorant and verbally abusive . . . But where could she have gone? Back to Cork where her mother wouldn't want her? It had been the cattle – the pedigrees – that had kept her sane then. They had been the ticket to what respect he gave her – training calves to the halter from an early age so's they would be quiet at shows, picking the ones with real potential – her strength – helping wash the bulls or cows that were going to be exhibited, curry-combing, trimming . . .yet it was always only Abraham Stephenson's name that had appeared on the show entries. Still, lots of people knew the real story.

After reading the instructions she took the envelope upstairs. She would pull out a hair when he was in a deep, snoring sleep . . .

She tried to overcome her distaste at getting into the same bed as him. He had betrayed her but he would deny everything until faced with evidence. How would he react when he found out?

She had it planned. If the test was positive she would tell him in the presence of his sister Vera – and others if necessary. That would protect her physically. Vera would not tolerate violence against her. Abe would also be facing his sister's wrath . . . . . .

The evening dragged by – a silent supper after he came back from an IFA meeting then him in front of the television and muttering about beet factories under threat and what the fuck was the world coming to and she pretending to be working on the Day Centre project but the words kept running together . . .

She delayed as long as possible before going to bed, letting him go first for what if, seeing her in their double bed again, he decided to go to the spare room? Her plan would be out the window then. Better to bide her time . . .

Eventually he came in after his last check of the yard. There was no 'goodnight' as he headed up the stairs, just an admonition to shut off the Aga for the night. As if she'd ever forgotten . . .

When she heard the bedroom door eventually close Florrie took her mobile phone out of her trouser pocket and sent the text. To Hannah Casey.

"Meet me in the Riverside Park Hotel car park tomorrow at 11 a.m. Pls confirm."

Florrie delayed several minutes before pressing 'send.' Once she did it that was it – she was on her way to taking Hannah Casey's side against her husband.

She panicked momentarily. What if he was innocent? What if Hannah was a liar and a trouble-maker? She could lose everything for what she was about to do . . .

If he was surprised that she got into the double bed with him at eleven twenty p.m. he said nothing.

Hadn't that always been the pattern? If he'd been hurtful and she was upset she slept in the spare room until the hurt had eased and she would somehow square his behaviour, putting it down to fatigue or stress or it being a heat of the moment outburst that meant nothing. Eventually she would go back to their bed and it was if it had never happened. And she was glad that normality had resumed.

He would never apologize but he would perhaps mention a day or so later that he would make that flowerbed she wanted or buy some tree he knew she'd like to add to the garden.

"I just happened to be passing," he'd say. "They were going cheap."

And she would thank him and there would be peace between them again. And more self-hatred would set in for letting herself be bought off once again . . .

She turned her back to him now, not talking. When he stretched a hand forward to touch her she flinched and he took it away.

She listened to the rain as she watched the hours tick forward. The volume on the TV monitor was switched down low so that at the far end of the room she could watch the cows in the calving shed. The camera switched every so often from one pen to the next. It would be days yet before Knocklannon Gem would calve but you had to keep an eye . . .

3.45 . . . She knew from his breathing that he was now in a deep sleep.

She could feel herself sweat as she built up the courage to pull out a hair. She moved her hand forward . . . Taking one from nearest his bald patch would be best – it would be the easiest to isolate.

She must do it quickly – decisively – because she might not get a second chance. She felt the dampness of his pate as she caught one hair between her thumb and first finger nails close to the scalp. Abe snored suddenly and she froze, her fingers still holding on.

As his snore spluttered to a fall she pulled quickly – and hard. He jumped in the bed as she pulled her hand back, immediately feigning sleep. She stayed very still until he settled again and the snores became regular again. She waited several minutes before getting out of the bed to go to the bathroom. There she put the hairs – two of them – now almost frozen between her fingers into the plastic sealable bag. It was done! She hid the bag now under clothes in the wash basket . . .

He woke as she got back into bed, his head out of habit lifting off the pillow so that he could look at the calving monitor.

"Nothing's happening," she said. "Go back to sleep."

He grunted and turned over on his left side.

She found it difficult to go to sleep. The cows in the pens moving around silently preoccupied her. They were all near their time. Near their time . . . what would that be like? She'd never known what it was like to be about to give birth.

Anger ran through her again at the thought of her husband and Lil Casey, of sperm meeting egg and fertilizing it, not like in her barren body . . .

Hannah would have been a beautiful baby . . .

She prayed for sleep that would help her forget.

7.15 a.m. Abe was getting out of bed, taking time to straighten up properly before he went to the bathroom. He looks like an old scarecrow in his pyjamas, she thought.

She felt very tired but also oddly elated. She would dress well this morning, do her hair carefully . . . Saying her prayers she asked again for guidance. Maybe she shouldn't be praying at all – maybe the devil had got into her. Maybe she should be a dutiful wife and pretend no accusation had been made and stand on the right hand of her husband's denial. No. That was impossible. She would not be able to live with herself unless she knew for sure.

"Where are you off to?"

Abe was in after feeding the cattle.

"Enniscorthy. Dental appointment."

"What time will you be back?"

Never. That's what she wanted to say but she forced herself to sound normal.

"Lunchtime," she said, putting on her coat and picking up her bag with the stamped, addressed envelope already in it.

When Hannah Casey came off duty the first thing she did was check her mobile phone. It was 8 a.m. and the night on duty at the nursing home had been tedious and tiring.

Several of the residents had been uneasy in the night and she had found herself on the go all the time. As well as that one of the staff hadn't turned in for work so they'd all been overstretched.

There was a text message from Beryl saying very little. 'Busy. Talk at weekend'. Either Beryl was out with her or she was preoccupied with work. Not hearing from her regularly was painful. There was such a chasm between them that she had not told her about Leo Kemp's harassment. Maybe Beryl was right – she needed to get on with her own life and who was she to be dumping her problems on her friend all the time?

She read the second message as she pulled on her coat. It was from Florrie Stephenson! Frantically she scrolled to get details of when it had been sent. After she started work last night . . . 'Confirm pls'. She checked her watch. Ten past eight. Her fingers fumbled, making mistakes as she answered the message.

"Will be there.'

Was she too late? She hoped not.

Getting into her car she wondered why Florrie wanted to meet. What if Florrie was off her head, just pretending to be sympathetic but really wanting to murder her in cold blood in a hotel car park . . . No, get real . . . Florrie was ok. She wanted to meet at eleven o'clock . . . Hannah decided to go back to the cottage and have a shower and breakfast first. Maybe it would wake her up a bit.

Her head ached. Ever since the blaring radio incident three days before and the hassle of talking to the gardai she hadn't been able to sleep properly during the daytime.

Peg Travers had offered her a bed but she couldn't go running to someone every time something happened.

Hannah was only out of the shower when she saw Peg's car drive in.

"How are you, love? Any more trouble since?"

Hannah ushered Peg into the heat of the kitchen.

"No, thank goodness."

"Let's hope he's learned his lesson. The guards'll have put the frighteners on him."

"I'm trying to forget about it."

"That's it – head up. Show you don't care."

Hannah put the kettle on.

"Busy at Springtown?"

"Never a dull moment."

Hannah wondered if could she trust Peg. Was she the one who sent the poison pen letter? Surely not, she was her mother's childhood friend, for God's sake. Still, right now she didn't know who to trust . . .

Over tea, Hannah kept the conversation light – the weather, work, Peg's aches and pains . . . She couldn't resist asking her about Maimie though.

"Peg – do you know if my mother kept in touch with Maimie Breen? Would you know if they kept up the friendship over the years?"

"Not that I know of but they did work together for years and were neighbours so there could have been contact for all I know. Why do you ask?"

"Maimie's in the nursing home. She gets me mixed up with my mother sometimes. She seemed to know her well, that's all."

"You're wondering if your mother told her about you?"

There was no codding Peg.

"I suppose."

"Maybe she did. Who knows? Still, I wouldn't put money on it. What did Maimie say exactly?"

"Nothing of any use. She's doo-lally most of the time."

"It's terrible how the mind goes all right but I wouldn't get my hopes up, love, if I was you."

"How do you mean?"

"Thinking that she might say there was something between your mother and himself . . ."

"I didn't say I was hoping that . . ."

"It'd be only natural if you did. It's just that Maimie wouldn't be taken as a reliable witness – not the way she is at the moment anyway . . ."

"You're right. No point clutching at straws."

Hannah glanced at the clock. She would have to hurry . . .

"Are you not going straight to bed? You must be knackered."

"I am but I just have to pop into town first."

Hannah could see the expectation in Peg's eyes but she said no more.

"Anyway I'll see you soon."

"And I'll get out of your way and let you get ready, love . . ."

"Thanks.

Switching on the car she saw that she was low in diesel. Damn! She'd have to stop in the village to get some. The last thing she wanted was to be stuck on the road between here and Enniscorthy . . .

Coming up to queue at the checkout the back of the woman bending to write out a cheque looked familiar.

It was Vera Kemp. Hannah was shocked to be so close to her. She hadn't seen her since New Year's Eve.

Hannah couldn't help glancing at the handwriting. She gulped. Was it similar to the handwriting in the threatening letter? Vera Kemp would have the motive. She could have done it . . .

Hannah bit her lip to stop herself shouting at Vera Kemp there and then.

She watched Tom Carthy give Vera Kemp a handful of notes along with the groceries. Then he turned his attention to his next customer.

"Hannah – what can I do for you?"

She saw Vera Kemp's back stiffen. She didn't look back as she left the shop.

"Diesel . . ."

If Tom Carthy had noticed Vera Kemp's reaction at knowing Hannah Casey was behind her he said nothing.

"See you again."

Hannah was still feeling uptight when she got to her car outside.

"Keep your cool," she told herself. "The guards can deal with this . . ."

She had the key in the car lock when she heard the voice beside her.

"You have some nerve staying around here."

Hannah turned to see Vera Kemp's lemon tight mouth.

"I've as much right to be here as anyone else, now excuse me."

Vera Kemp's hand was holding the door.

"You'll get nothing out of him – do you hear? My brother's more than able for gold-diggers like you."

Hannah forced herself to look Vera Kemp straight in the eye. She had a good three inches in height on her which helped.

"Your brother knows the truth. One of these days he'll have to admit it if he's to die with an easy conscience."

Spittle appeared at the corners of the older woman's mouth.

Hannah had enough.

"I don't want to destroy him. I just want him to admit the truth! As a human being I have the right to know my father . . ."

"He's not your father."

"And maybe you don't know him as well as you think you do."

"You . . . you . . . you . . . !"

Hannah paused getting into the car.

"I got a threatening letter the other day. The Gardai have it and are on the track of whoever sent it. Handwriting is traceable, you know. And the pen . . ."

"I don't know what you're talking about."

"You've nothing to worry about then. Excuse me . . ."

Vera Kemp had grabbed the door even tighter.

"Is it money you want – is that it? Name your price . . . It'd be worth it to get you out of here."

Hannah shoved the door, making Vera loosen her grip.

"You make me sick!"

Heart pounding she started the car and drove off leaving Vera Kemp standing there in her worn brown coat, fists clenched and Tom Carthy watching out the window.

Ten to eleven. She was on time to meet Florrie. Where exactly did she want to meet? Suspecting that she meant the undercover car park Hannah swung in to the right and parked in a corner spot.

"This is like one of those American spy movies," she thought.

Ten minutes later she saw Florrie drive in. Florrie put up her hand. What was going to happen now?

She saw Florrie get out of her car and walk over to her, glancing round as she did so.

"May I sit in?"

"Yes, of course."

"It's good to see you."

Florrie seemed tense.

She heard her voice tremble as she told Hannah how she'd gone up to the attic to find the statements.

"There is a strong possibility that money went out around each time it was lodged by your mother," Florrie said. "There is no definite paper trail but there's enough for me to know that money is unaccounted for at those times."

Hannah felt herself choke up. She was getting somewhere.

Now she watched Florrie Stephenson take a brown envelope from her bag.

"I did a DNA test. There are two hair samples of his there."

"What?"

Hannah was shocked.

"He did the test?"

"I got the samples while he was asleep."

Jesus! What if he'd woken up . . .

"If you will give me a hair sample as well I will include them here. Five days they said it'd take to get the results back – express."

A DNA test – Florrie had done one on the quiet! Hannah stared at the plastic bags.

"Why would you do this for me? After the way he's hurt you?"

"I'm not doing it for you. I'm doing it for myself, to put an end to these lies, if lies they are. He won't be able to deny it any longer and then I will be able to decide how to move forward."

"Will you leave him?"

"I don't know."

"What do I have to do exactly?"

Florrie explained the process of needing the follicle and handed Hannah the sterile bag.

Hannah isolated a hair in her head then tugged sharply. Had she got a follicle? Yes. Carefully she inserted the hair into the plastic bag and sealed it.

She watched Florrie place the items in the envelope along with Abe Stephenson's. She couldn't believe it – in a few days she would know for certain.

A dreadful thought struck her. Mabye Florrie was in league with Abe, going through this charade in order to tell Hannah that the tests were negative.

"This isn't a con, is it?" she said. "Just to make me think that he's not . . ."

"You have my word."

"Thank you."

Hannah watched another hotel-user get out of his car. If he knew what drama was going on feet away from him . . .

"I'd better go. I'm sending this by courier. When I get an answer I'll be in touch."

Hannah sat in her own car for several minutes before she felt ready to drive. Exhaustion mixed with emotion – she felt high, as if she'd drank several glasses of wine. She needed to talk to Beryl. Too much was happening not to contact her . . .

It went to voicemail again.

Hannah threw the phone down on the car seat almost in tears. It had been an astounding morning and she had no one to share it with. Grabbing the phone she tried to ring Beryl a second time. No luck this time either. She must be working. She would go home and get some sleep now and try her later. She even thought of ringing Matt. No, that was over.

"It'll be a long five days," she thought as she left the town.

Maybe she shouldn't even talk to Beryl about it – not when Roy Kemp, her cousin, was staying at the hotel. What if Beryl mentioned something to him in passing and let the cat out of the bag? She couldn't betray Florrie's trust like that. It could put her in real danger. No, she wouldn't tell Beryl.

Not that Beryl would have even been talking to Roy while he was there. He'd be just another guest. She wondered how he'd react.

Reaching the cottage at last, Hannah sat in the car for a few minutes, head back against the head rest. It had been a long few days, a long few months but the next week would be even longer...

Vera Kemp took several deep breaths after stopping the car in the yard. Her head ached after her meeting with the Casey one at the shop.

Shock had run through her when she realized that Hannah Casey was behind her at the counter.

She had tried hard to keep her dignity, walking calmly out of the shop without looking round but control had gone out the window when she saw her swanning out of the shop, as if butter wouldn't melt.

Right now she regretted going near her.

"Maybe you don't know your brother as well as you think you do . . ."

The gall of her!

No, easy, she told herself, she's only trying to rile me.

Why had she blurted out about the money – about wanting to pay her off? Lord, was she mad! It made it look as if Abe was to blame. Out of control – that's what she'd been. The talk of the letter had done it. Had Hannah Casey been looking over her shoulder as she signed the cheque in the shop? The pen! God Almighty, she'd used the same pen! If the guards came after her they could find her pen and know the letter had been written with it. Vera got out of the car, walked down to the yard, down the back lane, her good shoes getting covered in muck.

Opening her handbag she rooted there until she found the pen then she threw it as far as she could into the marl hole behind the ditch. Good riddance . . .

Back in the house she put on the kettle. Hot, sweet tea – that's what she needed to steady herself. 10.45. Leo would soon be in – that's if he wasn't gone to Abe's. The Gardai being in the yard a few days before had been a shock and Leo guessing who'd written the letter. She mustn't have been thinking straight when she sent it.

When Leo hadn't returned by eleven thirty she rang him.

"What?"

His tone was sharp.

"Whereabouts are you?"

He named a parts supplier in town.

"I'll be back when I'm good and ready."

She could have done without a lash of his tongue.

Putting on her Wellington boots and her yard coat and headscarf she went outside again. What would she do? Should she go see Abe and tell him about meeting yer one? No, better to calm herself down a bit first or she might say something else she'd regret . . .

The yard was more untidy with Roy away. Roy hated the yard being messy. Leo called it his 'green streak'. Every time either she or Leo gave out about all the new environmental regulations he would defend the need for them, stutter out an argument for seeing the bigger picture, caring for the planet.

'Effin bunny-hugger', Leo called him.

Vera wished Roy was back. She couldn't remember him ever being gone for a whole week before – maybe a weekend here and there with Macra before he got too old for it.

He had phoned early this morning – stuttering worse than ever.

"I-I'm d-doing this d-d-deliberately to get the f-f-fear out of it," he said.

Didn't make sense to her. And after spending all that money . . . He had sounded in good form though. She had stopped short of telling him all that was going on. Time enough when he came back.

When she got to Knocklannon only Abe was to be seen.

"Gone to town," Abe said when she asked where Florrie was. Vera glanced at Florrie's car in the yard.

"She got a lift," he said.

"Right."

Why was he telling lies? If the car was there Florrie was there too. Did Florrie just not want to talk to her?

Vera followed Abe across the yard after he locked the back door of the house. He didn't seem to be in the humour for talking but she'd make him. She needed answers. She followed him into the shed where barley was stored for cattle feed in the winter.

"The guards were at our place the other day," she said. She was talking to his back.

"So I heard."

"They said the Casey one made a complaint."

Her brother still had his back to her. She wished she could see his face. Read it.

"Aye?" he said.

"I met her in the shop this morning."

Her brother stopped what he was doing – but only for a second.

"Oh?"

"I know I was stupid – I shouldn't have gone near her . . ."

Her brother swung round – too quickly.

"What did you do?"

"I had to say something – she as good as accused me of sending her some poison pen letter! I told her I knew nothing about it. She was all up in herself saying stuff about you and that you'd be better telling the truth than dying with a guilty conscience."

"I told you to stay away from her!"

"She got me so angry! What was I supposed to do – just let her away with it?"

"Just stay away from her."

"You said the solicitor's letter would work . . ."

"It will. I'll go to court if I have to."

"Court . . ."

The thought made Vera feel sick.

"She's getting a kick out of upsetting people – can you not see that?" he said before turning on the meal grinder. Vera covered her ears to deaden the noise.

There was no point in trying to talk to him. She drove out of the yard angrier than when she came in. And with a bigger lump in the pit of her stomach. She knew her brother. And she could tell when he wasn't being honest . . .

Crotch control – that's what this comes down to. Had he had it or not? She tried to not let the pictures into her head – her brother with Lil Casey . . . The thoughts of it sickened her but would any man resist if it was handed to him on a plate?

As she switched on the window wipers to a faster speed she thought of the opportunity her brother would have had to play away – Spring Shows and agricultural shows in the early days anyway. Lil Casey would have known that too. Maybe she looked him up, flaunted herself at him . . . That was it. Her kind were always the same. No . . . God knows who that one's father was. Lil Casey could have named her brother and he not be to blame at all.

Her head throbbed. Lie down for a few hours – that's what she would do and block all this out for a while.

"What time will you be back? Will you make church?"

It was Sunday morning and she was talking to Roy on the phone. Leo was at the kitchen table, a glass of water in front of him, hungover.

"Stop shouting, for fuck's sake!"

"The line's bad," she said, struggling to make out what Roy was saying.

"Good. We'll see you then. I'll put the meat in the oven so it'll be ready when we get home . . ."

Roy had already rung off.

"He hardly wants to know about fuckin' meat."

"And you won't want your dinner when it's put in front of you I suppose?"

She wished God would give her patience. Would Leo have been reared better if his father had lived longer, she wondered?

Harry! What would he think if he was alive right now – of a lot of things?

Her husband had never liked Abe. She knew that. What would he say now that Abe was in trouble? No, Abe wasn't in trouble! It was all lies!

Vera snapped her handbag shut.

"Church isn't for another hour – where are you off to?" Leo said.

"To make sure it's presentable for a service," Vera said. "Mabel Archer wouldn't know dust if it flew up and bit her. I don't know why the rector puts her on the roster at all. Will you be there?"

"Yeah, yeah."

"And have a wash. You can't go to church smelling like a brewery."

When she got to the church she was surprised to see the door already open but there was no car to be seen. Had the place been broken into? No. The door would have been burst in if it had. It was probably the rector – his wife might have dropped him off early.

She opened the interior door very quietly so as not to disturb him if he was praying before the service.

There was no one at the altar. Looking sideways she saw the figure of her sister-in-law, Florrie, in a seat she didn't normally sit in, head down, hands clasped in prayer. A shiver ran down Vera's spine. What had happened?

Bang! The door clunked heavily into place. She saw Florrie's head swivel.

"The hinges need oil. I didn't see you there."

Florrie was getting up.

"I brought some greenery – Mabel rang to ask. She hadn't got anything good enough in her garden.

"Right."

Vera was running her finger along the pew beside her then looking at her fingers.

"It's clean," Florrie said.

"Makes a change . . . You're tired looking."

Florrie was putting the communion cloth on the altar.

"I'm not sleeping well these days."

"None of us are. I hope God forgives that one for her lies because I can't."

Her sister-in-law was smoothing the altar cloth out with her right hand.

"And if it isn't lies?"

"What? Of course it is – pure filth!"

She saw her sister-in-law smile a weird smile.

Vera scrawked a kneeler back into its place in the second pew in torment.

"I'm not listening to this! You of all people not believing him! That one's polluting your mind too – that's it. She's evil, I'm telling you!"

"She's a human being, just like the rest of us."

"And a schemer. In this for what she can get out of it! If you let her get to you you're thicker than I thought. That's what the likes of her wants – to come between man and wife, break up families. She probably gets a kick out of it."

Florrie seemed to be smiling. Was she going daft or what?

"Have you ever talked to her?"

"I wouldn't lower myself. And neither should you!"

Florrie was standing looking up at the stained glass window behind the altar. It depicted Jesus carrying a lamb.

"A lost sheep – that could be what Hannah is. Or Abe."

"You're losing it! Can't you see what's staring you in the face – that she's making all this up and that her mother has filled her head with lies to line her up for a few bob?"

Florrie was unnerving her now, standing there so still and speaking so quietly.

"What if there was proof?"

Vera felt sick.

"What proof?"

Vera knew she was almost screeching now.

Florrie shrugged her shoulders.

"Who knows? Maybe the real truth isn't out yet."

Vera's heart was thumping in her chest.

"Truth be damned!"

The door banged. It was Reverend Mundy and his wife.

"Great to see a few early birds," he said, looking from one to the other. "How are you both?"

Vera's heart was still pounding. What was Florrie getting at?

She struggled through small talk with the rector, cutting it short by bowing her head to pray. *Lord God, lift this trouble from us* . . .

Florrie began playing the organ as people started to arrive.

Vera glanced toward the door.

Where was Abe? He seldom missed church. What would people think?

Proof . . . what was Florrie going on about? Vera felt sick to the stomach again.

Roy arrived as the first hymn was about to start. She had forgotten how well he could look when he was dressed up.

She saw him smile at Florrie when she turned and spotted him. He hadn't smiled at her.

He was singing now, the words of *Be Thou My Vision* coming out deep and sweet. He never stammered when he sang. It had always amazed her.

Leo turned up when the prayers had started. Did he ever go anywhere on time?

Vera Kemp got more and more narked as she listened to the sermon. The rector was going on about honesty in business, honesty in relationships and how scarce a commodity it was. It was something we should all be striving for, he was saying. Was he hinting at something? Picking that topic thinking Abe would be here? No, the sermons were based on the readings for the day – it was all laid out beforehand. Anyway he was on their side, wasn't he? She was over-reacting.

She saw Florrie smile at Roy again as he took up the collection. She felt excluded.

After the blessing the twenty or so people at the service made their way out of the church.

Roy was talking to Florrie.

"How did it go?" she'd asked too, but he had heard Florrie first.

"Gr-reat."

"I hope it was worth the money?" Vera asked.

Her son looked embarrassed at the question.

"Has it done you any good?"

"Y-y-yes."

"A bit of encouragement – that's what Roy needs," Florrie was saying.

"I think I know what my own son needs."

She saw Florrie turn away. Who did her sister-in-law think she was, lecturing her like that?

"H-have you g-got the c-car?" Roy was saying as he looked around.

"No, I walked."

"I'm right, she is going daft," Vera said to herself.

"Where's Abe? It's not like him to miss church."

Florrie looked straight at her.

"You'd have to ask him."

"The meat'll be cremated," Leo said as he came up behind them, "and you making a fuss about it."

Vera glanced behind her. The rector had come out to talk to Florrie. What was going on?

"I-I-I'll s-s-see if Aunt F-florrie needs a lift home," Roy said. And he was gone.

Roy putting his clothes in the washing machine so soon after he came home surprised her. He was whistling as he did so.

"Don't turn that thing on until the dinner's over – the motor is going in it so it'd deafen you."

"O-Ok."

Vera looked at Leo and he at her.

She knew her eldest son had caught it.

"W-w-what's going on?"

"The Casey one's going to court and she's had the guards here accusing us of harassment – is that enough for you?"

She saw Roy put down his knife and fork, his face turning suddenly red.

"What the fuck are you reddening for?"

"Leo!"

"Wh-hat does U-Uncle Abe say?"

"He says she can go be fucked."

"Scum of the earth!"

She saw Roy sit there, eating silently.

"What – did you think the problem was just going to go away because you were away on holiday?"

"No-o."

Vera pushed her plate away.

"How did your Aunt Florrie seem to you today?" she asked Roy.

Roy didn't make eye contact.

"A-all r-right."

"Odd as two left feet, if you ask me. Walked to church, if you don't mind."

"Ho-w is Un-ncle A-Abe?"

"A bad colour last time I saw him. It wouldn't surprise me if his blood pressure was up."

"It's not today or yesterday he's had that trouble . . ." Leo said.

"How do you mean? He only went to the doctor with it before Christmas."

"Yeah, right!"

"Come on – spit it out – what are you getting at?"

"He didn't tell you because you'd be fussing."

"Tell me what?"

"That he went to see a consultant in Dublin in October. No . . . November – the day I got the new loader for the John Deere."

"And you never said a word? "

Leo got up and went over to the windowsill where last year's calendar still sat.

"It was the third of November – a Tuesday."

"He never said a word . . ."

"Well, I'm telling you now. He'd been in Dublin anyhow. He said something about seeing a quack and to say nothing."

November third – why did that date seem familiar to Vera? Try as she might she couldn't remember.

When Roy had gone out to the yard and Leo had fallen asleep on the sofa Vera went to the washing machine to switch it on.

One of these days she'd have to get a new one, with the noise it was making. Always something needing money spent on it . . . The lads put too much in it at one time – that's what had probably caused it. You couldn't watch them. Had Roy filled it too full this time? She opened the door and put her hand in to see if the drum of the machine moved freely. It was all right – he hadn't overloaded it.

Still bent down, her nose twitched. What was the smell? She took one of Roy's shirts and put it to her nose. Perfume! Roy had met a woman. That was why he was whistling and grinning . . . That's all she needed – him meeting up with some slapper! What next would be sent to torment her?

November third – she was still thinking of the date. Why did it seem familiar? God! Heart pounding she rushed to the cupboard under the stairs where she kept the old newspapers. Five minutes later she found it – the *Irish Times* from November 1st, open on the death notices page. Lil Casey's burial was the third of November. And her brother had gone to Dublin that day . . .

There was no smell of dinner. Abe Stephenson checked his watch. It was after 1 p.m. and he was hungry. He knew Florrie was back from church because he had seen Roy drop her home yet the kitchen was quiet.

He had eaten no breakfast and had a restless night full of bad dreams that he awoke from in a lather of sweat. It was as much as he could do to drag himself out of bed to feed the cattle then he had returned to it to lie on it fully clothed and sleep.

When he woke, his wife wasn't in the house yet the car was there. Strange . . . A note on the table said she was gone to church. What fool notion had she taken to walk? She'd been acting weird all weekend, saying very little, just looking at him, walking out of a room soon after he came in to it like she couldn't bear to breathe the same air as him. Say nothing – that's what he had to do and it would all blow over . . .

Hearing her come down the stairs now he put the kettle on to boil.

"You walked to Rathbrandon?"

"I needed some air."

Her voice sounded strange. When he looked round he saw the holdall on the table.

"Where are you going?"

She had picked up the bag.

"I'm not exactly sure but right now I need some space."

His heart started to pound . . . Was she leaving him?

"Space! The heifer . . . what about her?"

"It'll be a while yet. I checked her earlier on."

She was still staring at him.

"We've been man and wife a long time. I'm asking you now . . ."

Christ! What was coming?

His hand shook so much he had to hold onto the kettle.

"If there's something you want to tell me, now's the time . . . Before . . ."

Christ!

"Before what?"

He saw his wife shrug.

"Before the truth comes out some other way maybe . . ."

"Ah, will you whist! There's nothing to tell – I told you before!"
She was still staring at him.

"I'm giving you the chance . . . . . ."

Her voice trailed off and relief flooded through him. Attack – it would his best form of defence.

"Shut up to hell! It's a dog's life I have with you – accusing me of this, that and the other! You'll end up in the red brick, the way you're going!"

He regretted it the moment he said it.

She had her hand on the door now.

"I didn't see it for years, you know, the way you treated me – making little of me, undermining me . . . It's abuse, did you know that? And I didn't even allow myself to see it."

The back door closed behind her. Abe felt his chest tighten as he opened it and shouted after her.

"Abuse, my arse! Go on! Get out of here! You'll soon find out what side your bread is buttered on! You'll be back with your tail between your legs – you'll see!"

She was staring again at him after she had let down the car window.

"I'll be back. When I know where I stand."

Abe stood in the yard for several minutes after she left, breathing hard. Where was she gone and for how long? His chest still felt tight. He needed to sit down. Fuck! He bent down, his hands on his knees, breathing in and out. It was a panic attack – that was all.

He eventually got back into the kitchen and slumped down in his armchair. Max was keening, head cocked on one side.

Where was she gone? To her? To the cottage? Were the two of them in cahoots? He closed his eyes tight to shut out the image of her – the child – her, staring at him that day on Mount Leinster, defiance dancing in her eyes . . .

Florrie gone – where? What was he going to tell Vera and the lads? That she'd gone daft, that she'd gone to Cork to some relative's funeral – that's it, they'd believe that . . . No, she'd be back. She said that, didn't she? Knocklannon Gem was her heifer – she wouldn't miss the calving . . . Never . . .

He switched on the television to break the silence, zapping from channel to channel. Family films . . . Shut your eyes . . . rest, he told himself . . .

He opened them to see a black and white film on the screen, an old black guy soft shoe dancing. Now there was a child beside him wearing dungarees and ringlets. Shirley Temple . . . Where had they dug that up from? He wanted to turn it off but he couldn't . . . *An-i-mal crack-ers in my soup* . . . she sang. What age was she – nine? Ten?

She had dimples. Like her . . . Fuck! He thought of her, the child, in the drawing room singing, the shock he'd got seeing her there . . . He'd end up in the red brick himself if he went on like this . . . His fingers fumbled to find the 'off' button.

The evening dragged. He thought about ringing Florrie but stopped himself. He had never run after anyone in his life and he wasn't starting now.

What if she had more stuff in the car and he just didn't realize it, though? That she was really clearing out . . . He went upstairs, resting after every few steps. First he checked the wardrobe in their own bedroom. No, there wasn't much missing . . . She had stuff in the spare room, too, though – had she cleared that out? Terrified, he went to look. Her dressing gown was on the bed. She wouldn't be gone for long without that. As relief flooded through him he picked it up and held it to his face. It smelled of her – warm, familiar . . .

He checked the wardrobe – there were a few items still hanging there, including her best coat. She'd have brought that with her surely if she was really going?

It was then he noticed the boxes on the floor. The dates on the labels jumped out at him – 1964 and 1965. Accounts from years ago – what were they doing down here? Lord God Almighty – she'd gone through them! She knew money had gone somewhere. Her bookkeeper's eye would have picked it up in minutes. She knew! Abe sat down on the bed, his legs unable to hold him up anymore.

No wonder she had been acting strangely. Her – the child . . . Hannah . . . must have told her about the money paid to Lil . . .

He buried his head in his hands. Lord God Almighty! It was all coming down around his ears.

Chapter
TEN

Florrie accepted the cup of tea that the rector handed her. She was glad of the warmth of it – and the heat of the fire in his study.

"I can't pray . . . That's not right, is it? Not to be able."

"God understands. Right now you're overwhelmed . . ."

"I had to get out of there, even for a while. The walls were closing in on me. And he going about his business as if nothing was wrong . . . I felt such anger . . . Doesn't make me a great Christian, does it?"

"We're all human and you're a better Christian than a great many people I know."

"I thought he'd admit it if I asked him straight out."

"Maybe he wanted to but couldn't. Sometimes we block out what we don't want to remember. As a way of coping."

"Even if it causes more hurt to everyone else by denying it . . . His own child . . . Me . . . It doesn't make it easier to forgive."

"I know, but time can heal. You've seen that before in so many people's lives – your own too."

"It's hard to see that right now."

"Pray your anger . . . Shout, rail against God, let it out, tell him what you think of him . . . We all feel forsaken sometimes – think of Jesus on the cross . . . Eli. Eli . . . lama sabacthani . . . but the pulse of your faith is strong – I've known that from the first day I met you. You always see beyond what seems to be – in everyone. That's a gift and it won't let you down."

"I don't feel very blessed right now."

"The pain will pass."

Florrie thought of the DNA test and the arrangement to meet the courier in the village the next morning.

"Do you think I was wrong to do it?"

"It's not for me to judge. You did what you thought was right."

"I thought he'd admit it. Then there wouldn't have been any need."

"Is there any chance that he may not be the father?"

Florrie shook her head.

"No. I saw it in his eyes. The accounts only confirmed it."

"Had you ever suspected that he was keeping something from you?"

"I knew there was something over the years. Always some kind of cloud in his face. It'd disappear sometimes, of course, but then I'd look at him sometimes when he wouldn't know I was watching and I'd see it. As soon as he'd realize I was looking it'd clear again."

"It must have been a burden for him . . ."

"The truth will set you free – isn't that what John says? Secrets – they rot your soul."

"Yes. Maybe this truth coming out is a new starting point . . . Think about it – there's nothing more to hurt you. There is freedom in that."

"Forgiveness is a big ask. To think of him with someone else . . ."

"Of course it is. Right now, you should rest and heal. Stay here tonight. We have a spare room. There's absolutely no need for you to go anywhere else."

"Sanctuary . . ."

"We all need it sometimes."

"You're very kind."

She watched the rector put more coal on the fire before sitting down opposite her again.

"And Hannah – how do you feel about her?"

Florrie stared at the fire.

"I should have seen it before I did . . . I liked her from day one. I've often thought about it since. Was I attracted to some part of him reflected in her – physical resemblance maybe – his child, on a subconscious level? Maybe that was God's way of helping me – by letting me get to know her a bit before I found out . . . Mysterious ways and all that . . ."

"Perhaps. It'll probably all come clearer as time goes on. What will you do – tomorrow – when you get the results?"

"Get everyone together. Vera, the boys . . . It concerns us all. That's the best thing to do, isn't it – talk it out at a family meeting . . .? No matter how much he doesn't want it, he'll have to face up to it then, won't he?"

The rector's hand touched hers.

Our Father, who art in heaven . . .

Abe woke in a sweat for a second time. No, it was all her fault. If her tubes hadn't been blocked none of this would have happened . . . The harshness of his breathing shocked him. Were his lungs clapping up on him too?

The silence in the house frightened him. Florrie was gone. What if she never came back? How would he explain to people that his wife had deserted him and why she had gone? She'd given him a chance to own up . . . Jesus!

Feeling panicky he rang her number on his mobile phone. Unavailable . . . She didn't want to talk to him . . .

What would he do if she never came back?

He tried to figure out what money she had. She had access to the household account all the time, but there was never more than a thousand euro in it at any one time. He rang Banking 365. No, she hadn't taken anything out – not yet anyway.

He sat up in the bed in fright. What if she had money of her own that he didn't know anything about? God, she could have! She could have salted away some over the years. No, she wouldn't do that – she wasn't the type . . .

Shutting his eyes, he cursed himself for having had anything to do with Lil Casey. He hadn't even enjoyed it, for God's sake. Fuck it! Why hadn't he been able to control himself? He was no better than the beasts in the field.

At 6 a.m. he couldn't bear to stay in bed any longer.

He had fed the stock when Vera arrived in the yard. That was all he needed!

"Abe!"

She was blowing the horn now. Florrie had hardly gone to her place . . .

The shed door creaked as he pulled it shut. He should have oiled it ages ago . . .

"There you are!"

"What?"

"Is Florrie not up? There's no answer."

Abe didn't speak as he unlocked the back door of the farmhouse. Vera followed him in. His sister's voice was higher-pitched than usual.

"She's hardly gone to town this early? The car's not there."

"She's gone off for the day – some day care thing," he said, washing his hands.

"She never said . . ."

Now he saw his sister take an old newspaper out of her pocket and lay it on the table in front of him, her hand shaking.

"What?"

Was it some land sale that was advertised?

"Look at it!"

He picked it up and glanced at the date – November first 2004 . . . . Death notices. He scanned the list. Casey. Elizabeth . . .Christ!

"What are you showing me this for?"

His sister's lips were pursed.

"I showed it to you a few months ago, remember? I talked about Lil Casey dying and about it saying she had a daughter."

"So?"

"You were away the day of that funeral."

God Almighty!

"Away where? What are you talking about?"

"You told Leo you went to Dublin to see a consultant. It was the day Leo got the new loader. Think!"

"So what if I did. What's it to you?"

"Nothing as long as you didn't go somewhere else as well . . ."

"What are you saying?"

"Did you go to that funeral?"

Abe snorted.

"I don't have to answer you! Coming in here, into my own house, like some kind of inquisitor! What would I go there for?"

His sister was screeching now.

"If you'd discovered you'd a daughter you might. Or if you knew all along you had one you might . . ."

"Shut up!"

Calm, he had to stay calm. She has no proof – bluster it out . . .

"Your imagination is running away with you!"

"You think? Where's Florrie then? Answer me that! And why was she acting so strange in church yesterday?"

"What?"

"Asking me what would I do if it was the truth about you and that one!"

"Get out of here if that's what you want to believe!"

His sister's hands were clutching the back of the chair.

"Tell me you didn't go! Tell me!"

Abe felt the sweat pour down his face. He couldn't speak.

"You can't, can you?"

"Believe what you want. Now get out!"

"Me? Get out of what was my own home? The place that should have been mine? Do you think I liked being passed over, seeing you assuming that all this was coming to you just because you were a boy? Do you think I had no feelings?"

"That's years ago!"

"To you maybe! Do you think I wanted to leave this house because there was nothing for me here . . . To see you get everything? Leo getting this place is the only thing that keeps me going. So you had better be telling the truth!"

Abe slumped down in his armchair after she'd gone. As the twinge of pain started in his chest, his hand rushed to his trouser pocket for his tablets.

The radio was on . . . More talk about Carlow sugar beet factory closing and speculation about the industry being wiped out in this country . . .

Abe felt nauseous. Everything was falling apart. The tightness was getting worse. Should he call the doctor? He had the number on his mobile. No, not yet. It was only something he'd eaten. Indigestion. Florrie – where was she? His fingers fumbled to ring her, but he couldn't do it.

The cattle – were they all right? He tried to get up but his legs wouldn't move. Rest – that's what he had to do . . . He closed his eyes but he could still see the pictures – her, the child, her eyes, her walk, the look of his grandmother about her.

Hannah suddenly felt terrified.

"What if it *is* all a setup?" she said to Beryl, who had just arrived at the cottage. "What if she put someone else's hair sample in the bag so that the test would come out negative and I'd stop thinking he's my father?"

"She wouldn't do that," Beryl said, "unless we're all very bad judges of character. No, she wouldn't!"

Hannah took her phone out of her jeans pocket to check the screen again.

"I keep looking at it even though I know she won't have the results till the morning. She's meeting the courier in the village."

"I hope she's ok . . ."

"She's not at home. She said she'd be back to meet him in the village . . . That means she's away somewhere. Maybe he threatened her . . ."

Hannah put her head in her hands.

"God, I've brought a lot down on her! And she doesn't deserve any of it!"

"It isn't your fault."

Hannah gave Beryl a hug.

"God, it's good to see you! It felt like my right arm's been chopped off with you not around. I was so scared during that Leo tractor thing . . ."

Hannah explained about the blaring radio.

Beryl looked shocked.

"Roy would have stopped him – if he'd been here."

"How do you know what Roy would have done?"

Was Beryl blushing? The penny dropped.

"Roy? You? You're joking!"

Now Beryl was grinning.

"You think that's not possible?"

"I didn't say that! You saw him at the hotel?"

"Quite a lot of him actually!"

"You didn't!"

"I really like him."

"You're an item?"

"Yes."

Hannah found it difficult to take in. Beryl and Roy . . . They were well matched, though.

"Good on you! I'm really happy for you! More power! Did you talk to him about me? Jesus! There I go again — talking about myself . . ."

"Not at first but it was a bit hard to avoid, given all that's happened. He doesn't really know what to believe with his uncle denying it and all, but he said that if it is true he'd prefer his uncle would own up rather than go on lying about it. I know he likes you. He said at least you'd have singing in common."

Hannah had a lump in her throat.

"At least one of them doesn't hate me . . . When are you seeing him again?"

"I'm not sure but he knows I'm here – we're texting all the time. I'd love it if he'd call over . . ."

Hannah laughed.

"And have the two of you going at it like rabbits when Auntie Vera arrives at the door with a big stick to beat her big, bad son all the way home!"

"He's forty-two, for God's sake! She'll have to let him grow up sometime."

Getting ready for bed, Hannah checked her phone again.

"Try to forget about it until the morning. She'll be in touch when she has the results."

Her friend was looking worried.

"What happens when you get them?

"I don't know . . . I just want to see his face. When he can't deny it anymore."

Hannah felt sick. "He wouldn't hurt Florrie, would he, when he realizes what she's done?"

"Roy won't let him. There'll be others around. He wouldn't be that stupid."

Hannah had a knot in her stomach.

"God, I'm walking in and upending people's lives but I can't stop it . . . it's like there's something primal driving me. I'm really glad you're here – you know that?"

Hannah climbed into the bed in her mother's old room and switched off the light. At least she'd be resting, though she doubted if sleep would come. Not tonight.

Leo Kemp was shouting at his mother.

"Spit it out! Something's up with you!"

"L-leave h-her a-a-alone!"

He almost spat in his brother's face.

"I will not! She's been going around as if she's shell-shocked for the past two days and I want to know what for. Are you sick – is that it?"

Leo saw his mother sit down as if her legs could no longer carry her.

"I'm not sick . . ."

"Well? You're as white as a fucking ghost then – what for?"

"S-stop sh-shouting at her . . ."

"You fuck up! Come on, I'm waiting!"

Seeing his mother sitting there squashing bread between her fingers made him feel even angrier.

"Well . . . ?"

"He went to the funeral."

"What funeral?"

"L-l-leave h-her a-alone!"

"Lil Casey's."

Fuck!

"He told you he did?"

"He didn't have to."

"Jesus!"

"W-Wh-at's the big deal?"

"He went to the funeral, you thick, because there was something between him and that bitch!"

"H-he was th-there."

Leo looked at his brother in amazement.

"How would you know where he was?"

He watched his brother's face redden.

"B-Beryl."

"Yer one's mate?"

Leo watched in amazement as Roy nodded.

"S-s-he h-h-has a n-n-name – B-b-beryl. Sh-she saw h-him there."

"What?"

"How the hell would you know what . . . Beryl saw – unless you've been getting pally with her – is that it?"

"So-s-so what?"

"You've been off doing a course and all the time you were shagging the enemy . . . is that it? You bastard!"

Leo had hit Roy a box before he realized what he had done. Roy looked stunned for a second, then Leo felt a punch in his guts.

He could hear his mother screeching at them to stop as they landed punches on one another. Now they were on the ground wrestling like when they were kids . . .

He had grabbed Roy by the throat when the water hit him. His mother had thrown a bucketful over them.

"Dogs in the street – that's what you're like! Dear God, what's happening?"

Leo sat back on the floor, breathing heavily. He hurt in several places and there was blood running from his nose – fuck!

His mother's mobile phone was ringing on the table.

He watched her squint to read the caller's name.

"It's Florrie!"

Leo watched his mother's hand shake as she answered the phone.

"What? Where are you? A meeting? What sort of meeting?"

Fuck! What was happening now?

"She's called a family meeting in Knocklannon. Now! To talk about the proof! Lord God Almighty . . . He is the father!"

"What proof? There isn't any – you hear! Where is she – Aunt Florrie – right now?"

His mother was sitting there still looking dazed.

"In the pub car park in the village. She's got some results. The meeting is in Knocklannon now. She'll be coming to the meeting too."

"Who? That bitch? Over my dead body!"

His mother was screeching now.

"Leo! Come back! Where are you going?"

Leo nearly took the door off the hinges as he went out.

"To put a stop to this once and for all!"

"Leo!"

He spun the wheels as he left the yard.

In the rearview mirror he saw his brother and mother get into Roy's car and follow him. They could fuck off. He'd leave them standing . . .

It was ten minutes past twelve when the call finally came. Hannah's hand shook as she answered it.

"The pub car park. We'll be there in five minutes. Yes, Beryl is with me, is that ok with you?"

Hannah was hardly aware she was driving.

"There she is!"

She could see Florrie's car.

Hannah tried to read Florrie's face as they approached the car, but the visor was down. What if the result was negative? Jesus!

She and Beryl sat into Florrie's car.

Florrie handed Hannah the open brown envelope. Hannah scanned the paper. 99.9% certainty . . .

Hannah's body heaved. Beryl's hand was on her shoulder.

"She wasn't lying . . . !" Hannah said. She grabbed onto Beryl's hand.

"Thank you for doing this," Hannah said, when she could finally speak. "I know it can't have been easy."

Florrie was staring out through the windscreen now.

"What's right is right. There's no way round it."

"What happens now?"

"I've called a meeting. I rang him – and the others. We'll all go to Knocklannon."

Hannah looked round as a van swung into the car park and screeched to a stop beside them.

"It's Leo!"

Florrie's hand was on her arm.

"Stay where you are."

Leo was now pulling the door open and grabbing the envelope from Florrie's hands. "Give me that!"

"It's not your property," Florrie was saying.

Hannah got out of the car.

"Give that back!"

Leo was reading the sheet of paper.

"No fucking way! No fucking way, you hear?"

"It's the truth!"

"It's not – and it never will be!"

He was tearing up the sheet of paper.

"Keep your voice down," Florrie said. "We're all going home to talk about this . . . now calm down. Hannah and Beryl – get into your car – now!"

Hannah got into the driver's seat. Before he hit her . . .

"No one's taking what's mine – you hear?"

Florrie was driving out of the car park. Hannah started the engine and moved off to follow her.

"GO! NOW!" Beryl was shouting.

Thump! Leo had belted the car on the bonnet with his fist as she moved off.

"He's mad!"

"Go!"

As Hannah moved out to follow Florrie, Beryl could hear Leo curse at them. In the mirror she saw him jump into his van . . .

"He's after us!" Beryl was shouting.

Leo was tailgating them.

"He's driving too close!" Beryl said.

The road was narrow, but Hannah increased her speed to try get rid of him.

"He's trying to pass!"

"Or run us off the road – Christ!"

Hannah was checking her mirror every few seconds. She felt terrified.

"The bollocks!"

"Ignore him," Beryl was saying. "Concentrate on following Florrie. It's not far now. Roy's car's behind – he won't let him do anything stupid . . ."

Hannah's heart was pounding.

They were coming to a wider stretch of road now.

"Jesus!" Hannah screamed. Leo had made to pass out but was staying abreast of them. The car mirrors were almost touching. She slowed the car. Beryl screamed. Hannah felt the van clip the wing of the car. She braked as the car slithered in on the grass verge, bumping over the uneven surface for several yards, briars and sceachs scratching the side. They'd stopped! A horn blowing non-stop behind them. Bang! They'd hit the ditch . . . Hannah gripped the steering wheel. When she looked up she could see Leo's van disappearing up the road. Florrie was reversing back to them.

"You all right?"

Beryl had her face in her hands.

"I think so."

Hannah switched off the engine. Her legs felt numb.

Florrie was hurrying towards them.

Hannah had her head down on the steering wheel.

"He was trying to kill us!"

"He's gone. You're safe now."

"B-bastard!"

Roy and Florrie were at the door.

"Are you all right?" Florrie was saying. "Are either of you hurt?"

"No."

Shit! Was the car wrecked?

Roy held the door open. Beryl climbed out the driver's side after Hannah.

Roy was hugging Beryl. Hannah looked at Vera standing there white-faced and dazed.

Florrie was talking to her.

"It's a DNA test. He is Hannah's father."

"God Almighty!"

"Leo could be gone after him . . ."

Roy was beckoning to them to get into his car.

"C-C-come on. W-we-ll get the cars later."

Hannah was still shaking as the five of them headed for Knocklannon in Roy's car. This wasn't happening . . .

It seemed an eternity until they reached the avenue . . . What if her father became violent? What if Leo had attacked him . . . ?

Leo's van wasn't there . . .

"Thank God!"

"H-h-he'll have gone somewhere to cool down . . ."

"Come on," Florrie was saying, heading for the backdoor of the farmhouse. It was locked.

"He can't be far. The jeep's there . . ."

The sound of a cow roaring broke the silence.

"Gem's calving! He'll be in the shed!"

"What if Leo's done something foolish . . . ?" Vera's voice was only a whisper.

"H-he's n-not that s-s-s-tupid . . ."

"Dear Lord, help us . . ."

Hannah followed Florrie into the cattle shed. She saw her father in one of the pens. Two calf's legs were sticking out of the heifer in front of him. He had a rope tied to them, sweat pouring down his face as he pulled his level best . . .

Abe Stephenson staggered backwards when he saw them all coming into the shed.

Tests . . . meetings . . . they were coming to get him . . .

"Get to fuck out of here – the whole lot of you!"

His voice sounded odd to him – distant.

Florrie was in the pen beside him.

"How long is she like this?"

He had to catch his breath before he could answer.

"An hour or so . . ."

Florrie was examining the water bag.

"The calf must be too big or she'd have delivered before now. It's under stress. Did you call the vet?"

"A few minutes ago."

"He could be ages. Did you examine her?"

"No."

"The head could be backwards. "It was her, the child, standing right beside him. "It can't be left or it'll run out of oxygen. Let me!"

Christ! She was standing right beside him . . .

"I'm a nurse, for God's sake. I'll feel where the head is."

Florrie was instructing Vera to get soapy water and rinsing water and Roy to tie the cow's tail up out of the way.

Abe stood back, feeling weak. What was she doing here, near the pedigrees . . . in this place?

He tried to catch his breath as his chest tightened . . . Fuck! He hadn't got a puff . . .

She was putting on calving gloves and his wife was squeezing obstetrical lubricant onto her palms. Now she – the child – was putting her right hand into the cow's birth canal above the protruding feet.

"We're ok, the head is there – I can feel the nose and the forehead so it's coming the right way."

"Thank God for that," Florrie was saying. "Good girl."

Abe felt dizzy. Was she saying that to the cow or the child?

"First calf, isn't it?"

"Yes."

She – the child – still had her arm up the cow.

"It's just hung up on the hymen. It's a tight fit, that's all. Common enough in heifers."

How would she know . . . Abe felt weird, like all the talk was miles away from him. The tightness in his chest was getting worse.

He could hear her giving orders.

"She'll need a good pull to get it out of there. Roy, would you stretch the vulva while we pull on her next contraction?"

"Y-Yep."

Now she was handing him the rope.

"I'll pull with you. Pull straight until the head's out. It has to arc over the pelvis . . ."

She was giving him orders . . . Fuck! He could see Florrie at the cow's head, calming her.

Abe tried to pull but felt too weak. Most of the strength was coming from her . . .

"Head's coming . . . A bit more."

He saw her change position to pull down on the rope now – how did she know to do that?

"She'll do it herself now . . . Easy . . ."

They both staggered backwards as the calf whooshed out onto the pile of straw.

Abe put his hands on his knees to steady himself. Christ, the pain had shot up into his right arm . . . Fuck! Focus on the calf – that's what he had to do.

"Well done!"

The calf . . . it was shaking its head to clear the fluid out of its nose . . .

Roy and Florrie had stepped away quickly to give the cow her space.

She – the child – was taking the rope off the calf's front feet.

The pain had now shot up into his jaw – FUCK!

"We'd better get out."

The heifer was already turning to lick the calf.

"It's a heifer. Another champion, please God!" Florrie was saying.

The sounds seemed further away now. Abe wanted to vomit. The vice was tightening again. He slumped to his knees.

"Abe!"

"You ok?" someone was asking.

The sounds were coming through a fog. Fuck! The pain!

Hannah saw him fall. Vera was screeching.

"Abe!"

Hannah could see her father clutching his chest and groaning. She was beside him immediately.

"Get an ambulance – now! Keep back!"

Hannah was on her knees beside him, listening for breaths and feeling his pulse.

"Can you hear me?"

No response . . .

She tore open his shirt then angled his head.

CPR . . . The routine – that's all she had to remember . . .

She put the heel of her right hand on the centre of his chest and the heel of the left on top of it. She pushed straight down, hard and fast, releasing after each one to let his chest come back to its normal position.

She stooped to tilt his head and lift his chin. Pinching his nose closed, she stooped to cover his mouth with hers and breathed twice, watching for his chest to rise as she did so, then it was back to the chest compressions . . .

"Count to 30! One, two, three . . ."

Florrie was on the ground beside her. Roy was giving the ambulance directions.

"Twenty-five, twenty-six, twenty-seven . . ."

Hannah moved to give two more breaths then more compressions . . . As the minutes passed her arms ached – 100 compressions a minute – that was what was needed to keep him alive . . .

Someone was praying – was it Vera . . . *Our Father, who art in heaven.*

Her arms felt like lead now.

"You – can't – die – you – bastard!" Hannah heard herself say. "You can't – get – out – of – it this way . . ."

"Let me . . . you're exhausted . . . tell me what to do . . ."

Florrie was on the shed floor beside her.

"Keep the rhythm . . . When I stop be – ready – to – press . . ."

Hannah almost fainted with relief and exhaustion when the ambulance screeched into the yard fifteen minutes later. Within seconds the paramedics had the defibrillator ready to use. Stand back . . . Shock . . .

"Oxygen."

She watched through a blur as they administered medication, all the time talking calmly.

"He's breathing . . . we'll get him to hospital now . . ."

Hannah could feel someone's arm around her, pulling her up off the ground. Was it Beryl's or Florrie's?

"Thank God!"

"Good work!" one of the ambulance men said as they closed the door of the ambulance. "He's a lucky man."

"Will he be all right?" Vera Kemp was asking.

"We hope so. Got to get him to hospital now."

They all stood in the yard in silent shock as the ambulance disappeared up the avenue, siren blaring.

"W-w-e'll follow on in a f-few minutes," Roy was saying as he put his arm around Florrie.

"Let's go inside."

Hannah was glad of Beryl linking arms with her as they went into the kitchen. She sat down and put her head between her knees, instinctively, in case she fainted.

"She hasn't eaten much all day," she could hear Beryl saying.

"There's bread there . . . biscuits. Get whatever she needs. Put the kettle on. Vera! We need tea with lots of sugar in it."

Hannah felt a bit better after eating. God, what had just happened . . .

"He was never sick a day in his life . . ."

Vera was at one end of the table, sitting very still.

"Would they be there yet?"

"Soon."

"What if . . ."

"He'll get priority in A&E. Coronary cases always do," Hannah said.

Florrie was back in the room with a packed bag.

"Lord God, this is terrible!" Vera was mumbling again.

"Are you going to the hospital?"

"We'll all go. It's better than sitting here. Roy, will you ring Aidan and ask him to come over to keep an eye on the cattle? Maybe he would get a bit of help and pick up the cars first, though . . . if Hannah and I leave our keys here . . ."

"Y-yes."

Florrie's hand was on her shoulder.

"You must come too."

Hannah felt a lump in her throat.

"Are you sure?"

"Yes."

Hannah looked down at the state of her jeans.

"They're filthy. I should change first . . ."

"It'll only take a few minutes," Florrie was saying.

"Leo – he should know." Vera said. "He's not answering his phone . . . Where is he?"

"H-h-he's lucky he's not in jail."

At the cottage Hannah still felt shaky as she changed her clothes. Beryl helped her on with her coat.

"You ok?"

"I think so."

"God, what a day!"

Hannah sat on the edge of the bed for a minute.

"What if he dies? He could be dead already for all we know. One cardiac arrest often follows another. Where will I be then?"

"Don't think about it! They'll look after him. You were marvellous – the calving and all. I could see him looking at you."

"I should have seen it quicker. His breathing . . . I should have noticed the minute we walked in . . ."

"You did your best. More than that . . ."

"Yeah – but for what? He probably hates me. Maybe he'd prefer if I'd let him die . . ."

Chapter
ELEVEN

Abe Stephenson drifted in and out of sleep. Everything seemed very bright and he closed his eyes against the harshness of the ceiling lights. He was back in secondary school and the lads in his class were jeering him about the meaning of his name. *Abraham – father of a multitude. Jaysus, Stephenson'll be worse than an AI bull, what? Can't ye see him – sprogs around him like sand on the seashore . . .*

Abe opened his eyes again. Someone was talking to him?

"Are you awake, Mr Stephenson? Abraham – can you hear me?"

He opened his eyes again. A woman in a blue uniform was looking down at him. He tried to speak but he couldn't.

"You're in Wexford Hospital, Mr Stephenson. You've been here since yesterday."

Abe found it difficult to concentrate. Hospital? He moved his head to look round. There were machines everywhere and beeping sounds and wires on his chest. Where were his clothes? What was he doing here?

"Have you any pain, Mr Stephenson? Abraham – can you hear me?"

Pain . . . He tried to lift his head but it sank back into his pillow like a lead weight. He closed his eyes again to block out the light – and the strangeness. Was he going to die? Foggy images of the calving shed suddenly came back to him – them all coming in through the door, her pulling the rope, inches in front of him, then pain . . .

"I have to get up . . ."

Abe made an attempt to get out of the bed, hands flailing. The nurse grabbed them. He could hear her voice – calm . . .

"No, you have to stay in bed, Abraham. Rest is very important. You have to give yourself a chance to get better. The doctor will be here soon to talk to you."

Abe lay back, breathless. Hospital . . . Nurses . . . Get better . . .

"What happened?"

"You had a cardiac incident, Mr Stephenson – to do with your heart – but you're recovering now. The ambulance brought you in yesterday afternoon."

Cardiac incident . . . Cardiac . . . Heart . . . Heart attack? God Almighty. He thought of his father dying young . . . *Runs in the family* . . . He could hear the people talking at the funeral . . . *Our Father, which art in* . . . Was he saying those words or were they in his head?

He remembered the green uniforms and the inside of the ambulance and the noise of an animal in pain – or had those sounds come from him?

"Florrie . . ."

"Your family's outside. They'll be glad to hear you're awake. I'll let your wife and daughter know."

Daughter!

Abe gripped the nurse's wrist in panic but couldn't speak.

"You don't want any visitors just yet, is that it? That's all right. We'll give them an update on how you are and suggest they go home and have some rest and come back later. Is that ok?"

Abe blinked, unable to make a sound.

Family . . . She was outside . . . He shut his eyes tight. What had Florrie told the nurses? Her . . . The bleeps – when were they going to stop? He closed his eyes trying to block out what had happened yesterday . . . Florrie's voice on the phone, telling him about test results and about how there would be no more lies . . . Fuck! If it was a heart attack he mightn't pull through . . . *Fellas with a dicky ticker don't live long* . . . Again he could hear the talk of people at his father's funeral.

Death . . . Clogs popped . . . He closed his eyes as another wave of fear washed over him.

Florrie Stephenson wished she could open the windows in the relatives' room off the coronary care unit to let in some air. The room was packed and stuffy now, another family as well as themselves waiting for news.

She could see that Vera was still asleep on one of the pull-out bed chairs, a blanket over her. The longer she stayed asleep the better . . .

Hannah was awake. Florrie looked at her, pointed at the door and Hannah nodded.

Telling the nurse that they would be in the foyer they walked together downstairs. 5.20 a.m. Abe was still asleep, the nurse said. Yes, they would let them know . . .

The tea from the machine was as black as tar, but it helped. Florrie's head felt heavy and her neck ached from dozing in an awkward position. There were people queuing at the admissions desk and down the hall they could see that the A&E department was still busy even at this hour.

"Places like this never sleep, do they?" she said.

"No."

"Do you miss it? Work? In Waterford?"

"Sort of. I'll have to go back soon."

"Yes."

Silence fell again as they sat watching two people go out through the automatic door in their dressing gowns to smoke. It was still dark and cold.

It seemed an eternity since coming here. Abe was being monitored all the time, she knew, drugs to dilate the arteries and blood tests and ECGs every few hours . . .

Right now she just wanted to know that he was ok. Hannah had been able to talk to the nurses and explain the whole process.

"They'll know more when they do the angiogram – what's blocked and the degree of it . . . They can't really say much until then."

Heart attack . . . It was difficult to take in. She had experienced a lot of emotions during the night – fear, guilt . . . Had she caused the heart attack by calling the meeting? No! A heart attack wouldn't happen just like that. Still, it had shocked her to see him in so much pain . . . She took several deep breaths to calm herself.

The rector had been in. Roy too – what would she have done without him? He'd been a rock – in an out, checking on both the farms, organizing everything, bringing in food last night, though none of them ate much. It was obvious he liked Beryl very much. Florrie liked her too. She was genuine, caring . . . Just what he needed.

It had been awkward explaining who was who to the nursing staff. In the end, she'd told the truth. What was the point in telling lies? They were looking after him. They should know what the situation was. Delicate . . . Complicated . . . Yes, his daughter was here as well . . . Yes, there was conflict . . .

"They're used to it," Hannah said. "There's no such thing as a normal family any more. We see lots of situations – the wife in one room, the partner in another, two sets of children maybe, trying to go between them – walking on eggshells stuff . . . I never thought I'd be on this side of it, though."

"No."

Florrie thought of how everyone they knew must be talking about them. Tongues wagging . . . The drama of it . . . What were they doing – pitying her? Condemning him? Blaming Hannah for turning up? No, it's no one's business but ours, she told herself. What other people think has nothing to do with us. She had learned to live by that a long time ago.

"Will you go in and see him?" Hannah was asking. "They wouldn't let you stay for long . . . a few minutes . . ."

Florrie paused before she answered.

"I'm not sure. Right now, I just want to know that he's pulled through. I can't think that far ahead."

Part of her wanted to shout at him – tear him apart in his hospital bed.

"Mrs Stephenson?"

The girl from the admissions desk was coming towards her.

"CCU just rang down. Your husband's asking for you."

Hannah shivered while she waited for the nurse to finish talking to Florrie.

She could see Vera Kemp at the relatives' room door, white faced and dishevelled-looking. She looked away when their eyes met. She hadn't said two words all night except to ask Roy several times if he'd heard from Leo. At least she hadn't been abusive even when Beryl had brought cups of tea up for them and she and Roy had held hands as they sat and waited.

"We should all go home for a while. He's not well enough for visitors yet," Florrie said.

"He'll be all right?"

Vera was beside them now.

"The doctor is hopeful. His chances get better as time goes on. Let's see what tomorrow brings. They'll be in touch every few hours to keep us updated. We all need some rest . . ."

"Someone should stay . . ."

Vera's voice was a squeak.

"No, Vera. There'll be time enough for talk. We all need rest at the moment. Perhaps Hannah would drop the two of us home . . ."

Home . . .

"Of course."

"Thank you."

Beryl's car was in Kemp's yard when she dropped off Vera. Beryl, wearing Wellingtons, came across Kemps' yard with Roy. Vera went into the house without speaking.

"I'll see you back at the cottage soon."

"Yes."

Hannah felt jittery and exhausted as she drove down the avenue to Knocklannon to drop Florrie back. There was a red car in the yard.

"Aidan's here," Florrie was saying. "Good. He'll do the yard work. Would you like to have a look in on Gem and her calf before you go – and have some breakfast with me? You must be hungry."

"Are you sure?"

"Yes."

"Sounds good, thank you."

Florrie was heading for the kennel near the back door.

"I'll let Max out first. Poor dog doesn't know what's going on, do you, lad?"

The sheepdog's tail was wagging madly as they walked to the shed.

"Come on, let's go see the cattle . . ."

Knocklannon Gem was suckling her new calf.

"Looks like she's grown since last night!"

"They grow like steam alright," Florrie said. "Mother's milk is powerful stuff."

Hannah watched Florrie stroke the cow's head from outside the pen.

"You're beautiful girls, aren't you, eh? The pair of you?"

Hannah looked round. That was where he'd fallen. She could still see the marks of the gurney . . .

Florrie was now following her gaze.

"Seems a long time since yesterday . . ."

"Yes."

She shivered slightly as she followed Florrie into the farmhouse a few minutes later. Heat! She was glad of it as she stood by the cooker warming her hands over the hot plate.

"Can I help with anything?"

"There bread's there – maybe stick some in the toaster while I get the kettle on."

"No problem."

Now Hannah sat down at the table and waited while Florrie found mugs, milk and butter. He probably sat in the chair at the top of the table . . .

"You've been very kind . . . There's lots'd — I don't know . . . run me maybe . . ."

Florrie had now poured the tea.

"What good would condemning you do? You did nothing wrong."

Hannah warmed her hands on her mug.

"My mother couldn't even look me in the face sometimes – it was like I was inseparable from her shame. Maybe that was the hardest part . . ."

"I'm sure she loved you in her own way."

"She probably did. The meeting yesterday – what were you going to say to him . . ."

"Lots of things . . . It's strange. I had it all worked out in my head – wanting to hear him admit it. Tell the truth at last . . ."

"And now?"

"I still want to hear that – yes! But he needs to let it out – for his own good too. Most of what I feel now, though, is sadness – that he was never able to tell. That is had to come to this . . ."

"You knew it was true?"

Hannah saw Florrie nod.

"I didn't want to believe it at first, of course, who would?"

"How did you know?"

Florrie was staring into space.

"His eyes. You don't know a person this long without being able to read his face."

"I suppose."

Hannah wrapped her hands round the mug to heat them again.

"What happens now? He may not be out of the woods for a while . . ."

"I don't know. I don't think there's any instruction manual for this one, is there?"

"No."

Abe woke again to see a man in black leaning over him.

"Abe . . ."

He tried to focus on the face, the place, the white ceiling . . .

"Rector . . . ?"

"Yes. They said I could have a few minutes. How are you feeling?"

More questions . . .

Abe closed his eyes.

"Yes . . . well . . . the doctors say you are making progress, so that's good . . . Florrie told me what happened, so I thought I'd call in. You're a lucky man and you're being well looked after."

Abe wished the talking would stop. He could feel water leak out of the corner of his eyes again. Florrie told him . . . told him what? How much did he know? What was going on? Abe tried to raise his head but couldn't. Christ, he felt so weak. Would he soon be pushing up daisies? He stared at the ceiling to avoid the rector's eyes.

"You've had a shock – of course you have – but in a few days time you won't know yourself. Time is a great healer . . . I've seen a lot of people worse than you do very well and be home in no time at all."

"Abraham!"

The nurse's voice coming at him now irritated him.

"Abraham, do you have any pain at all?"

Why did they always shout as if you were deaf . . . ?

"No."

How many times had he been asked that?

The rector was touching his arm.

"Right well, I'll call another time. And you'll all be in my prayers."

His eyes were leaking again and he couldn't wipe the water away.

Our Father who art in heaven . . . Hallowed be Thy name . . .

It was his mother's voice he was hearing now and he was a child, kneeling beside his bed and she was saying the words and patting his head when he'd finished.

"My boy – Abe – and able – that's how you'll be when you grow up . . ."

Now he was seeing her – the child – her red coat on, her stare burning a hole in his soul . . .

Deliver us from evil, For Thine is the Kingdom, the power and the glory . . .

Abe closed his eyes tightly.

It was the rector's voice again. He was still there.

"If there's anything troubling you, I'm here to talk to – anytime – you know that . . ."

Abe turned his head away.

"Just tell the nurse and she'll ring me if you need me."

Abe felt the rector's hand touch him again. He pulled away.

"Good can come of difficult times if we leave ourselves open to that possibility . . . and to God's grace . . . Florrie will be in soon, I'm sure . . ."

Florrie . . .

Abe closed his eyes tightly to squash the water and the brightness out.

"Have you heard from Leo?"

Vera Kemp was trying to concentrate on what Reverend Mundy was saying.

She fiddled with the mobile phone on her lap and shook her head.

"No? Well . . . he'll be back soon, I'm sure . . . once he's come to terms with things . . . Perhaps he needed a bit of space. We all need that sometimes."

Vera stared at the television oblivious of what programme was on. Three days and no word . . .

"And Abe is making progress, I hear? Getting stronger every day . . . He'll be going to Waterford Hospital for the angiogram soon, Florrie was saying . . ."

Angiogram . . . what did that mean? Vera tried to remember about the dye and the vein and how they could see the blockages.

"Will you go in to see him? I'm sure he'd like to see you – when you're both a bit stronger . . ."

"I don't know."

"Yes, well . . . Roy is a marvel – looking after everything, I believe. You've a good son there, but you know that I'm sure."

The clergyman's voice sounded distant.

"Have you thought about seeing the doctor yourself, I wonder? Roy tells me you're not eating much but you have to keep your strength up. Shock can affect us all in different ways. Abe will be out and about soon, I'm sure, and he wouldn't want to see you poorly . . ."

Vera felt as if the cold had entered her bones.

"Thank you very much for calling."

Roy was now showing the rector out.

"Will you try him again – Leo?"

"I-I-t's p-powered off."

Vera's stomach felt sick. Where was Leo? Was he all right? Everything was falling apart. She'd seen them all staring – the neighbours she'd met on the road, having a right laugh probably, the whole lot of them . . . She couldn't take it in. Her brother the father of that one . . .

Vera closed the prayer book the rector had left open beside her. There was no God – not if this had happened. What had she lived well for and gone to church on a Sunday for if life could turn upside down like this?

"The n-nurse said he was a-a-asking for you . . ."

Vera stared straight ahead.

"Has Florrie gone in yet?"

She saw her son look away.

"N-no."

"I'll never forgive him."

"T-t-that's how you f-f-feel now . . . T-hink of what Aunt F-Florrie has to c-c-cope with . . ."

"Talking to that one – having her in there!"

"It's n-not her fault s-she was b-born . . ."

"Coming back here upsetting decent people with her accusations. Your grandparents would turn in their graves!"

"J-Jesus!"

She jumped as Roy's hand slapped the table.

Vera sat up straight. Roy shouting?

"Y-you d-don't know that! Every f-family has sk-eletons in the c-cupboard, if you d-d-dig d-deep enough. T-this one's n-n-no d-d-ifferent!"

She could see the veins standing out in her son's neck as he shouted.

"I-it's n-not the end of the w-world! W-We're not a cut above b-buttermilk like you always made us think. We're as g-good or b-bad as the n-next person. P-p-pride – that's all that's been h-hurt around h-here. M-Maybe it's time a lot of people came down off their high h-h-h-horses and joined the real world."

Vera sat there in shock. One son gone and now Roy talking to her like this . . .

He was heading for the door.

"Where are you going?"

Had her voice been a shriek?

"T-t-to see B-beryl. A-and y-you may as well g-g-get u-used to it."

Vera sat up very straight in the chair. Brother against brother . . . Son against mother . . .

The tick of the clock was very loud. She wanted to get up and make it stop but she couldn't. She was too tired.

Florrie handed the bag with the clean pyjamas in it to the nurse.

"He's been asking for you."

"What did he say exactly?"

The nurse was looking at her oddly.

"He was asking if you'd been in, and when you would be in next, things like that. He's a bit emotional, but that's perfectly normal . . ."

Florrie almost smiled.

"Not for him."

"Oh . . . It's just that most people are fragile enough for the first few weeks after a heart attack . . . You realize you're not invincible, I suppose. That's probably hard for a man like your husband to take in. You can come in now if you want . . . You know he'll be going to Waterford tomorrow in the ambulance for the angiogram?"

"Yes."

Florrie took several deep breaths as she followed the nurse into CCU.

He looked old. And paler than she'd ever seen him. She looked at him but could say nothing.

The nurse pulled the curtain round.

"Give you a bit of privacy . . . There's a chair there."

"Thank you."

She saw his hand move as if to take hers. She kept hers away.

"How are you?"

He had turned his head away. Was he tearful? The sight shocked her. She'd only ever seen him cry once before – at his mother's funeral.

She waited until he eventually spoke.

"The cattle – are they all right?"

"They're fine. Aidan is keeping a good eye on them – and Roy."

"Max?"

"He's looking up the lane a lot – like he's expecting you back."

He was staring at the ceiling again.

Asking about the animals . . . What about the humans? Her head pounded as she sat there. She didn't want to look at him, but she forced herself to.

"You'll be going to Waterford hospital tomorrow . . ."

"Aye."

"They've explained what's involved?"

"Yes."

"At least you don't have to wait too long . . ."

"Aye."

"They should have a better idea what the situation is when they do that."

"So they say."

They were staying on the surface of words . . .

Florrie couldn't resist saying it.

"That's where she nurses . . . Hannah . . . in Waterford Hospital . . . in a ward like this. She'll be going back to work soon, she says."

She kept looking straight at him.

Was it fear she saw in his eyes?

She watched his IV hand clutch at the top of the sheet. She waited until he spoke again.

"Wha-t are you going to do?"

She took a deep breath before answering.

"I haven't decided yet. When I do I'll let you know. In the meantime you'll have your own feelings to figure out."

Florrie stood up.

"The hospital will let me know when the test's done – and what the outcome is."

His hand was making grabs at the sheet and his eyes had filled up again.

"Vera?"

"She's taking it hard."

Was it fear she saw flash in his eyes again? And shame? He was looking away again.

"We've all got a lot of thinking to do."

Outside she took several deep breaths as she walked down the long corridor toward the stairs. God had given her strength. He would continue to do so. All she had to do was ask for it.

What the hell was the noise? Leo Kemp turned over in his hotel bed. The phone on the locker was ringing.

"What?"

His head ached as he blinked and listened to the receptionist with the foreign accent as she asked if housekeeping could service his room and would sir be staying another night.

He tried to concentrate.

"I'll be down in a few minutes," he said and slammed the phone down.

He tried to remember where he was – a hotel . . . where? Bray. Yes, he'd driven there after . . . God, his head was splitting. What time was it? What day was it? The receptionist had asked him if he was staying a fourth night so that meant – fuck! It was three days since he'd checked in! Throwing back the clothes, he struggled out of the bed to go to the toilet, almost stepping on a tray he'd left beside the bed. His stomach heaved at the sight of congealed fat around rinds of rasher. There were beer bottles everywhere, the mini-bar door was wide open and there were several other trays of room service food remains that he had forgotten to leave outside the door. All he had wanted to do was get plastered and shut out everything that had happened. He'd run her off the road – Jesus!

He caught his reflection in the mirror. God! He looked rough – three days' stubble, greasy hair and bloodshot eyes. Fuck! He smelled under his arms. He stank to high heaven. Shit! Three days . . . What had happened since he holed up here?

He winced, thinking of how he'd driven back to the bungalow and grabbed his wallet and a few things in a bag, heart thumping thinking the guards would be after him any minute. Her car had gone into the ditch – he had seen it in the rearview mirror. What if she was dead?

He vomited into the toilet, his stomach heaving again and again until it was empty.

"No, it wouldn't be that bad," he said to himself after wiping his mouth with toilet tissue. "She wasn't going that fast, her and that other one – the friend."

All he could remember was his Aunt Florrie's face as he passed her by. Contempt. And Roy after him too . . .

He sat down on the edge of the bath. He could have killed her – any of them . . . What was he thinking of? Christ!

He picked his mobile phone up off the wash-hand basin. It was switched off. No . . . he couldn't look at it yet. He was sick of this room. The sooner he was out of here the better.

He stood face up under the shower, scrambling to adjust the heat as the cold water assaulted his body . . . He grabbed the small bar of soap from the wash hand basin. As he scrubbed his body, the reality of what had happened came back to him. The DNA test – She was his cousin! The bastard! His uncle had been lying all along! He'd got Lil Casey up the duff all right. Damn him to hell!

Leo wanted to vomit again. It wasn't meant to happen like this. He lashed out at the shower door. Fuck! His hand hurt. He stood still, letting the water fall on the back of his neck to calm him . . .

The guards could be after him – fuck! And they'd believe her now about the harassment when they heard about the car chase. Of course she'd ring them – his Aunt Florrie might even have done it . . . He closed his eyes again. Turning off the shower, he grabbed a towel. What was there for him in this goddam country now? He had to get out of here. Roy Boy was welcome to their mother and the handkerchief of a farm and his fucking stonework. England – he'd get work there easy enough on the buildings, he thought, driving a digger or a tractor. If it came to it he could do labouring for a while – anything at all to keep him going. Maybe he'd go to the States later on . . .corn cutting in Kansas maybe. It'd be better than staying here. He was a fucking eejit. He should have cleared out the minute he was eighteen instead of hanging on at home and doing tractor jobs for other farmers to keep a few bob in his pocket while he waited to inherit sweet fuck all! He was a second son – what did any of them ever get? He panicked now as he thought of the guards – if he had a police record he could go nowhere. Christ! He had to go quick . . .

He grabbed the pair of jeans he had in the bag before opening the curtains and windows wide to let out the stink. He grabbed his wallet and phone. The television had been on all night. 11 a.m. it said in the bottom right-hand corner. He grabbed the zapper to turn it off but stopped when he caught sight of footage of Carlow beet factory on the news. He turned up the volume. A shiver ran up his spine as he took in what the newsreader was saying. Greencore was closing Carlow – the factory he'd hauled sugar beet to since he was a chap. And sugar beet had provided most of his contracting work . . . He sat down on the bed in a daze. The IFA person was saying what a bad day this was for the country and the farmers of Ireland. The EU wants to end sugar beet growing in Ireland, he was saying . . . So, the rumours were right . . . it was only a matter of time and the rug would be pulled out from under every beet farmer in the country. There was definitely nothing in this country for him now. He could give his beet sower and harvester up for scrap.

Getting into the van, he threw his bag in on top of the new oil filters for the John Deere that he'd bought a few days ago. He might never use them.

He took out his mobile phone, switched it on to see 35 missed calls on the screen. He rang his brother.

He had to hold it away from his ear as Roy stuttered at him about where was he and where had he been and did he have any idea that their mother was up the walls with worry and what did he think he was playing at and their uncle being moved to Waterford Hospital.

"Hospital? What?"

He listened again to Roy telling him about the heart attack. Fuck! About them all going there after he tried to run Hannah Casey off the road . . . About the cow calving and the ambulance coming . . .

Them all going there . . . That meant she wasn't hurt when he ran her car into the ditch.

He tried to think straight. How bad was the heart attack? They wouldn't know until later today, Roy said. No, Aunt Florrie hadn't been in to see him. Or their mother. She didn't want to. Roy said he'd been in for a few minutes but he wouldn't talk and seemed very weak.

"Y-y-ou could have a-a-answered your ph-phone! And the b-b-beet – did you h-hear?"

Leo pressed the red button then turned the phone off. He couldn't listen to any more. Heart attack . . . his uncle could die. What'd happen then? His aunt would have the place – and yer one . . . There was no way round it. He was out on his ear. The building development would never happen either without his uncle's start-up money. And her in that cottage . . . Leo felt like vomiting again. He'd never be rich. He'd be sixty and still struggling with only a goddamn bungalow to his name, if it was ever paid for, and not another square inch of ground belonging to him. He was up the creek without a paddle . . . He tried to concentrate. What would he do now? He'd have to go home and get his passport and his driver's licence and pack a case. Money . . . He spotted the farm account cheque book on the floor of the van. His mother had signed an open cheque in it meant to pay for two new gates in the co-op. He was supposed to pay for them the other day. He picked up the book and stared at her signature. There was money in the farm account . . . He would write the cheque out to himself and lodge it to his own account. Three thousand – that would keep him going while he looked for work in the UK. No, it wouldn't be stealing if he took the money – he'd earned it and more, the work he did at home. And his mother wouldn't say a thing about it. She'd rather he had money wherever he was going than be worrying that he was short.

As he pulled out of the car park onto the busy street he couldn't wait to see the back of Rathbrandon, to shake the dust of Wexford off his feet – the dust of the whole fucking island.

"The guy who's going down to theatre for an angiogram this morning is your father?"

Hannah was in her boss's, Emer Boyle's office in Waterford Hospital.

"Yes."

"I see!"

She had gone there to talk about going back to work but she knew herself it was more than that. Maybe she'd see him. He'd be in one of the beds that she had nursed heart patients in for years.

"And how are you in the middle of all this?"

Hannah had to think before answering.

"A bit fragile. I didn't think I would be, but . . ."

"That's one of your strengths – and weaknesses – thinking you can handle anything, but you're human just like the rest of us."

She had filled her boss in on some of the detail.

"And you've had no contact with him since the cardiac arrest?"

"He knows I've been in the hospital, but no . . ."

"What is it you're hoping for?"

Hannah shrugged.

"That he'd say something that'd make a difference . . ."

"Maybe it's early days. He'll be all over the place because of the heart attack – you know what heart patients are like – and he has a lot more on his mind than most. Maybe you should give it time."

Hannah shrugged again.

Her boss was staring at her.

"Have you ever considered counselling? I know, it's not for everyone, but it can help. You've had a lot to cope with – overwhelming stuff, actually . . ."

"I haven't thought about it."

"Maybe you should, but I'll leave that to yourself. You should try to get some rest. Take a few more days off. We're under pressure without you, but it's important you be able for work when you come back."

Hannah felt heat pricking her eyes. Jesus! The last thing she wanted to do was start bawling here. She was exhausted, that was all . . . strung out . . .

"Everyone feels fragile when they're exhausted. Can I get you a cup of tea or anything?"

"No, thanks. I should go."

Emer Boyle was checking some list.

"He'll be ready to go back to Wexford General in the morning. The ambulance is booked for 8.30. A&E door."

Why was she telling her this? So that she could . . .?

"Thank you."

Hannah started the car to go home to her house in Waterford. Tomorrow morning . . . would she have the guts to try see him?

"Anything's better than this limbo," she said to herself as she put the car in gear.

It was over. The procedure. The doctor was explaining about there being partial blockage in one of his arteries and how they'd put a prop in to keep the artery open and let the blood flow. Abe thought of drains being blocked on the farm and shoving a stick back and forth to clear the gunge.

Fear gathered in his chest again. He could barely concentrate on what the doctor was saying now – something about rehabilitation team and lifestyle change . . .

"So I'm not going to . . .?"

He couldn't say the word.

"No, you'll have a good few years left in you yet if you do what you're told. You're one of the luckier ones."

Abe closed his eyes as relief flooded through him. A good few years . . .

"Are you ok?"

"Yes."

Thanks to who . . .

"The porter will be here soon to take you back up to the ambulance guys. Best of luck."

Abe closed his eyes again. She worked here in this ward – wasn't that what Florrie had said? You'd have to have your wits about you to do this sort of job, he knew, from watching the staff in both hospitals since he came in. He didn't know how they did it – reading the machines, calming people down, cleaning up vomit, toileting, talking . . . He jumped as an image of her came back to him – her in the shed, giving orders, knowing what to do . . . And she'd worked here for years . . . He tried to fill in the blank bits – where did she train? He tried to push the thoughts out of his head, but he couldn't . . .

Florrie . . . The staff had phoned her, he knew. She'd know he'd be back in Wexford Hospital soon. Time to think, she said . . . he'd had plenty of it in here all right. What he wouldn't give to be out of here . . . Home . . . He felt suddenly anxious. What if Florrie didn't want him home? If she wanted him gone because of what he'd done . . . He closed his eyes again to shut out the mess . . .

He was at the ambulance entrance doors in a wheelchair now, ready to go back to Wexford General. He wanted to walk, but they wouldn't let him.

"You have to take it easy, Abraham," the chattier of the two paramedics said. "Don't run before you can walk, so to speak."

"We'll get you in, in a minute."

The A&E area was quieter than when he'd come in. People were sitting around waiting for someone belonging to them to be treated or to get news of them.

"Hannah! Long time, no see!"

His head swivelled as the paramedic spoke to someone sitting on one of the A&E seats. He stared as the tall woman came towards him.

"Des . . . Phil . . . Yes. How are you?"

"Good. And you?"

"Fine, thanks."

"You back to work?"

"Not yet. Soon. Just sorting that out today."

"Well for some, what? Able to live it up and the rest of us killing ourselves, what?"

She was looking at him.

"Yes."

He tried to look away, but he couldn't.

"Mr Stephenson."

"You two know each other?"

"You could say that."

Abe felt himself nod.

"Right . . . We'll give you a minute then while we get sorted."

"Thanks."

She was looking down at him, her hands stuffed into the pockets of her red coat.

He had a lump in his throat that he couldn't clear.

"How are you?" she was asking. Her eyes were the same colour as his grandmother's.

"So-so."

"They've sorted you out?"

"Yes."

"Florrie . . . your wife . . . she rang . . ."

She'd been talking to her?

The silence was awkward, but his head felt too heavy and confused and he couldn't make his mouth form any words.

"It's a good hospital . . ."

Abe could think of nothing but her pulling on the rope in the cow house . . .

His voice seemed at a distance from him.

"You've . . . calved cows before . . ."

She looked shocked.

He tried to remember what he'd said as he stared at the floor.

"Yes. Years ago. We helped out on farms at holiday time – I liked it."

She was holding out her hand to give him some kind of book. It was a small photograph album.

"They're photos of me. All the time you didn't know me . . ."

He tried to speak but couldn't as he placed it on his lap.

"Florrie – your wife – she's a remarkable woman," she said.

"Right! We'd better get this man back to the purple and gold. Now that he's got all the pipes flushed, isn't that right?"

The paramedics were now coming back, all green uniforms and efficiency.

"We'll have to talk soon . . ." she was saying. "You owe me that."

Abe tried to stand up straight and step out of the wheelchair but one of the paramedics had a hand on his shoulder.

"No, no, stay there, good man. We'll push you in this. Don't want you toppling over on your head, do we?"

Walk tall, walk straight and look the world right in the eye. The words of the Val Doonican song came back to him as he was pushed up the ramp of the ambulance and his eyes started to leak again, as he opened the first page of the album – it was a photo of her stooking square bales, age 10 or so, two small hands holding the baler twines, one plait undone and squinting at the sun as she lifted . . .

"H-he's gone." Roy Kemp watched his mother's shoulders droop.

"For good?"

"T-to look for work, b-but he's all r-right."

Leo had sent a text to say that he was leaving. He had collected some things from the bungalow the night before and had got a flight to the UK that morning. He didn't mention the bit about Leo saying that he wanted to get away from the whole fucking lot of them, their uncle particularly.

"T-h-here's lots of work over there – he'll be ok."

His mother was squashing a piece of bread between her fingers again. Why did she always do that?

"He took money."

"W-what?"

"Out of the farm account. I checked it on the phone this morning – he drew a cheque on it."

"H-h-he f-f-f-forged your name?"

"I don't know."

"How much?"

"Three thousand."

"W-h-hat about the b-bills?"

His mother seemed to be staring into space and her voice was low.

"He needed it."

"Still doesn't g-give him the right . . ."

"I raised expectations in him, all his life, that weren't mine to raise. A good mother wouldn't have done that, would she?"

"Y-y-you're not a bad . . ."

His mother's voice was even lower now.

"I should have let him go . . . Made him go – years ago –so he could carve a life out for himself somewhere else . . ."

Roy went outside to feed the sheep in order to clear his head. Leo – robbing from his mother, from this place . . . His mother's admission . . . She was in bad shape . . .

His uncle was coming back to Wexford Hospital today too . . . The stent was in. Would that mean that he'd be discharged in a few days . . .? What would his Aunt Florrie do then? Christ, what a mess! Right now he hated his uncle for bringing all this trouble on her. Beryl – he wished she was here. Maybe he could drive down in a day or two and stay over . . . Concentrate on getting the yard work done – that's what he had to do. It would keep his mind off everything. Maybe then he'd be able to go to the shed for an hour.

The tapping away at the piece of stone calmed him. He inhaled deeply. The stone had a smell of its own, he thought, and veins and a skin . . . He looked at the piece he was working on. Already he could see the finished piece in his mind . . .

The door suddenly opening startled him. It was his mother. She reminded him of an old seabird that had been forced to ground because of illness.

She was sitting down now on a pile of pallets near him, wrapping her coat around her.

"Y-y-you should have s-s-stayed inside in the h-h-eat."

"I couldn't stand the silence. Your Aunt Florrie rang. He'll be let home in a few days."

"R-right. G-go back inside . . . You'll c-c-catch your death."

Seeing that she wouldn't go, he moved the gas heater nearer to her. Back at the stone now, Roy continued to chip away.

"Your father had the measure of him, you know . . ."

His father? She had mentioned his father!

"Too big for his boots, he always said. Riding for a fall . . . It's only a matter of when it happens, he'd say, because that's the way the world works and the ones at the top have the furthest to come down . . ."

Roy felt rooted to the spot. She had never talked about his father before. His mother's voice was quieter now.

"And I made little of him for saying it. I used to think he was jealous, but I couldn't see what was under my own nose . . . He could always see through people . . . to the good and the bad . . ."

"D-D-Dad?"

"Yes. I should have seen it too."

"S-sometimes we d-don't want to see s-s-stuff."

"No."

Roy tried to focus on the chisel and the stone, but he couldn't.

"You're a lot like him . . ."

"Who?"

"Your father. He was sound – that's the way they'd say it now. What you saw was what you got. Like looking into clear water."

Roy's hand shook so much he couldn't continue. Eventually he sat down beside his mother on the pile of wooden pallets.

"E-very f-family has its t-troubles . . ."

His mother's bottom lip was quivering and she was now gripping his hand – hard.

"Your Aunt Florrie – what if she won't have him back?"

"I-It's b-between the two of them. W-w-we can't interfere."

His mother's grip was now tighter.

"I can still see your face that day, you know . . . Running into the yard – and me shouting at you to make sense – and all the time there was no sense in it. No sense at all . . ."

Chapter
TWELVE

Hannah was shocked by how frail he looked.

Watching him being pushed, in nightclothes, down the A&E corridor in a wheelchair by a porter, she barely recognized him.

Photo album in her hand, she wondered if she had the guts to go through with it. She eyed the door – she could still escape if she wanted to . . .

Florrie had told her he'd failed a lot, but she hadn't expected this much. Still, she should have known. She'd seen enough people after heart attacks and the way it could knock the stuffing out of them.

She forced herself to stand up when she saw the porter reach the door and talk to the waiting paramedics, who were going to take her father back to Wexford Hospital.

"Hannah! Long time no see!"

"Des . . . Phil . . . How are you?"

"Good. And you?"

"Fine, thanks."

"You back to work?"

"Soon."

"Well for some, eh? On the doss and the rest of us killing ourselves, what?"

She looked down at her father.

"Mr Stephenson."

It seemed odd, saying the name out loud.

"You two know each other?"

Hannah kept her voice steady.

"You could say that."

Did her father nod, even slightly?

She looked at Des, who picked up that she needed a minute.

"Thanks."

Hannah stuffed one hand into a pocket so that he wouldn't see it clench.

"How are you?"

The question seemed shallow, inadequate. She could barely hear his answer.

"They've sorted you out?"

"Yes."

He was finally making eye contact.

"You've . . . calved cows before . . ."

Cows!

"Yes. I've spent time on farms . . .holiday time. I liked it."

She waited for him to say more, but he didn't.

She heard herself make a comment about Florrie – about how he should appreciate how good a person she was. Why had she said that, of all the things she could have said? Was this going to be it?

"We need to talk."

He looked about to speak, but his mouth closed again as Des and Phil came back, all green uniforms and efficiency, letting the lock off the wheelchair.

"Right – we'd better get this man back to his home county. Now that he's got all the pipes flushed, isn't that right?"

She handed him the photo album and watched him try to get up out of the wheelchair, but he was told to stay where he was.

Hannah stood at the door staring as he was pushed up the ambulance ramp.

Seven words – that's all he'd said. God!

When the ambulance had gone she sat for several minutes in the car. No, she was stupid – what did she expect, confronting him like that? What was he going to say, for God's sake? Make up for forty years of lost talk in a public place? Now he'd think her weird . . . Still, he hadn't blanked her. And the question – cows . . . Maybe cows were all he could talk about . . . She thought of Florrie saying that she was sad that he'd never felt able to tell. What was it like for him carrying the secret around . . . ? Had it been a burden to him?

Back at the house in Waterford she waited for Beryl to come home from work. The bottle of wine in the fridge drew her, but she put it back in the door. What was that going to solve? She'd drunk herself silly enough times over him. She was glad of the call from Florrie a few minutes later to tell her about the angiogram results. She had the right to know, she said. Technically she was his next of kin. Hannah swallowed hard, as Florrie told her that she was finally going in to see him today. He'd have a room of his own now, she said. What would Florrie say to him? Hannah wished she could be a fly on the wall.

Peg had left a message on her phone asking if she was ok. Ok . . . What did that mean? At least she was good enough to enquire. She would text her later.

She knew the minute she saw Beryl that she had news.

"Leo's gone. To England."

Hannah listened while Beryl related all that Roy had told her on the phone. Work over there . . .

"How does Roy feel about that?"

"It's for the best, maybe, he says."

"His mother?"

"She's ok. Relieved that he hadn't . . ."

"Topped himself?"

"Maybe."

"Christ . . ."

Hannah was glad Beryl was home.

"Roy is getting on better with his mother – that's a positive, isn't it? Sometimes change for the better comes out of crisis . . ."

"She's probably blaming me."

"It's her own baggage if she does. The only one she should feel let down by is her brother. He should have told her years ago. She'll have to come to terms with it as best she can."

Hannah sat down. God, she felt jittery. Beryl looked shocked when she told her that she had gone to the hospital.

"What happened?"

"I'm not sure."

Her friend's voice was low.

"The whites of his eyes – did you see them?"

"Maybe . . . He looked scared. It's odd . . . I should have felt powerful – but all I felt was . . . pity. And scared that I'd give him another heart attack and he'd die there in front of me and then there'd be . . . nothing. Where would I be then . . . Me, wanting to back off! Christ, I'm losing it!"

Beryl's hand was in hers.

"No, you're not. You're just feeling stuff you've never allowed yourself to feel before or weren't ready to feel. Compassion is a sign of transformation . . . a stepping stone to forgiveness . . ."

Hannah breathed deeply several times.

"She loves him . . ."

"Who?"

"Florrie. I know by the way she talks about him. There must be some good in him if she loves him, mustn't there?"

The sobs took her by surprise – big, hard ones that caught in her throat and made her chest heave.

"Let it go. It's ok . . . Ssh."

It was a long time before she spoke again.

"He may never want me – I have to face up to that. You said I shouldn't push it in case I got hurt, but I wouldn't listen – oh no, I had to go bull-headed after him and for what? Just to feel like this?"

"At least the truth is out – that has to be better in the long run – for everyone."

"Is it, though? Even my own mother told me not to go after him. I didn't even respect her wishes properly by coming down here ..."

"You did what you felt was right. Had the guts to do it ..."

"Then why do I feel so rotten now?"

She'd come! Abe could see his wife standing at the door of the private room he'd been moved to.

It shocked him how well she looked.

"You're back ..."

"This morning."

"So – no bypass?"

"No."

"You've a lot to be thankful for, then ..."

Abe couldn't speak.

She had walked to the window now and was staring out of it onto the car park. Could she not even bear to look at him?

"The social worker ... she asked about your home situation ... whether or not you had one to go to."

A wave of fear hit him as he took in what she said.

He tried to get the words out.

"What did you say?"

"I told her it depends."

He swallowed.

"On?"

"I'd be within my rights to throw you out, of course. Some women'd have nailed your testicles to a tree for less ... I can't say it hasn't crossed my mind."

Jesus!

Abe tried to force the words out.

"If I could go back ..."

His eyes were leaking again.

She was staring at him.

"If you could go back, what would you do? Never let it happen? Have more sense? But you can't, can you? We're at where we're at – that's the long and short of it ..."

"I'm sorry."

She was still staring.

"I wondered if you'd be man enough to say it. Sorry's not a word that has featured much in your vocabulary ..."

"I am. More than I can say."

He tried to get out of the bed to go over to her, but he felt suddenly weak and lay back down again. She hadn't stirred.

"It's funny the way tables turn in life . . . In relationships . . . Things are going to be different now – you know that, of course. You'll be coming home because I let you."

He gripped the sheets to steady himself. He could go home . . . He wished she would come to him and hug him and let him bury his face in her breasts and have her arms wrap round him, but she was staying where she was . . .

He could hear the clatter of a food trolley outside the silent room. She had turned to face him again.

"I'd have reared her, you know."

"What?"

God Almighty . . .

Her eyes were boring into his soul.

"I'd have loved her. And you couldn't even see that . . . That's the tragedy in all this – we all lost out. I'd have screamed blue murder at first, of course, but I'd have taken her. You have no idea what it's like to want a child so badly . . ."

She was still looking at him.

"Or maybe you do . . ."

"A lifetime's work – in these . . ."

Abe Stephenson watched the rector walk from each of the aerial photographs to each of the cattle prize-winning ones in the study in Knocklannon.

"Yes."

"We all want to achieve something – make a difference, don't we, whatever our field of interest. You and Florrie can certainly be proud of your work. The place is a credit to you."

Abe sat down in his armchair feeling suddenly tired. Potter around the place for a few weeks, the doctor said. Potter . . . He'd never pottered in his life.

He watched the reverend take another sip of the cup of the coffee that Florrie had brought him.

"You won't be able to drive for a while yet?"

"Another few weeks."

"That's normal enough. Give the body time to heal properly. How are things between you and Florrie?"

Abe moved the fountain pen round on his desk.

"As good as can be expected."

"Yes, indeed. And Vera looks a bit stronger – I called in on her yesterday."

"Aye?"

"Yes. Roy is keeping an eye on her. Leo has got a job, I hear?"

"Yes."

Abe closed his eyes, thinking of how much Leo must hate him and wishing the clergyman would go.

"And yourself – how are you doing?"

Abe fussed with the pen, finally putting it in a drawer where it was never kept. Beside the photo album she'd given him . . .

"Getting by."

"Good. Good. One step at a time."

The rector's finger was tracing the rim of his cup.

"Life throws a lot of challenges at us all, of course, at all stages of our lives. Sometimes we think they're going to paralyze us, but most times they end up teaching us something about ourselves – and the world. All we have to find is the courage to be open to the lessons."

The rector was smiling.

"There was a time you'd have told me where to stick my preaching."

Abe breathed deeply to stop his voice from shaking.

"Aye . . ."

"Yes indeed. You're tired – I can see that. Of course you are . . . I can call another time. I'm sure you've had a lot of visitors since you came home."

Visitors . . . Abe could count them on the fingers of one hand. Three neighbours had called. They'd talked awkwardly of hospital and heart attacks and how the frying pan can be a gravedigger and the price of cattle and mostly about the beet industry going . . .

"I'll let myself out," the rector was saying. "Florrie said she was going out to the cattle. The new calf is doing well, I hear – the makings of another champion."

"Yes."

Abe saw the rector pause at the door.

"Hannah – she's going back to Waterford today, I hear . . . Back to work."

"You hear a lot of things, Reverend . . ."

The rector smiled.

"All part of the job. '

Air! He needed some fresh air. The study suddenly seeming oppressive, Abe walked up to the kitchen, when he heard the back door close. Where had Florrie gone? To the shed? It was only across the yard. If he took it easy he'd be all right.

Max came running towards him when he heard him coming.

"Good boy!"

The dog's head felt warm and familiar as he patted it. The sucklers were standing or lying in the pens, in clean straw, chewing their cud. He saw his wife checking the water in all the troughs in case any of them wasn't working properly. She glanced up but made no comment. No lecture about being outside when he shouldn't be or what the doctor might say. Still, she'd have been no different.

She was in the aisle now, fingers proking through a handful of feed ration that Aidan had fed them earlier.

"The new ration is working," she said. "They're doing well on it."

They'd changed the feed for the sucklers before Christmas.

"Yes."

He was at Knocklannon Gem's pen. He shivered as he remembered the last time he was here. He tried to concentrate on the pen where the calf was feeding, its head butting its mother's udder as it latched on.

Florrie was going into the pen now with a cattle brush.

"Easy, girl!"

The cow didn't stir. He watched his wife brush the heifer as if she was grooming a horse. She'd done it with all potential champions from the time they were calves.

"Who doesn't like to be stroked, eh, animal or human?"

Abe leaned over the gate, feeling soothed by the rhythm of the movements – forward . . . back . . . forward . . . as the calf sucked, its tail wagging all the time.

Florrie was now out of the pen, leaning on the gate too, watching Gem and her calf.

"Did you see it on the counter?"

"What?"

"The registration form for this little lady. You'll have to send it in soon . . ."

"Aye."

She was stroking the calf again.

"*Knocklannon Pearl* – it's a good name for her, don't you think? Something precious to come out of chaos."

Hannah packed the carton of sour milk and the out-of-date sausages into a plastic carrier bag. She would bin them when she got back to Waterford. Beryl wouldn't want them there stinking the fridge out when she came back to see Roy.

Work – she'd be starting again tomorrow. The normality of it would be good, she knew. Routine . . .

Upstairs she took out what clothes were in the wardrobe, folded them and packed them into a case. She picked up two paperbacks that were on the locker to put them in the case but changed her mind. Beryl might want to read them.

She reached up to take the framed newspaper cutting from over her bed. *The term illegitimacy will end . . .* The word bastard banished . . . She rubbed her forearm over the top of the frame to wipe the dust off it. *Someday I will know who I am . . .* She had succeeded but what more could she do? It was time to go . . .

Downstairs she laid the frame on the kitchen table beside a box of odds and ends that she was taking back to Waterford. Five minutes to load up and she'd be out of here . . .

A car . . . Who was coming now? That's all she needed – Peg Travers arriving, keeping her talking all day . . .

Her heart started to pound after looking out the window. It was Florrie. He – her father – was getting out of the passenger seat . . .

His shape seemed to fill the doorway.

"You're going?"

She heard him clear his throat.

"You're off . . ." he said.

"Yes."

"May I come in . . . ?"

"Suit yourself."

She stayed at the table, putting the last few items into the boxes, continuing to stare at him as he stooped to enter the room, his clothes hanging on him as he looked around the kitchen.

She thought he was never going to speak.

"Well?"

"You . . . You did a good job . . ."

What was he going on about?

"You came here to talk about me doing this place up?"

"The doctors – they said you knew what you were doing . . . the night . . ."

She continued packing the box.

"I'd have done the same for anyone."

He looked like she'd slapped him in the face.

"Of course."

She watched him open his mouth and close it again.

"Why have you come? I've things to do."

He was still saying nothing. She noticed that his right hand was shaking – the one that held a rolled up piece of paper.

"This . . . isn't easy . . ."

She shrugged before slamming her hairdryer into the box, where it clattered against a biscuit tin.

"Maybe if you hadn't left it so long it wouldn't be. You think it's easy for me?"

"You've the right . . ."

"To what? Be angry? Damn right I've the right!"

A lump in her throat stopped her from saying more. He was standing there – saying nothing! She breathed deeply to regain her composure.

"My mother – did you have any feelings for her? Ever? Go on, tell me!"

She forced herself to keep looking at him as she waited for an answer.

"Well?"

His hand was shaking again.

"She deserved better than me."

God . . .

She held his gaze and waited for him to speak again.

"I didn't do right by her. You either . . . I should've . . ."

She waited again, but he'd stopped . . .

"Go on! Say it! You should have reared me – given me your name but, oh no, you had to cover it all up and deny me – over and over! Do you know what that felt like – to have the truth thrown back in your face again and again? And you the liar the whole time! You're the bastard!"

Before she knew what she was doing, she had thrown the framed cutting at him. It struck him on the arm then landed on the ground beside the table, the glass shattering.

The words spilled out of her until they ran thin – how she hated him and how he'd screwed up her life by never being there for her and how even an animal would acknowledge its young and how his cattle were better treated than she was and how she hoped he'd rot in hell . . .

The sobs finally stopped her.

"You've the right . . ."

"Why couldn't you have just owned up? Why couldn't you?"

Was his hand shaking even more?

"I tried to bury it."

"Bury *it*? Bury me, you mean! Your own flesh and blood!"

She saw him slump down onto one of the kitchen chairs as if his weight was suddenly too much to hold up. Now he took the photo album she'd given him out of his coat pocket and opened the first page. She could see him fingering the photo of her stooking square bales at Watson's farm. What age was she then – nine, ten?

"I . . . never let myself imagine your face . . . I should have . . ."

She saw him bend now to pick up the framed cutting from the floor, shaking the broken glass off it. He was reading it. Hannah clenched her fists. *I can hold my head high . . .*

He was looking at her now, eyes watery and voice wavering.

"You weren't going to be walked over . . ."

She held his stare.

"I've a crooked streak in me. Maybe I didn't lick it up off the grass . . ."

Was that the glimmer of a smile as he fidgeted with the rolled up paper he'd brought with him again? Now he was holding the paper out to her.

"What is it?"

She stretched her hand out to take it. It was some kind of application form . . . Registration form. Pedigree calf registration . . . *The Irish Hereford Cattle Society Ltd . . .*

She read what was written there – Herd: *Knocklannon*, Date of birth . . . It was the day the new calf was born – the day of his heart attack . . .

"You've named her Knocklannon Pearl?"

"Florrie chose it."

She continued to read.

Genetic merit . . . Sire – *Bloomfield Major*, Dam *Knocklannon Gem* .

"What? What are you showing me this for?"

She saw his finger point at the top left hand corner of the page. His name was there as breeder. *Abraham Stephenson . . .*

"So what?"

Her eyes now followed his finger further down. Owner, she read. *Hannah Casey Stephenson.*

THE END

ACKNOWLEDGEMENTS

I would like to thank all my family and friends for their support and encouragement while writing this book and since I started putting pen to paper. Kind words and cups of tea make all the difference on long, draft-driven days.

Thanks, too, to my copyeditor, Penny Osborne, for polishing my punctuation and to Catherine Ryan Howard for inspiring me to take *Deny Me Not* to the world.

www.margarethawkins.ie

Facebook/MargaretHawkinsAuthor

Twitter @MargaretHawki10